HIDDEN THREAT

A.J. TATA

VARIANCE
USA

Variance Publishing
1610 South Pine St.
Cabot, AR 72023,
(501) 843-BOOK

Published by Variance LLC (USA).
www.variancepublishing.com

Library of Congress Catalog Number 2010939966

ISBN: 1-935142-17-8
ISBN-13: 978-1-935142-17-1

Cover Illustration by Larry Rostant
Jacket Design by Stanley J. Tremblay
Interior layout by Stanley J. Tremblay
Map by Jackie McDermott

Visit A.J. Tata on the web at: www.ajtata.com.
10 9 8 7 6 5 4 3 2 1 0

For Brooke and Zachary, two great kids

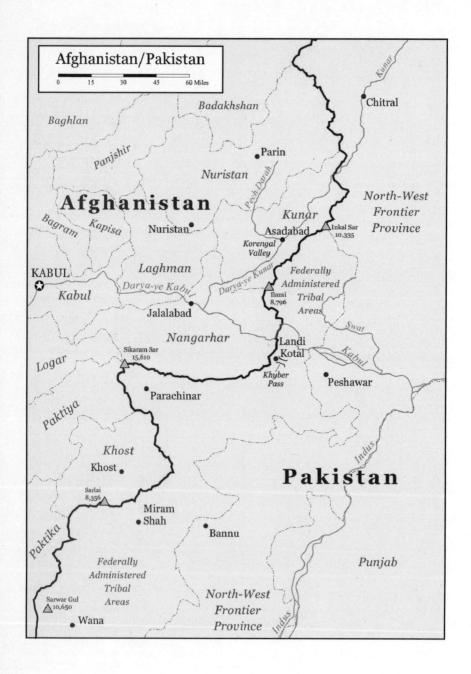

THE INDIRECT APPROACH

CHAPTER 1
HINDU KUSH, AFGHANISTAN

MAY, FRIDAY MORNING, 0400 HOURS

He was born for combat. Fighting wars was his lot in life. He found a sense of purpose in this calling like no other. Only once had he tempted fate by seeking another course, and yet here he was, back in the fight where he belonged.

In a sense he had been fighting his entire adult life.

Napoleon had called it *coup d'oeil*, literally "at a glance." It was the ability to see the battlefield in an instant and understand what needed to be done. Part innate ability and part learned skill, the talent was as rare amongst military commanders as true cunning and Machiavellian business acumen in the corporate world.

Whatever people wanted to call it, Colonel Zachary Garrett possessed this unique skill set, so much so that the United States defense community had entrusted much of the hunt for the most notable terrorists to him.

Standing in ankle-deep snow in a forgotten saddle of the Afghan Hindu Kush Mountains, Colonel Garrett looked down at the black radio handset, satisfied that he understood his mission.

"Operation Searing Gorge is a go." The general's voice was crisp and authoritative. "I say again, Operation Searing Gorge is a go."

"This is Raider six. Roger, understand Searing Gorge is a go, over." Zachary relayed his acknowledgement to Major General Jack Rampert, the commander of U.S. forces in Afghanistan.

"See you on the high ground, son."

"Roger, out."

Zachary stood beside his up-armored Humvee, the coiled radio handset cord trailing through the window, connecting to the satellite receiver affixed to the center console. The Afghan firmament was a never-ending blanket of darkness, interrupted only by the jagged white peaks that sprawled into Pakistan and farther north until they ultimately linked up with the Himalayas. Millions of stars were pinpricks in the black sheaf, offset by a waxing gibbous moon setting to the west.

The Hindu Kush Mountains made the Rocky Mountains in the United States look like foothills. Pike's Peak, hovering just above fourteen thousand feet, was the highest peak on the Front Range in Colorado. By comparison, summits in Afghanistan commonly reached eighteen thousand to twenty thousand feet. *The enemy lived and fought at these altitudes.*

A crisp breeze snapped past him, stinging his face. He shrugged off the historical fact that the literal interpretation of Hindu Kush was "Hindu Slaughter." In 1382 the Muslims had routed the Hindus in one of the interminable wars that plagued this land. There had been no survivors.

What was more difficult to dismiss was his testy relationship with his boss, Major General Rampert, the commander of all special operations forces in Afghanistan. Yesterday they had gone toe to toe over the utility of this mission and Rampert hadn't budged.

"It's suicide and you know it, General," Colonel Garrett had said.

"I thought you said you'd follow me to hell and back, Zach," Rampert quipped, signature grimace acting as a smile.

"Last time I checked the manifest, you weren't on it."

"You got me there, son. But you know how important this mission is. Hell, your brother Matt's the one who's pushing it."

That comment had stopped Zach cold. If true, his brother, a high level CIA operative, would have something worth getting after.

"Bullshit . . . sir," Zach responded, testing the commander. They had been standing in his sparsely furnished command office on Bagram Air Base.

"Wouldn't bullshit you about Matt. Someone needs to get up there and that someone needs to leave something behind."

Zach had stared at Rampert for a long while and then said, "If Matt's pushing this thing, then that someone will be me."

It amazed Zach that over nine years after the 9-11 attacks, nearly seventy thousand United States and NATO troops continued to fight now resurgent Taliban and Al Qaeda movements along the Afghanistan and Pakistan border. Colonel Garrett was not part of that blend of conventional soldiers conducting combat operations and reconstruction missions. He and his men were not supposed to exist. Like ghosts, one moment they were present, and the next they were gone. They moved seamlessly around the battlefield in search of the most worthy targets.

He looked at his driver, Sergeant Lance Eversoll.

"Looks like tonight we're going to give it another shot, Solls."

Eversoll's skeptical grin told the story of several raids on Al Qaeda safe houses that had resulted in little to no results.

"It's like fishing, sir. We keep pulling up sticks and tires instead of the big 'un. We need to find us a honey hole."

Eversoll was raised in central Kentucky on a family farm. He was a broad-shouldered, square-jawed man who had done two years of college on a wrestling scholarship at Louisville University and then got bored with the entire scene. One morning he walked into the recruiting station in downtown Louisville. He'd stood tall and told the recruiter, "If you give me airborne and ranger, with a shot at Special Forces, I'll sign up right now."

Now, at twenty-five years old, Eversoll was a Special Forces paratrooper. He had landed the impossibly difficult job of being the radio operator, driver, bodyguard, and virtual aide-de-camp for the group commander, Colonel Garrett.

"Well, they don't come any bigger than what we're going after here with this one. It's not so much what we're hoping to bring back, but what we hope to leave up there." He felt the weight of his M4 hanging loosely on the snap link affixed to his outer tactical vest, and found himself hoping the plan *would* work.

A moment of silence followed, before Eversoll replied, "I know I'm not supposed to know about this, but I overhear a lot, you know, sir."

"That's why I picked you. I can trust you."

Colonel Garrett nodded in the darkness. The less said about this mission the better. Sure, they were going into the teeth of a known Al Qaeda hideout in the undefined border region, but they had come up empty so many times that Zach figured if Matt had any hand in the plan, it had to be worth it, no matter how dangerous. Garrett watched his driver Sergeant Eversoll scan the horizon, M4 carbine at the ready. He saw him spit some tobacco juice into the snow beneath their feet and say, "No issues there, sir."

"Raider six, this is Tiger six, over." Garrett and Eversoll looked at the radio handset.

"It's time, sir."

Garrett gave him a nod and placed the handset to his ear.

"Tiger six, this is Raider six. Searing Gorge is a go. Execute now, over." Garrett spoke with certainty.

"Confirm Searing Gorge is a go, over."

"Roger, Searing Gorge is a go."

"Roger that." The tone of Commander Jeffrey Montrose was high pitched and excited. Zachary visualized the Navy SEAL gathering his men on the other side of the valley from where he and Eversoll stood. His own eight-man security team was situated within two hundred meters of his command vehicle, occupying positions of dominance along the ridge in order to protect their esteemed commander. The team had been inserted last night into this valley, not too far from the fabled Tora Bora cave complex. An Afghan citizen, a poppy farmer, had been captured a week ago and, after some tough questioning, had delivered a pearl of intelligence.

Senior Al Qaeda leadership was re-forming in the rugged northeastern Afghan mountains for the spring offensive, maybe even Osama bin Laden himself.

Garrett knew that Rampert had been waiting for a two-fer: conducting the Searing Gorge mission and also kill or capture some senior al-Qaeda leadership.

Despite his misgivings, Garrett was confident in the overall plan. He still had some concerns, which he had voiced to Rampert. But Rampert, again, had been unrelenting. He refused to budge on the time. Given the sensitivity of the mission and its myopic purpose, Rampert had dictated the landing zone times and the loads in each helicopter. Accordingly, Zach had his team rehearse the mission several times at their base camp in the relatively secure compound in central Afghanistan. After they worked out the kinks, he liked everything about the concept except for the fact that they were attacking just before dawn. He would have preferred the middle of the night, with the cover of total darkness. The helicopter pilots had also expressed concern about getting into the fourteen-thousand-foot landing zone during the 'goggle transition time'—they would have preferred either full darkness to completely use their goggles or enough light to discard them as they flew the narrow canyons of the Hindu Kush.

It was risky, but Garrett had chosen an offset landing zone no less than a half mile from the objective. With Predator unmanned aerial vehicle coverage and U.S. Air Force F-15s, A-10s and AC-130 gunships, he was confident their insertion would be well protected. The Predator would be flying at thousands of feet above ground level, piping real-time video into the joint operations center at an airbase in Afghanistan. Meanwhile, the AC-130 gunship would orbit silently above the objective, ready to destroy the enemy with its 105mm cannon. The A-10s and F-15s would orbit tens of thousands of feet above the target and drop precision-guided munitions when called for.

However, as usual they could not be completely certain of the terrain, and if the enemy had hidden surveillance positions near the landing zone that went undetected by the overhead sensors, then the mission would become significantly riskier. All or nothing.

The exact timing of the mission still nagged at him, but he knew that this was a time-sensitive target. They had to move now.

The pressure to capture a senior Al Qaeda leader was intensifying every day. The eight-thousand-mile screwdriver, as Zachary called the Pentagon and other bureaucrat-laden government agencies inside the Beltway, had gone cordless. The squeeze was on, and they needed to produce. Searing

Gorge seemed to be the best option.

His plan was to insert Montrose's team first, and then his own team would come in to secure the exfiltration landing zone. They would also be a reserve force, a backup, to support Montrose.

Zachary looked west. The moon looked as though it was splitting into two jagged pieces as the Gulam Gar peak, the highest mountain between his men and the center of Afghanistan, jutted irregularly upward.

"Raider six, this is Tiger six. Marco, over."

"Marco, out." Garrett quickly responded to Montrose's signal that they were airborne in the Special Operations MH-47. Now he would anxiously await the code word "Polo," meaning they had safely secured the landing zone.

"Sir, we're all set," Eversoll said. "Here comes the second aircraft now."

"Okay, you're staying here with the XO, right?"

"Roger, the bird is bringing in Charlie team. We've rehearsed it, sir; no worries. Just get back here safely."

Garrett looked at Eversoll with pride. *Where do we get these guys?* He was always amazed at the courage of American soldiers who, before their enlistments, were just high school kids playing soccer or football or writing computer programs. Now here was Eversoll, watching his back, a colonel with over twenty years in the military. Eversoll was in third grade when Garrett had served as a lieutenant in Desert Storm.

He gave Sergeant Eversoll half a hug with his right arm. "We'll bring you back something to mount on the wall."

"Make it a big 'un." Eversoll smiled and then walked with his colonel into the middle of the snow field and guided the MH-47 into the landing zone. He flashed a small infrared light several times, indicating the lead touchdown point for the aircraft.

Garrett smiled, reached into his pocket and thumbed his Saint Michael medal, which was secured in a plastic sleeve with a faded and worn, but clearly visible, picture of his daughter, Amanda. He flipped it over and kissed Amanda's photo. Saint Michael was the patron saint of paratroopers, and Garrett's ritual since his days in the Eighty-second Airborne Division had been to touch the medal and kiss Amanda's picture prior to a jump. He placed the medallion and the photo back into the Velcro pocket on his army combat uniform.

"Maybe old Saint Michael there will give us a hand this time." Eversoll nodded in the darkness toward the medal, having watched his commander go through the routine. He had seen it many times, never before commenting, but understanding the soldiers' need to feel connected to something larger than themselves as they embark on a dangerous mission. Eversoll absently placed his hand atop his individual body armor near his sternum, where his Saint Michael medal hung beneath his uniform with his dog tags.

Garrett looked at Eversoll, his face lighted by the moon. "He's never failed us so far." That was true, he thought. He and his men had come back from every mission, and that was something to be thankful for.

They watched as the twin-overhead-rotor aircraft descended into the tight valley, pushing loose snow into the air and creating a miniature blizzard. Always a nervous moment for pilots landing in snow, Garrett watched the skilled special-operations aviators settle the aircraft into the newly formed white cloud.

Through his night-vision goggles, he watched his Alpha team gather onto the outer perimeter of the LZ. The yawning ramp of the MH-47 opened, spilling into the bone-white snow another eight Special Forces troops who came sprinting forward. They were wearing PVS-14 night-vision goggles and advanced combat helmets, and had their assorted weaponry at the ready.

Garrett saw the darkened silhouette of a tall man jogging toward him.

"Sir, we've got the Pickup Zone secure. Have a good mission."

"Thanks, Mike. Watch out for Eversoll here. We'll be back soon, we hope. I want you listening to the reconnaissance and fires net to make sure you know where General Rampert is directing those aircraft."

"Roger, sir."

Garrett left Lieutenant Colonel Mike Chizinski standing next to the Humvee and did a half jog, half walk to the back of the helicopter, hovering menacingly in the pick-up zone. He turned and looked at Eversoll, who was saluting. He returned the gesture, but quickly. Saluting in enemy territory was a faux pas, but he understood; it was dark, Eversoll didn't think he'd be looking, and the young man looked up to him as a father figure.

Garrett looked into the dimly lit cabin of the roaring helicopter, saw he had all eight of his Alpha team, and then nodded at the loadmaster crew chief. He watched as his men were pulling charging handles back on their M4s. Lock and load.

He slipped the communications headset on as the behemoth aircraft lifted into the black void above the Hindu Kush.

Before he could call in his code word to General Rampert, he received a radio call from Montrose. There was trouble, which was not unexpected.

"Raider six, this is Tiger six! We're taking fire. We're hit. We're hit!"

MULLAH RAHMAN, AKA the Scientist, sighted down his weapon and pulled the trigger as many times as he could. He could hear the Predator overhead and another airplane that he figured was the AC-130, which he knew would be especially deadly. He watched the MH-47 hover and then land before screaming, "Now!"

His fellow mujahidin raised the rocket propelled grenade launcher against his face, aligned the tube, and squeezed the trigger mechanism, sending a high explosive warhead screaming through the frigid air into the side of the thin skinned aircraft. He saw the explosion and more importantly saw the American fall from the back of the helicopter.

A wall of steel began raining down upon them from the AC-130 as they focused their fire on the departing aircraft. Surely they would come back for their fallen comrade, Rahman thought.

He looked to his right and saw four of his men, dressed in white parkas designed to conceal them in the snow. Their sentries had heard the loud chopping of the twin bladed Chinooks from miles away and had radioed in the direction and probable landing zones. Rahman knew another of the helicopters was on the way as he peered through his night-vision goggles.

"One hostage is what we need," Rahman said to his second in command, Hoxha, a fighter from the Balkans.

Hoxha nodded and gathered three of his men. The snow was driving down on them now and Rahman heard the second aircraft inbound. They had damaged but not destroyed the first and so the second was coming in to rescue the stranded fighter.

"Go now," Rahman ordered, his voice struggling to rise above the din of the 105mm artillery rounds that were exploding 100 meters to their front. They were relatively protected in the trench they had dug, but Rahman knew that the thermal radar on the AC-130 and just about every other American aircraft could see the heat from their body mass, which was impossible to disguise in the frigid temperatures. He could only hope for some timid commanders who were hesitant to inflict collateral damage until they had positive identification of hostile intent. Even though they had just put a rocket through the first aircraft, he had been previously amazed at the Americans' restraint in such situations. He had presumed they would search for women and children before returning fire and Rahman had obliged. He had ten mannequins in blue burqas huddled around a small fire about fifty meters to their rear near the cave complex. Not a complicated deception scheme, but sometimes a little bit was all it took. And for the moment, the American fire was focusing on separating them from the wounded soldier, not on killing them.

Hoxha looked at Rahman, stared at the virtual wall of steel, and nodded again. He muttered something in a Balkan language that Rahman did not understand.

Hoxha and his men followed the trench to the steep southern edge of the ridge, popped out on the perimeter of the AC-130 fire and knelt. Rahman watched as Hoxha patted a tall man, who opened his vest, which Rahman knew was a suicide bomber vest full of C4 explosives and other maiming detritus. He pointed at the inbound helicopter then quickly turned to another of his team and pointed at the isolated soldier. Hoxha then grabbed the third member of his team and pointed at the ground.

Rahman understood the plan. The suicide bomber was going to hug the aircraft. The second man was going to secure the hostage and Hoxha and his wingman were going to lay down a base of fire. Good plan. Rahman liked these Balkan fighters. They were tough and smart.

Rahman watched the action unfold and thought to himself, if we can capture one American, then we can unlock the rest of the plan.

"TIGER SIX, THIS is Raider six, give me a status, over." Zach Garrett's calm voice hid the anxiety and tension he felt regarding the last spot report he had received. "I say again, send spot report, over."

The MH-47 in which he and his team rode chopped against the thin air in the highland range. Garrett stared out of the small circular porthole, barely able to discern the jagged mountain peaks against the first wisps of what sailors call "before morning nautical twilight," or BMNT — that first moment of a new day when things aren't completely black, but close to it. A ball of fear burned in his stomach. He was not afraid for himself, rather for the unknown fate of Commander Montrose and his team. Garrett had not lost a single man to the fight after five months in Afghanistan. Now was not the time to start, he thought to himself. He looked over at his men, all staring at him, waiting for the word. He had written on a small piece of Plexiglas with a grease pencil: *Landing Zone Hot*, then passed it around to his team members. They understood.

The crew chief got Garrett's attention by waving a Nomex-gloved hand in his face. "Two minutes, sir!"

Garrett pressed a button on the small black switch connected by a cable to his headset. "Rampage one, this is Warrior six. What do you see?"

Rampage was the AC-130 gunship patrolling in the sky directly above the landing zone. The aircraft could deliver deadly accurate fire with its 105mm cannon and high-tech guidance systems. Its infrared and thermal sighting apparatus allowed the pilots to magnify and zoom in close enough to read a name tag from four thousand feet above ground level.

"This is Rampage one. We've got one MH-47 returning fire on the landing zone. We are suppressing an enemy element two hundred meters to the west."

"Roger, has the team secured the landing zone? Over."

Garrett waited for the response and then heard a short beep, followed by the static of the radio.

"Negative. Two operators have left the aircraft. Wait a second . . ."

This was painful. He knew they were two minutes out, less than that by now, and wanted to know whether to abort the mission. He needed to see the action. His fist clenched around the push-talk button of his headset.

"We've got one man down on the ground and another lying on the ramp, shot. The aircraft is taking off. Don't go! Don't leave him! Shoot right there, right there! They're coming after him."

Garrett listened as the AC-130 pilot talked both to him and his own crew, expressing operational precision and human emotion all wrapped together. Sometimes it was impossible to keep the two from colliding.

The crew chief came over to Garrett holding up his thumb and forefinger barely spread apart. "Thirty seconds, sir!"

Garrett acknowledged with a nod then got back to the AC-130. "Status, over."

"We've got you inbound. Tiger six team is outbound—Oh shit! RPG just hit their back rotor. They're going down!"

"Status of the LZ?" Garrett asked. He was focused. He zeroed in on the previous report of one man missing from the aircraft. He could still save the mission, especially if there was one man stranded on the landing zone.

"This is Rampage. We've got one friendly on the LZ. The enemy is trying to close on him fast. We're pouring 105 onto the landing zone. Tiger six aircraft is hit, but still flying. Thermals show a smoke trail, but it is stable. Recommend you extract friendly combatant and abort."

"Roger, continue to separate enemy from friendly. We will extract the friendly."

Garrett switched a toggle on his headset and spoke to the pilot flying his aircraft.

"Pete—"

"We monitored the entire transmission, sir. We've got the friendly in sight. We're landing now. We will take off once we have everyone on board."

"Roger, thanks." Garrett tore his headset off, pulled on his helmet and gathered his men on the back ramp of the aircraft as it lowered into the blinding snow billowing in the gaping ramp door like fog rolling into San Francisco Bay. They heard the dreadful and distinct metallic clink of bullets off the thin metal of the airframe.

"One man down on the LZ!" Garrett was screaming over the din of the rotors. "We grab him and get back on this aircraft! The other aircraft is hit and has departed! One man! Team one, you secure left side. Team two, you secure right side. Honeywell, you come with me to secure the friendly. Never leave a fallen comrade!"

Honeywell, the largest man on the team at six foot seven inches, ducked as they exited the ramp running into calf-deep snow. The twin rotors continued to create a snow blizzard, and soon Zach lost sight of everyone except Honeywell until they got outside of the blinding sphere of snow.

Orange and green tracers whipped around them like a laser light show. The enemy was close. He saw one spot where orange tracers were emitting closer than any of his team could be. Orange tracers were usually 5.56mm rounds fired by U.S. or NATO forces.

"This way!" he screamed to Honeywell, who was following him closely, lumbering through the snow. Honeywell stopped, lifted his M4 carbine, which looked like a child's toy in his large hands, and fired five shots at the enemy. They both continued until they were behind a small rock.

"That's him!" About ten meters away was a single U.S. Navy SEAL wearing a parka and a skullcap, firing his weapon at six Al Qaeda combatants who were braving the wall of raining steel emitting from the AC-130. Deafening explosions rocked the small saddle of land situated between two rugged cliffs. It was the only flat land in the area and, therefore, had been well defended by the enemy.

"Cover me!" Garrett shouted. Honeywell lifted his weapon and began firing short three- to six-round bursts, having toggled his selector switch to automatic. Zach crouched and rolled forward, dodging the return fire. He ducked behind a small outcropping of rocks and then leapt to the tight depression where the SEAL had taken up his defense.

"Friendly!" Garrett smacked his kneecap as he landed next to the SEAL, and then he pulled out his identification tags from around his neck. Shaking the dog tags as if to prove who he was, he hollered above the gunfire, "Colonel Garrett!"

"I know who you are, sir! I knew you'd be here!"

They both laid down a heavy volume of fire as the enemy increased their accuracy. Was Honeywell hit, Garrett wondered?

"Are you okay?" He looked at the SEAL, whose eyes were wide with fear.

"I'm hit, sir. Not sure I can walk." Garrett recognized the man as Petty Officer Sam Jergens from somewhere in Wisconsin. He knew the man well enough to understand that he was a tremendously fit individual. If he said he couldn't walk, Garrett knew he was going to have to carry him.

Never leave a fallen comrade.

"Okay! I'll put you in a fireman's carry as long as you continue to shoot at the enemy. Honeywell is covering us!" He hoped that was still the case.

Suddenly Garrett noticed a movement above Jergens's head. He stood, and in one continuous motion pulled his knife from its sheath and raised it up through the throat of the attacker who had made a suicide charge through the AC-130 suppressive fire. The man, practically wrapped in sheets, fell between them, blood staining the white snow like a blossoming rose petal.

"Let's get out of here, sir!"

Garrett sheathed his knife and snapped his M4 onto his outer tactical vest. In what was akin to a wrestling move, he swiftly lifted Jergens onto his back and began to run through the snow. He found Honeywell, who was changing magazines. *Thank God he's alright.* "Cover us!"

Honeywell looked up and continued firing, then moved into a crouching position. He began backpedaling as Garrett sped past him carrying Jergens. Zach felt a stinging sensation in his leg that made him buckle but not fall. He knew he was hit. It wasn't the first time. It probably would not be the last.

They entered the blinding snow tornado that remained suspended in the minute or two they had been on the ground. Zach could see that both team one and team two were collapsing into the aircraft like a well-rehearsed football play. He counted four from team one and three from team two. He had Honeywell with him, which meant he had all of his men.

Another stinging sensation caught him in the triceps, causing him to spin and lurch forward. He dropped Jergens onto the ramp of the aircraft as Honeywell passed him, leaping up. Garrett's body twisted and dropped, his dog tags flapping loosely around his neck. He wrestled with the snap link securing his M4 carbine to his outer tactical vest. It was a fully functional weapon with close combat optics, infrared aiming devices, and other high tech gear lashed to its rail.

It was also important that he leave it on the landing zone.

But the helicopter was taking off.

"No! No! No!" Someone was screaming and then Garrett felt a hand ripping at his body armor as he unclipped the snaplink. He was confused. There was another man running toward them. The aircraft was off the ground, hovering just above the snow. *It's the enemy.*

A figure closed on him, tore at his neck, and then ripped his dog tags from atop his outer tactical vest as Garrett was attempting to retrieve the weapon he had just dropped into the snowstorm. Garrett looked into the man's eyes, which curiously glanced at the two pieces of thin metal he was clasping in his olive hand. The man then looked up at Honeywell, who had pulled the Al Qaeda combatant off Colonel Garrett. Honeywell was leaning over as the aircraft began to ascend rapidly into the sky.

The pilot was hearing "Go! Go! Go!" when in fact, as Honeywell was slitting the throat of the Al Qaeda combatant, he was screaming, "No! No! No!" Honeywell looked over his shoulder at the crew chief and kept screaming, "Colonel Garrett is still on the ground!"

Then Honeywell looked down at the man with a grin frozen on his face and at the same time thought he saw Colonel Garrett through the snow. He pulled back the man dress wrapped around him and saw small packets of C4 explosive secured to his abdomen, nails stuck in the putty-like material.

They were about two hundred meters above the ground and nosing over a cliff when Honeywell looked back at the cockpit and muttered, "Shit," under his breath. Then the helicopter exploded in a bright fireball.

CHAPTER 2
SPARTANBURG HIGH SCHOOL, SOUTH CAROLINA

FRIDAY (EASTERN TIME ZONE)

Unaware of either the 9.5-hour time difference between South Carolina and Afghanistan or that her father was facing horrific combat, Amanda Garrett stood nervously in front of the class, two blonde-streaked tendrils of hair framing her face. She had her father's sea green eyes and her mother's movie star smile. She was wearing a brown American Eagle shirt with three buttons open to show her yellow stretch halter. Her stone-washed jeans flared just enough to cover the heels of her platform sandals. She was five and a half feet tall with the broad shoulders of a champion swimmer and the honey-blonde hair of someone who spent too much time in the sun and chlorinated pools. Having been called upon to read her poem, she balled up her fist and cleared her throat.

She glanced at her teacher, the ever popular Lenard Dagus, as he crossed his legs and clasped his knee with laced fingers. Dagus was a tall man with a mustache, a skinny Tom Selleck. A moderate in his journalism teachings, he had already self-published one book, titled *Policing the Fourth Estate: Publish or Perish*. It wasn't exactly original, but he never let his students forget it was the foundation of his doctoral thesis. The media should be held accountable for their reporting; otherwise, credibility would wane and the institution would crumble, he argued. The book had received moderate acclaim that had made him somewhat of a celebrity in the high school. He also organized and led an online media watchdog group he called MediaHunt, which resulted in the occasional guest spot on Fox News or CNN as a media expert. In his "spare time," he taught literature and chaired the high school drama club.

She could smell the light scent of his aftershave as she stood before the class. Amanda, like many students, found him to be approachable and genuinely concerned. Given the fact that she was the editor of the school magazine, the *Venture,* she had spent many hours with him going over layouts and copy prior to sending them to print. In a way, he was a mentor to her, as he was for many other students. In some respects, he had even filled the void her father had left behind.

"Go ahead, Amanda," Dagus said with a gentle smile. She was nervous and felt an invisible finger trace her spine, unsure of what it meant. She turned toward the piece of paper in her hand and began to read in a slow cadence, carefully inflecting every comma and line change.

Good To Go

Biology may deem it so,

But I can't pretend to know

Who you are,

What you do,

Or how you came to be

Related

To me.

Memories may reside,

But I've never cried

Over you,

To you.

As I've grown

I've not known

You.

Where have you been?

Never mind,

I don't want to know,

Because I'm good to go.

No Dad?

I'm glad.

The class was still. Then one of the students started a slow clap, as if he was in a bad teenage movie, and the rest of the class joined in. Amanda rolled her eyes, gave a "whatever" shrug and moved back to her chair.

"Well, Amanda," Dagus began, clearly uncomfortable, "we might be able to fit that one in the *Venture* graduation edition. We'll have to see." He looked away as he spoke.

"Good poem, Amanda," Brianna Simpson whispered in her ear. "You're such a bitch. Who needs a dad anyway?" It was more of a statement than a question.

Amanda smiled.

"Mom helped me write it, so I can't take all the credit," she whispered back.

"Who cares? You're getting published in the *Venture*. That's, like, so cool."

Amanda looked at Brianna and gave her a fake smile. The bell rang and she grabbed her pack as she hollered over her shoulder, "See you later, Bree. Party tomorrow night. Don't be late."

As she passed Dagus, she gave him a nonchalant wave and kept going. Once in the hall, she hooked a left toward the main entrance. Merging with the steady stream of bodies moving in all directions at all speeds, Amanda began checking off a mental list of things to do before everybody showed up tomorrow evening: get the ice, wrap the gag gifts, and get Gus to tap the keg. She was underage, but hey, this was graduation.

Exiting the school through the wide double doors, she spilled out onto the concrete apron that ran the length of the school. She stopped to readjust her book bag when she felt someone staring at her. Looking up, she saw Principal Rugsdale looking in her direction.

"Okay, Garrett, how you doing?" The retired Marine wore an aqua golf shirt with shark fins at all different angles and khaki pants. He was trim and muscular, looking every bit the Desert Storm veteran that he was. He had left active duty with the Marines shortly after that war and pursued his degree in educational administration. In his early forties, he was often mistaken for someone much younger. Generally speaking, the students admired him despite the universal incongruity of bearing affection for one's principal.

"Hi, Mister Rugsdale," Amanda said, smiling. "I'm fine. You?" she added, as she walked past him holding up a hand, which he high-fived.

"Great season, champ. Almost had it this year."

"Horseshoes and hand grenades," she called over her shoulder as she waved with one hand, wiggling her fingers. She continued walking past his new red Mustang convertible in the number one parking spot.

"Watch the car, Garrett!" Rugsdale smiled.

She tossed him a playful look and pretended to touch the car with a finger, removing it quickly as if the red paint had burned her. "You and your cars!"

WATCHING AMANDA BLEND into the antlike swarm in the parking lot, he frowned. He wasn't sure what it was, but it was something. Her touch, maybe. Yes, that had been it. The simple slapping of the hand, he thought, had transmitted a signal to him. The way some people with arthritis can feel a low-pressure system coming, he had a sixth sense about him regarding danger.

"I know all about hand grenades," he muttered out of her earshot. He had started out as a basic grunt in Desert Storm, wounded once in that war. In 2003 he had been recalled in the reserves and sent to Iraq to serve as a public affairs officer, of all things, in Operation Iraqi Freedom. Essentially he escorted the press around and wrote the occasional article for public consumption.

Standing in front of the school, watching his flock, he nodded to himself.

Yes, he knew all about danger.

AMANDA NAVIGATED HER way through the parking lot, where she saw her mother's Mercedes idling directly behind her car. As she approached she noticed the passenger side window silently lowered and stuck her head in.

"Hi, mom, what's up?"

"Doctors appointment. Come on, jump in. I'll give you a lift." Her mother was wearing a white silk blouse atop a navy skirt. Amanda noticed the blue blazer was carefully hanging in the back behind the driver's seat. Her mother's Rolex watch hung loosely from her slender left wrist as she leaned over and rested her arm on the two o'clock position of the steering wheel.

"What doctors appointment? I don't need to see the doctor." She was really confused now, as she had to get home to make final preparations for tomorrow night's party the party. "And what about prepping for tomorrow?"

"Just hop in. It's a follow-up. Nina's got the house about ready anyway."

Amanda got in the car and turned her head to the right and laid it against the headrest as she closed her eyes. Maybe this doctors visit would be the one, she sighed. Maybe they would figure out what was wrong with her.

"So, did Gus get the keg?" Amanda asked, breaking the silence.

Her mother continued staring straight ahead. Her most recent boyfriend, Gustavson D. Randel III, was a writer for *Charlotte Magazine*. A bona fide Charlotte bachelor, Gus Randel was handsome and smooth. She didn't particularly care for him, although he had sided with her when she had approached her mom about the party. Still, she wasn't sure, but she always felt as though he was interested in something besides her mother.

"I don't know anything about that, Amanda, remember?"

"Oh, right. That's our deal. Gotta keep you clean," she responded sarcastically. "I'll take that as a yes."

Thirty minutes later they were at the doctor's office, where she went through a series of blood tests, which she had just had performed six months ago. As she was gathering her backpack to leave, she saw her mother talking to the office assistant at the billing counter. The lady had a round face and whitish blonde hair that was starched in place with hairspray. She had to be over fifty, Amanda thought.

"Okay, now I need the total bill. I know insurance is going to pay for eighty percent of this, right?"

"Yes, ma'am, but we will take care of all of that. You don't need the bill."

"You're new here, aren't you?" Melanie grimaced at the woman, losing patience.

"Well, I've been here a few months."

"I keep very detailed records. Amanda's father is pretty bad about, you know, keeping up with child support payments and insurance, so I need it all."

The office assistant considered her comment and said, "I understand. I've had to deal with some of the same stuff."

"We have to stick together, don't we?" Melanie commented as the lady handed her the paperwork in an envelope.

On the ride back from the doctor, Amanda asked her mother, "What was that all about?"

Melanie, seemingly occupied with driving, said, "Hmmm? What was what all about?"

"The doctor visit. Did they figure anything out?"

"We still don't know. In the meantime, though, you've got to stay healthy, Amanda. Your lipids are terrible. So we'll keep doing these visits as long as we need to."

Amanda stared out of the window to her right as her mother returned her to the school parking lot. She could feel her mother's eyes on her as she wondered what the hell lipids might be and what it might mean if they were "terrible."

"Don't you worry about anything. We've got the party tomorrow night. That's what you need to be focused on."

CHAPTER 3
NORTHWEST FRONTIER PROVINCE, PAKISTAN

FRIDAY EVENING

Mullah Rahman had led his team into the cave after he watched the second helicopter explode early Friday morning. He wasn't certain about the first one, but there was no question about the second one. The Balkan operators had done well.

Indeed, very well.

As they had made haste through the labyrinth from one side of the mountain to the back, through nearly a half mile of complex tunnels, dead-ends, and guarded posts, Rahman made the decision that they would keep going until they were deep inside their Pakistan sanctuary.

So they walked, carrying their wounded and their spoils of victory, until nightfall. Now they rested in a small village several miles from where the combat took place. Rahman directed his men to conduct triage, secure the prizes from the landing zone, and reload their ammunition quickly.

The snow had been deep on the top of the mountain but they had been descending most of their trek and now were in relatively bearable temperatures for May. The small village was nondescript with several adobe huts that had been reinforced with mud and straw over the years and now could withstand a 500-pound bomb. He walked into the structure where the wounded were being treated by a team of two doctors. Both men had thick, untrimmed beards and wore scrubs, surgical gloves and surgical masks. The doctors' compliance with Sharia law was as important as saving lives, thus the long, unsanitary beards.

On the first table, he saw one of his Pakistani Taliban fighters bleeding from a severed leg. Rahman himself had tied the tourniquet, which the doctor had loosened, but he doubted the young man would survive. On the second table he saw Commander Hoxha, who had taken several shrapnel wounds to the chest. Blood was blowing in bubbles from the right lung as the doctor had removed the battlefield dressing and now worked furiously to patch the sucking chest wound.

Rahman looked at Hoxha's gear, piled in the corner on the dirt floor. He saw the tactical vest with empty AK-47 magazines, the AK-47, and an M4. Hoxha had radioed in to Rahman that he had captured an American rifle, always a prized possession of Al Qaeda and Taliban fighters. Often these weapons hung over the fireplaces of Muslim fighter homes the way American Civil War muskets hung over mantels in Virginia. Rahman picked up the M4 with all of its high tech gadgetry. He popped out the magazine, which still had several rounds packed against the spring. He pulled back on the charging handle and ejected a solitary 5.56 mm round which tumbled across the room.

"Not in here," the doctor working on Hoxha called over his shoulder to Rahman.

Rahman nodded and left the operating room, moving into the room he used as his headquarters when they were operating from this village.

He sat on the rug cross-legged and placed the M4 in his lap, studying it. He was experienced with its predecessor, the M16, and the two weapons looked essentially the same other than size. Rahman held the M4 up, the single light bulb hanging from the ceiling providing a weak yellow hue. There was no name that he could see on the weapon, but it did have a serial number just above the magazine well. The numbers were meaningless to him. He adjusted the weapon so that the light would shine on the opposite side. As he turned the rifle, he heard a sliding, scraping noise in the butt-stock, as if something were loose.

He turned the weapon so that the muzzle was pointed down at the floor and he was staring at the machined backing of the telescoping stock. He saw a detent button and a cutaway portion of the butt. Similar to the M16, but smaller again, he knew this was where the soldiers normally carried their weapons cleaning gear.

He pushed on the button, pulled on the miniature trap door and turned the weapon upside down.

Into his lap fell a 4 GB flash drive.

CHAPTER 4
HINDU KUSH, AFGHANISTAN

SATURDAY

Sergeant Lance Eversoll sat inside Colonel Zachary Garrett's command Humvee as it idled in the daylight. A bright sun had squeezed the purplish gray from the morning and now reflected off the white snow, making him thankful that he had his dark Wiley X sunglasses. He had parked the vehicle at the base of the mountain where the helicopter had crashed, and he had been monitoring radio transmissions for a full day since.

As soon as they'd gotten word of the crash, another helicopter had ferried in a full platoon of infantry to secure the site. There were nearly one hundred people floating around the area, and with the enemy about four thousand feet above them in the mountains, no less.

Right up there, he thought, looking at the top of the inhospitable ridge. He visualized the explosion and then the aircraft plummeting into the crevice below. He had listened to the entire fight on the radio, and his heart sank when he heard the reports from the AC-130 pilot that Colonel Garrett's aircraft had gone down in a fireball. Moments before the crash, the radio had crackled with the constant stream of spot reports that the team had rescued the Navy SEAL. Eversoll had pumped his fist with a definitive *Yes!*

Then came Rampage's excited voice from the AC-130 gunship that they were concentrating fire on approximately twenty Al Qaeda moving toward the aircraft.

Seconds later the pilot reported the explosion.

He had participated in the subsequent rescue mission that had taken all of Friday and now into Saturday. Mortuary affairs soldiers milled around the wreckage like scavengers looking for scraps. There wasn't much left. The Kunar River raged and tumbled at the bottom of the abyss. Some of the bodies had been found a mile downstream. Still others had yet to be located.

Then the call came over the radio that the rescue operation had officially changed to a *recovery* operation. There was no one to rescue.

Sergeant Eversoll wiped his forehead with his sleeve and then placed his advanced combat helmet back on, snapping the chinstrap tight. He gritted his teeth as he whispered the warrior ethos to himself. *Always place the mission first. Never accept defeat. Never quit. Never leave a fallen comrade.* These were words for a soldier to live by, he thought to himself. And to die by.

He refused to believe that his role model was gone.

"Sir," he said, turning to Lieutenant Colonel Chizinski. "Sir, are they certain that they found Colonel Garrett's dog tags?"

Chizinski looked at Eversoll with sullen eyes.

"Chopper exploded with a full tank of gas then fell four thousand feet into a damn crevice. They've only found the remains of four people."

"What about the other ten?"

"Still looking." Chizinski coughed into one hand and opened the other to reveal a charred piece of metal half the size of a credit card. "The colonel's dog tags were in the wreckage."

Eversoll took the identification tag in his gloved hand and stared at it, touching the last remains of his commander: Zachary A. Garrett; O-Pos; 227-54-0987; Methodist.

"His buddies called him ZAG," Eversoll whispered more to himself than to Chizinski. He handed the piece of metal back to the lieutenant colonel. He stared into the sun and looked at the ground two hundred feet below them.

He returned his gaze to the high mountain from which the helicopter had fallen. "What did the team up there see, anything?"

"Not a damn thing other than some blown up mannequins in burqas." Chizinski was angry too. "They went up there after the Air Force bombed the hell out of the place, though, so you might say they disturbed the crime scene."

"Damned AQ probably already snuck out the back door, don't ya think?"

"Probably."

After a moment, Eversoll had a thought. He looked at Chizinski and then back up at the ridge. "Sir, you think we can do an op up there?"

"No need. Everything we're looking for is down there." Chizinski pointed into the gorge. Two rappel stations had been set up, nylon ropes tied around the winches of two Humvees. They actually had to climb down ropes to get to the crash site. "That's the only op we're going to be doing for the next few days."

Eversoll never removed his eyes from the top of the mountain towering over them like an impenetrable fortress.

I don't believe it, Eversoll thought to himself.

Just then, a soldier clawed his way over the edge. He was a black sergeant whose face was streaked with mud. He scrambled over the lip of the cliff and went to one knee, then stood. Brushing himself off, he loosened the back-pack he was carrying, then slipped it off his shoulders.

Eversoll watched him as he carried the bag toward them and then pulled several baggies from the inside, laying them on the hood of the Humvee.

"Five more identification tags. No more bodies. That thing burned, exploded, and then burned again, it looks like. After that, everything washed downriver."

Sergeant Eversoll looked at the tags. He knew them all. Driscoll (married with a baby on the way); Burns (father owned a cattle ranch in Wyoming); Svitek (loved to write, even did some poetry); Jackson (his first roommate at Fort Bragg, just bought a house with his new wife).

And Garrett. It was the other tag. Soldiers carried two, one on the long chain and one on the short chain.

There was no doubt, Colonel Garrett was dead.

CHAPTER 5
SPARTANBURG, SOUTH CAROLINA

SATURDAY EVENING (EASTERN TIME ZONE)

Saturday for Amanda was filled with the brisk handling of chores to set up the house for the party. Finally, with a chance to relax, she pulled on the lever of the keg.

"Whoo-hoo!" Amanda screamed, as foam sprayed everyone near her, mostly young high school males seeking her affection. "Another one bites the dust!" She sang the lyrics to the Queen song as if she'd been raised during that era thirty years ago. "Another one down and another one down, another one bites the dust, hey, hey!"

Suddenly there were two football players wearing Hawaiian shirts doing the bump with her, but not to the lyrics she was singing. Rather, they were grinding to the heavy bass rap chatter of Snoop Dog filling her plush suburban home.

"Hey, guys," Amanda said, teasing just a bit and then sliding from between them. She wore a see-through lace blouse over a light-green satin camisole that offset hip-hugger jeans. She was showing about six inches of midriff, which was enough to display the diamond belly-button ring and a lean, narrow-hip figure honed by the best swimming coaches money could buy.

"Gus! The keg's broken," she called into the study. She opened the door and saw him intently focused on the computer.

"Broken?" Gus looked up with a smile on his face. "Is this your Southern way of asking for help?"

"Maybe." She gave him a sheepish smile.

"Okay, I'll get right on it." Then he lifted a small digital camera off his desk and pointed it at her. "Hold it right there."

Amanda hammed it up by scrunching up her hair in a mock sultry pose. He snapped one photo as Brianna Simpson came walking in the room.

"This would be better out by your new Alfa," Amanda quipped. She was referring to Gus's "other girlfriend," the Alfa Romeo Spider parked at the curb.

"Not getting near Spidee," he said, stowing the camera.

"Amanda, phone's ringing," Brianna said, waving the handset at her. Amanda turned and looked at her. They had been best friends since elementary school. Brianna was her swimming partner in the Spartanburg Swimming Club since either could remember. She was an average swimmer whose mother had ambitions beyond her daughter's true potential. Amanda easily bested her in their races, making the friendship a challenge at times. Moreover, Brianna had once lived near Amanda but had moved away, as her mother had fallen on hard times when Brianna's father had left them. Somehow, though, she was able to keep the swimming lessons going.

"Phone," Brianna said, shoving her hand at Amanda as they exited the study.

Amanda's look was either, how could you hear the phone over this noise? or, there's a party going on, why do I care?

Either way, she grabbed the phone and waved at Gus to remind him. "*Keg?*" she mouthed, then did a pirouette and shuffled toward the hallway.

"How's acting class coming along?" Brianna asked. It was the one activity that they did not do together.

Amanda stopped and placed the back of her wrist against her forehead, as if in distress. "Rhett, Rhett, what am I going to do? Where shall I go?"

One of the anonymous boys passing by stuck his face in between the two girls, looking a bit like Chris Rock, and said in a squeaky Pee Wee Herman voice, "Frankly, my dear, I don't give a damn." Then, as he walked away, he muttered, "She's pretty good." And she was.

"Another one down and another one . . ." Amanda continued to sing as she made her way down the hall, shook her hair, and then put the phone to her ear. "Dominos, how may we help you?" Another teenage boy wearing dungarees that defied gravity by *not* falling below his buttocks smiled at her as she danced a small jig toward the foyer and out onto the front porch. Two white columns framed the entry.

"Hey, babe, how's the party going?" Amanda shifted from dancing to swaying slowly as she maneuvered down the steps toward the perfectly man-icured Saint Augustine grass lawn. A few guys and girls came and went freely in either direction. If there was one thing in her life that could keep her focused, it was the quarterback of the football team—and longtime boy-friend—Jake Devereaux.

"Great. When you getting here?"

"I'm here, pulling up now."

Amanda walked down to the driveway, moved an orange cone she had placed behind her metallic silver Mercedes SLK-350 Roadster, and waved Jake's Ford pickup truck into the circular drive. She ran up to the driver's side, opened the door and threw her arms around his big neck.

"Three weeks to graduation, babe. Can you believe it!" Amanda had downed four beers and was a bit tipsy. Jake had secured a scholarship to the University of South Carolina, just down the road in Columbia, where Amanda planned to attend on a swimming scholarship.

"I know. Coach Rogers told me today that the Einstein who was going to be our graduation speaker cancelled."

Amanda was uninterested. "As long as we get our diplomas, who cares?"

Jake cracked a grin. "Ever the deep one, aren't we?"

"Nooo," she said with a smile. "Take a poll. You know I'm right."

"Probably, but you know I've always been a sucker for that kind of thing. Stuff has to have meaning, you know?"

"That's why we're the most awesomest couple," Amanda said cutely. "Besides, we'll be graduating, genius; that has meaning."

She nuzzled her head into Jake's chest, then pulled up and kissed him softly on the lips. "We have meaning," she whispered.

After a moment, Jake's demeanor changed slightly, taking on a more serious tone. "We need to talk about something."

"Please don't tell me you're pregnant," she said, pulling away in mock horror.

Jake smiled a devilish grin briefly and then turned serious. "I got a call from The Citadel today. They've had a cancellation. I'm in if I want it."

"What!" She pushed away from Jake, an unusual move. Her outstretched fingers reached up and pulled at her hair from either side of her head. Amanda heard the words but was unable to allow them any validity. They'd had this discussion before, and Jake had turned down the academy's offer. He had never been entirely comfortable with the decision, primarily because he had felt enormous pressure from Amanda not to go, but now it was back on the table. "You can't be serious!"

"I haven't made up my—"

"That's not an option!" She was screaming now. A couple standing on the porch stopped talking and looked in her direction. "We talked about this."

Jake shook his head and started to close the door to the truck. "Hey, I just wanted you to know."

"Wait a minute. You can't just drive off."

"Then settle down, Amanda. You're making an ass out of yourself." Jake was characteristically firm. Eminem's "Eight Mile" was banging through the walls of the dining room. Someone had obviously turned up the bass, if not the volume. Jake looked over his shoulder. "Gettin' out of control in there?"

"Quit trying to change the subject, Jake." She was calmer now, more in control, honestly wanting to discuss the matter. Her resistance to Jake's going to The Citadel was based on more than well-founded fears of a dreaded long-distance relationship or an ensuing assignment in the Army.

Amanda could not fathom her boyfriend, and hopefully future fiancé, going to a school that would train him in the same profession as her father.

"Is this about your dad?" Again, direct and firm.

Amanda tensed at the mention of the word "dad."

"I don't have a dad," she muttered under her breath.

"That may be, Amanda, but you shouldn't take it out on me." Jake stood from the driver's seat of his pickup and stretched. He was six foot three inches tall, weighed 230 pounds, and he had the best arm in the southern United States. If Jake Devereaux were to show up unannounced on The Citadel's doorstep in a few days, not only would SEC football scratch its collective head, but the Bulldogs alumni would possibly be heard from the beyond sounding off with a thunderous *Yesss!*

Amanda stepped toward him, placing her thin hands on his jacket. She slid her arms as far as she could around his chest and laid her head against him.

"I know, baby. I just want you near me." She spoke quietly into the soft leatherette of his coat.

Jake pulled her closer. "You know I love you, Amanda, and I want us to be together forever. You know that."

He paused before broaching what he knew was another tough subject.

"And if we are going to be together forever, you need to sort out this thing with your dad."

Again she flinched. "Let's not talk about that, okay? There are just three weeks to graduation. My dad has only caused problems in my life. It's like he never existed except when he was missing child support or threatening my mom, or whatever."

"Come on. Don't you think that if those things were really happening, he'd be in jail?"

"That's where he belongs." Amanda's words were quick and decisive. There was no doubt about her sentiment.

"I hear what you're saying, but I'm here for you. And you can count on me to stand by you. My only request is that we talk to somebody about it, you know?"

Amanda pulled away. "You mean like a shrink?"

"Something like that," Jake said, less sure this time.

"Get out of here." Of course, she didn't mean for him to leave. Rather, she was calling into question the entire foundation of his last comment.

"If we're going to one day get married, like we've talked about, I don't want you having all these man-hating feelings." Jake had thought his way through this part of the discussion several times, though he had not expected to have it this night. He was operating purely on instinct, and it seemed right to talk about it. He had read that most couples who fail did so because of miscommunication. And he wasn't going to have any of that.

The headlights from a white minivan cut across them like a prison searchlight. Jake looked up and saw who it was.

"I think you probably need to get inside. I'll check you later."

"No, don't leave," Amanda said, pulling on his arm lightly. A matronly figure with bleached-blonde hair, not thin, not fat, wearing a matching coral pantsuit with a triple string of pearls around her neck emerged from the minivan that was now hemming Jake's truck into the driveway. "At least say hi."

"Hey there, Jake," the woman said in a whiny, Southern accent with mock enthusiasm.

Jake shuffled, looked at the ground, and then looked up at Mrs. Gabrielle Hastings—Hastings being the surname of her fourth husband. "Hi, Miss Gabrielle, nice to see you."

"You can call me Nina, Jake. How many times have I told you that? Anyway, if I didn't know better, I'd think you were lying to me." The expression she painted on looked curiously like a smile, but for the emptiness in her eyes. "Are you taking care of this pretty girl here?" Without giving him a chance to answer, she continued. "Of course not. Nobody can take care of my Manda Wanda like her Nina." With that she hugged Amanda, pulling her away from Jake. "Isn't that right?"

"Hey, Nina." Amanda's persona changed measurably, assuming the role of a child, becoming sheepish, cowing. Nina was the nickname that Amanda had known for her since she was born. Her grandmother had told her that she could never utter the words "grandma," and it always came out "Nina." Though she had no recollection of that, she presumed it was true.

"Where's your momma?"

"Be home in a few minutes. Went to get more ice or something."

"With a party like this going on? What are you, crazy?"

"They're being good in there, Nina. Don't worry."

"Let's just go see about that." Nina Hastings pulled Amanda away by the arm toward the porch.

"Wait, Nina, I'm talking to Jake about something. The Citadel's accepted him."

The grandmother stopped walking and turned slowly toward Jake, who was sitting in the driver's seat of his truck with one foot on the cobblestone driveway, elbow leaning on the steering wheel. Nina's face contorted into an evil mask, the light from the porch casting across half of her face then slowly shining across the entire tortured countenance.

She locked eyes with Jake, who held her stare. He had never liked the woman. He thought she was bad for Amanda and her mother, quite frankly. He saw her as selfish and controlling, using Amanda to fill her own egotistical needs. They held their locked gaze for a moment. Nina narrowed her eyes.

Jake smiled. "I think I just made up my mind."

Nina snatched Amanda's arm again and dragged her toward the house.

Amanda's eyes widened. "No!" she screamed as Nina hauled her to the porch and into the house.

Jake listened as someone had stopped the music and there was a collective moan from the party crowd. Then, he heard Nina's voice say, "Come on y'all, let's have a party." The music suddenly cranked back up and thumped at the walls.

Jake slid behind the wheel of his truck, closed the door and muttered, "Citadel, here I come," under his breath. He pulled forward into the grass and then back onto the circular driveway.

A leathery hand pulled apart two of the dining room window blinds, allowing Nina Hastings' hawkish eye to watch Jake Devereaux drive away.

CHAPTER 6
SPARTANBURG, SOUTH CAROLINA

SUNDAY MORNING

Amanda Garrett rolled in her bed, the bright morning sun cutting like a knife through the razor-thin slits in the miniblinds. She looked at the clock and moaned. *Why am I awake at eight a.m.?* Her head pounded from the vestiges of last night's beer, and she pressed her hands into her temples.

There was a noise from downstairs. She thought she heard two people arguing. One of the voices was her mother's, she knew that much. Even in her groggy condition she recognized the smooth Southern drawl. When had she come home? Had Nina spent the night? She couldn't remember. And Jake?

Oh, Jake. The Citadel. *No way*, she thought to herself. Her stomach got weak at the thought.

"Amanda." It was her mother's voice.

"Not now, Mom. I'm sleeping." She half screamed through her closed door.

She could hear feet coming up the oak hardwood steps.

"Now, Amanda, this is important."

"Nothing important happens Sunday morning at eight, Mom."

The door cracked open, and her mother peered in. She was still mildly attractive as she neared forty. A face-lift and continuous dye job on the hair seemed to keep her looking somewhat younger.

"No, this is important, Amanda. Now put on some decent clothes and come down."

Amanda took about ten minutes, tolerated another visit from her mother, and then came downstairs wearing jeans and a USC sweatshirt with the silk-screened image of a rooster on the front. As she bounced down the steps, she slowed her pace as she saw two uniformed men standing in the foyer.

She looked at her mother. "Is this about the party?" With arms crossed, her mother shook her head. Amanda noticed Nina in the dining room watching the drama unfold.

"Then what?" Amanda looked at the two men, both in green uniforms that she vaguely recognized as something she had seen her father wear at one point in time. She shrugged her shoulders and looked at them as if to say, "Okay, get on with it."

One of the men was a tall, handsome soldier holding a green beret in one hand and some papers in the other. The other man was shorter and stout. He was clearly older, balding some, and Amanda noticed he had a silver cross on his lapel.

The tall, handsome Green Beret looked her in the eyes and began to speak. "Are you Miss Amanda Rose Garrett?"

"That's me, all day long. You know ARG, like a pirate," she said impatiently, making a play on her initials.

"Ma'am, I am Major Ross Blair, and I regret to inform you that your father has been killed in action in Afghanistan."

Amanda stared at the man, without really seeing him. She was searching for some kind of response inside. There was nothing coming to her mind, no connection between thought and emotion. Simply, there was no emotion.

She turned to her mother for guidance and saw that she was exchanging a look with Nina. She then looked across the foyer into the dining room at Nina, who remained silent, her thin lips curled upward just a bit. *What is that look?* Amanda wondered to herself.

"Miss Garrett, we are notifying you because your parents are divorced, and you are listed as the next of kin. I am the casualty assistance officer and will be able to help guide you through the process as we honor Colonel Garrett and lay his remains to rest. I hope you understand why we had to notify you personally and could not simply tell your mother."

Amanda noticed the man spoke without prepared remarks; however, the words seemed well rehearsed. Perhaps he had done this before, she thought.

"While I know you are understandably upset, Chaplain Jones and I will be outside after you have had a chance to discuss the matter with your mother. Do you have any questions for either of us right now?"

Amanda looked at Major Blair and then at Chaplain Jones.

"No," she responded to the major. She tapped her foot and looked at her fingernails, then turned to her mother. "Can I go back to sleep now?" She spoke with an irritated edge, as if she had been needlessly awakened.

The major and chaplain exchanged glances, and then Blair looked at Amanda's mother. "Ma'am, we'll be outside if she needs us."

"I won't need you," Amanda said. "I'm fine." She turned around and ran up the steps, stopping at the midlevel landing. "Just one question."

By now Nina and Amanda's mother were ushering the two soldiers to the door. They stopped and looked up at her.

"What was he doing? I mean how was he killed?"

Blair had one foot in the house and one foot on the porch. Nina stepped in front of him and continued their momentum outside, but he was a large man and didn't budge. He looked up at Amanda. "Miss Garrett, your father died rescuing another soldier."

"That's enough, major. Can't you see she's upset? Let's just get going here." Nina's voice was loud and shrill. Finally, Blair's good manners overcame his stubborn desire to make sure that Colonel Garrett's daughter knew he died a hero, and he stepped outside.

Amanda turned and continued to climb the stairs. She heard the door close and glanced over her shoulder. She saw her mother and Nina leaning against the door as if to keep an intruder at bay. They turned and looked at each other, both smiling just a bit, as Amanda rounded the corner into her room.

She shut the door and stood motionless in the center of her room, staring at the full-length mirror against the far wall. She saw her image, that of a nearly grown woman, and she continued to wonder why she felt nothing at all. Surely she should be sad, upset, mad, or overcome by some other raging emotion. She didn't even feel happy, which she had actually thought about before. Did that mean she wanted him dead?

Regardless, that day had come. Colonel Zachary Garrett would no longer fight with her mother, miss a swim meet or birthday, skip a child support payment, or inconvenience her life with unplanned visits. Well, good, she thought.

She walked over to her window and looked out at the street where the two soldiers' car was parked. She saw the chaplain hugging the major, who had his face buried in his shoulder.

Amanda Garrett sat on her bed and looked at her clock. The entire episode had taken nine minutes, which was more time than she had thought about her father in a long while. She kicked off her sandals, slid under her sheets, and rested her head on her pillow.

LOUDOUN COUNTY, VIRGINIA

Matt Garrett stood at the door of his Loudoun County home and stared at the man standing before him. The soldier was dressed in Army blue uniform, creased perfectly along the front seams of the pants. His face was stern, stoic, and unrelenting in its gaze.

"So either my brother's dead or you're lost," Matt said.

"Sir, I regret to inform you that your brother, Colonel Zachary Garrett, is reported as killed in action in Kunar Province, Afghanistan."

The rest of the visit was a blur. Matt had been down this dark trail previously in the Philippines. And now again? True, both he and Zach operated in the thin margins of life where danger continuously lurked, waiting like a rabid puma, eyes glistening, mouth foaming, ready to kill at random. His role with the CIA had put Matt in a series of difficult situations while Zach's eagerness to get back into the fight after 9-11 had led to fights in the Philippines, Canada and now Afghanistan. Men like Matt and Zach operated in the netherworld of spies and operatives that few Americans understood but from which all benefited, whether they knew it or not.

Zach dead?

"I'll believe it when I see it," Matt muttered. He dismissed the officer and walked through his small brick rambler sitting on three acres of rolling hills. He picked up the phone, thought about calling his sister Karen and his father, but then put the receiver down and decided to wait. They were probably at church anyway. Instead he grabbed a Budweiser from its dominant and nearly solitary place in the refrigerator, and walked through the back door onto his wood deck. From the deck he could see his land slope away to the south and west, toward the Blue Ridge and toward Stanardsville, his family home 90 miles away.

He could also see his makeshift batting cage about 100 feet away. It was Sunday morning and he figured he did his best thinking down in that mesh netting so he bounced down the steps, pulled the gate closed behind him as he stepped into the cage, and grabbed his Pete Rose 34. He dialed the pitch speed to 95 miles per hour and said, "Screw the helmet."

Standing in the batter's box, the first pitch blew crazily past him as if it were a knuckle ball. The tires kept spinning and the cantilevered chain driven arm dropped another ball into the jugs machine and he saw this one coming high and inside, took a slight step into the bucket, and ripped a solid line drive to what would be left field, maybe even over the green monster at Fenway Park in Boston.

He was juiced. Zach dead? No way. He didn't care what some puke stateside officer told him. His brother had proven his own indestructibility in the Philippines and then had damn near saved the world during the Ballantine incident a few years ago. He continued to groove what he called "frozen ropes" into the back of the net. As he did so, he developed his plan.

First he would call Karen and tell her what the uniform had told him, but he would ensure she didn't say anything unless the media got hold of the information. Then she could tell their father. Next he would get on the first plane smoking to Afghanistan, link up with Major General Jack Rampert, who owed him a mountain of favors after what he had done to Zach post-Philippines. And who knows what kind of tight spot Rampert just put Zach into in Afghanistan that supposedly got him killed.

Lastly, if indeed Zach were dead, he would exact revenge. He would do it coolly and professionally. He would find the offending bastards and kill them. It was his blood promise with Zach, who had dragged him dying off the Philippine battlefield.

He took one last cut, got that weightless moment between bat and ball, felt the rawhide launch into the netting and watched it punch a hole through the taut material and keep going. He doubted three acres would contain that anger management swing.

He punched the red button, watched the tires slow, and flipped his bat against the back of the cage. He walked back to his deck, halfway expecting to see Peyton O'Hara reappear, but knowing she was forever gone into the terrorist underground. He drained his Bud, walked into his bedroom, grabbed his go-bag full of weapons, knives, and night-vision goggles, locked his house, and tossed his equipment into the passenger side of the Porsche. He cranked the engine, slammed the stick into first gear, and floored the gas pedal so that his 15 year old sports car spat gravel from his driveway like the rooster tail of a cigarette boat as he rocketed toward Dulles Airport

Retrieving his Blackberry, he punched the Agency director's number and said, "I'm going to Afghanistan."

"I heard. I'm sorry, Matt." Roger Houghton, the director of the CIA, spoke over their secure line in somber tones.

"He's not dead. Save your sympathy."

"I've got the Afghan team running the reports. It sounds . . . conclusive, Matt."

"You don't know Zach like I do."

"I know Zach, but I understand. We'll send you on tonight's milk run."

"Thanks. It's Sunday. Usual time?"

"I told them to get ready. They'll be waiting for you when you get to IAD."

"Thanks, Roger."

"Least we can do."

"I'll be back when I'm back. No sooner."

"No sooner. And Matt?"

"What?"

"You know Rampert gave your brother the Operation Searing Gorge mission right?"

Matt hesitated. Searing Gorge was his idea, but he certainly didn't anticipate that Zach would be the mule.

"No idea." After a pause, he added. "Though it makes sense. He's the best."

"That he was," Houghton added.

"Is," Matt corrected and hung up.

Matt pulled into the private parking lot that the agency leased at Dulles International Airport. He found the crew chief to the Boeing 757, shook his hand, and said, "Let's get on with it."

As he boarded the nondescript Boeing 757, he noticed four rows of seats and then pallets stacked to the ceiling. The Agency ran an airplane weekly to Afghanistan to resupply the operatives on the ground. It was affectionately known as "The Milk Run."

There were a couple of logisticians with Ipod earbuds hanging from their ears sitting in the small passenger section. Matt nodded at them as they immediately offered to move.

He fixed a killer's grimace onto his face and sat in one of the comfortable seats in the front row, strapping his go-bag in the seat next to him. Anyone looking at the expression on his face would have figured him for a deranged psychotic. He went through a checklist in his mind: recover Zach, kill whoever did this, and complete the Searing Gorge mission himself.

Matt Garrett was on the move.

CHAPTER 7
SPARTANBURG, SOUTH CAROLINA

Jake Devereaux pulled into Amanda's driveway, slamming the door as he rushed from his truck and sprung up the steps of the brick Georgian home two at a time. He knocked furiously on the door and rang the doorbell twice, then again.

The door swung open, and he was face to face with Nina Hastings.

"She's not accepting visitors."

"She called me and told me what happened. Let me in." Jake stood tall in the doorway. He'd had enough of Nina Hastings for a lifetime. He wasn't going to be deterred when Amanda needed him. "Ma'am, we can do this the hard way or the easy way."

"Nina, let him in. I called him," Amanda said, pushing her way past her grandmother.

Always one to pick her fights, Nina relented, but added, "See what happens when you go to The Citadel, Jake?"

Jake, hugging Amanda in the hardwood foyer, looked over his shoulder and said, "Have some respect, please."

He took Amanda's hand and walked her outside, curving around the two-car garage with finished bonus room above. He led her into the backyard and beyond the fence into an isolated spot in the woods. Amanda was wearing her Clemson sweatshirt and had put on a pair of jeans. Jake was wearing a T-shirt that said "Fandango" on a movie ticket stub. His biceps were pushing at the material as he rested a hand on a small dogwood branch. Two hummingbirds hovered around an open knot in a tree that was filled with water.

"You okay?"

"Yeah, what's not to be okay with?"

"Don't give me that tough girl act, Amanda. This is your father we're talking about." Jake pulled her close.

"Like I said last night, he's just been a thorn in my side. So maybe this is for the best."

Jake looked at her, shaking his head. "Don't ever say that again. Your father loved you."

"How would you know?"

"I saw him come to your swim meets and cheer you on."

"Yeah, well, where's he been since then?"

"How about trying to keep us safe over here?"

"You don't really believe that, do you? That fighting solves anything? That going—going over there to wherever helps?" She was nearly screaming at him.

He could see she wanted to cry, but that she was afraid. Afraid of what, he didn't know, so he just talked.

"Amanda, for the last four years I've seen you struggle with this issue about your father. At times, I can almost see a star-struck daddy's girl deep inside of you, though you never let it out. Mostly, though, you are hateful and spiteful towards him, even manipulative."

"That's not true," she said, pushing away to emphasize the point.

"I think your grandmother and mother have made you the point man in their fight against your father. That's not a fight any sane person would want."

"My grandmother helped raise me in his absence."

"Maybe, but don't you think you owe it to yourself to learn something about him? Maybe honor him just a bit. After all, you only die once."

Amanda stepped away. "I know everything I need to know about my biological father. Everything!"

Jake lowered his head. "I'm just trying to help here."

A long moment of silence passed between them. The hummingbirds continued their yo-yo around the small pool of water. The wind tossed Amanda's highlighted hair, and the sun shone in a single ray through the forest canopy behind Jake's head.

The shrill voice of Nina Hastings pierced the moment. "Amanda, telephone!" Jake shook his head slowly.

"I've gotta go deal with this. The army guy told my mom he needed me to sign some paperwork. Something about insurance."

"Okay, go do your thing, Amanda. Just remember, I'm trying to make us better, and you need to work with me to do that."

"You're being naïve, Jake. You weren't there when all of this happened."

Jake looked at her. "Were you?"

Amanda walked away, saying, "Don't cause a fight anymore than you have, Jake. This is not your business."

"Amanda, phone!" Nina's echoing squawk was the shrill call of an angry shepherd.

Jake kicked at the underbrush as Amanda walked past the pool, up the deck steps, and then disappeared into the backdoor of the house. Amanda was the first and only love in his young life. He enjoyed curling her up into his arms for hours as they mapped out their future together. But now, he was beginning to see—no, had seen for a long time—an unseemly materialistic side to her.

She'd been taught to believe that love was a wisp of air, and that money and things were forever. Did she really love him, he wondered? Or were they together just because he was the quarterback and she was beautiful?

CHAPTER 8
BAGRAM AIR BASE, AFGHANISTAN

MONDAY

Sergeant Eversoll parked Colonel Garrett's Humvee next to the headquarters building at the old air base. The location had been a MiG fighter base during the Soviet Afghan invasion. The invaders had constructed some rudimentary cinderblock buildings, which now served as respectable makeshift headquarters for the Joint Task Force.

He was exhausted from two days of participating in the search for remains of the fallen soldiers. They had collected either actual remains, pieces of bone mostly, or the identification tags of all but one soldier. Sergeant Honeywell was unaccounted for and was listed as duty status whereabouts unknown, or DUSTWUN in Army acronym parlance. Eversoll wondered about Honeywell, one of his closer friends in the unit, as he locked up the vehicle and walked into the command headquarters.

He unsnapped his helmet and dumped it on the ratty chair that sat outside Colonel Garrett's office, then walked in. The large window splashed the 6 a.m. sunlight across the dusty room. An old desk, two equally ratty chairs, and a table were situated around the room. Eversoll walked past the desk, eyeing the pictures of Colonel Garrett's daughter scattered about in different frames, and stopped at the wall with a large map of Afghanistan spread from side to side. He ran his hand absently along the terrain he knew so well, the very area where Colonel Garrett's helicopter had crashed.

"Hard to believe, isn't it, son?"

Eversoll quickly turned and stood to attention at the sound of Major General Jack Rampert's voice. He saw Rampert standing just inside the office, holding a combat helmet under his arm. Rampert's bristly gray hair covered his head like shaved porcupine quills.

"Yes, sir," Eversoll responded. Then he added, "Actually, I don't believe it."

"You don't believe that he's dead, or you refuse to believe it?" Rampert's voice was crisp and authoritative. It was the voice of someone well practiced in the command of soldiers in tough situations.

Eversoll walked away from the map and toward the desk. He was about ten feet from Rampert. "Sir, let's just say I need more than a dog tag to go by."

"They found both of them, Sergeant Eversoll. That isn't good enough?"

Rampert knew Eversoll from spending time with Colonel Garrett during so many long missions through lonely nights waiting for situation reports. Sometimes senior leaders got to know quite well the young men who drove, answered radios for, and protected leaders such as Garrett as they led the Army. Rampert respected Eversoll's relationship with Colonel Garrett. The conversation was not confrontational; rather, it was intended as comforting.

"I understand what you're saying, sir. Maybe I'm in denial; I don't know. But you always tell us to use our instincts, and something just doesn't feel right about this." Eversoll lowered his eyes, unable to hold the general's gaze. Maybe he was in denial. Maybe he was not being honest with himself.

"Come here, son. Follow me." Rampert turned and walked toward the hallway.

Five minutes later, Sergeant Eversoll found himself in the bowels of the Joint Task Force headquarters. He was standing with Major General Rampert in a windowless room. Two large plasma television screens sat atop a long table. Eversoll thought to himself that it looked like a small home movie theater. The general motioned him into one of the comfortable-looking chairs.

"On the left, Sergeant, you will see the unmanned aerial vehicle video of the action that night. On the right will be the AC-130 video."

"Rampage." Eversoll's voice was a whisper. He wasn't sure he was prepared for this. Wouldn't he rather live with the slim hope, however misguided, that his boss had somehow miraculously survived the explosion of the helicopter? It was too late. As he was pondering the notion of getting up and walking out, Kill TV, as the soldiers called it, began to show on both screens. They called it that because typically they were watching their team kill the Taliban or AQ in large numbers. Reviewing this reversal of fortune was not supposed to be part of the moniker.

"You can see there, we've got heavy fire on the landing zone, with the first aircraft taking a hit in the tail rotor engine housing." Rampert used a green laser pointer to circle the MH-47's smoking tail rotor. He shifted to the AC-130 gun tape. "Here, you see Rampage laying down heavy 105 suppressive fire."

Eversoll remembered sitting in his Humvee listening to the fight. So far this tracked with what he knew. Though, it was different seeing it actually happen.

"Here you see Jergens falling out of the aircraft as it lands, then pulls up. We lose him for about twenty seconds because of the whiteout from the snow. Watch."

Sure enough, the helicopter was kicking snow high into the air. The twin rotors pushed down and then pulled up the snow, creating a white cloud that surrounded the helicopter and everything within one hundred feet. Eversoll knew that pilots called this whiteout, and he absently wondered how they could possibly control an aircraft in those conditions. These Special Forces pilots were good; he knew that much. Watching this video, he saw they had to be. He could not see the aircraft or Jergens.

"You see the 47 take off here," Rampert continued. "It almost falls, but maintains control off that ledge. Now that the whiteout is gone, you can see Jergens, here, and AQ coming at him, here." He used the pointer to highlight Jergens on the left side of the screen and the Al Qaeda on the right. There were about fifteen men wearing white sheets and wielding AK-47s and rocket-propelled grenade launchers. The grainy, gray video painted an unmistakable picture.

Navy SEAL Jergens was a dead man if something didn't happen in the next two minutes. Eversoll felt like he was watching a thriller movie. His palms were sweating, and he could feel himself wishing someone would help the American trapped on the mountaintop.

"Here comes Colonel Garrett's aircraft." Rampert pointed to the UAV video feed. "You can see the AC-130 is still focused on separating the AQ from Jergens."

"Doing a pretty good job, sir." Eversoll had not followed this portion of the picture when he had originally listened to the fight. The AC-130 was providing pinpoint accurate fires, killing the enemy. He could see six or seven dark masses lying in the snow.

"Roger, now watch what happens here."

Eversoll saw the second MH-47 come hurtling in toward the very same landing zone the first helicopter had tried. As the aircraft slowed and flared in its descent, the ramp was already down. Four men spilled out of the aircraft to the left and three to the right. About the time Eversoll noticed two men running straight off the back ramp, snow enveloped the entire helicopter.

"That has to be Colonel Garrett and Sergeant Honeywell," Eversoll said with conviction.

"I agree. Honeywell's the biggest soldier we've got, and Garrett's the kind of guy who would go get Jergens. The radio transmissions tell us that Colonel Garrett ordered Rampage to continue to isolate the enemy. We heard the MH-47 pilots from Garrett's aircraft tell the pilots from the first aircraft that they were recovering Jergens and then aborting the mission."

The video streams continued. The AC-130 was clearly focused on destroying the enemy, though they seemed to be able to find good cover and then rush for a few seconds, finding good protection again. The UAV video was solely focused on the helicopter. The blurring white snow would fade just a second and then become thicker than before. Eversoll could clearly see Colonel Garrett emerge from the whiteout with Honeywell at his side.

Honeywell stopped to shoot as the colonel rushed toward a dark spot in the snow—the man that was probably Jergens. The UAV operator must have zoomed in during this section of the film, because Eversoll could see Colonel Garrett clearly now, yelling and shaking something near his chest. Suddenly a suicide Al Qaeda slipped through Rampage's wall of fire, leaping over the rock providing cover for the two Americans. Eversoll clenched his fists in pride as Colonel Garrett whipped out his knife and impaled the would-be attacker on its sharp edge. Colonel Garrett quickly slipped Jergens into a fireman's carry. Jergens was firing his M4 as best he could. They ran past Honeywell, who then began to backpedal.

"Way to go, sir," Eversoll whispered. He noticed he was sweating now. The film was coming to the part he wasn't sure he was ready to see. He remembered seeing replays of the Challenger shuttle explosion, and even though he had only been one or two when the tragedy had occurred, he still found it hard to watch. There was something unsettling to him about the confirmation that comes with witnessing the moment of tragic death.

Honeywell, Jergens, and Colonel Garrett all reentered the snow haze around the aircraft. The AC-130 tape remained focused on the Al Qaeda fighters. Eversoll could see about twelve dark masses lying on the ground, presumably dead. On the UAV video, the whiteout had ebbed enough for him to see Honeywell leap up onto the ramp, pulling the wounded Jergens from Colonel Garrett's shoulders.

Eversoll found himself thinking, *What could go wrong; the hard part is over? Just take off.* He was clutching the table now with both of his hands. He felt Rampert's hand on his shoulder.

The whiteout reappeared in full force, blocking any visibility from the video feed as the MH-47 throttled up and began to torque straight up into the sky. The video followed the aircraft up, watching it nose forward over the ledge and speed off, ramp still open.

"They're away—"

The UAV video suddenly erupted with a billowing, grey and white image when the MH-47 exploded just above the landing zone. Burning pieces of the debris wafted into the deep crevice beyond the mountaintop.

Eversoll pushed away from the table and stood up. "Where did that come from?"

Rampert looked at him. "Do you really want to know, son?"

He was afraid for his commander. He was personally devastated. "Yes, sir. Damn right I do."

"Rerun it, VD," Rampert said to Van Dreeves, sitting in the dark corner of the room.

The video picked up again where Eversoll could see Honeywell on the ramp, Jergens being flopped onto the ramp, and Colonel Garrett on one knee in the snow. The operator had enlarged the picture. It wasn't great, but it was good enough to see the three men through the snow tornado created by the rotor blades. As the aircraft lifted off, the whiteout thickened, and there was no way to tell what happened next.

"Stop it," Rampert ordered. "See there. That's got to be Colonel Garrett getting on the aircraft."

Eversoll followed Rampert's green laser. Through the snow, it was possible to make out a dark mass moving quickly onto the aircraft. As the video played in slow motion, the aircraft took off, nosed over, and then two streaks of light cut across the feed from right to left. Then the helicopter exploded.

"Those could be RPGs or maybe even surface to air missiles," Rampert said. "We're not really sure. There could have even been an explosion inside the aircraft."

Eversoll sat speechless for a moment. On one hand it seemed undeniable. Colonel Garrett was on the aircraft, and it exploded, killing him and the rest of his friends.

"Sir, does the UAV ever go back to the landing zone?"

"No. It follows the aircraft into the gorge. Why?"

"How about Rampage?"

"Watch it," he said, motioning.

The AC-130 video continued to focus on the enemy that seemed to come pouring from nowhere. There were at least thirty on the mountaintop, cheering wildly as the helicopter exploded. Rampage's 105 rounds expedited their meeting with Allah.

"So, nothing ever gets back to the landing zone? The UAV and the

AC-130, they never look at the LZ? Rampage couldn't have killed everyone up there." Eversoll's mind was in high gear.

"No, but we killed about forty AQ. Rampage had to break station about five minutes after this. They were out of gas. The team that went in Saturday afternoon saw some blood trails and a lot of shell casings from the firefight. That's about it, son." Rampert paused, then continued. "We never kill them all, that's for sure. And there's a cave complex up there. That's where all those guys came from. I think we were onto something."

"But we don't know for sure that Colonel Garrett got on that helicopter, General."

"We know it, son. It's hard for me to accept, too, but we know it."

"The last image in the video that we know for sure is that of Colonel Garrett was on the ground."

"We found his dog tags in the wreckage, son." Rampert stood. "We'll talk more about this later. It's been a rough couple of days."

Eversoll stood, thanked the general and walked out.

As Eversoll departed, Rampert looked at Van Dreeves and said, "The real question is did he leave behind what he needed to?"

Van Dreeves looked at the general and said, "Actually, we can be pretty sure of that. What we really need to know is if the bad guys found it."

CHAPTER 9
SPARTANBURG, SOUTH CAROLINA

SUNDAY EVENING

The major sitting across from her had a serious tone. They had returned from their earlier visit in the morning in accordance with military protocol. He was now there to tell her about what her father had left behind, facts and figures that she really didn't care about. But when Amanda Garrett heard him say, "Five hundred thousand dollars," her heart skipped a beat.

"Surely that's not all for me?" she said.

"Ma'am, Colonel Garrett left you that much money. It was every bit of his life insurance. He had savings accounts out of which we are paying for things such as his mortgage in North Carolina and other expenses. This money is yours." The major looked away briefly.

Amanda was dressed in a black pantsuit that her mother had purchased. "You're in mourning and we need you to appear to be," she had said. Amanda and the major sat in the dining room, papers spread out between them. Nina Hastings watched from the living room, while Amanda's mother sat pensively at the other end of the table.

Amanda looked at her mother, whom she caught eyeing Nina at the sound of the words "Five hundred thousand dollars."

"Why would he do that? I hated him. I couldn't even stand for him to be around, and he leaves me all of this? It doesn't make sense."

"Well, clearly, ma'am, he didn't hate you," the major said.

"I think what Amanda is trying to say," her mother chirped, "is that relations between her and her father had been strained in recent years."

"Strained? You wouldn't let me—"

Nina Hastings raised a hand and said, "Child, we'll have none of that. Your father's dead, and it isn't right to talk about him like this."

Major Blair and the chaplain exchanged glances. Perhaps they had seen it before; Amanda didn't know.

"When does Amanda get the money?" Melanie Garrett asked.

"Well, there's one catch," Major Blair said.

"I knew it," Nina muttered under her breath. Amanda turned and looked at her and then back at the major.

"Amanda, you're not eighteen yet." The major clearly preferred talking to her as opposed to her mother or grandmother. She watched her mother out of the corner of her eye as the major began to speak. Her face was twitching, as if she was trying to not smile. Interesting. The major reached across the table and touched Amanda's hand lightly.

"Your father put a stipulation in his will that if you were under eighteen when he passed, you'd have to talk to someone before receiving the money. And then, on your eighteenth birthday, the insurance would be paid out to you. Because he passed before you turned eighteen, this stipulation endures. You must comply with it to receive the death gratuity. In other words, even after you turn eighteen, you have to follow the instructions as detailed by your father if you wish to receive the money."

"What is this?" Melanie Garrett spat. "Some cruel joke from beyond the grave? He has to manipulate Amanda even when he's gone, is that it? I'm getting a lawyer here now!" Amanda's mother jumped up from the table, knocking some of the papers onto the floor.

"Just goes to figure," Nina Hastings said, shaking her head.

Amanda sat in her chair and looked at the major. "I turn eighteen the day after graduation. That's two weeks. Who do I need to talk to?"

Major Blair handed her an envelope. "The name and address are in here with some other instructions. This has all been thoroughly checked out by our judge advocate general. That's a military term for a lawyer. Colonel Garrett obviously put a lot of thought into this, ma'am. The least you can do is to follow it through."

"And if I don't?" Amanda removed her hand from the major's light grasp.

"He has named a secondary beneficiary, whose name I cannot disclose."

"I heard that!" Melanie Garrett was back now, pointing her finger at the major. "I heard that bullshit. He's breaking his court order. He was supposed to always keep at least one hundred thousand dollars life insurance on her until she was eighteen."

"Ma'am, I don't think this is helpful. Our lawyers, as I mentioned, have looked at this. His last child support payment to you was at the beginning of this month. He used that date as the date to—"

"The effective date is her birthday!" Nina Hastings had joined the fray. "He can't do that!"

Amanda watched her mother and grandmother circle like hawks around the major and chaplain. Each would take turns diving and swiping their talons at the two uniformed officers. She let it go on for about two minutes, then stood and screamed, "Stop it!"

She stared at her mother and then turned toward her grandmother. "Stop it!"

Amanda Garrett took the envelope the major had passed her, turned and bolted up the stairs, leaving the others frozen in time, as if in a wax museum, staring at her as she fled.

She closed the door behind her and leaned against it. *This is crazy. Five hundred thousand dollars?*

She found her cell phone, dialed, and said, "Hey, can you come get me. I need to talk to you."

★ ★ ★

NINA HASTINGS LOOKED at her daughter, Melanie Garrett, from across the dining room table with a purposeful stare.

"Well, what are you going to do?" Her voice had the tenor of a high-pitched fire engine alarm, both pleading and accusatory at once.

"About what, Mother?"

"What do you mean, about what? You have no idea what's going on with this situation, and you know you stand a good chance of getting screwed out of that money. Probably Amanda, too."

"I know, Mama. I have a plan." And she did. Melanie quickly conjured an image of the mansion at The Cliffs on Keowee Falls. The idea had been careening around in her mind for months, and she figured that this was the last best chance to do something about it.

"I've been right all along about him. Ever since Amanda was born. I knew he was bad news. Thank God I was standing right there when she came into this world." She looked away through the window as if staring at an apparition. In a lower voice not necessarily directed at Melanie, she continued, "God sure gave me what I wanted."

Melanie shot her mother a glance. Whose life was she living, Melanie wondered, hers or her mother's?

"You've got to remind Amanda who raised her. You've got to keep repeating it so that she understands. She needs to know in her heart that it was us." Nina was punching her chest with a wrinkled finger.

"Mama, just let me work this, okay? It will all be under control. Things are moving fast, and I'm just trying to sort everything out. I've got my eye on a few things, so trust me when I say that the insurance money will work itself out."

"Work itself out? How dare you! How many times do I have to tell you that you don't get anything out of life that you don't take? Everything's already been had; it just moves around, and you have to go after it." Nina uncrossed her arms and hovered next to her daughter. "I spend my entire life raising you and then raising Amanda, and you have the nerve to challenge me at this time?" She leaned across the table. "The money is the only thing that loser will have ever produced for you or Amanda. If you don't get that, then what was it all for?"

"What *was* it all for, Mother?"

"What are you talking about? Wasn't it me that encouraged you to move back here instead of uprooting every two or three years? Wasn't it me that supported you when we had to go to court to get more child support? Wasn't it me that wined and dined the judge of your divorce case so that you could get the best deal? Who did you live with after the divorce? What the hell are you talking about?"

Melanie dropped her head. She had heard it all before so many times.

"You're right, Mama, you've been there for me and Amanda."

"You're damn right I have. Now is not the time to forget it. We've got to make sure we get that money . . . for Amanda's sake." Nina then changed her inflection, having won her point. "Poor, innocent Amanda. No father to take care of her. Just like me and you," she cooed in almost mocking tones.

Melanie could relate. Gabrielle Hastings, her mother, had been married to four different men. Her big takeaway from those years was that each time her mother divorced, they somehow wound up in a bigger house and with a new car. In the confusing world of a teenage girl, one thing was very clear: feelings were fleeting, unimportant, while material things and status were enduring. Her mother's comment made her think about her own father.

Jack Clarke had been raised in South Carolina the son of a farmer, land merchant, and general businessman. Jack had graduated from the University of South Carolina with a business management degree and had fallen in love with young Gabrielle Williams, also from a small Southern town. As a Gamecock freshman, so the story went, her mother had made herself popular with the boys early in her college career. Having neither the interest nor the patience for college, she trolled the fraternity houses and found a willing graduating senior in Jack Clarke. Before long, she was pregnant, and she married quickly soon after.

Melanie had been about ten years old when suddenly her father had disappeared. It was a few months later that she learned her parents had separated. She later heard from her mother that Jack Clarke, which is how she referred to him now, had had a male paramour. While Melanie had never seen her father with another man, the rumor had taken flight and was generally accepted as fact in Columbia, South Carolina, where they were living at the time.

She had no relationship with him today, nor did she care to. Adapting well to the lifestyle for which she had been trained, Melanie Garrett had discarded long ago any notion of what a father might be.

Likewise, she had watched her mother rotate through husbands the way some people flip real estate for profit. Melanie mused that it was not a bad gig if you could remove the emotion from the situation; everyone had to be a means to *your* end.

So, in the final analysis, Melanie viewed men, whether they were fathers or husbands, through a sterile prism devoid of any emotion. In a way, she had inherited the family business and had proven herself a worthy heir.

Coming back to the moment, Melanie sighed. "Maybe I can call Mark Russell, the lawyer that I arranged to help out Kimmie Carpenter," she said absently.

Her mother stared at her a moment, indicating she was unclear on what Melanie was discussing.

"You know, the case where her ex-husband lost two legs in Iraq, and the Army reclassified his retirement pay as disability pay, which meant she didn't get her fifty percent."

"Yeah, I remember, but I thought it was because they were only married a few years."

Melanie chuckled, back in stride. "Well, that's the law, but it doesn't matter. There's plenty of ways around that. And the nerve of those bastards to try and steal that money from her."

"Who won the case?"

"That's what I'm saying. Russell took them to the cleaners. He argued that the Army had world-class medical care—her ex would be able to enjoy that for life—and prosthetic limbs were so high tech today that most people could hardly tell the difference anymore. Kimmie told me that they were trying the old whiplash trick where, instead of wearing the fake neck brace, every day in court her ex would show up in a wheelchair or using crutches. The nerve."

"Who was the judge? That's what makes the real difference. If we could get Russell and that judge lined up—"

"It's a different county, but not impossible. Anyway, Kimmie got to keep her half, and she won attorney's fees. So she didn't have to pay a dime."

"No risk."

"That's right."

★ ★ ★

AMANDA QUIETLY EXITED through the back stairway that led to the garage. She padded through the darkness down the street to Jake's truck and opened the passenger door.

"Hey, babe, what gives?" Jake was wearing his blue-and-gold letterman jacket over a set of gray sweats. His hair was tossed in an unintentional way, as if he had come straight to her from running sprints.

Amanda hugged him. "Thanks for coming," she said pulling away. She slid across the bench seat, her knees touching the stick shift. "It just got too crazy for me in there."

Jake looked down. "How so? What's that?"

Amanda looked at the envelope in her hand. "Can we go somewhere?"

Jake didn't utter another word. He pushed in the clutch, punched the stick shift into first gear, and sped down the road.

Twenty minutes later they were in King's Mountain Battlefield Park, overlooking the battlefield where Brigadier General Daniel Morgan had finally routed Lord Cornwallis, stopping the British advance and pushing them back into Charleston Harbor.

It was a warm spring night, though cooler at the top of the mountain. Jake let Amanda out of the truck and walked her to the scenic overlook. He kept his arm around her, knowing she just needed him close. This had been his first clue about two years ago. He saw the storm raging in Amanda's life: two dominant, materialistic women continually putting Amanda between them and whatever problem arose.

"North Carolina's in that direction," Jake said, pointing to the north. "And Spartanburg's back over that way, across the parking lot. See how the night sky is brighter."

He knew she was listening and that his voice gave her a measure of peace. Sometimes she would encourage him to just talk for hours. She listened and cuddled up to him, finding safety in his presence.

"Keep talking," she whimpered into his chest. She was crying. "Please keep talking."

He pushed his face into her hair and whispered to her. "It's going to be okay. I know what you need. When you're ready, *you* just talk to *me*, okay? But here goes . . ."

He told her about Morgan's defense of King's Mountain and the later battle at Cowpens about 30 miles to the east for nearly an hour before she abruptly began speaking.

"I don't understand what's happening, Jake." She went on to tell him about the major and the chaplain discussing the insurance money. She didn't understand why her mother and grandmother had acted the way they did. "It's so unlike them."

Jake listened and privately seethed. Finally, he said, "Can I see the envelope?"

She handed him a sealed manila-colored page-length envelope. "I'm afraid to open it. I want you to do it."

Jake stared into Amanda's eyes. "Are you sure? Do you want your mother to be with you?"

"No. I want you to do it, right now. Just do it before I change my mind!" She emphasized her words with her hands, pushing outward, to provide herself reassurance. Jake could see she was uncertain, but he pressed on.

He pulled a dull Buck knife from a sheath he wore on his belt, popped open the blade and slid it beneath the seal and the top of the envelope. He produced two sheets of white paper with large writing. The ample moon hanging low in the west provided sufficient light for him to read the documents.

Jake looked at Amanda, who was covering her face with her hands, as if she were watching a horror flick. "It's a lady's name and address. There's a date and time." Jake looked at the date on his watch with the flick of his wrist. "The date's for tomorrow. Tomorrow at four p.m. Miss Riley Dwyer. Tryon Street, Dilworth Office Complex, Charlotte, North Carolina."

Amanda looked at him. "That's it?"

"No, the second sheet of paper has a Sanford address. No date and time on this one. Just says that you have to do it in the next week. 6212 Haymarket Court, Sanford, North Carolina. That's near Raleigh, right?"

"That's his address."

"Your dad's? Well, you're supposed to be there in the next seven days."

"No way am I doing that."

Jake paused. "Amanda, I think he's talking to you."

"What about after all that Ballantine stuff when the country was supposed to be under attack. My dad was supposed to be dead then. I went to a funeral, Jake! There had been no life insurance, no nothing for a year. Everything was supposedly put into a trust for me when I turned eighteen, and my mom told me that's not even true."

Amanda was right. There had been a funeral at the Garrett farm near Charlottesville, Virginia. She'd never seen any Army people show up at the door. She just knew that her mother had signed all of the paperwork.

"I remember. Your uncle Matt saved him, and then they both took down Ballantine."

"That's your version. Some people think that my dad and uncle were in on it. That's what I'm saying, Jake. I don't know what the truth is."

"I also remember when it was announced that your father was alive."

"Bastard never even had the decency to contact me."

"Amanda, he did come to see you."

"Once. That's it. What good is that? He's just a deadbeat like all the others."

"You don't know that. He's talking to you now, Amanda. Just listen to him, for once."

Amanda turned and looked at Jake. Damn, he was handsome, she thought. His square jaw, high cheekbones, and thick, dark hair that matched his deep coffee eyes made her melt in his arms. She was too tired to fight anymore. That was just it. At every turn with her father there was a fight. Her entire life, it seemed, had been a constant skirmish for child support or visitation rights or medical benefits. Her mother had fought the good fight, of that much she was sure.

CHAPTER 10
SOUTH CAROLINA

MONDAY MORNING (EASTERN TIME)

THE SLEEPLESS NIGHT and following morning brought more confusion for Amanda, though she attempted to play the role that she knew she needed to perform. As she sat in her journalism class, her best friend Brianna Simpson smiled at her.

"Hey, bitch, sorry to hear about your dad," Brianna said.

Amanda shrugged. "Nothing to be sorry about. It's like it happened to someone else, you know? Like something that happened on a TV show I didn't watch very much."

"Cool. Know what you mean."

It was Monday morning and the two girlfriends sat in the back of Dagus's class watching their journalism teacher bend over the DVD player, pressing some buttons.

"He's got a nice ass, don't you think?" Brianna whispered to Amanda.

"Hey, Len, you ever think of becoming a plumber with a crack like that?" one of their fellow students commented to broad laughter from the rest of the class.

Dagus got the movie started, then turned, and said, "Actually, I do some plumbing in my spare time, Mister Johnston, and I will be happy to discuss this with you after school today. Say for an hour?"

The kid groaned. "Come on, teach. You know I was just kidding."

"And Amanda and Brianna, you two have been talking all class. I think you can join young Mister Johnston here. Graduation's in a week and a half; I'd hate for any of you to jeopardize that."

Amanda slumped in her chair. "No fricking way," she whispered. "You don't think he heard what you said . . ." She raised her hand and said, "Mister Dagus? I was the one who was talking to Brianna. It was my fault. She shouldn't have to stay."

Dagus seemed to consider this a moment. He was rubbing a well-manicured hand across his strong jawline, as if to elicit thoughts directly from his brain like a genie from a lantern.

"I'll tell you what, Amanda, if you can answer one question, none of you have to stay. Deal?"

Amanda threw a quick glance around the room and nodded.

"Better get it right, bitch," Brianna whispered, smiling.

"What is the Fourth Estate's worst enemy? And why?"

Amanda smiled. He had tossed her a softball. She knew the answer because she had discussed the notion with Dagus at length while editing the school magazine one day. She scratched her chin a moment, as if she had to think about it.

"Why that would be an unverifiable source. Use of unverifiable sources leads to indiscipline in journalism. This indiscipline discredits the institution."

"You are correct," Dagus grinned. "Clemency granted."

Mike Johnston and Brianna slapped palms.

Amanda lowered herself in her chair, avoiding any further attention. Dagus dimmed the lights and began the movie, which was a documentary on war reporting. The basic themes were that the Afghan and Iraq wars were wrong and that the media had become too embedded with the soldiers—reporters failing in their duties to report responsibly during the buildup of each. They went native, so to speak, and did not objectively report the news. Dagus stopped the film twice and highlighted that all journalism should be reinforced by verifiable sources.

"A story without sources is bad fiction," he said.

Most of the class snoozed through the forty-five-minute film, but

Amanda was curiously drawn to its images. She found herself asking questions in her mind, never out loud. Her father had just been killed in one of those wars. She couldn't remember which one right now.

As the film concluded, with a few minutes of class remaining, Dagus leaned against his desk. Cotton tan pants were cuffed at the hems above khaki socks and copper-colored Rockport deck shoes. He wore an Egyptian cotton golf shirt. Soft, dark chest hair was visible as it peeked out of his open collar. His arms sported the same thick hair as well. Turning to the class, he asked, "So, what do you guys think? Did the media in these wars report and inform us? Or did they reinforce The Big Lie by pumping out unverified stories? Do you even care?"

The class sat silent.

Brianna's hand shot up for the first time in perhaps a year.

"Yes, Brianna?"

"Well, I think this was particularly relevant since Amanda's biological father was just killed over there."

Amanda whipped her head toward Brianna. "Shut up! I didn't want anyone to know."

After an awkward pause, Dagus spoke softly. "Amanda, I'm so sorry. This must be a very challenging time."

She looked at Dagus and felt the staring eyes of the entire class on her as if she were center stage with a spotlight trained on her.

"Class, dismissed." Dagus said softly. "Amanda, if you could stay behind just a second, please?" He turned his attention to something on his desk as the students tumbled out of the classroom.

"Brianna, why did you have to do that?" Amanda sighed.

Brianna stuck her tongue out at Amanda. "You said you didn't care, right? So what's the big deal?"

"Nothing. I just didn't want any attention over this, you know? Bad enough he was such a loser."

"I'll call you later. Don't let Dagus get fresh." Brianna winked as she looked over her shoulder at Amanda. She walked along the row of empty desks, and Amanda noticed her and Dagus exchange a glance.

Amanda's view of Brianna had oscillated from best friend to white trash over the course of their ten-year friendship. Today it was somewhere in between. Lately Brianna's mother had been demoted at her work, which left them struggling to survive in the high-cost I-85 corridor serving Greenville, Spartanburg and Charlotte. Nobly, Brianna's mother continued to send her to Spartanburg High School even though they had moved out of the district, and it cost her dearly. Amanda knew that Brianna's mother, whom she liked, either had to keep Brianna in Spartanburg High or risk losing her along with the husband and job that had already departed.

Amanda was still sitting in her desk when Mike Johnston, who really was a nice guy, rapped her desk lightly with his knuckles, as if to knock. "Hey, Amanda, sorry about your dad. Really."

As Mike walked away, she found herself wondering why anyone else would care if she didn't. As the class emptied out, Dagus was turning a digital camera in his hands as if it was a space rock. He stared at it a second and then placed it back on his desk. Standing, he closed the door and walked over to Amanda. He sat in Brianna's chair next to her and leveled his dark-brown eyes on her.

"I'm so sorry." He reached his hand forward on the desk toward her but avoided contact.

"Mister Dagus, there's nothing to talk about. I hated my father with a passion. He was a worthless son of a bitch, and what I don't get is why I should feel guilty about his death."

"You shouldn't, Amanda. But perhaps you should grieve. Maybe just open your mind a bit about this. I know you said he hasn't been there for you. I remember the few times that you mentioned him it was always in a negative light. But, you know, you only die once."

She wasn't sure what he meant by that comment. *You only die once.* She was trying to understand what he was saying, but her mind had long ago shut like a vault door when it came to her father. She recalled that Jake had also said the same thing.

"This is really no big deal."

"Okay. I understand. Just know that I'm a good listener if you need to talk to someone."

She watched him for a moment as he seemed to consider something. He had wavy brown hair and a thin, handsome face. Many of her girlfriends were attracted to him in a "cool teacher" way, and she had to admit that she had her moments as well. But she loved Jake and always considered her pull toward Dagus a natural student-teacher thing.

"But be careful, Amanda. This may catch up with you when you least expect it to."

She tried to consider this, but was unsure what he was saying. "What are you talking about?"

"The mind, Amanda. The mind." He pointed at his temple and then began to emphasize with his hands again. "Try to imagine that you are the tip of a laser beam moving through the darkness penetrating untapped space. You have no idea what's in front of you. In the same way, you have no idea how this is going to affect you one minute from now, an hour from now, or even a year from now. This may not be as inconsequential as you make it seem."

Dagus lifted his head as the door to his classroom opened.

"Anyway, I think between Jake and me, you've got two men that you can talk to."

"Hey, Mister Dagus," Jake said.

"Hi, Jake."

"Jake," Amanda said, standing. She pecked him on the cheek and then turned to her teacher. "I'm okay. I can guarantee you that this deal will not affect me in any way a minute from now or even a year from now."

CHAPTER 11
BAGRAM AIRBASE, AFGHANISTAN

MONDAY EVENING

Sergeant Eversoll flipped open the blade of his Duane Dieter SpecOps knife and tossed it lazily into the dirt at his feet. He was sitting on an ammo crate outside of the Special Operations headquarters at the former Russian air base. Tall mountains loomed all around him, snow still capping their jagged peaks. He wore a black skullcap to keep his head warm and a black and gray Army physical training sweatsuit with running shoes.

Eversoll picked up the knife and tossed it into the ground again with a flip of the wrist. He repeated the process time and again. He thought about his many conversations with Colonel Garrett over the past eighteen months. A year and a half in and out of combat was enough to make two men relatives. They knew each other completely; therefore, they trusted one another completely.

Again with the knife. Eversoll remembered Colonel Garrett telling him about his brother, Matt. He had heard of Matt Garrett during the Ballantine attacks, as the nation referred to them now. Jacques Ballantine, a former Iraqi general, had unleashed a deadly series of attacks on the United States, and then followed up with the most surprising form of attack.

Freakin' nuclear and chemical Predators on a damn Chinese merchant ship, like an aircraft carrier, Eversoll thought to himself. It was ingenious, and, for that reason, scary. Colonel Garrett told him that his brother had come to rescue him in a fishing hole in Canada after Ballantine had captured him. Matt Garrett was a CIA big shot now.

Maybe that's my duty, Eversoll figured. Why can't I seem to accept the fact that he's dead? Is it denial?

"Sergeant Eversoll!"

The voice was from Command Sergeant Major Tom Palmen.

"Yes, Sergeant Major," Eversoll said, picking up his knife and standing.

Palmen was a large man with a completely shaved head. There appeared to be no neck connecting his head to his shoulders. The man spoke with a distinct Chicago accent, a physically fit John Candy.

"Pack your shit. You've got escort duty for some VIP. He specifically requested you."

"But, Sergeant Major . . ."

"No buts, Eversoll, this is your mission."

Fifteen minutes later, Sergeant Eversoll appeared back at the headquarters in his army combat uniform, pistol strapped to his leg and Humvee keys in his hand.

"Where's your M4?" Palmen barked. "And lose the keys; you're not driving."

Eversoll was confused. "M4's in the arms room, Sergeant Major."

"Go grab it. And pick up those two radios over there on your way back. Oh yeah, and make sure you've got a ruck packed for at least forty-eight hours."

Ten minutes later, Sergeant Eversoll returned. He popped his full rucksack off his shoulder and quickly stuffed the two satellite radios in its special compartments. He stood and watched across the room as Palmen, Major General Rampert and a third man, dressed in civilian clothes, stared at the large map on the wall. Rampert was pointing and talking.

Palmen looked over his shoulder and said, "Eversoll, get over here."

Sergeant Eversoll laid his M4 carbine on his rucksack and walked across the room. As he neared the group, his eyes remained fixed on the civilian. He had seen him somewhere before, but couldn't place him.

"And this is where we've been searching," Rampert said, pointing at the location on the map of the gorge where Eversoll had spent two long days and nights.

"Well, I want to go right there," the civilian said. The man pressed his finger on the map about two inches to the right and above the place where Rampert had just pointed.

Sergeant Eversoll looked at Rampert and then at the civilian.

"We've been down this road before, Matt."

"And we'll go down it again."

Sergeant Major Palmen noticed Sergeant Eversoll standing behind them. He grabbed him by the shoulder. "Sergeant Eversoll, meet Assistant Director of the CIA Matthew Garrett."

★ ★ ★

MATT SHOOK SERGEANT Eversoll's hand and took measure of the young man, quickly surmising that he had served his brother well.

"Good to meet you, Sergeant."

He turned to Rampert and said, "We need to talk in private."

Rampert nodded, saying, "Follow me."

They walked into a plywood paneled office with maps hanging all over the walls. Rampert sat behind his gray metal desk and Matt took a wooden chair opposite Rampert.

"Searing Gorge?" Matt said.

Rampert hesitated. "Yeah, they told me that was you."

"Why'd you give it to Zach?"

"That's a stupid question. He's the best. That simple."

"You put him in a bad spot. Going in daylight. What gives?"

"We needed a fight for it to work."

"You got a bunch of men killed, General."

"It was combat. We had it under control but Jergens fell out of the damned chopper."

Matt backed off and changed his tack.

"Do you know what will happen if the enemy gets the report on these minerals that these State Department weenies made public?"

"You think I'm an idiot?"

"You sure you want me to answer that, General?"

Rampert paused. Matt knew that the man had a complex history with Zach and him. Just before the beginning of Operation Iraqi Freedom, Zach had fought a resurgent Japanese army in the Philippines and was reported as killed in action. Rampert and some of his Delta Force troops had been part of that fight and had rescued Zach, kept him alive, and clandestinely evacuated him to Fort Bragg where the special operations doctors nursed him back to health under a pseudonym. As Zach recovered from his coma, former Iraqi general Jacques Ballantine decided to attack the United States with the missing weapons of mass destruction that he had been stockpiling in Canada. The Canadians refused to allow U.S. military action on their soil, leaving Ballantine's team free to operate. So Rampert had Zach Garrett, operating under the nom de guerre, Winslow Boudreaux, jump into Ballantine's Canadian fishing hole where he dueled with the Iraqi general before being captured.

Complex, Matt thought, was probably an understatement.

"There's definitely some things we don't want them to get," Rampert said.

"Well, all we can hope is that Zach and his team did what they needed to do."

"We'll know soon enough."

Matt studied Rampert a minute, pushing his feet off the front of his desk and leaning his chair back. He turned his head toward the map that was a blow up of the Kunar and Nuristan areas.

"Biggest Lapis mines in the world right in there," Matt said.

"A lot of timber, too," Rampert added.

"Have you looked at that mineral map?"

Rampert paused. Matt could tell he had only scanned it with passing interest.

"You know what the term Searing Gorge means?"

"Like a hot valley," Rampert said.

Matt grimaced and stood, the legs from his chair sounding like a gunshot.

"Searing Gorge is an online gaming name coined by World of Warcraft," Matt said.

"Why do I give a rat's ass about that?"

"The Searing Gorge is where the Thorium Brotherhood have their base of operations."

Rampert shrugged.

"Check your periodic chart, General." Matt walked to the map and pointed at the border between Kunar and Nuristan along the Pakistan border. "Thorium itself is not fissile, but it is a close kin to Uranium, but it doesn't sterilize you when you handle it. Except for one kind—Thorium232—which *is* considered fissile."

Rampert stared at Matt.

"That means the bad guys can make nukes out of it."

"No shit." Rampert stood and walked to the map.

"And the deepest, richest Thorium 232 mine in the world is right there," Matt said.

He was pointing at a spot near the Kunar River where it scraped against the border of Pakistan.

"What was on that flash drive, Garrett?" Rampert asked.

"A two phased plan."

"That we want the enemy to know?"

Matt nodded.

"Absolutely."

CHAPTER 12
CHARLOTTE, NORTH CAROLINA

MONDAY AFTERNOON

"Dagus is only trying to help you, Amanda."

"I know, but everyone's making way too big a deal out of this," Amanda replied as Jake drove her into Dilworth to meet with Ms. Riley Dwyer for the first time.

"I don't know him that well, but you've been working with him for a couple of years now. So, cut him some slack."

She considered his comment. "Fine. You deal with him, then."

Jake gave Amanda an amused look. "Well, I've got to turn in a review of Aerosmith for him. So maybe I'll try to explain some things to him then."

"I was being a smart ass, Jake. He's fine. Let's change the topic. So tell me again why I am doing this?"

"You know why." Jake put his truck on cruise control at 70 mph as they sped along I-85, looped onto I-485, and then took I-77 south into Dilworth. They passed Charlotte Coliseum, which was nearly rebuilt after the bombing. A solitary crane arched over the north end of the sports complex like a heron in the marsh, the only indication that reconstruction was taking place.

"See that?" Jake said, pointing at the crane. "That's why. Terrorists tried to blow up these malls almost exactly two years ago. Your dad was killed fighting those guys so they can't do that anymore . . . or at least the bad guys will die trying."

"Honestly, Jake, I have never felt threatened. Even when 9-11 happened, it was so far away. Even when this thing supposedly happened, I mean I felt bad for the families and everything, but it just kind of went away."

Jake wore jeans and a black T-shirt that said "Gavin McGraw—Security" on the front and had a list of sponsors on the back. He had picked up an odd job working security for the McGraw concert at Clemson last spring. The T-shirt had been part of the benefits package. Since then he had been invited back as a regular.

The temperature was comfortably warm, a beautiful South Carolina spring day. Amanda was dressed in a tight pink T-shirt with the number 10 on the front and back, indicating her high school graduation year. Hip-hugger jeans belied the fact that she was en route to a meeting in a brick-and-chrome office building in Charlotte's swankiest section. She still had her school books in her lap.

"Your dad is the kind of guy who makes those things 'kind of go away,' Amanda."

"Was."

"Was, what?"

"You said 'is,' and you meant 'was.' He's dead, for real this time."

"Right. Kind of a stupid point to make, don't you think?"

He had parked in front of a tan brick building with a sign that said, "DWYER AND ASSOCIATES."

"I'm not going in," Amanda said with conviction.

"And I'm not leaving until you do." Jake pulled the parking brake up, leaned back into his seat, and looked into her eyes. "Listen, Amanda. If you're not going to do this for your dad, then do it for me. I've been troubled about this. Part of me just wants to hold you and support you, which you know I do all the time. Another part of me, though, feels like I need to lead you here. It's like I'm with you for that reason. Like, your dad's asking me to help you."

"That's good, because he never helped me," she quipped. Amanda lifted the door handle, jumped out, and then leaned back in. "For you," she said with a smile. Then she added, "Be back in a few."

After taking an elevator to the fourth floor, Amanda found the restroom, went in, applied makeup and smiled at herself in the mirror. *Don't you look good*, she said to herself. She pulled at the two strands of hair on either side of her face, sucked her cheeks in, and smacked her lips.

She exited the bathroom, found the correct office, and introduced herself to the clerk at the front desk. "Hi, my name is Amanda Garrett, and I'm supposed to meet Miss Dwyer now."

"Miss Dwyer has a client in her office," the clerk announced. "Fill out this paperwork and bring it back to me when you're done, please."

Amanda gave her a snobbish look then glanced at the paperwork. "I'm not filling out any papers. This thing didn't mention any of that. It just said to be here at this time, and I'm here." She shook her own paperwork in her hand.

"Young lady, if you don't fill out *this* paperwork, I'm not even going to know who you are." The woman, probably in her fifties, used a school-teacher's voice to scold Amanda.

"I don't need this crap. I didn't even want to come today. See ya, wouldn't want to be ya." Amanda did a light-footed pirouette, waved nonchalantly over her shoulder, and strode for the door.

The office door to the side of the receptionist opened, producing two women who were casually chatting. Amanda looked back, briefly catching the eye of the younger of the two women. She looked vaguely familiar, Amanda thought, although she couldn't place her.

Amanda placed her hand on the chrome door pull and was leaning backward when she heard, "Amanda Garrett?"

She dropped her head and muttered, "Busted." She turned around, stepped to the side as the previous "client" brushed past her, and said, "That's me. Who wants to know?"

Amanda watched a strikingly beautiful woman walk toward her. Auburn hair, light, almost sky blue, eyes, and a fresh, clean face. Slim figure, lots of thin gold bracelets on one arm, and trendy Chino pants with a tight-fitting light green blouse. An emerald necklace hung against the freckled skin at her neck.

"Wouldn't you like to know," the woman said with a smile, reaching her hand out.

"Not particularly," Amanda shot back, folding her arms across her chest.

"I'll give you three guesses." She put her arm around Amanda to walk her back toward the office.

"Don't touch me, lesbo," Amanda shrieked, pulling away.

The woman dropped her arm, then stuck it back at her, and said, "Hi, Amanda. I'm Riley Dwyer. Now let's cut the tough-guy act and get this over with."

"That's more like it," Amanda said, giving Ms. Dwyer's hand a limp shake. Riley was walking slowly with Amanda following. "I've got things to do."

"I'm sure you do. Graduation is just around the corner; college is coming up; your boyfriend is a football hero; swim meets going on . . ." Miss Dwyer was waving her arms in the air each time she mentioned an item.

"That's right, plus I was voted most popular and best looking, so I've got responsibilities there, too."

"Oh my, those are, like, the two best things," Miss Dwyer mocked, though it was lost on Amanda.

"Yeah, I lobbied for it pretty hard. It was competitive."

"All that and you've probably got a senior class trip on the way. I'm just so lucky you could fit me in."

"Yeah, we're going to the Bahamas." Amanda looked at her watch and said, "Well, I don't have much time, but I can give you a few minutes to check this off my list."

"I'm fortunate." Miss Dwyer gave Amanda a tight-lipped grin.

They were in her office. Three floor-to-ceiling windows were evenly spaced along the wall on the left. She had tastefully arranged a dozen plants, including two ficus trees and some elephant leaves, along the window wall. Splashes of light blazed through the glass, creating equally spaced rectangles along the floor. In the middle of the office was a large oak desk with papers on it. To the right were a sofa and two padded chairs. A smattering of pictures and degrees hung on the walls in no particular fashion or pattern. Several paintings of sand dunes and beach cottages were scattered throughout the office.

Amanda stopped and said, "Can you just sign this thing so I can get on my way?"

"And what thing would that be, dear?" Miss Dwyer came over to Amanda, again invading her personal space, to look over her shoulder at the paperwork.

"What is it with you? Really, are you gay?"

"No. Why would you think that?" Miss Dwyer took a step back. "You asked me to sign something. I just wanted to see what it was." Again, her mock offense was lost on Amanda.

"Okay." Amanda rolled her eyes warily.

"Why don't we sit down, Amanda, and we can see what it is that you've got in your hand there." Miss Dwyer motioned at the papers.

"Nah, I'd just rather you sign this and let me get out of here. There's nothing here for me."

Miss Dwyer walked around her slowly, sizing her up, looking at her with those pale blue eyes, and then sat down in one of the two overstuffed chairs.

"You're creeping me out, woman. Maybe you're the one who needs the shrink."

"Maybe so. Why don't you give me your analysis." Miss Dwyer waved her arm toward the sofa.

"Well, this could be kinda cool, but only if you sign this paperwork saying I'm good to go."

Miss Dwyer's head popped up. She stared at Amanda.

"What? Got a problem with that?"

"We'll see," Miss Dwyer said absently, regaining her composure. "Why don't you come down here and analyze me, young lady."

Amanda sat down in the chair across from Miss Dwyer, crossed her legs, and laced her fingers together over her knee as she leaned forward.

"Let's start with your childhood," Amanda said in melodramatic form. She drew on her theater training, bugging her eyes wide open.

"Normal. Two great parents, an older brother who protected me and plenty of friends. I'm close with them all today."

"Hmmm. Sounds like the famous African Normalcy Syndrome, or what we call ANS. It strikes in our sleep."

"But doctor, I'm not complaining of any issues," Miss Dwyer countered, smiling like a Stepford wife.

"Ahh, but therein lies the nastiness of this disease," Amanda said, wagging her finger. "You just don't know you have it."

Miss Dwyer drummed her fingers on her knee, smiling inwardly. "Wow, you may be on to something."

Enjoying herself, Amanda continued. "Now, the real test is how you have matured as an adult. So tell me about your relationships. I see no ring on your finger. You're passably cute, and you're probably only twice my age."

"Oh, girlfriend, you flatter me so."

"Tell me about your love life."

RILEY STIFFENED, EVEN though she knew the teenager was just playing a game. It was a natural reaction. She had exactly one love in her life, and he was no longer available. Her heart had been crushed, perhaps her soul as well.

"Come on, come on, out with it now," Amanda mocked.

"Your time is up, doctor. It's my turn."

"Oooh. Struck a nerve, did I? What is it, give him sex too early and he dumped you? That's what happens in high school. You gotta tease the guys and manipulate them so they stick around."

Riley smiled, but it looked more like a grimace. "Okay, young lady, I can see you've got a career in psychology ahead of you."

"Please," Amanda scoffed.

"Now that your father's dead, tell me about him, Amanda." Miss Dwyer's words were a bolt out of the sky, a momentum changer. In an instant, the well-practiced psychiatrist had seized control of the situation.

Amanda stared at her for a moment then looked down, pulling at her pink shirt with one hand, as if picking lint. "Nothing to say. He's dead." Then she thought a moment and said, "But he left me half a million dollars. Pretty cool, huh?"

"Why did he do that?"

"What do you mean? I'm his daughter; he had to. Mom told me that she had to get a court order."

"Really. When did your mom say this?"

"I don't know, a few years ago. Dad was always missing child support payments, never helping with anything. He just ignored me."

"I see. Why did he do that?"

"Just the way he is—was. A bastard."

"Pretty strong word."

"Pretty bad dad." Amanda acted impatient. "How much of this do I have to endure."

"None at all. You can go now. I've seen enough." Riley stood, brushing her pants off.

"So you agree, then, he was a bad father? That's cool. So we just sign the paperwork, and I'm good to go."

Riley stopped. There it was again. "No. You can go, Amanda, but I'm not signing the paperwork."

"What do you mean? I came down here to see you, and you're not even going to sign it?"

"I don't have to sign it, so why would I?"

"If you don't sign it, I have to wait two weeks to get my half mil," Amanda said, trying to act like she pulled off multimillion-dollar deals all the time.

"Oh, no, that's not true." Riley stood firm in front of her now. She was the dominant figure, not the pretending, aloof scatterbrain.

"Really! You mean I don't need your signature?"

"No, you need my signature. Actually, what your father's will states is that if I don't sign off on your paperwork, your take of his insurance is fifty thousand dollars."

"You lying bitch! It doesn't say that. I have the Army paperwork."

"You must not have reviewed it very carefully Amanda, because Major Ross handed me a copy as well."

Amanda fumed.

"So then, are we good to go?" Riley asked, turning away toward her desk.

Amanda balled her fists, wrinkling the documents she held in her hand.

A MINUTE PASSED where Amanda stood motionless, as if she were a mannequin in a storefront window. Riley sat at her desk, shuffled some papers, picked up the phone and made a call, saying, "Yes, about the Garrett case. I think we'll be able to wrap this up rather quickly. . . . No, I'm afraid not. She just really appears to despise her father. . . . That's fine. I'll finish the other paperwork and send her back."

"Who was that?"

"Hmm?" Riley looked up with a look of confusion, as if she had forgotten Amanda was still there.

"Who was that on the phone?"

"Oh, I'm sorry. You're not privy to that information. It's confidential." She wrinkled her nose and went back to the paperwork on her desk.

"What do I need to do?"

Again, feigning distraction, Riley looked up, and with aggravation said, "Do, for what?"

"To get the money. We're talking about four hundred and fifty thousand dollars here—money my dad wanted me to have. Who are you to say I can't have it, anyway?"

"I, young lady, have been named in your father's will as the person to determine whether or not you are mature enough to receive the money that he really does want you to have. That," she emphasized, "is who I am."

"We can sue, you know?"

"Of course, and by the time you're my age, God forbid, you may get the money."

Amanda tapped her foot as she stood in front of Riley's desk. With folded arms, she said again, "Okay, what do I have to do?"

"Well, Amanda, for starters, you have to take a seat over there and talk to me."

"Fine."

"Now, as long as you're doing this voluntarily, I'm happy to talk to you."

Amanda sat on the sofa this time. She crossed her legs and leaned back into the large tan cushion. The two females stared at one another for several minutes without speaking a word. Riley detected chemistry, both good and bad, on many levels. Running through her mind were so many thoughts about how she was going to complete her mission with Amanda. Her instructions were very specific.

Riley slid her chair back from her desk. Before standing, she opened a drawer. She slid her fingers across the glass of a picture frame. A smiling soldier stared up at her from the desk drawer. *God, give me strength*, she asked silently.

She had received the letter the same day that Amanda had been notified, she presumed. Major Ross had arrived at her office, sat down with her, and they had a good cry together. He had given her the relevant portion of Zachary Garrett's will, giving her the responsibility to conduct seven sessions with Amanda before the Army released the insurance money.

She slid the drawer closed, stood, and walked toward Amanda. "Anything to drink?" she asked.

"No, thank you," Amanda replied.

Riley summoned her courage and then asked a simple question.

"Can you tell me the seven worst things your father ever did to you?"

"Where do you want me to start? He was always missing child support; he never came to visit; he was mean to my mom and grandmother; he always created problems when we were together; he was always disrupting stuff I wanted to do . . . need me to continue?"

"Just pick one. Child support?"

"Sure." Amanda shrugged.

"When did he miss child support, Amanda?"

"I don't know, always, sometimes. Mom would tell me."

"Any chance mom wasn't being straight with you?"

Amanda stood up. "Don't ever say that! My mother and grandmother raised me."

"Sit down, Amanda, and I will throw you out of here if you do that again. Do you understand? It will cost you $450,000."

That seemed to get her attention.

"Sorry," she muttered. "It just kind of happened."

"I understand." And she did. Riley was beginning to get the picture. Not that there had been much doubt before, but seeing Amanda's reaction to a mild suggestion that her mother might have misled her convinced her that they had a lot of work to do.

"So tell me, again, Amanda, do you remember any one time that your mother told you that your father missed child support?"

Amanda seemed to be thinking, wrinkling her brow. "Well, I remember one time, because Jake and I were going to go up to the lake to go skiing, you know? And Mom said I couldn't go because there was no money, and that Dad had missed a child support payment."

Riley thought for a moment. "And so you could not put gas in your Mercedes, was that it?"

Amanda understood this jab and wasn't going to take it lying down. "Look, lady, he missed the child support that month. My grandmother bought me that car."

"Is that so? Okay, that would have been when?"

"June or July two years ago."

Riley stood, walked across her office and picked up a large brown box. She carried the box to her seat, placed it on the desk, and pulled from it a large accordion folder.

"In here is every one of your father's pay statements. Child support payments were deducted directly from his pay, sent to a clearing house in South Carolina, and then it was forwarded to your mother's bank account. Your father received a notice every time the transaction was completed. He kept all of the receipts. Now I want you to find the one he missed. They are in dated order. Go back as far as you like. I'll give you a few minutes."

Riley stood, leaving Amanda with the box. On her way out she sang, "Remember, $450,000."

She walked past her receptionist, into the hallway, and went into the same restroom Amanda had stopped in initially. She leaned against the sink, staring at herself in the mirror. *Please give me a sign of hope here, God.*

She walked outside, picked up a hot tea from the Starbucks next door and enjoyed the sunshine while sipping it slowly. On her way back in, she spied a young man across the parking lot leaning against a truck, and figured him for Amanda's boyfriend. Riding the elevator up, she tossed another thought around in her mind.

"So, what have we found?"

Amanda stared at her for a moment. After a long silence, she said, "Well, South Carolina probably screwed it up somewhere, because mom would never lie to me."

"So, he didn't miss a payment? Is that what you're saying?"

"I couldn't find anywhere he did, but that doesn't mean he didn't."

"Oh, I'm sorry, I came back too soon. Please, take some time and review all—"

"No. I don't need to do that. I looked at most of them . . ." she trailed off, looking away. After an awkward moment, she looked back up at Riley when she didn't say anything. "What?"

"You tell me."

"What do you want me to say, that he didn't miss a payment? Okay, he didn't."

"I just want you to say what you see, Amanda. What are the facts before you? Not filtered through anyone's eyes but only yours. If we were in court right now, and you were on the witness stand, I would approach you and say, 'Isn't it true, Miss Amanda Garrett, that your father never missed a child support payment?'" Riley deepened her voice and strode across the room with theatrical practice, waving her arms as she did so.

Amanda smiled, weakly wiped at her face, and said, "Funny."

"Judge, may I treat the young lady as a hostile witness?" Riley turned toward the window wall, as if there was a judge there.

"Okay. Okay. He didn't miss a child support payment."

Riley walked over to her desk, leaned forward with her hands on the matting, stared directly at a Peggy Hopper painting, and said, "Ladies and gentlemen of the jury, Colonel Zachary Garrett never missed a child support payment." Turning toward Amanda, she said, "Witness, you are excused until tomorrow."

With a long slender arm, full of bracelets, she pointed at the door. "Go see that hunk boyfriend of yours."

Amanda wrinkled her forehead, stood, and walked out of the door. "Whatever."

Riley watched her depart, waited a few minutes, and then sat at her desk. She opened her desk drawer and held the framed photo in her hands for what seemed an eternity. Tears were streaming down her face as she placed the photo back on her desk where it had been for two years.

Why, damnit? Why? Then, a moment later, after a few more tears, she shook her head. *I can't do this by myself.*

Riley punched her intercom box and told her assistant to go home. She pulled a bottle of red wine from the cabinet opposite the window wall, poured a glass, and took a long sip.

She cried and drank. Her thoughts swung from one end of the spectrum to the other. She was flattered and privileged that she could honor Zachary's death by helping his daughter. On the other hand, was it an unfair burden to place on her?

No, it was a privilege, she concluded. It was what he'd wanted, and she would give him that. There were so many other things she had wanted to give him.

She poured the last of the wine. Standing, she picked up her glass and walked to the window. *You get one shot at true love*, she thought to herself. *One shot.*

She recalled the day Zachary was leaving for Afghanistan. She was crying, holding him tight. She had driven him from his house in Sanford to Fort Bragg. He was dressed in his Army combat uniform with a Special Forces patch on his shoulder. They were parked outside of the headquarters.

He pulled her to him, kissed her on the lips and then the forehead.

"I'll miss you," she said, crying into his uniform, "again. Last time was hard, but this time, Zach. I don't know; just be careful."

"One last time, baby. I've got to go do this. Then I'll come down to Charlotte, we'll get married."

"I want that for us, Zach. I want to meet Amanda. And I want to give her a brother or sister, you know."

"We'll do that, Riley. That's what I want."

"You be careful."

Zach pulled away, grabbed his rucksack, and kissed her one more time. He got out of the car, walked around to the driver's side and leaned into the window to kiss her face, wet with tears. He smiled at her with his crooked grin as he pulled away.

"Don't worry, babe, I'm good to go."

CHAPTER 13
NORTHWEST FRONTIER PROVINCE, PAKISTAN

TUESDAY

Colonel Zachary Garrett opened his eyes. He had been dreaming about Amanda. She was five years old and wearing red shorts and a green T-shirt with a single flower in the center.

"Daddy's got to go to work, baby girl."

The young Amanda grabbed her daddy's watch and said, "Five minutes." She held up her small hand, spreading her fingers, and then she leaned into her father, hugging him. "You're not going anywhere for five minutes."

"Daddy's not going anywhere, ever, baby girl."

The pain surged through his body as if carried by an electrical current. He was wounded, but not in a debilitating way, he prayed. Amanda's face hovered in front of him for an instant, smiling, loving, and pure. What hurt more, his wounds or the memories?

To the best of his knowledge he had been held in this stone cave prison for at least three days. He remembered the helicopter taking off without him and the blinding whirl of snow all around. Had he been able to leave behind the weapon? Had they found it? Perhaps he would never find out. Then two men were upon him so quickly that he was unable to maneuver against them. He knew he had been shot twice as he was carrying Jergens to the helicopter. Then the explosion, and all hell broke loose. Two men, screaming Arabic at him, one holding a knife to his throat. He'd resisted, but one of the men had apparently butt-stroked him on the head, knocking him unconscious.

He heard unintelligible voices beyond the pile of rocks that blocked his egress. On three sides of his confines was solid rock, a cave. Stacked to his front were large boulders that allowed him only small slivers of light. Occasionally he would see a dark shadow pass across the tiny gaps between the rocks. Twice, he had been given food. The first time, a pair of hands had removed a flat rectangular rock about the size of a laptop and slid a tray of rice and cold lamb onto the ledge. The second time, he had been given an American combat ration, Meal Ready to Eat, or MRE.

Zach calculated that the preponderance of Arabic and lack of Pashto or Dari languages indicated he was being held by Al Qaeda. There were other groups operating in the area, such as the Taliban, but Al Qaeda was imported, and they spoke Arabic.

If it was Al Qaeda, then they had been right about their target. They had been onto bin Laden.

The rocks began shifting in front of him. One by one, two pairs of hands removed smaller rocks, followed by larger ones. Soon there was a hole large enough for him to crawl through. The bore of an AK-47 assault rifle poked through, then shook twice away from him. It was, he figured, the international symbol for "get over here, asshole."

He looked down at himself. His uniform was shredded, his feet bare. He had no weapon. They had even found the knife he kept strapped to his ankle. They had cut his pant leg, and someone had performed minor surgery on him. The bullet wounds were covered with dirty gauze.

Again, the weapon shook in front of him, followed by a voice ordering him forward. "Come. Come."

For a moment, he thought of grabbing the muzzle of the AK-47 and snatching it from his captor's hands. Surely though, there were others behind this one. He wouldn't stand a chance backed into the corner of this cave.

"Boots," Zach called out. "I need my boots."

A deafening blast exploded in his makeshift cell. The muzzle emitted flame, and the bullet struck the wall.

"Okay, okay, I'm coming." He looked through the hole and saw more than five men dressed in traditional tribal garb. The flowing white robes, sheepskin vests, and brown wool *Pakols*, or black turbans, all reinforced his conviction that his captors were Al Qaeda.

As he crawled through the hole, two men on either side roughly grabbed him and yanked him through. The sharp rock scraped at his bullet wounds, causing him to grimace. One of the guards immediately pushed him against the wall and snapped plastic flex cuffs around his wrists.

Once he was standing, another man came into the cave. He could see about fifty feet of large cavern to his front, then the tunnel took a turn to his right. He saw ammunition boxes stacked high along the walls. Every man he could see had at least one weapon. Light was minimal but passable. Everyone stared at him for a moment and then turned toward the new figure in the cave.

"Colonel Garrett, I am the Scientist. Our leader has instructed me to talk to you. Won't you follow me, please?"

Garrett paused. The Scientist? They had a complete dossier on this man, Mullah Rahman.

"Rahman?" Garrett's voice echoed in the cave.

Rahman, who had moved to within ten feet of him, smiled a yellow-toothed grin. "I see you have studied hard, Colonel. Knowing my name should only make you more fearful."

Zach was impressed with the man's English. It was practiced and smooth. He knew Rahman had studied in Great Britain. He knew that Rahman was revered by the jihadists as one of their most brutal leaders.

"Then I think I'll join you," he growled.

As he began to walk, the six guards fell in behind him. Rahman was to his immediate front, preceded by two more guards.

They stopped while the lead guard moved a large curtain out of the way and the other stood to the opposite side. Someone checked his flex cuff. It was secure.

Rahman led him past the drapes and into a brightly lit bowl of rock. They had exited the cave, for the most part, but were still surrounded on all four sides by solid granite.

There was an AK-47 leaning against the rocks next to a man sitting on a prayer mat. Zach could not determine how tall he was, but he seemed lanky. The man's face was covered so that only his eyes were visible. They were black holes against the dirty white sheet wrapped across his face.

This can't be happening. Is this bin Laden? Zach's mind reeled. He looked at Rahman and back at the man seated on the prayer mat. He knew that Rahman was just behind Zawahiri on the Al Qaeda organization chart and it was Rahman who was escorting him. *This is crazy!* Then he looked to his right and saw a man holding a small digital video camera. Again, looking down at the mat, he saw a newspaper with Arabic writing, and he quickly began to understand.

"Are you done taking in your surroundings?"

"Just wishing I had a GPS device on me right now," Garrett quipped.

"I want to introduce you to a man you have been seeking but are unable to find. You are in the presence of the great one, so pay proper respect. Please bow."

Zach looked at the Scientist and scoffed. "Kiss my ass."

He felt a swift blow to his rib cage. He gasped for air as he doubled over, hugging his stomach. He hadn't been hit like that since Billy Johnson took a cheap shot at him in high school football.

"Now, please bow," the Scientist said calmly, "or we will make you bow."

Zach stood erect again and remained motionless, spitting up small amounts of blood. Two men fell upon him in a torrent of boots and rifle butts, pushing him back down to the ground. He thought he saw the digital camera guy filming the entire scene.

Please don't let Amanda see this, was his first and only thought before a foot into his sternum forced the wind from his lungs. He buckled to his knees.

"Ah, I see you are a wise man, Colonel."

"Go to hell," he spat, blood seeping from the corners of his mouth.

"We are already there, my friend, trust me." The Scientist lowered his face to within an inch of Zach's.

The seated man on the mat waved his hand and said something that Zach did not understand. The guards moved forward and dragged Zach on his knees to within a few feet of the man on the mat.

They want to film me on my knees in front of bin Laden, Zach thought to himself. *No way in hell.* With his hands cuffed behind his back, he struggled to regain his footing, leaning forward and then lifting his right knee. The two men tackled him, beating him again, then lifting him to his knees again.

"I'm not kneeling, so you'll just have to keep beating the shit out of me," Zach groaned.

There were ten guards in the open area, all prepared to kill Colonel Garrett if he made a single move against the man on the mat.

A knife came from out of nowhere and pressed into his neck, drawing blood. He felt the warmth sliding down his chest.

"You will kneel before the master. America will kneel before the master."

And the camera rolled.

CHAPTER 14
SPARTANBURG, SOUTH CAROLINA

TUESDAY AFTERNOON

Amanda had endured another drama filled day at school, returned home quickly and now bounced down the steps from her bedroom, cinching her backpack over her shoulder. As she stepped into the foyer, her mother stood in front of the door, blocking her exit.

"I don't want you to go back to see this woman, Amanda."

Amanda stopped, looked at her mother, and then found it hard to hold her stare. Twenty-four hours had passed since Amanda's first visit with Riley Dwyer. During her classes today the child support issue clawed at the back of her mind like a dredge. She dismissed it, though, as inconsequential. What difference did it make?

"Mom, Jake's waiting in the driveway. I don't want to do this either, but if we want that money, I have to." Amanda was dressed in a long pink skirt with a tight-fitting, matching tee underneath a denim jacket. She had snapped a Tiffany bracelet on her left wrist. She looked at her mother and then at Gus Randel sitting next to her.

Gus had wavy, light-brown hair that was swept back onto his collar. He had a baby-smooth face that made Amanda wonder if he shaved. He was wearing a black polo shirt and Levis.

"What's her name?"

"What difference does it make? Just some lady in Charlotte. Gus, help me out here."

Gus held up his hands in surrender. "Hey, I'm staying out of this one."

"Thanks a lot."

"Hey, I got you the keg," he said with a smile.

"What have you done for me *lately*?" Amanda countered.

"Well, now that you mention it. Melanie, I do think you should let Amanda just deal with this on her own schedule, you know?"

"Stay out of this, Gus. It doesn't concern you."

Gus raised his eyebrows. "Think I'm getting another beer." He stood from the table and walked into the kitchen.

"You're not leaving until you tell me her name. I need to know, just to make sure you're safe."

Amanda fidgeted. Maybe it wasn't so inconsequential. She chewed on a nail and then looked up.

"Okay, but first, answer me this. Remember when you told me dad was always missing child support? Why did you say that?" She shifted her weight and looked at her nails.

After an uncomfortable pause, her mother replied, "Because he did."

"No, mom, he didn't. I saw the records yesterday. He never missed a single payment."

Amanda brushed past her mother, opened the door, and leapt into the truck.

"Everything okay?" Jake asked.

"Just go," she muttered. Amanda stared straight ahead during most of the drive, numbly watching the familiar landmarks tick past.

★ ★ ★

GUS RANDEL GAZED at them through the bay window on the second-floor landing. He stood there in full view, perfectly framed by the transom as if he were hovering.

He lightly stroked his jaw, deep in thought, wondering about this situation and what opportunities it might present. He decided he would drive to his upcoming meeting in Charlotte, NC. That would give him time to think and outline some writing. He was working on several articles for *Charlotte Magazine*, but a new idea had just come to him.

Turning to go back downstairs, he saw Melanie staring at him. How long had she been there, he wondered?

"We need to talk," she said.

And they did.

CHAPTER 15
CHARLOTTE, NORTH CAROLINA

RILEY STOOD AS Amanda was introduced by her assistant. She smiled weakly and said, "How's my expert witness today?"

Amanda looked at her and shrugged. "Jake's waiting. What do you need me to do today?"

Riley figured it was too much to ask to make any real progress in a week's time, but she would continue to try. She had not slept much last night, and the alcohol hangover still tugged at her brain even this late in the afternoon.

"Let's just have a seat, shall we?"

Amanda took the same seat she had before and remained silent. "Rough night?"

"You're so good for my esteem," Riley replied, smiling thinly.

After an awkward moment of silence, Riley made the first move.

"Amanda, I wrote down last night the four or five things you said bothered you most about your relationship with your father." She held up a yellow legal pad of paper. "Missed child support, no visitation, mean to your mother and grandmother, always created problems, and disrupting stuff, whatever that means."

"Well, exactly, like if I had something planned, he would plan something on top of it. That happened a lot, and it got to the point where I, you know, just had to put a stop to it."

"What do you mean?"

"Well, we took my dad to court to reduce his visitation."

"You did what?" Riley was open-jawed. Her arm dropped limply off the side of the chair. Her David Yurman bracelets rattled around her wrist like a slinky.

"It got to the point, like, I would want to go to a soccer game with some friends or maybe even a trip to the mall, and dad would say he had already planned stuff. So I just took control of my life."

"Took control of your life . . . by cutting your dad out of it? How is that taking control?"

"One less distraction."

Riley thought she might be ill. Clearly the evidence that Zachary had never missed a child support payment had not been enough to convince her that she needed help, though she had suspected this might be the case. Riley was now convinced that she had been a victim of what was called parental alienation syndrome or PAS. There were emerging fields of study that were making some, but not much, headway in the courts. A few judges were beginning to listen to arguments of noncustodial parents who were being carved out of their children's lives by scheming custodial parents. The child was nothing but a tool, a weapon, in the fight. The children were the hidden threat, the argument ran. They were unknowing spies who were taught to lead a life of double agency.

The custodial parent was able to shape the child's world and scale her prism the way an optometrist measures eyesight and fits a pair of glasses. The mother, in this case, *became* the lens through which Amanda viewed the world. Amanda's personality lived in the shadow of her mother's rage.

Riley had handled several similar cases and had even testified as a witness in family law court. After reviewing the files of the Amanda Garrett case, and now speaking to Amanda in person, she suspected that she had not seen any case quite so intricate or elaborate.

"Well, I made this list yesterday of bad stuff. Let's make a list of good stuff," Riley chirped cheerily. She grabbed her pen and rested her hand atop the legal pad.

"Short list."

"A short list is better than no list," she responded.

"No list. I was being sarcastic the first time."

"Boy, I missed that," Riley sighed. She thought to herself that she could rattle off pages of Zach Garrett's high quality attributes: honorable, loyal, loving, compassionate, funny, sensitive, strong . . .

"Hello?" Amanda was waving a hand in front of her face.

"I'm sorry. I just find it rather unbelievable that you have nothing good to say about your father. No good memories, nothing?"

Amanda shrugged. "There's nothing there, nothing to say."

After a moment, she relented. "Okay, let's do it your way, then. Tell me all the bad stuff." She leaned forward when she spoke, as if wanting to hear a secret. "What's the second worst thing he ever did to you?"

"Like I was saying, he would always be trying to pull me away from my friends and even stuff my mom and Nina had planned, especially in the summer."

"Did your father have any visitation rights in the summers? Most divorce decrees include at least a few weeks for the noncustodial parent."

"I guess he didn't want any block of time, but he would watch my schedule, you know, and then plan stuff over top of it."

"How does one watch your schedule, dear?" Riley sounded a bit like Audrey Hepburn when she asked the question. She even smiled at her own authentic throaty voiced impersonation.

Amanda looked at her and screwed up her face. "You can be really strange."

"I know, don't you love it?" It was all an act. It had to be. The weight she was carrying was so heavy that she had to skim along the surface. If, for an instant, she allowed herself to get in touch with her own feelings in the presence of Amanda, it would be fatal to any potential therapist-client relationship. Riley wasn't confident that one was going to develop, but Amanda was here today, and that was a good sign.

"Whatever. Mom would tell Dad when I had stuff planned and then at the last minute he would plan on top of that. He never asked for any blocks of time in the divorce decree; that's what mom said."

Amanda looked up at Riley, as if to recognize a point that Riley would make. Amanda continued. "But we did hide sometimes; you know, leave the house when he said he was coming, because I already had stuff locked in, you know, planned, paid for and all that good stuff."

"You hid from your dad? How long has that been going on?"

"Ever since I can remember. I mean, if he's not supposed to be there, then what was I supposed to do? He's in the Army, and Mom kept telling me he could get violent."

"Violent? Did you ever see anything like that?"

"No. Well, maybe once." Amanda seemed to reel back in time. Riley was particularly interested that she seemed to have only negative memories of her father. Parental alienation syndrome labeled this "the programming effect." If a parent repeats the same message over and over again to a child, they will emphatically believe it as true. If the Soviet Union could do it to millions of people, then certainly one parent could abuse the trust of a child and easily accomplish the same task, Riley had written in one of her books.

"Go ahead," Riley urged in a soft voice.

"Well, I don't remember it all that well, but Dad had come down and forced Mom to drive to the local elementary school to meet him. He was taking me for the weekend somewhere; I can't remember where, or when, for that matter. I just remember being in the back of Nina's car, and Mom getting out to talk to Dad like she was asking him for something. Dad was shaking his head, then Mom ran back into the car real quick, and Nina hauled ass in the car."

"What did you hear from the back seat, Amanda? Surely your mother and grandmother spoke of the incident as you drove away?"

Amanda sat speechless for a minute. Riley could see she was clearly struggling to recall the incident. She placed a box of tissues next to Amanda with the reach of an arm. Amanda looked at the Kleenex as if it were an unwanted nuisance.

"Something like, He wouldn't give me the money."

"How old were you?"

"I don't know. Maybe I remember something; I don't know!" She was emotional now. Amanda snatched several of the tissues and wiped her eyes. Her mascara was running.

"Ooh, Alice Cooper, I like that look," Riley quipped.

"What are you talking about?"

"You'll see. Now continue. Your mom gets out of the car, your grandmother is in the driver's seat, and you're locked in the back seat."

"I didn't say that."

"Not hard to fill in the blanks, Amanda. What then?"

"Well, when Nina started leaving, she was going real fast, you know? I turned around and saw my dad." She stopped talking. It appeared that she couldn't reestablish the memory, as if it was a radio signal losing strength when her mind collapsed back onto more comfortable thoughts.

"Go ahead."

"Nothing," she said. "He was just screaming. I remember him screaming."

"What were you doing?"

Amanda looked at her with teary eyes. "Nothing. I just sat there," she said, and sat still.

"Amanda?"

"Nothing, lady. I was cool. It was cool."

"Okay, we're cool," Riley responded, holding out her hands. "We're cool. How old were you?"

"I don't remember. I've tried to forget all of that."

"Did you try to forget, or were you expected to forget?"

"I don't know what you mean by that, but I do remember that it happened right after 4-H camp in Clemson."

"Yes, I know the 4-H camp. I was a counselor at that camp when I was an undergrad at Clemson. If I recall, it's mostly kids who are seven to ten."

"That'd be about right."

"You know, Amanda, that's the most impressionable time for a young lady."

"I'm exhausted. Can I go? Will you just sign this stupid piece of paper?"

"Not yet. But eventually, if we keep talking like this. First, though, I want you to take a look at something."

"Not again. Okay, he never missed a child support payment."

Riley laughed. "We got that point through last night, did we?"

"Maybe."

"Ah-ah. Do I need to put you back on the witness stand?"

"No, please, I've seen better acting in high school. I admit he didn't miss a child support payment."

"I'll have you know I was the drama queen of my high school. I played Annie." Riley held up a big swatch of her reddish-brown hair and then pointed at her fair skin. "It was almost blonde *way* back then."

Amanda laughed. "I took drama. Then I got into modeling. Revlon used my lips for lipstick advertisements." Amanda puckered her lips so that they were plump.

Riley looked about nervously, then leaned forward, her eyes darting back and forth. She held a finger up to her lips. "I think I hear the paparazzi. There's a back way out of here," she whispered.

Again, Amanda giggled.

Riley stood, and so did Amanda. "Not so fast, young lady, we've still got ten minutes. I want you to read something for me. Classwork, you know," she said looking down her nose. Riley handed Amanda a legal document. "Have you ever seen this?"

She eyed the first sentence that read: CASE #0456 MELANIE GARRETT PLAINTIFF vs. ZACHARY A. GARRETT RESPONDENT. "No, I don't think so. What's a plaintiff?"

"The plaintiff files for divorce. The respondent, your father, is the one who didn't want it." It was a leap, and it was a liberal interpretation, she knew, but it was a subtlety that Riley felt was important.

"That'd be about right. If my dad was abusive, Mom would have been the one to put her foot down and get out of it."

"We'll get to that later, dearie. There you go, getting ahead of yourself. Now, turn to page two and read paragraph one."

Amanda shuffled the pages and remained silent as she read.

"No, out loud, please. I want to hear it too."

Amanda looked at Riley and then back at the document. "Captain Zachary Garrett cedes all financial assets to include stocks, bonds, mutual funds, and present savings accounts to Melanie Garrett. The estimated sum of these accounts totals $98,042.00. In exchange for the lump sum grant, Melanie Garrett agrees to full joint custody of their daughter, Amanda Garrett, and that in addition to every other weekend, and every other major holiday visitation, Captain Garrett is granted, authorized, and awarded sixty days of residential custody in the summer months, provided there is no conflict with Amanda's schooling."

Amanda rested the paper in her lap.

"What do you think, sport? Did you know any of that before?"

A long moment of quiet passed between them. Amanda dabbed at her eyes with a few more tissues. Riley sat in the chair, allowing Amanda to have her moment.

Amanda's eyes moved to Riley's. "I cried," she said.

"Excuse me?"

"I screamed and cried, 'I want my daddy!' 'I want my daddy!' That's what happened in the back of that car!" She was sobbing now. "I can't believe they did that to him." She was convulsing. "I just wanted to spend some time with him, and all they wanted was money." She was heaving. "I just wanted my daddy. Why couldn't they let me be with him? And now he's dead. He's gone. He's really gone."

Riley moved over to the couch and pulled Amanda close to her. She was crying too.

A half an hour had passed when they heard a knock on the door. Riley stood and opened it.

"Hi, ma'am. I'm Jake, we spoke in the parking lot—"

"Yes, Jake, come in."

"Is everything okay? Her mom's freaking out, calling me every five seconds, telling me she's going to report Amanda as missing. Then her grandmother called, demanding to know where we were and who you are."

"I understand. Why don't you have a seat?"

Jake sat next to Amanda, whose head was in her hands. He could see she had been crying. "You okay, babe?"

Amanda lifted her head and slowly turned toward him.

"My father's dead. How could anything be okay?"

NINA HASTINGS DROVE her minivan hunched over the wheel, speeding up I-85. To an outside observer, she would have looked like Cruella De Ville with her silk scarf fluttering in the breeze from the open window.

She whipped onto I-485, then I-77, and shot like a rocket into Dilworth, finally screeching into the parking lot of Riley Dwyer's office building. She took a moment and gathered herself, checking her makeup in the visor mirror, eating her rage as she did so. Still simmering, she stepped outside of her van and gained her composure, pulling down on her turquoise top, straightening her shell necklace, and smoothing her satin white Capri pants.

She then marched into the building, found the office, and breezed into Riley Dwyer's office as if she held the deed.

Riley, Jake, and Amanda all looked up from the sofa, tissues littering the floor like peanut shells in a bar.

"We've had about enough of this nonsense. Amanda, get your things. Let's go," she barked.

"I'm sorry," Riley said, standing and placing herself between Amanda and Nina. "This is *my* office, and I don't believe you've got an appointment." Riley was moving slowly toward Nina, who stood her ground.

"Don't give me any of that crap, lady. Amanda doesn't have to be subjected to this. You will be hearing from an attorney in the morning." Nina was trying to look past Riley, but the therapist was doing a good job of cocking her head, blocking Nina's view.

"He'll have to make an appointment, too," she laughed.

Nina stood motionless, years of poison and Old South genetics boiling around inside her. Always get what you want. Damn the torpedoes. Leave no prisoners. If the truth doesn't give you what you want, create a new one that does. A lie is simply a truth waiting for the right opportunity.

The aphorisms rushed from her calculating mind like horses from the opening gate at the Preakness. They were off and running, racing toward a destination that only she knew. Nina Hastings had sniffed a vector from the moment she read the will and every other document related to Zachary Garrett's death she could obtain. She had taken them from Melanie, spent an hour at Kinko's, and made two copies of the will, the survivor benefit plan, the life insurance, the death gratuity, and the statement of action that Zachary had outlined in the event of his death.

Nina had not been prepared for his thoroughness. Having spent the better part of the morning combing over the documents, she became alarmed as she read the details. Her expectation had been that the $500,000 would go to Melanie with some weak provisions about her having to partition some of the money to Amanda over the years. With Amanda's eighteenth birthday nearing, she had believed Melanie would be able to get control of the money immediately.

Yet, Zachary had outmaneuvered them, at least for the moment. How hard could it be to do an end run on a dead guy? She had already energized her attorney to file a motion to stop the counseling sessions with the enigma standing before her. And she had hired a private investigator to begin digging into Riley Dwyer's background. She needed to know her enemy. That spade work had already produced one pearl, one juicy nugget.

"Listen you little tramp, I'm not sure what your angle is here, but just because you had an affair with that loser, Zachary, before Melanie's divorce was final doesn't mean you can lay claim to the insurance money."

Nina could see she had gotten the attention of the group. Riley Dwyer was speechless. Amanda Garrett shot up out of her seat, grabbing at Riley's shoulder.

"Is that true?"

Riley looked at Amanda, and then she looked back at Nina, who was wearing the smug, satisfied look of an attorney who had just introduced surprise, damning, and irrefutable evidence in a capital case.

"Is it true?" Amanda demanded again.

"Amanda, it's complicated, and I was going to—"

"You bitch!"

Amanda stormed out of the office, her boyfriend racing behind her.

Nina Hastings remained behind. This was the opportunity she was seeking. She walked a step closer to Riley, pouring stale breath into her face. "You have no idea who you're messing with here. Your life is about to become hell unless you decide to give up this little pop psychology garbage with Amanda."

Riley had regained her composure. "Lady, it's clear to me that you are a domineering, selfish woman. You only want what is best for you in this life. Your life is an alternate reality that somehow has placed you at the center of the universe. You do only enough good to fool people into thinking that, as they begin to see the real you, maybe there's hope that you're not the evil bitch that you are."

"Don't you ever talk to me like that, slut, or I'll take you down!"

Riley's slender arm lifted and pointed toward the door, like an arrow poised on a bow. "I think you better leave now, before you do something you regret."

"I can't remember the last time I regretted anything."

Nina Hastings's wicked smile gave the brief impression of a haunting jack o' lantern. None of the information she had announced was true, but she knew that the best lies were built around a kernel of the truth.

"Why doesn't that surprise me?"

"I'd be looking over my shoulder, if I were you," Nina squawked before turning and departing.

★ ★ ★

RILEY CLOSED THE door behind her and pressed her back against it. She so clearly envisioned first meeting Zachary that the images seemed almost lifelike.

Zachary had been leaving the courthouse after the hearing. Wearing his class A green uniform, he looked like an Army recruiting poster. Riley was coming down the steps of the courthouse, two loads of papers and books carelessly stacked in her arms after completing testimony as an expert witness in a different case. Without even looking at her face, Zachary instantly offered her some help, which Riley readily accepted. After getting everything into her car, she insisted on buying him a Starbucks, which he accepted.

Zachary had been up front with her. He was devastated about the divorce and could only focus on his daughter. Riley totally understood, gave Zachary her card, and said, "If Amanda ever needs anyone to talk to, you have her call me, no charge. I prefer doing pro bono for the right cause." She had shrugged and smiled. "I'll never get rich, but my soul will feel good."

Pulling out of the memory, Riley stared through her window, watching the old woman shake her finger at Jake. She saw Nina grab Amanda by the arm and pull her out of Jake's truck. *This might turn uglier than it already is,* Riley thought.

Jake came around the front of the truck and confronted Nina. The young man, she figured, had courage in confronting a woman who had so ferociously laid down a marker. There was no scenario where he could wind up the victor. Amanda was already in the passenger seat of the minivan, and, frankly, Riley believed that Nina would welcome Jake getting physical. More ammunition for the image, the big lie, the alternate reality.

She watched Nina step toward Jake, who wisely backed away and returned to his truck. There it was, Riley figured. Nina had provoked Jake, and the young man was able to keep his cool enough to walk away from what she knew to be an unbelievably frustrating situation.

Riley turned away from the window as the minivan pulled away. She crossed her arms, her bracelets rattling against one another. What could she do? What would Zachary want her to do?

She lifted the photo of her and Zach.

"Please help me," she whispered to him.

CHAPTER 16
NORTHWEST FRONTIER PROVINCE, PAKISTAN

EARLY WEDNESDAY MORNING

The whipping rotor blades from the MH-47 helicopter pushed warm air against Sergeant Eversoll's face as he stood on the airfield tarmac. Next to him was Matt Garrett, dressed in army combat equipment. Eversoll had on his standard army combat uniform, body armor, and helmet. He carried a rucksack full of radios, batteries, and ammo. Matt held an M4 carbine in one hand and a ground position locator in the other. He wore clear Oakley sunglasses and a small, form-fitting helmet that cut above his ears.

"Ready?" Matt said.

"Roger that, sir. Born ready."

They boarded the Special Operations helicopter as the sun dipped below the mountains to the west. Inside the aircraft they removed their headgear and donned communications headsets. Two other men, Army Special Forces commandos Hobart and Van Dreeves, were already seated in the back. Matt gave them a wink.

"Team, how we doing?"

"Good to see you, Matt." Hobart was first.

"Rog'." Van Dreeves was second, and always a man of few words. Matt, Hobart, and Van Dreeves had participated in the Ballantine takedown in Canada two years ago along with then-Colonel Jack Rampert. Matt looked at Eversoll, who was watching the three comrades. He could see that he might feel like an outsider.

"Okay, Sergeant, you know we're going into Pakistan, right?"

"Roger that." Eversoll turned toward Matt from across the helicopter.

"Our plan is to land and hit a cave complex where we picked up some communications intercepts. The helicopter will circle while we do our mission. We are to be on the ground for no more than thirty minutes."

"Yes, sir, I understand."

"And, Sergeant?" Matt's eyes drifted from Eversoll back to Hobart and Van Dreeves, who were both staring at Eversoll, and then locked onto the sergeant.

"Yes, sir?"

"We are going in light, because the Pakistanis don't know what we're doing. And they will never know. They'll just know something happened. We've got no air cover and no way out except this helicopter. These bastards killed my brother. I want to kill all that we find. You are rear security. Hobart and Van Dreeves have left and right, respectively, as we go into the tunnel. I have the center."

"I understand, sir."

The helicopter climbed and banked for an hour. They flew mostly in silence. All lost in their own private thoughts, each with their own rituals for preparing for combat.

Matt closed his eyes and thought about his brother, Zach. Was he going out purely for revenge? Maybe. But he *could* defend the decision under the guise of an intelligence-gathering mission. He wasn't having second thoughts at all. He was just making sure he could cover for the others if things went bad.

The aircraft bucked and swayed heavily once as they did the first in-flight refuel. The MH-47 yawed as it was tethered to the refuel aircraft before it.

"Five minutes!" The crew chief hollered. He was wearing an oxygen mask and helmet. They were attacking a cave complex fifteen thousand feet high in the Hindu Kush Mountains just across the Pakistani border in an area called the Northwest Frontier Province.

The four men pulled back the charging handles on their M4s. Sergeant Eversoll licked his lips. For all the time he had been working with Colonel

Garrett, he had never been on a mission like this. He had always minded the store. Sure, he'd been in a few firefights, and had acquitted himself well. He was a good shot and a brave young man, but this was different. They were launching into the heart of Al Qaeda territory. He was glad to be in on it, for sure.

The two men to his left looked like mercenaries, even though they wore subdued American flag patches on their right shoulder. Hobart had dark hair, a long face, and broad shoulders. Van Dreeves was blond, more boyish looking. He could fit in on Sunset Beach in Hawaii.

"One minute!" The helicopter began to flair. Eversoll could tell the pilots were struggling with the altitude as the Chinook yawed back and forth. A loud bang rapped into the side. They were hit, but they kept going.

The ramp to the back of the aircraft opened. The crew chief shouted, "Go! Go!" as he pointed to the yawning hole. He was on one knee, holding an M240B machine gun on his hip. Suddenly the machinegun roared to life, spitting flame and lead at the enemy.

Sergeant Eversoll let Matt Garrett, Hobart, and Van Dreeves exit the aircraft, in accordance with the plan, before he charged out the back. They were in thigh-deep snow with green tracers whipping all around them. The MH-47 shot straight up, pushing snow everywhere, obscuring the team on the ground, and providing them a moment to maneuver. Eversoll watched as two rocket-propelled grenades left smoking trails on their way toward the helicopter.

"The fight's down here, son," Matt Garrett shouted to him. "Let's go."

The Chinook dove quickly as the grenades missed their mark, exploding into the mountainside.

The four men ran to the rock wall, shuffling as best they could through the snow. When they reached the entrance to the cave, Hobart and Van Dreeves tossed grenades into the opening and then peeled around the corner, firing their weapons.

Hobart broke left while Van Dreeves broke to the right, their shoulders rubbing the sides of the tunnel. Matt Garrett stayed about ten feet behind Hobart, aiming his weapon between his lead team.

Sergeant Eversoll turned his back to Matt, reaching with his hand to ensure he was close. Walking backward slowly, Eversoll saw two men run into the mouth of the cave, one holding a rocket launcher, the other an AK-47. Weapon at the ready, he fired two quick shots at the Al Qaeda carrying the rifle, and then he trained his weapon on the man with the grenade launcher.

He squeezed the trigger, knocking the enemy backward, but not before a rocket-propelled grenade launched from the tube. Eversoll yelled, "RPG!" The entire team ducked as the grenade flew high over their heads into the top of the cave. Smoke filled the tunnel to their immediate front.

His heart was pounding, adrenaline surging through his body. His mouth dry, he counted out, "Two AQ down!"

"Good job. Keep moving," Garrett said calmly.

The team reached a four-way intersection. Hobart peeked around his corner at the same time Van Dreeves looked to the right. Green tracers flew from left to right, chipping the rock around their heads.

Eversoll turned briefly and saw Garrett motion to the left. They were there to kill the enemy. Move to the fire. He calculated in his mind that, as the team turned to the left, he would have to quickly cover in three directions for a few seconds. He committed to watching the long axis to the right.

Quickly, they were already moving into the left section of the cave. They moved in a tight-knit diamond, like synchronized swimming, Eversoll thought. An RPG flew past them, this time from right to left, before anyone could say anything. Eversoll hit the dirt, sighted his weapon, and fired repetitive bursts into the darkness. He flipped on his night-vision goggles and saw one body on the ground, a rocket launcher next to him. Looking to his rear, the team had continued to move. They were about fifty feet from him now.

He was out of the four-way intersection and gaining on the team, quickly looking back. He kept his PVS-14 night-vision monocle on. Hobart and Van Dreeves were using flashlights which cast enough light to allow his goggles to work better. More shots from the front of the team echoed through the cave. Those sounded like M4 muzzle blasts to Eversoll.

Eversoll had caught up with Garrett. He was about ten feet from him.

"Doing good, son." Garrett's reassuring words were a boost. He continued to scan the rear of the formation. More shots from up front.

"RPG!" Hobart called out. Again, the team dove into the dirt. Eversoll felt the heat from the rocket lick at the back of his neck. He quickly pushed his goggles atop his helmet to prevent whiteout. The explosion was deafening. In its brightness, Eversoll saw three men running toward them. It was one flash of a strobe light. They were there, and then they were gone. He flipped his goggles back down, but his eyes were having a hard time adjusting. Smoke was billowing and pieces of rock were falling everywhere.

There they were, coming right at him. He resisted the urge to spray in machine-gun fashion, and instead fired well-aimed, double-tap shots at the enemy. His PAQ-4C laser aiming light shone directly onto the chest of one of the Al Qaeda as he pulled the trigger. He hit the next man as well.

The third was on top of him, screaming. Eversoll rolled to his left, pulling his knife from his boot. Arcing it upward, he caught the man in the stomach and felt warm blood pour across his hand. The man's face was close enough for him to see it in the dark. It was the face of an insane zealot. His eyes were wide open, a toothless grin locked on his face, stale breath engulfed him. Blood began to seep from his mouth as the man muttered, "Die."

Eversoll looked down and saw a grenade roll from the man's limp hand. The spoon popped off, flipping into the air in what seemed like slow motion. Eversoll shouted, "Grenade!" He suspected, though, that the team had continued to move and was safely away. He mustered his strength and rolled toward the grenade, holding tightly onto the Al Qaeda zealot. As he completed his roll, the grenade exploded, sending him five feet into the air.

He waited. He was still alive. The man's body had absorbed most of the grenade. A few flecks of burning metal protruded from his body armor.

"Eversoll, you okay?" It was Matt Garrett. "Let's move." Garrett's hand was under his arm, lifting him.

"Yes sir. I'm good." Eversoll got to one knee, took a second, and then stood, Matt's steady hand helping him up.

They continued to move, catching up with Hobart and Van Dreeves.

"We're at an open area," Hobart said. "Looks like a circle. A fire is still smoldering."

"Okay, we've been here long enough. It's time to call in the aircraft. Everyone put on their SPIES seats." The team took a minute to wrap a twelve-foot section of rope around their chests and then insert a metal climbing snap link into the loop.

Hobart moved left while Van Dreeves went right. Machine-gun fire pushed them back into the tunnel. Van Dreeves loaded a grenade into the M203 grenade launcher, stowed beneath the muzzle of his M4.

Stepping into the circle, he fired directly at the muzzle of the machine gun and stumbled back. He was hit. A flurry of machine-gun rounds had pelted him in the chest. The only question was whether his body armor had dissipated the bullets' energy at such short range.

The grenade worked its magic, silencing the gunner. Hobart took a knee next to Van Dreeves while Matt and Eversoll trained their weapons upward at the lip of the opening. One man looked over the edge, and Matt quickly fired into his forehead. Then another came from the other direction. Eversoll shot him.

"We've got to get up there. We're ducks in a barrel here," Eversoll said.

"Roger. How's Van Dreeves?"

"Alive, but not ambulatory. We have to carry him."

"Okay, Eversoll and I will secure the ridge, and then one of us will come down to help you."

With that, Eversoll quickly climbed the steep slope, his weapon slung on his back. Garrett covered him. At the top, he slid on his belly and then pulled his weapon to the ready. He could see clearly through his goggles. Two men were about fifty meters to his front climbing a steep slope. He shot them both. Another group of about ten men was at the top of the next ridge, maybe two hundred meters away. Inaccurate fire from that location swung wildly overhead. He didn't return fire.

"Secure," he called down to Matt. In an instant, Garrett was next to him on the ledge.

"Go help Hobart. I'm calling the helicopter."

"See there," Eversoll pointed. "About ten of them."

"Got it."

Eversoll slid back down the ridge and knelt next to Hobart. "How bad?"

"He'll make it. Let's go."

His knee pad had slid down around his ankle, and as he knelt, something crunched into his knee.

He looked down as he was reaching for Van Dreeves. A piece of paper or something plastic was under his knee. He grabbed at it, pawing at it with his gloved hand, unable to pick it up.

"Come on, let's go, Eversoll." Hobart was impatient. Eversoll heard the whirring blades of the helicopter as it approached.

"Hang on." He slipped his glove off, reached down, and picked up the piece of plastic, slipping it into his pocket.

"Let's go, damn it!"

"Come on." Eversoll helped Hobart, pulling Van Dreeves up the ledge as Hobart pushed.

The helicopter hovered. Matt fired randomly at the retreating enemy to keep them at bay. A rope dropped from the middle of the helicopter's under-belly. Each man hooked into a metal loop affixed to the rope. Hobart was first, then Van Dreeves, then Eversoll, and finally Garrett. The three capable men fired their weapons at the Al Qaeda as the helicopter lifted off and slung them away from the cave complex.

Bullets whipped past Sergeant Eversoll as he tried to return effective, aimed fire, but it was nearly impossible as he circled from the rope. As they swung below the helicopter tethered by the hoist cable, the winch slowly pulled them upward into the three-foot by three-foot square in the bottom of the helicopter known as the "hell hole."

They were flying so fast that water seeped from Eversoll's eyes. He looked up. Hobart was in the helicopter helping pull Van Dreeves in also. A moment later, it was his turn. He was in and helping Garrett before he knew it.

The crew chief gave them all a thumbs-up and walked around hugging them. They had made it.

The helicopter wove through the steep valleys of the Hindu Kush at one hundred fifty miles per hour. They had killed a bunch of Al Qaeda, and, if nothing else, that felt pretty good.

After about thirty minutes, once the adrenaline had slowed, Eversoll removed his glove and reached into his pocket. He had nearly forgotten about the piece of plastic he had retrieved. Any intelligence was useful, he figured. Expecting to see Arabic writing, he held up a plastic sleeve with a photo on one side and a small medallion on the other.

Speechless, he stood and walked over to where Matt Garrett was sitting, his head in his hands.

"Sir?"

"Not now, Eversoll. Now's not the time."

He imagined what Matt Garrett was going through. He had just exacted the very revenge he had come to Afghanistan to seek. Now there was nothing left, or so he thought.

"Sir, I don't know how to say this, other than I think your brother's still alive."

CHAPTER 17
CHARLOTTE, NORTH CAROLINA

TUESDAY EVENING (EASTERN TIME)

The man waiting for Melanie Garrett, whom he knew well, called himself Del Dangurs. Of course, it wasn't his real name, but a worthy nom de plume, perhaps even nom de guerre. He had arrived at the restaurant early, picking the perfect table sequestered away from the flowing throng at Ripster's high-end steak house. He had his back to the wall, like always, and watched as Melanie entered, checked with the maitre d', who nodded in his direction. Their eyes met, and he gave her a slight nod. They knew each other well and he was going to enjoy this new phase of their relationship.

He stood as she approached and he gave her an air kiss as he pulled her chair away from the table. She sat and smoothed the white linen napkin in her lap as he sat across from her. He had her favorite cabernet already poured and so he lifted his glass and she reciprocated. He watched as she held the rim just below her eye level and stared back at him.

"Melanie," he said.

"So, Del Dangurs, very nice to meet you here."

"And you as well," Del said. "Like my nom de plume?"

"Kinda sexy, in a bad boy sort of way." He watched as she swirled the maroon wine in her glass. Staring at the whirlpool he guessed she was trying to determine if it really was a good wine. She tilted the glass. The legs looked okay. He could smell the heavy bouquet of the cabernet.

"Gives me more freedom of license, if you know what I mean," Dangurs said, as he looked around the crowded restaurant.

"Who else knows who you are?"

"Just you, my attorney, and two people at the paper. There's a non-disclosure clause in my contract."

"Okay, so why does it matter to me? Why the secret rendezvous?"

Del put his glass on the table and scratched his chin pensively. "Well, aside from the fact that I thought I'd enjoy an evening with you, I wanted to make a proposal."

Melanie's loud cackle caused the couple at the next table to look curiously in their direction. "But I hardly knew ya," she joked.

Del smiled at her jab. He placed his hand on the base of his wine glass, two fingers on either side of the stem. Making small circles, he patiently waited for her to be done with herself. It was a small price to pay for getting his story.

Tiring of her routine, he decided then that he would take her home and enjoy her tonight if she was willing. Then, a dark cloud passed across the imagery in his thoughts. Maybe, he thought, he would take her even if she wasn't willing. He had created an entirely different persona that *did* allow him more room to maneuver, especially given his tiresome day job. Besides, he considered, he had so much talent and so much desire that he believed he required two identities.

"I'm thinking that I can help you, and you, in turn, can help me."

"So this isn't about marriage?"

"I thought you were through. Do you need a minute?"

"Uh, no. Sorry."

"So, as I was saying, you've seen my byline before in the papers. I do human interest articles, some reviews of the arts, and so forth."

Even he didn't consider his journalistic dalliances so far anything note-worthy, which brought him to this point. He saw the possibility to combine his drive for fame with her need to completely and utterly destroy her dead ex-husband. He understood her myopic desire to cruelly and utterly defame Colonel Garrett and would play into her need.

"Okay, go on," she said.

"I think there's a good story with Amanda, and her father being killed. This could be huge, and it could be mutually beneficial."

He was barely able to finish his sentence. He held up his hands as she put down her wine glass and got into her mental three-point stance for counter-attack.

"Just hear me out, okay?"

"This better be good."

"It is, trust me."

Del Dangurs told her his plan. She listened intently . . . and he could tell she liked it. Something was missing, though. Always quick on her feet, he watched her mind shift gears and she saw the unspoken angle.

He smiled as she said, "Okay, but now you have to listen to my plan."

And he did.

Later that evening, as they were lying in his bed, she leaned over to him and whispered in his ear. "If you do this, I will really make it worth your while."

Del Dangurs gave her a wicked grin.

"I'll make it so he wouldn't even *want* to be alive."

CHAPTER 18
NORTHWEST FRONTIER PROVINCE

WEDNESDAY

Mullah Rahman considered his good fortune. They had survived not one, but two, significant fights with a heavily armed American special operations team while inflicting the heaviest casualties on the first group since Ahmad Shah had downed the American MH-47 in Kunar several years ago killing a total of 19 Americans. In the initial fight, the Balkan fighters had died, but that was their misfortune. This time, they had merely escaped with their prisoner and the mysterious flash drive. It bothered him that the Americans had known to attack the specific cave complex he was using at the time. His instinct, though, told him that the Americans had simply gotten lucky. Maybe the campfire in the cave opening had been too bold, but he wanted that for the money shot on the video.

Killing Americans was the sweet spot when it came to funding. Having video of that killing, as Shah had taken, was the bull's-eye of the sweet spot. And now having video of his prisoner was even better. He had spliced together his own shoot down of the MH-47 and Colonel Garrett's "confession." Getting that video to the Al Qaeda diasporas would bring in hundreds of thousands of dollars, if not millions.

The truth was that Rahman was tired of fighting. Just as the Americans were growing weary of the war, so were the Arabs. The initial blows from the 9-11 attacks had led to euphoria in the Muslim world. David had struck Goliath solidly. After 10 years of combat, though, the sensation had numbed.

The fact was that combat was simply hard work. Fighting the Americans was even harder.

Sure, Rahman could continue to train a bunch of wayward, homeless Pakistanis plucked from refugee camps and processed through the Madrassas to attack the Americans, but he often thought about life beyond the Northwest Frontier Province.

He held in his hand the video that would provide him that passage. Perhaps he would find a plush pad in Dubai or Oman or Bahrain. He could blend into the ebb and flow of life there, changing his identity, get some plastic surgery, and rest, perhaps even return to the battlefield when he felt the time was right. But, really, who was he kidding?

He did the calculations. Say they gave him a million for this video. He would take a third of that and fund the next series of operations while setting in place the logistics for his escape. He had to stay off the American intelligence radar while navigating who he could still trust in the Pakistani Intelligence Service (ISI). Maybe he would just jump in a truck headed to Karachi.

But that was a long way both geographically and figuratively from Chitral, Pakistan, one of the most protected zones in the country. The Pakistan Army knew better than to venture into the tight valleys there; the security rings were too formidable, thanks to Rahman.

As the operations officer of Al Qaeda in Pakistan and Afghanistan he was the equivalent of an American three or four star general. But here he was living hand to mouth, in squalor mostly, on the fringes of humanity, fighting the good, righteous fight, but when, he wondered, did Allah provide that reprieve? He knew it was blasphemous to question Allah, but they all did, even Zawahiri, who was a two-faced prick in Rahman's mind. The Egyptian hid behind the smoked glass of SUVs and put others in danger by using doubles. No man was indispensable.

He held the DVD in his hand, trying to understand how such a weightless item could carry so much import. But he knew it was all about information. And the information contained on this piece of plastic would be shocking. The words spoken would be devastating to the Americans and their cause.

And it would be wildly enriching to Mullah Rahman, one of the new breed of opportunistic Al Qaeda/Taliban leaders. Fight some, live some.

Just don't get soft.

And watch your back, Rahman thought.

He stuffed the disk in the padded envelope and called the two couriers into the adobe hut. One was tall and dark, Mansur, a Pakistani from Karachi who knew the routes the best. The other was smaller and wore thin spectacles, Kamil. Rahman thought of him as a bookworm, but both men had proven reliable couriers.

"To Dubai. Base headquarters. The message is that we need two million to keep the momentum."

The tall one nodded and grasped the envelope.

"We will report back in a few days."

Rahman continued to hold onto the envelope and said, "They die if you don't, you know. But I'm giving you a week because of the amount of money we are asking for."

Both men nodded.

Their families lived a good life in the town of Chitral, realizing they were part prisoner and part teammate. If the men failed, their wives and children would be slaughtered. Rahman had already been through three couriers who had botched runs. All had been found and killed after, of course, they had been brought back to "identify" the remains of their families.

"Understood. We have not failed you."

And they had not, yet. Two million was the highest amount Rahman had asked for to date and he was curious what would come back.

The Diaspora would want to show the video on world wide television and they would generate revenue from selling it to major cable networks. So he thought two million might be feasible.

He watched the couriers leave and his mind drifted to the activity in the room next to him in the small adobe hut.

Before going to take care of that business, planning what to do with the spoils of the last attack, Rahman's mind drifted and he thought, *Maybe*

Morocco. Good beaches. Lots of Muslims.

He ran his hand through his beard and moved to the next room.

Rahman sat at his computer and saw that Asad Mohammed, his information technology specialist, had left him a note, indicating that he had cracked a small portion of the thumb drive, but was still frustrated that the encryption was so complex.

Nonetheless he had downloaded one Microsoft PowerPoint presentation to Rahman's laptop. Rahman smiled. He had heard that the U.S. Army used the PowerPoint program to run its command and decision briefings as well as for simple information updates. Rahman refused to put anything sensitive on any kind of digital media for exactly this reason; someone who shouldn't be looking at it ultimately would.

But he was glad the Americans were careless in this regard.

He opened the briefing and saw the title: Thorium Locations in Afghanistan.

Rahman's interest immediately piqued for two reasons. First, Thorium was an alternative to Uranium in the nuclear world, though considered much safer. Second, as one of the master bomb makers throughout all of Pakistan, Rahman had been discreetly searching for Thorium fields where he could get enough to create a nuclear bomb with sufficient yield.

He had been reading with interest the widely publicized reports that over one trillion dollars worth of minerals lay beneath Afghanistan's soil. Surely, he figured, there was Thorium in there somewhere.

He flipped to the next slide and was not surprised to see a map of Kunar and Nuristan Provinces with small dots of possible Thorium fields.

Then he saw one dark red dot just across the border near the town of Naray where the mountains were steep and the river charged through tight valleys.

Above the red dot someone had typed: Known Thorium Location.

Rahman summoned his aide, Habib, and said, "I want to conduct a raid on the forward operating base near Naray. But it will be a diversionary tactic."

Habib, wearing his white man-dress and worn tan sandals, nodded obediently awaiting the ensuing wisdom.

"I want you to find the villagers nearest this point," he said pointing at the map, "and pay them whatever it takes to reopen the mine indicated here on the map. Tell them we are looking for Lapis."

"What do we want with a bunch of Lapis?"

"They can find the Lapis, but you will lead the team that will find the Thorium," Rahman said.

"Thorium? There's a Thorium mine in Afghanistan just across the border? Is it the right kind? We've gone after this before."

"I've got a document that says the Americans believe it is Thorium two thirty-two. If they're right, we could quickly get enough to make high-yield explosive bombs for Bagram, Kabul, and Kandahar."

"You know this is radioactive material, Mullah Rahman?"

Rahman laughed. "Of course I know. That's the entire point."

Habib nodded.

"I will take thirty fighters with me. We will need ample funds. The Americans are heavily involved in that area. So it will take some money to pay off the Nuristani Tribe."

"That will leave me with only a small force, but we will manage. Leave Aktar in charge and come back once they are in place. Have him use the locals to dig and use the fighters to secure the location and probe at Firebase Naray to keep the Americans off balance. Take a half million dollars."

Habib nodded again.

"I want this done quickly. I know what I'm doing."

"No one has ever doubted that, Mullah Rahman, not even the great one."

"We shall make him happy," Rahman said, wistfully. "Now go and hurry back."

CHAPTER 19
SPARTANBURG, SOUTH CAROLINA

THURSDAY, EASTERN TIME

An uneventful Wednesday had passed for Amanda. Her mother had banned her from seeing Dwyer, not that she wanted to after Nina's disclosure about Dwyer's relationship with her father.

Pleasant spring weather held a tenuous grasp on the foothills in which Spartanburg lay. It was only a matter of time before the humidity and searing summer heat arrived.

Thursday, Amanda flowed through her classes, settling from a boil to a low simmer over Tuesday night's revelation about Riley Dwyer and her father. The woman had violated her trust. "See what we're saying, Amanda? This is all a sham," her mother had said.

"Your father is manipulating you from the grave," Nina had added.

Her sleep had been restless, which set the tone for an anxiety-ridden day. Only learning that her grades were good enough that she wouldn't have to take any finals had put the Dwyer issue on a back burner.

She was surprised, however, that she was slowly becoming preoccupied with the insurance payout from her father's will and sensed she was beginning to question a few things. In class she found herself attempting to recall memories of her father, but kept coming up blank. She thought to herself that it was like when she would try to pull up a Web site and would get the "cannot find server" page instead. No information, just frustration.

She contemplated what she was about to do with some deliberation.

Where she had, in recent memory at least, never questioned the women who raised her, now she was beginning to feel a need to at least explore the *possibility*, however remote, that her father's last request merited consideration. There was one way to find out.

"Jake, I need to talk to you." Amanda was surprised at how agitated her own voice sounded.

"I can be there in fifteen."

"Okay, that's good," she said. Walking to her window, she looked outside where she saw Nina's van parked. "Pack an overnight bag. This thing might be getting out of control."

"Just hang tight. I'll be there soon."

Amanda hung up her cell phone and walked to her door. She opened it partially and could hear Nina talking in a low whisper to her mother.

"Well, this has gone too far. I'm surprised you're not more aggressive about this. If you're not careful, all this money could get away from you."

"Mama, I'm just trying not to be too obvious. Zach's up to no good, but I'd rather let this play out a bit."

"Play out?" Nina scoffed. "They'll be dancing all around you, shaking fistfuls of money at you while you stand there like a lost kid on the playground."

"Mama, come on. I told you. I've got a plan, but you're wearing me down here, making me tired."

"You're too tired to go after a half a million dollars after all you did to raise Amanda? After all I . . ."

"After what, Mama?"

"Nothing, forget I said anything."

"No, after what?"

Nina didn't take the bait.

"After all that you did? Is that what you're all hot and bothered about?"

Nina crossed her arms and fumed.

"Besides, I've got someone coming to see the house soon."

"The house?"

"I've got a plan for the money. It's a good investment. Trust me."

Nina studied her daughter for a moment.

"Okay, I'm listening," Nina said.

Amanda had rarely heard her mother challenge Nina the way she did tonight. It occurred to her that the money was having an impact on her family that worried her. She remembered reading an old John Steinbeck book called *The Pearl* in high school English. A diver in Mexico finds the mother of all pearls, as he describes it, and suddenly everything changes in their family, their village, and their lives.

Was that happening here? Or was that what had been happening all along? Like a focusing telescope, was she beginning to see things more clearly? Or was it her father playing tricks on her from the grave?

She backed quietly into her room and shut her door. Before leaving, she clicked on her e-mail account and sent a message to Len Dagus saying she would not be in class tomorrow. She copied Principal Rugsdale, thanking both men for giving her time to "grieve over the death of my father."

Grabbing her small satchel and cell phone, she opened the window that led to a terrace. She dropped it over the rail before she turned around and climbed backwards over the wrought-iron lattice. She hung on the ledge, let go, and landed nimbly as a cat just behind the mulched boxwood hedgerow. She picked up her satchel and, staying low, jogged to her car, backed out with the headlights off and drove to the high school parking lot.

Sure enough, his truck rounded the corner as she locked up her car. She flagged him down, jumped in the passenger seat, and gave him a kiss on the cheek.

"Hi, handsome."

"So, where we going?"

"Gotta map?"

"Sure, why?"

"I think we need to get on 85, then from there, we can find Sanford."

"Your dad's house?"

CHAPTER 20
DUBAI

FRIDAY

The Scientist's two messengers, Mansur and Kamil, took extra precaution in Peshawar and linked up with their pilot who flew them to Karachi. There wasn't much to worry about, but the two men loved their families and they knew that Mullah Rahman would absolutely follow through on his promise to kill them if they weren't back in a week.

Once in Karachi, they maneuvered through the chaotic port and linked up with a contact who demanded double the payment. "ISI is turning up the heat, my friend." Mansur, who carried the money, paid the man, who led them to a rusty merchant ship headed for Fujairah, an Emirate on the Gulf of Oman and geographically opposite the seven others on the Persian Gulf. Their barely seaworthy vessel had moved quickly though and magically weathered the seas. By docking in Fujairah they had avoided the contentious Straights of Hormuz. Sometimes the Iranian patrol boats sank merchant ships, sometimes they just shot at them, and other times, rarely, they let them pass unmolested.

In Fujairah, they picked up an old Chevy Blazer with tinted windows and drove across the peninsula toward Dubai, but stopped short in Al Dhaid, an Emirate capital town about 30 miles from Fujairah and 30 miles from Dubai, perfectly centered in obscurity.

Pulling up to the compound, Kamil slowed the Blazer and flicked the headlights twice. Night had fallen but it was still over 100 degrees outside.

They had kept the air conditioner blasting during the short trip, as the ship's engine had been overheating and the sun had beat upon them without mercy.

"Gate is opening," Mansur said to Kamil. The two Pakistanis talked about how this was the time when they both got nervous. The information controller for Al Qaeda lived inside the compound. When there was word of a high priority piece of usable information, the Technician, as he called himself, required personal delivery. Certainly Mullah Rahman could have fired the digits over satellite and the Technician could have downloaded them. There would have been no certainty, though, that he was the only one with the information.

Thus, the need for Mansur and Kamil, who had proven very reliable so far. They pulled into the circular drive beneath video cameras and floodlights brighter than a Friday night football game in Texas. The two messengers stepped from the vehicle, knowing the drill, held up the DVD for the camera to see, and, presumably for the Technician's recognition software to do its magic, confirming their identities.

Soon, two guards with Uzis came out and whisked them inside through the stucco façade of the house and all the way into a secure chamber in the basement where the technician was waiting.

"What do you have for me, boys?"

"Sir," Mansur said. "We have a special video from Mullah Rahman who reports that progress is going very well."

"I'll be the judge of that," the Technician said. "How much is he asking for?"

Mansur and Kamil exchanged glances, a bad move they knew.

"How much?" This was another voice, from the recesses. Mansur knew this was the voice of the man who handled the finances. He was rarely seen in public and even Mansur and Kamil had only seen the back of his head in the dark. He was even now seated in a high back chair facing away from them apparently staring at a bookcase full of bound volumes.

"Two million," Mansur said. He choked out the words though, as if he couldn't even believe them.

The Technician laughed.

"Really?" It came out more as a sneer. "And what might Rahman have captured for two million?"

Mansur felt a flash of anger, as he knew that at least Mullah Rahman fought for the cause while these men lived in plush homes like this one, sending young Muslims from around the world to their deaths.

"I will let you be the judge, sir. Mullah Rahman believes you will be fully satisfied, in shallah."

The Technician snatched the DVD from Mansur's hand and said, "You are dismissed for now."

Mansur and Kamil were escorted by the Uzi carrying bouncers into an anteroom filled with a fully stocked bar, a large cigar humidor, and a large screen television. They waited fifteen tense minutes, wondering if they were going to be shot. The Uzi men reappeared, not that they had gone far, and brought the two men back into the basement library, as Mansur called it.

"Here is one million," the Technician said, handing a bag of U.S. dollars to Mansur. "Is this the only copy?"

Mansur grasped the bag, feeling the heft of one million dollars.

"The only DVD. Of course, Mullah Rahman has the original."

"Of course. Tell Mullah Rahman he did well and that while the video may well be worth two million, all we had available for now is one million and we will take the second million under advisement."

Mansur knew that this meant Rahman would not get the second million, but one million was twice as much as they had ever carried, so this was new territory for them.

"I will pass the message."

The Uzis escorted Mansur and Kamil back to their Chevy Blazer where they would reverse their route.

Then Mansur spoke.

"I have a better idea."

CHAPTER 21
SPARTANBURG, SOUTH CAROLINA

THURSDAY EVENING (EASTERN TIME)

"Your plan might work, but you better watch your ass," Nina Hastings spat. She was walking now, bright yellow blouse shifting against the white clam diggers, sounding like the rustle of insects on a tile floor. "You let this get away from you, it will all be for naught."

"I'm already ahead of you on this, Mama." Melanie Garrett stood her ground, perhaps out of pure exhaustion. There was the possibility that she was afraid to back down. Her mother was a violent person, though not physically so. Mental torture and gamesmanship were her areas of expertise. And while Melanie had willingly been the alternate cop to whatever her mother had chosen with respect to Amanda, eighteen years of shifting personalities and roles had taken their toll. She was, in fact, tired of the game, though still in it, still alive with the passion for making money the easy way.

"How so?"

As if on cue, the doorbell rang. Melanie smoothed her pink jumpsuit; had it been orange she may have been mistaken for an escaped convict. The white coral necklace hanging loose around her neck accented the outfit.

Opening the door, Melanie saw a tall, handsome man with blond hair, a strikingly pretty woman with hair the color of a setting sun, and two children who appeared to be twins.

"Hey, y'all, come on in." Melanie was cheerful. "I'm glad you could see the place before it goes on the market tomorrow."

"Hi, I'm John and this is Laura. This is Sam and Sally." Nina watched the husband speak and then look at his wife, who spoke next.

"Well, we have the same agent, it appears. Tad Johnson gave us a heads-up you might be selling. We are interested in a premarket viewing."

"Hi, I'm Nina, Melanie's mother. We're so happy to see you." Two good cops, a role they could both play until the time was necessary to mix it up, get them off balance.

After thirty minutes of touring the house, the yard, the garage, and back through the house, the children were already picking bedrooms.

"We're ready to make an offer. We understand that you're asking three hundred and ninety thousand, is that correct?"

Melanie paused, looking at her mother. "Well, we hadn't actually listed a price yet. I think the assessment is going to come in more around the four hundred and twenty thousand range," she countered.

Melanie watched the husband and wife look at one another with a knowing glance, as if they'd been down this road so many times. Before they could think, *Back to the drawing board*, Nina intervened. The real-estate markets in the greater Charlotte and Spartanburg areas seemed to be bouncing back and getting in premarket was the way to go, for sure. But it gave the seller some leverage.

"So I think we can reach some kind of agreement between what you heard and what we think the assessment will be," Nina offered.

New life came to the couple's eyes. "We can't go over four o five."

"We really need four ten," Melanie countered again.

The twins came running into the house from the backyard. "Mommy, Daddy, you have to see the pool in the back! I want to go for a swim right now!"

Resigned, Laura looked at John and said, "I'll probably be able to get a raise after six months of teaching. Coke promised you a review after a year."

He nodded, and then she turned to Melanie and Nina. "Four ten it is, but we want to sign a contract right now. We will put down the earnest money today, and we want to close in a week."

Melanie and Nina exchanged glances. They had made $15,000 more than they thought that they could get on the house, and it was just too easy, like everything they did. Closing within the week, no problem. They had bigger plans. Doing the math, Melanie calculated that with the money they would net on the house after paying down the mortgage plus the $500,000 from Zach's life insurance, she was $240,000 away from owning a mansion on Lake Keowee. She determined she could do that with some effort.

"Tad gave us these papers to sign if we got a quick contract. We can give him a call and get him over here, if necessary."

"I don't think it will be a problem. Tad said that if you made an offer we could sign the contract, and that he would expedite everything from there," Melanie said, taking the documents. She spent about five minutes reading through the offer. In big, bold letters on each page were the words, "**This contract is binding and irrevocable upon signature of both parties and transfer of good faith earnest money equal to 10% of the agreed upon price.**"

No getting out of it, but she didn't think she'd be able to get a better price for the house.

"You're ready to give me $41,000?"

"Checkbook right here," Laura said, retrieving the billfold from her purse. Placing the checkbook on the kitchen island she pulled out a pen. "Make it out to?" she asked with gritted teeth. She held the top of the pen in her lips.

"Melanie Garrett."

She finished signing, tore the check from the book, and handed it to Melanie, who studied it for a second. Laura handed her the pen as if to say, "Okay, it's your turn."

Melanie took the pen, looked at it, and then said, "Well, here goes."

After filling in the blanks for the agreed-upon purchase price and what appliances would convey, she signed the document, and handed the pen back to Laura. John and Laura completed the transaction with their signatures.

The deal was done.

NINA WATCHED HER daughter follow the couple out of the house and walk them to their car. Nightfall was approaching with a gray hue. Melanie waved as they departed and then opened the door to her Mercedes. The top pulled back on the car to reveal her daughter looking in the mirror, smacking her lips, and then inserting the key.

Nina knew exactly where she was going. It would be about an hour roundtrip, at least, for Melanie to go to the mansion on Lake Keowee, stare at it for a while, and then return.

She walked into Amanda's room and called out her name. After checking the entire house, she became concerned. Returning to Amanda's room, Nina entered the password to her computer and scanned her e-mail inbox. Seeing nothing of import, she clicked on the Sent folder. Immediately she saw written in bold black letters, "**Tomorrow.**"

She opened the e-mail that Amanda had sent less than an hour ago.

After reading it, she quickly retrieved her cell phone. Punching speed dial, she listened as Del Dangurs picked up on the first ring.

"How soon can you get here?"

"I'm about five minutes out, why?"

"It's happening."

She hung up the phone without saying good-bye. She turned and looked in the foyer. She would have many memories from this house, though none that would matter much to her. Life moved along objectively for Nina Hastings. One chess move at a time.

She looked up at the second-floor landing and knew what she was going to do. Swiftly moving upstairs, she changed into something more provocative and came back down about the time Del Dangurs was ringing the doorbell.

"Come on in," she said in a hoarse Mae West voice.

"Whoah, Gabrielle, not here! What are you thinking?"

"Just do what I say, slave." She grabbed him by his lapel and kissed him hard on the lips. She may have been fifty-nine years old, but she could turn it on when she needed to. "You said you wanted some risk in your life. Well, here it is."

"I just usually prefer women much younger," Del responded, Nina still holding on to him.

She smacked him across the face. "I can see you want to play it rough. Is that what you want?" Again, she smacked him and then ran her hand up his thigh. "You like that?" she whispered in his ear, then bit his lobe hard.

"I do," he said with a smile.

She guided him upstairs into Melanie's bedroom and pushed him down on the bed. Pulling down the bustier she had snatched from her daughter's bureau, she disrobed. She fumbled with Del's belt buckle and then made quick work of the rest of his clothes. For thirty minutes she pleased him in every way possible.

"This gets better each time," Dangurs said. "I liked the rough act."

Nina looked at him. They were not snuggling or spooning. Each was lying on their side of the bed. The only bond between these two was the recently negotiated agreement. To Nina, sleeping with a man to achieve a personal agenda was no different than any other transaction. It was purely objective.

"I guess you should with your background. You do what I say, and we'll keep your anger management issues to ourselves. Understand? For now."

He shifted to look at her, his eyes turning to stone. She watched him transform in front of her. His neck muscles tensed and his face seemed to become thinner, almost skeletal. His smile was wicked.

"That's what you want, isn't it? Keep your little rape incident a secret? Be a bitch to explain, wouldn't it? Given your line of work?"

Dangurs continued to morph. One moment he was the consoling, inquisitive man of his profession and the next he was in a sinister trance. This was the Del Dangurs she wanted on the mission *she* had negotiated.

"They're going to North Carolina tonight. Your *real* mission starts now."

"Okay." He was nearly catatonic. Nina's manipulations had placed him in the zone where she needed him. Violence might be necessary, and the man lying in bed next to her was proven to be as violent as they come.

Nina looked at the alarm clock on the nightstand. They had about ten minutes. She wanted to provide him some positive motivation—a dog biscuit in advance.

"Want to really risk it?"

Of course he did. And so they repeated the process.

As they were finishing, Nina heard a car door shut outside.

"Guess who's home." She grinned as she slipped out of bed and into the bathroom. Smoothing her clam diggers with her hands, she arrived at the top of the landing in time to hear Melanie greeting the man who called himself Del Dangurs.

"Hey there. What are you doing here?" Melanie said, smiling as she climbed the porch steps.

He leaned into her to steal a kiss. Not expecting the move, she received him stiffly. He noticed and pulled away. Not wanting her to smell Nina on him, he moved quickly down the steps. He spoke to her over his shoulder and then stopped on the sidewalk.

"I'm off to North Carolina to do some research for the story. Was just nailing everything down, if you know what I mean."

"You're leaving this late?"

"Listen, I *am* late, but I'll call you to let you know how, you know, everything's going."

"Do that." She smiled.

He looked around quickly, then blew her a kiss. He walked briskly across the yard toward his automobile—the one he called his "sweet ride."

Del Dangurs was on the move.

CHAPTER 22
BAGRAM AIR BASE, AFGHANISTAN

FRIDAY

Matt Garrett, Major General Jack Rampert, Sergeant Eversoll, Hobart, and Van Dreeves, sufficiently bandaged around the shoulder, huddled around the wooden table inside the headquarters at the air base.

"Sir, I saw your brother kiss this picture of Amanda and the Saint Michael medal a hundred times before missions. And he did it directly before he got on that helicopter."

"We've reviewed the tapes now fifty times, and it doesn't look like anyone was left behind, but there is the whiteout," Hobart said.

"Maybe the picture fell out of his pocket when he rescued Jergens. AQ snatched it up, thinking it might be intel?" Van Dreeves said what everyone was thinking. They all wanted to believe that Zachary Garrett was alive, but it seemed so unlikely that no one wanted to get their hopes up too soon.

"No." Eversoll was getting excited. He believed all along that Colonel Garrett had not been killed. "He secured that photo and medallion in the Velcro of his army combat uniform. He was captured and questioned right there in that circle. That was probably AQ taking him away when we popped out of the hole at the end of the tunnel."

Matt Garrett looked at him. He saw an eager, fresh-faced young man who had a bit of a country look to him. He could see Eversoll's bottom lip bulge, no doubt full of "worm dirt," what he and Zachary had called smokeless tobacco. Eversoll wore the newer version of the army combat uniform, a tan-and-olive computerized checkerboard outfit. Velcro pockets and zippers seemed to be in all the right places. He saw the three-chevron rank of sergeant squarely in the center of Eversoll's chest on a small piece of square cloth about an inch across.

"Zach mentioned that you were pretty squared away," Matt said. "Think you're up for another mission?"

"If it involves getting Colonel Garrett back, yes sir."

Matt looked at Rampert, the consummate warrior king. Rapidly promoted to two-star general after the Ballantine mission a couple of years ago, Rampert was recognized throughout the defense and foreign policy communities as the Special Operations guru. Some were already calling for his accelerated promotion to four-star general so that he could be the chairman of the Joint Chiefs of Staff. Rampert would have none of that, Matt was sure. He looked at his rugged friend, crew cut somehow making him look younger than his fifty years.

"What do you think, General?"

"Going into Pakistan once without telling anyone was a huge risk. Going in twice, is what we call a gamble."

"Know the difference, Eversoll?" Hobart had turned to Sergeant Eversoll. Clearly the three special operators saw something in the young sergeant they liked. Matt's impression was that they had already made the decision to groom him for qualification school and ultimate acceptance into their elite band of warriors.

"Only gambling I know about is in Memphis on the riverboats."

Hobart smiled a thin, wicked grin. His face was stern with a ruddy complexion. A full head of dark hair fell over his ears with no distinguishable part on either side.

"Can't recover from a gamble if you lose. Lose all your chips. A risk, that's something you can bounce back from if it doesn't work out."

"And the shirt off your back," Rampert added. "Point being, we've blazed that trail once. No doubt AQ has already leaked to Pakistani intel that we invaded their space. So, provided we didn't get shot down going in again, well, we'd all be put in the brig, most likely. State Department weenies wouldn't have any of that."

"I might be able to work something there," Matt countered. Matt felt at ease with these men. He had been a CIA combat field operative. Although he had fully recovered from his wounds in the Philippines and Canada, at thirty-five he had begun to feel the pull of scar tissue. The damage he'd incurred to his body had cut his career short well before he was ready to switch to the policy side of business.

Two years ago, after the Ballantine incident, Matt had been confirmed by the Senate as the assistant director of the CIA. The job wasn't really his cup of tea, but it kept him in the loop.

"How so?" Rampert asked.

"Know a few people," Matt said, moving over to the large map. Van Dreeves had drawn a circle around the location of the raid which they had just conducted. Matt stared at the tight contour interval lines that indicated rugged terrain in the lawless northwest province of Pakistan.

"The Paks would never allow it," Rampert said.

"They don't have to know," Matt countered. "Until it's too late."

Matt watched Rampert study him for a minute.

"I know what you're thinking."

"You can't possibly know, General, what I'm thinking," Matt countered.

"I sent your brother into Canada two years ago without anyone, to include the Canadians, knowing about it. Now you want to know if I've lost my cojones."

"Assuming that promotion to general doesn't involve any surgery, then I'm going to put my money on the table that you've still got 'em. Sir," Matt replied.

The five men stood in the operations center, radios occasionally chirping spot reports, large flat-panel monitors scrolling significant activities, and the giant map on the wall with Van Dreeves's circles on them screaming at them.

Matt's voice was firm and decisive.

"I'm ready to gamble, but you've got to tell me one thing first."

"What's that?" Rampert asked.

"Did the enemy find the flash drive?"

MOMENT OF TRUTH

CHAPTER 23
CHARLOTTE, NORTH CAROLINA

THURSDAY EVENING

Riley Dwyer walked slowly back and forth in her office. The Hawaiian ladies peering down from the Peggy Hoppers dotting the wall watched her pace the floor with uncharacteristic tension. Large, leafy plants waved at her as she passed, her vapor trail causing just the slightest turbulence.

In her right hand she held a piece of paper. She had memorized the document. Heck, she had written it and had it published in several magazines. Her fifteen minutes of fame had been derived from the words contained on this document. She had neither sought the fame nor the attention that followed. She had to admit, though, that it had been good for her business.

Riley was one of the leading experts in the country on the emerging field of parental alienation syndrome. It seemed that one of the primary byproducts of divorces with children had become the use of those children as weapons. The paradox had always intrigued her. Here a defenseless child frequently became the most used weapon in a parent's arsenal. Like any combat, there was suffering, and in this particular form of combat the weapon systems themselves, the children, suffered the most. They were slung at the intended target with all the ferocity of any arrow or bullet or missile.

Riley could see it so much in Amanda Garrett that it ripped out her heart. While her relationship with Zach had ebbed and flowed with the demands of each of their careers, his presence had always been with her. She carried him inside her heart the way many carried their first love. There were no bad memories, only happy thoughts and times that were sometimes interrupted by deployments. They had been happiest when Zach had left the service and worked the farm in Virginia. He did some defense consulting with a firm in Charlotte, and he had traveled regularly to South Carolina to try to see Amanda. They each had found peace, and in the summer of 2001 Zach began preparations to move to Charlotte for a full-time position with the company. It would keep him close to Amanda and place him with the woman he loved. They were ready.

Then 9-11 happened. Riley and Zach had spent the Labor Day weekend together, and Zach had stayed on for another week. He would head over to Spartanburg Swim Center to watch Amanda compete and then meet up with Riley afterward. She respected Zach's decision not to introduce Amanda to her until he was ready. Privately she believed that it would be healthy for Amanda to see her father in a strong relationship with another woman. The absence of Amanda, such a large part of Zach's life, had left a hole in their relationship. They would drift apart for a while and then come rushing back together. Not Amanda's fault at all, but Zach would not be whole until he could integrate his entire life, she knew that much.

She watched him struggle with the abuse that his ex-wife would levy upon him and Amanda. He would come home from an attempted visitation shaking with rage. For a while Riley didn't know what to do. Zach said very little, internalizing the pain, the frustration, and the injustice. She had wondered what was truly happening. Surely, no one could be that bad.

But it appeared that Amanda's mother and grandmother had been worse than anyone could have anticipated. Perhaps in the early days when Amanda was much younger, after she had first met Zach, she had been inspired to study the disaffected child of divorce. She had surprised herself when she began to mine the uncharted caverns of maternal abuse of custodial children.

Riley had been laughed at, screamed at, and ridiculed by mothers and the media. She was cutting across the current of hate framed by such monikers as "deadbeat dads." She had written an article for *Parents* magazine that, much to her surprise, had been published. The basic theme of the article was the existing inequity of the law where generally a father was forced to pay child support, but the woman was not compelled to honor the visitation schedule. She had explored reams of evidence in county courthouses around North and South Carolina where well-meaning fathers were gunned down by ignorant judges and attorneys who strung out cases so long that most men just gave up. It was a trap, she determined. The man, once divorced, was swimming upstream against the flooding waters of bias and stereotype. The courthouses were the floodgates, governing the tide against which the fathers braced.

She had once violated Zach's rule about staying out of sight of Amanda. She wanted to confirm in her mind what Zach had not so much told her, but what she had witnessed in his stoicism. He was an enigma in her mind when it came to Amanda. She watched him wrestle with uncommon angst and pain, knowing that Amanda had been launched at him the way an insurgent presses the key fob of an improvised explosive device as a military truck passes by. In a flash, pain and suffering occur, while the terrorist walks away, whistling and looking innocently at the sky. So it was with the enabling parental alienator.

That day a few years ago, before the Ballantine event, when Zach had re-entered the service and was stationed at Fort Bragg, Riley had taken it upon herself to watch a swim meet in Spartanburg. Not fearing identification, she sat in the bleachers near Amanda's mother and grandmother, listening to their conversation while Amanda glided to victories in all five of her races over worthy opponents. For a moment, Riley had forgotten her mission as she had become engrossed in the splashing and yelling as the competitors churned through the water.

It was the conversation, though, that had amazed her the most. The swimming was pure amateur hour compared to the well-practiced smoothness of the mother and grandmother, who openly derided the father, both in the presence of others as well as Amanda. It was a constant subtext to all that was done or said. Yet, none of it was obvious or overt.

"Don't you know that Speedo race suit cost one hundred and eighty dollars?"

"Well, I know who didn't pay for it."

"You got that right."

And so on.

And then, when Amanda was leaving with her mother.

"Good meet, Manda."

"Thanks."

"Too bad what's-his-name wasn't here."

"Yeah, too bad."

Then everyone was laughing.

She looked down at the paper, pondering her next move. The one positive sign was Amanda's ability to unlock the secret compartment in her mind. She had been brave enough to go where she really wanted to go, which was to be allowed to love her father. Having been denied that opportunity since she was a small child, was it really possible, she wondered, for Amanda to love anyone at all? The transference and blockage that had occurred surely must skew any existing or future relationship. If you're not allowed to love the father that you *know* is a good, decent man, then where is your baseline? What was her metric for attachment?

Her role models, the mother and grandmother, were clearly sociopaths, and had put Amanda in a canoe in that same river, giving her a good shove into the current. The distorted and pained contortions of Deep South love, Riley determined.

She had been gelling and crystallizing the two brief sessions with Amanda. She realized that she was basing her conclusions more on what she knew about Zach than on her interactions with his daughter. She had tried hard not to allow that to happen, but her love for Zach was a fixture in her life she couldn't easily rearrange to make room for fresh analysis.

Nor did she think she had time.

CHAPTER 24
NORTH CAROLINA

EARLY FRIDAY MORNING, EASTERN TIME

Amanda startled awake.

"What was that?"

She rubbed her eyes, pulling herself up out of Jake's lap. She had been asleep, soundly, thoughts thrashing around in her mind not necessarily as dreams, but rather as lightning bolts. Her mind was the equivalent of an electrical storm, static electricity lighting the night sky. Thunder and lightning ripped through her mind and shook the windows of her soul.

"Nothing babe, go back to sleep. We've got another thirty minutes or so."

Jake had stopped in Ashboro, North Carolina, grabbed a giant coffee, straight up, taken a leak, and then jumped back into the truck for the remaining leg into Sanford, North Carolina.

"We must have hit a bump."

"No bump, babe, just smooth sailing." Jake put a strong hand on her arm. Amanda looked out the window into the darkness.

"Well, I felt something." She remained unconvinced. Always a sound sleeper, she didn't understand the storm raging in her slumber or the anxiety she now felt. She watched a few drops of rain slap against the windshield of Jake's truck, followed by a gaining steady rhythm of rain pellets. "See there."

"Okay, babe, as usual, you're right." Jake smiled, looking down at her quickly as she lowered herself back onto his leg. Suddenly, lightning struck with a loud bang less than a mile away. This was not a distant rumble, but an explosion.

And so it went for the remainder of the trip. It was one o'clock in the morning, and they pulled into a motel in Sanford not far from the address that Riley Dwyer had provided him. Missing school would be the least of his problems, he had told her. Given what he knew about Nina Hastings and Amanda's mother, he fully expected to find himself facing kidnapping charges within the week, if that long.

"Why don't we just go to the house?" Amanda asked, as Jake fumbled with the key to the motel room. It was a Hampton Inn and had decent parking lot lighting, so he felt it was a safe choice.

"You don't think I just drove for four hours to not get lucky, do you?"

"Please." Amanda forced back a weak smile.

"Just kidding, babe. We'll get some rest, and then we'll go to the house. I've got the key. Miss Dwyer gave it to me."

"Don't mention that slut's name, okay? I'm just doing this because I have to. It's part of the plan, okay? So don't go native on me and team up with her."

They walked into the basic room, spied the single king-sized bed and each sat down. Amanda lay all the way back, her feet still touching the floor and her body making an inverted L on the bed. Jake leaned on an elbow and looked at her, sliding up toward her head.

"Don't do this, Jake. I've never been close to my dad, and I don't know what kind of cruel trick this is, but if I had to drive four hours to get the half million, then so be it."

"I drove."

"Whatever."

"Why are you being a bitch?"

Amanda stared at the ceiling. There was a slight tugging somewhere in the deep recesses of her soul, but she passed it off as the faint pull of fatigue.

"I'm being myself, Jake. You know, for the past fifteen years, as long as I can remember, he's never been there. He rarely made this trip the other way, you know. He was just never there for me. It's been my mother and my grandmother. Always. So, I don't know what we're going to see a few hours from now in that house, but whatever it is will leave me disappointed, as usual, I'm sure."

Jake studied her, remaining silent.

"When he was alive, I was better off without him. Why, when he's dead, should I be better off with his memory? He's dead. It's as simple as that. It's like I'm reading it on the news. If I didn't care about him when he was alive, why would I care now? I really don't see what the big deal is."

"Well, what was that all about back in you-know-who's office? Was it an act?"

Amanda looked at him and smiled. "Yeah, pretty good, don't you think? I mean, how else am I going to get the half mil if I don't convince the gatekeeper?"

Jake felt a chill race up his spine. The smile looked menacing, and he had seen it before . . . on Nina Hastings. At that moment, Amanda Garrett's facial expressions contorted into a mask, the blood rushing to the back of her head, pulling down on her skin, making her appear years older. He saw the family resemblance between Amanda, her mother, and her grandmother. He suddenly felt as if he were merely another pawn in her game.

"What?" Amanda asked.

"So what am I? Taxi service?" Jake had never been good at holding his thoughts in abeyance. He was more of a here and now kind of person. He didn't have the patience for the atmospherics.

"What do you mean?"

"Well, if Miss Dwyer is the gatekeeper, and you're just on a mission to get this money, I guess I'm being used, too?"

"Come on, Jake. I love you. We're in love. I've never used you for anything."

There was an awkward pause. He wanted to believe her, but didn't know if he should. They had been together for four years, but he had never seen her presented with any major life challenge, until now. He was learning about her, and himself. So, it was best to be supportive and not inject his feelings into this critical time. She was the one who had lost her father, not him. Still, he felt a calling to be more forceful with her, but in a subtle way. He wanted to guide her. Toward what, he wasn't sure. But the feeling was palpable. He needed to be a steady hand for her as she navigated these waters.

"I know. I love you, too."

They laid their heads back onto the bed and were asleep in each other's arms within the minute.

★ ★ ★

AMANDA'S MIND SWIRLED with confusion, a stormy sea tossing the vessel of her soul against competing swells. Tears of anguish flowed inside her soul. Something stirred within her, something hidden. Eyes peeking from a dark corner, wondering, wanting. Sleep washed over her, but as night spread through her body, a nocturnal entity shifted, perhaps feeling it might be safe to come out.

Those eyes, innocent and frightened, searched for a glimmer of light, a sliver of hope. So many times trying to emerge from hibernation, so many times pushed back, forced into submission. A head lifted in the night, lumbering, listening, checking, and holding still. Like a tamed animal, the eyes turned away from the swirling fury, back toward the inner sanctum where blackness painted over any hope. Where there was no pain.

Inside her tormented soul, distant music began to echo, minute sounds pulsing against the storm. A song, a female voice, a bit bluesy, a bit country—she'd heard it before, a long time ago. The hibernating eyes blinked again in the darkness, brief shutters opening and closing once, as if in acknowledgement of the music that only it could hear. Though competing with the maelstrom that raged in Amanda's mind, Jessi Alexander's sweet voice ascended in the private sanctum:

"*Every time you smile, I smile with you/Every time you cry, I'm crying too/And if you fall, my arms are open wide/When your night is dark, I'll light your way/When you've lost the spark, don't be afraid/I'm here for you, just close your eyes/I'm a part of you/You're a part of me too/Take refuge in me.*"

The eyes closed. Her soul snuggled deeply into the darkness where it had been taught to hide. Alexander's words providing the only hope . . . the only promise.

The only way.

Then, suddenly, the eyes opened, alert and scanning.

Connected.

CHAPTER 25

FRIDAY MORNING

Del Dangurs had downed two Rock Star energy drinks. His mind was racing. The inside information he had received on Colonel Zachary Garrett was priceless.

"Can you say, 'Pulitzer Prize'?" he said loudly but to himself as he stared through the windshield of his vehicle. He was on top of the world, his ego surging from the possibilities and the prey.

His talents were too great, in his view, to waste on proclaiming that *Les Miserables* was passé or that Aerosmith Reunited was, like, totally awesome. The story on which he was presently working would blow away the competition. No one would come close. He recalled seeing the *Charlotte Observer* intranet notice about Colonel Garrett's death. That was when his genius moment had crystallized. He was at the time finishing a review of Morgan Fairchild's Mrs. Robinson in *The Graduate. Steamy, seductive, and sexy!*

The editor had decided to post the email from the *Charlotte Observer* Afghanistan embed, Mary Ann Singlaub, on the intranet.

Have significant lead on MH-47 crash in Afg. where Colonel Garrett was killed with 15 others. Garrett has Charlotte-Spartanburg connection. Have good source. Story to follow.

His story would center on the grieving daughter. He could care less what Singlaub was going to do.

Dangurs ran a smooth hand across the dash of his excellent automobile, petting it. He hadn't relished the thought of eating something in this car, but he laid a towel across his lap as he munched on a buffalo chicken wrap from Smoothie Plus in Sanford. He would have to move quickly once he saw them leave.

Drumming his fingers on the dashboard, he cycled through several thoughts in his mind. First, they had been in the house now for over an hour. Were they taking inventory? Dangurs smiled as he thought to himself that he would have missed the two if good old Nina hadn't given him the heads-up. He would have eventually gotten the message, but it might have been too late by then. Thankfully they had decided to spend the night and not go straight to the house. *I've got a day job, you know.*

He watched two young female Central Carolina Community College students walk past his car. They were carrying books in their arms and chatting as if they didn't have a care in the world. One was dark-haired, and the other had what appeared to be naturally red hair. The redhead had on Daisy Duke shorts and a tube top. The other, he could see now, had an Asian look. She was wearing a bikini top and running shorts.

Dangurs licked his lips. He watched them through his windshield as they walked into the Smoothie Plus. The Asian girl held the door for the redhead, who wiggled through the gap. She then turned her head and stared directly at him. Her almond eyes locked onto his. He was an attractive man, he knew, so he understood.

She smiled at him and held the gaze as if to invite him. There was a slight turn of her head toward the inside of the restaurant. At that moment, he considered abandoning his assignment.

Instead, he turned his head to his left, beckoning her toward him. She smiled, held up one finger and disappeared inside for a moment. She re-emerged, and he pushed the down button on his automatic window.

"Nice wheels," she said with a smile.

"Nice smile." He stuck out his hand and gave his name. "Del."

"Nice to meet you. I'm Julie Nguyen. Are you going to be around later?"

"I might be. You got a cell number?"

Of course she did. She wrote it on a napkin for him and carefully placed it in his palm. "Call me. Let's hook up."

"You got it." Dangurs pulled a digital camera from the front seat and said, "Give me that world-class smile again."

She grinned, and he clicked a photo.

Turning, she walked slowly into the store, offering him a protracted view of the olive skin of her naked back. As she disappeared into Smoothie Plus, he checked the photo in the display and grinned. *Spring is in the air!* This was turning out to be a good trip after all.

Too many distractions, he determined. He needed to move to remain focused on his mission. *Then* he could enjoy the spoils. So he repositioned his car to a Texaco food mart farther down the road. The new location was just across from the only entrance into Tobacco Road subdivision.

As he waited in the Texaco parking lot, he powered up his Dell Notebook. He began writing the story right there in his front seat, funneling brilliant thoughts onto the screen. Sometimes when he was driving, he would rotate the screen to the vertical position and use the handwriting software and touch pen to scribble digital notes. So many genius moments occurred to him alone on the highway. The cigarette lighter charger was an absolute must for him.

He completed entering his thoughts into the computer and then finished the sandwich. Dangurs tossed the wrapper into a trash can and put his auto in gear. He eased slowly out of the parking lot and crossed the street toward the Tobacco Road neighborhood.

As he made the turn into the subdivision, passing between the rock walls, a dark van closed on his rear end. Paranoid for no reason, he kept telling himself, he made the first turn he could, which was a left.

He watched the van in the rearview mirror as it continued along the primary route.

He remained parked for a few minutes, acting as if he was playing with a radio dial. The Beatles' "Yesterday" was playing on one station. Because he enjoyed the song, he decided to leave that station tuned.

Yesterday, all my troubles seemed so far away . . .

That's right, he thought. Today, they seem even further away. *This story is my big break.* He grinned.

And the young girls would flock to him like bees to honey. Just like Julie Nguyen.

CHAPTER 26
SANFORD, NORTH CAROLINA

Jake, for his part, wasn't sure what to think. Amanda's moods—no, her personalities—were swinging between some pretty wide margins. He pulled the key out of the bag and opened his door, thinking that he truly loved Amanda and wanted her to sort through all of this. He wasn't planning on being a psych major, but could plainly see that she was about as conflicted as a person could possibly be. Football and baseball were his things, but he was a leader, and he knew that she needed him to be steady for her right now. Oscillating between intense feelings of love for her father and stone-cold hatred, Amanda could explode, depending on what they found in the house.

He lightly let her down from the truck's passenger side, led her to the breezeway, and inserted the key. "Okay, we're in."

He opened the door that led directly into the breakfast nook.

"I always hated that wallpaper. Look how ugly that is."

Jake remained silent as he looked through the nook windows into the expansive backyard that was covered with the same crawling-style grass, though the blades looked thicker. The dogwoods were in full flowering brilliance, and the azaleas were losing their pink flowers, the tail end of their bloom. He turned his attention to the wallpaper. Nothing unusual, he thought.

"Must have had a woman pick it out."

"Probably when he was cheating on my mom."

"C'mon, Amanda, lighten up a bit, will you. This hatred, it's like a poison just eating you up. Let it go."

"Sure thing, buddy."

Jake noticed that the kitchen was clean, as if her father had someone come in to neaten it every month or so while he was away.

"What are we supposed to find? Is this like a treasure hunt?"

"I'm not sure, but if you keep being a smart ass you're going to be looking for it by yourself." Jake leaned against the taupe kitchen counter with the sink window behind him.

"What?"

"You're being a bitch. Lighten up. Last time I'm going to ask you."

She walked over to him and leaned against him playfully. "C'mon, you lighten up. We're here." She threw her hands up in the air. "At least we made it here, so let's go do whatever it is we're supposed to do."

Jake paused a moment. Still leaning against the kitchen sink, he said, "Listen, I am here supporting you in this. I have no selfish motive here and have actually put myself at risk to bring you up here. So, if you can't do it for your father, then do it for me."

That was leadership, right there. Get her in the right frame of mind to at least begin the process. Open her mind just a bit.

She softly bounced her forehead on his chest, grabbing his large biceps with each of her hands, pushing against him. "I'm sorry. You're right. Why don't we just walk around the house and see what's here."

"Good idea."

She led him by the hand through the kitchen, and they made a right into a hardwood hallway.

"And this is the lavatory," she said somewhat theatrically, as if she was showing him the home for his purchase. "Notice the beautiful oak hardwood floors." She swept her hand across what really was well-appointed flooring. "And to the right," she declared before reaching the next room, "will be the den."

They turned into the den, which was carpeted, and stopped.

Two burgundy sofas were situated on the left of the room, spaced apart by cherry end tables. Four floor-to-ceiling windows punctuated the two walls. A wood-burning fireplace with oak mantle was centered on the wall directly in front of them. To the right was a plasma television framed by bookshelves. The room looked absolutely normal.

"Well, this isn't so bad," Jake commented.

Amanda was silent, just staring at the fireplace.

Jake gave her a moment, trying to figure out what had transfixed her.

"I used to read to him right there," she said, pointing at a small child's wicker chair next to the fireplace.

"You mean that he would read to you, right?"

She shook her head quickly. "It was our thing. He would read to me in bed, or tell me stories, is more like it. He told the greatest stories." She stopped and took a deep breath. "But I would read to him down here. He'd just lie there on the floor tossing a baseball, maybe pushing the fire around, and I would read."

Jake was trying to figure out his role once she got into the rhythm. What was he supposed to do? Step back and let her immerse herself in her memories, or should he direct her to something, like a counselor. Miss Dwyer should be here, but she wasn't, and there must be a reason for that, he figured.

As he watched Amanda kneel down and touch the rocker with her hand, a shiver went up his spine. This was like returning to the scene of a crime, he thought to himself.

★ ★ ★

AMANDA REACHED HER hand out, picturing herself rocking and giggling, her father lying on his back with that silly baseball. She would playfully kick him in the ribs when he was trying to catch the ball. He was too quick for her, and he would grab her small leg, stopping her from rocking.

She stroked the wicker seat knowing that she was the last person to ever sit in that chair. "Maybe he wants me to have this," she whispered. "Maybe that's all this is about."

"We've got room in the truck."

She slowly put her hand to her mouth and started to weep. *What a beautiful memory*, she thought to herself. *Where has it been? Why haven't I thought about this until now?* Like a white dove released from the magician's hands, the memory darted from a black trap door in the back of her mind.

"He should be right there," she said through wet eyes, pointing at the place where her father would lie on his back. "Why can't he be right there?" She collapsed onto the chair, convulsing, crying hard.

Jake was upon her in an instant, holding her. This was his mission, he realized. Nobody but him could hold her and make her feel protected.

"C'mon, Amanda, we'll get the chair and go."

"No! We're staying until I'm done." She stood, clumsily pushing against him, but holding onto him at the same time.

She turned toward the bookshelves and stared at the plasma-screen television.

"What's this?" Her tears had stopped for the moment, but there was no guarantee that would last. She pulled a taped message from the bottom of the television. It was her father's handwriting, but it seemed dated. She lifted the note, the Scotch tape resisting her pull. Holding it up so they both could read it, she read the words aloud: "Amanda, watch this last. Love, Dad."

The hand came to the mouth again. Tears came pooling up again. Jake took the note from her hand and hugged her.

"Let's go, babe, this is too hard."

She pushed away. "I said we're staying."

She regained her composure and placed the note on one of the bookshelves. Interspersed amongst the different shelves were pictures of Amanda and her father and a few of Zachary and his family.

"That's my uncle, Matt. He's the one who saved my dad during that whole Ballantine thing. Remember the coliseum being bombed and all that?"

"I reminded you about that, remember? So that's him? They look a lot alike."

"I should call him. I wonder where Uncle Matt is right now."

CHAPTER 27
SANFORD, NORTH CAROLINA

She led him up the stairs. Each step was a lightly stained oak that had retained its lacquer sheen. Amanda turned immediately to the left as she reached the small, carpeted landing.

"My room," she said. "He never changed it."

They were standing in a small eleven-foot by eleven-foot room. A white-and-yellow bedspread lay crisply atop the twin bed, which was beneath a window against the far wall. Amanda recognized the little sunshine patterns, the reason she had selected the bedding. To her left was the dormer window, and to her right was the cherry bureau with a large mirror. To the left of the dormer was a small desk with a computer. Next to the desk was a closet door that also doubled as the middle dormer of the house. Accordingly, it was well lit.

The door was slightly ajar, inviting.

Amanda pulled on the doorknob and stared into the sun-washed walk-in. She eyed clothes that she had long forgotten, perhaps never even been given the chance to remember. She reached out and pawed a small green velvet dress.

"Christmas," she whispered. "In Virginia."

She stroked the material as if it were the finest silk. Her sullen gaze moved incrementally to another garment, this one a bit larger. She took the T-shirt and jeans combo from the hanging bar and held it at arm's length.

The T-shirt said on the front, "This Kiss." She flipped it over. "Faith Hill Rocks Fort Bragg."

"I forgot all about this. Matt and my dad took me to see Faith Hill." She dropped her arm and turned to Jake. "How could I have no memory of this," she said, holding up the T-shirt in one hand. "Until now?"

"I've got some ideas."

Amanda turned back into the closet. More clothes, shoes, and miscellaneous girl stuff were neatly arrayed along each side of the closet. She walked all the way to the end of the dormer and looked out into the front yard.

"He used to like to work on the yard. I'd work in the garden over there," she said, pointing to her left where a row of boxwood shrubs angled along the property line. "But sometimes I'd be in my room here, and I would just watch him from right here. It was just nice, you know? Safe. I could keep an eye on him. And he would look up and wave without even knowing I was in here. I mean, he just knew. I never told him."

She felt Jake's hands on her shoulders and leaned back into him, closing her eyes.

"He's got a nice house."

"*Our* house," she corrected. "He always called it *our* house."

"Sorry. It's just so perfect, you know, for you and him."

"That's all there was."

"He sounds like he was really dedicated to you." Amanda didn't respond. She simply closed her eyes, pulled away, and then slid past him, walking out of the closet.

She walked across the landing and into the master bedroom. To the right was her father's dark walnut double bed. She immediately recognized everything. The matching bureau and chest of drawers were on the two opposite walls. The third dormer separated the bureau from a small television stand with a fifteen-inch TV. Sunlight splashed in a long rectangular shape across the bed. She smiled at the sight of the green and maroon bedspread she had picked out for him many years ago. She walked to the left, where the bathroom and wash area was located.

Everything looked as if he would be walking in the door any second, saying, "Amanda, let's go track some wild animals."

But that wasn't going to happen, and she wasn't quite sure how she felt about anything right now. She leaned against the sink area that separated the walk-in closet from the master bath and shower. Looking in the mirror, she saw her face reflect the confusion, which she felt. What had happened to her?

The powerful scent of her father surrounded her and raised the hair on the back of her neck. She turned quickly, expecting him to be there. Emotions were rushing through her, tumbling over one another like a theater crowd escaping a blaze. She gasped, then caught her breath, placing her hand over her heart.

It took her a second to realize that the bathroom smelled of the shaving cream that he always used. That was his smell.

She realized that Jake had not followed her into the room. Wanting to scream, Amanda suppressed the urge and ran her hands through her hair, momentarily pausing as if to pull it all out. What was going on? Like some chemical reaction, the memories of her father and her came rushing back as if someone had just hit the rewind button on the DVD player, sometimes pausing, sometimes skipping along at speeds that made the images unrecognizable.

Suddenly she was sitting atop her father's shoulders at the Faith Hill concert waving her arms in time with the music.

Skipping, blurred images . . .

Next she was hiking with him in the woods of Fort Jackson, South Carolina, believing they were following bear tracks along a sandy creek.

Skipping and blurring . . .

Now she was at the farm in Virginia, chasing the cattle that roamed freely throughout the hundred and twenty acres of Blue Ridge foothills.

Then summer camps in North Carolina.

Then trips to the Outer Banks.

The stories he would tell her at night.

Then—

"Hey, babe?" Jake called from an adjacent room. Amanda was vaguely aware of Jake's voice, having been lost in the maze of memories springing forth like a newly tapped geyser. "Think you should probably see this."

Her face was slick with perspiration. She pushed herself away from the sink to move out of the captivating aroma of her father. Like some invisible potion, the lingering scent of her father had spellbound her, if only for a moment. She took one step and then another, unsteadily making her way to the guest bedroom.

"Look at this," Jake said without looking up at her.

Amanda saw that he was focused on stacks of paper neatly organized on the double bed in the center of the room and a small desk beneath the sole window, which provided a panoramic view of the backyard.

"What is it?" Her voice was weak, shaky.

"I don't know—hey, you okay?"

Amanda began to falter, placed her hand on the bed for support, and then leaned into Jake, wrapping her arms around him. She felt Jake's arms pull her toward him, almost lifting her up.

"It's okay, Amanda. It's okay."

She buried her face into his chest and then muttered, "I'm fine. I'm okay."

"Just say the word—"

"No, I have to do this. Something's happening and I'm just . . . just confused, that's all."

"Okay, I'm with you."

She pulled away from him and looked into his eyes. She studied him for a moment, reappraising his handsome features. The square jaw, deep-set brown eyes and dark hair were all so perfect. He was perfect. She felt something stir inside of her chest, a fluttering of her heart perhaps. What was happening?

"Have you ever felt like you don't know who you are?"

She watched Jake consider her question. Of course not, she figured, he was Jake Devereaux, star athlete. Everyone wanted to be him, so it was only obvious that he knew exactly who he was and where he came from.

"Sometimes, you know, I wonder how I'm so lucky to be blessed with the things I have. Athletic ability, decent grades in school, good family." He paused. "You."

"Jake, I'm really struggling with something here." She crossed her arms, not really considering his comment. "I feel like half of me has been hiding. I feel like, I don't know, I've been ashamed of who I am, so I just cover it all up with this shallow bitch act."

Jake dropped his eyes and looked at the floor. "I wouldn't love you if I felt like I should be ashamed of you." Jake's words were reassuring to her. She felt his hands gently cup her face.

"You're way too good for me," she muttered against his hand, kissing his palm with a scrunched-up lip. "I don't deserve you."

"Hey, what kind of talk is that? We deserve each other." His whispered words sounded sophomoric, he knew, but they somehow seemed appropriate.

"No, Jake, I'm a shallow, manipulating bitch. You're a good person. I mean, look at you," she said stepping back. "You're here with me, skipping school, so you can help me deal with my dead father's belongings, or whatever it is we're doing."

"You would have done the same for me."

Amanda stared at him for a long time.

"Maybe I would have been there, but not like this. You're the only thing I can rely on right now, you know. That and my mom and Nina."

Jake stuttered for a second. It was obvious he was uncomfortable, as if he wanted to say something. Finally he did.

"I think you may be missing the point here. Take a look at some of this." He waved his hand across the stacks of paper on the bed. There were about fifteen different stacks, some higher than others. On the tops of several were small yellow pieces of note paper. The titles read: Medical Insurance Fraud, Denied Visitation, Child Support Payments, Court Cases, Attorney's Fees, Life Insurance Payout, Visitation Expenses, Grandmother Interference, Parental Alienation, One Day."

Amanda was speechless.

"I think this is what he wants you to see," Jake said. "It's proof of something. Evidence."

"Evidence of what?"

"Well, Amanda, all I've ever heard you say is that your father was a louse, you did that 'No Dad' poem for the school magazine and you keep saying your mother and grandmother *completely* raised you. I flipped through some of the Visitation Expenses files; your father spent over $52,000 just coming to see you over the past decade."

"No way."

"The evidence is there. Plane tickets, rental cars, hotel rooms, you name it."

"I can't believe this," she said, looking at the papers and then back at Jake. She could feel herself going numb.

"Look at the 'medical insurance fraud' stack, the one that's twice as high as any of the others."

"What about it?"

"You know how you're always going to the doctor for some reason or another?"

"I have lots of medical issues."

"No, Amanda, you don't."

"Yes I do. What about my bursitis? My acne? My back pain? My—"

"Amanda—"

"Shut up! Stop it! Just shut up!" She looked away, grabbing her bottom lip with her thumb and forefinger, squeezing off and on. Amanda looked through the large window into the backyard. Perfectly green stems of grass poked upward throughout the backyard. The grass in the back, she remembered, was different than the centipede grass out front. She and her father had dug holes and placed sprigs of Saint Augustine grass, another crawler that thrived in warm climates and sandy soils.

"It's called psychosomatic. You're led to believe it's true and, therefore, it becomes true. Your mind tricks your body into thinking you have a bad knee or back or whatever, and you can actually feel the pain. But it's not real."

"What brought this up, anyway? Big deal. What can you prove?" Amanda felt herself slipping back into shallow bitch mode. She was defending her mother and grandmother, as she had been trained. "How do we know that all of this isn't just a bunch of my dad's creation?"

"Well, some of it might be," Jake replied, pointing at the stack of papers labeled One Day.

Amanda reached over and thumbed through the stack of pages. She began to read:

One Day (15 June 1999/Amanda/Brooke/Megan/Christa sleepover)

One day, Amanda and Brooke and Megan and Christa were driving in a blue car really fast along the Auto Strada near Rome, Italy. Their driver was a nice Italian man named Antonio who let them play really loud Italian rock music from the radio. The girls didn't understand the words, but Amanda in particular was having fun shaking her hair and bouncing in the car, giggling with her best buddies. . . .

"Oh my gosh, I remember that night like it was yesterday. My dad used to make up these stories all the time. In this one, we went to the Coliseum and there was this thief—'the bad man'—who had stolen Caesar's chalice and we helped the *polizia* capture him. And there was a dog. And they made us princesses of Italy forever."

"What's this?" Jake asked, pointing to the bottom of the page.

(Amanda said, Good story, Dad. The others chimed in with, Yeah, Mr. Garrett, great story. I asked them what was the moral of the story. Amanda said, Even though the dog looked mean, if you were nice to it, it could help you. Brooke said, Always carry dog biscuits. Beautiful night with the girls. Remember to tell Brooke's dad what a funny girl he has.)

"Wow," Jake muttered.

Amanda wiped a tear from her face. "He was always such a great storyteller. I never knew he went back and wrote all of this down. Brooke was great, too. Her dad was Army and divorced just like mine. We got along great, though her mom lived in Georgia and Brooke wasn't here much."

She flipped through the ream of stories: "German Castle," "Bear Tracks," "Underwater Cave," "Beach Crabbing," and so on. Each story, she noticed, began with the line "One Day, Amanda . . ." and would follow with whatever friends she seemed to be associating with at the time.

"It's like he knew his time with you was slipping away. He wanted to capture the good memories." Again he waved his hand over the reams of paper. "As great as that story is, and what it means about your *real* relationship with your father, take a look at this."

Amanda haltingly took the manila folder from Jake's hand. The title on the folder read: Insurance Fraud: How it Works.

She gave Jake a quizzical stare; he simply nodded at her to continue. She opened the folder and saw both writing and calculations. She read what she presumed her father had written.

"Melanie Garrett maintains three forms of health insurance on Amanda. First, is her own insurance through Beacham Advertising Company; that pays 80 percent of any doctor visit by Amanda. Then, of course, is her current husband's insurance policy with Humana; that also pays 80 percent of all of Amanda's doctor visits. Lastly, there is the military TRICARE system; that will pay 80 percent also. The insured must inform the insurance companies of the existence of other insurance. Melanie has craftily been bilking all of these companies, and Major Garrett, for many years, using Amanda as an automatic teller machine, of sorts. Whenever Melanie wants more money, she takes Amanda to the doctor and then bills all of the different insurances to include telling Major Garrett he owes her the remainder of the 20 percent not covered by the policy. For example, if there were a $100 doctor bill, Melanie sends separate bills (see enclosures) to each of the three insurance companies, who each send her an $80 check. Then, she forwards to Major Garrett one of the doctor bills telling him he owes her $20. So her gross on a legitimate $100 health insurance claim is $260. We have catalogued over 126 separate doctor visits that have been exploited in this manner for a total of $17,394 in illegally obtained reimbursements. — Insurance Fraud Division."

Amanda dropped the piece of paper on the bed and stared at Jake. "We need to go through all of this."

"You think you can?"

"Let's get it over with."

He handed her the folder labeled Life Insurance. "Brace yourself."

She opened the folder and saw on top the words: "$250,000 payout to Amanda Garrett will be paid instead to Melanie Garrett, based upon the legal findings of this court. Further, the court finds that sufficient time had passed during Major Garrett's alleged death such that it was a reasonable conclusion that he was dead, and that the money shall remain paid and be considered irrevocable."

"This was from when we thought Dad was killed in the Philippines."

There were other important sounding words, but it was clear to her. Her mother had lied to her. The life insurance payout from his supposed death nearly two years ago *had* been paid to her, yet her mother somehow got it changed into her own name. No wonder they could afford the house, the trips, and the cars.

Amanda's phone began to ring and her mother's picture popped up on the display, as if she were in the room watching.

Jake stared at the stack of papers and then said exactly what was on his mind.

"You're nothing but your mother's money bitch."

Then he made the mistake of walking downstairs.

CHAPTER 28
SANFORD, NORTH CAROLINA

Hanging up from the phone call with her mother, she ran down the steps into the foyer to find the front door open and two men in black windbreakers with NCBI stenciled on them. One man stuffed his weapon into a holster inside his jacket and walked over to her. He was about six and a half feet tall, muscular, and wore his hair in a tight blond crew cut.

"Miss Amanda Garrett? Are you okay?"

Amanda looked at the man and then noticed that the other man was handcuffing Jake, who was face-first against the foyer wall.

"What are you doing!" Amanda screamed, and moved toward Jake.

The tall blond man stepped in front of her, holding up a hand to keep her back. "Don't touch me! Who are you? What are you doing here?" Her words were crashing together. "Jake are you okay?"

"Ma'am, I have to ask you to not communicate with the suspect." By now the tall man's partner was escorting Jake out of the house.

"What the hell is going on?" Amanda ran past the tall man to the front porch, chasing after Jake. The man escorting Jake was a powerfully built African American with a shaved head. "Jake, what's happening?"

The black man stared at her with fierce eyes and then gave an annoying look at his partner.

"Ask your mom," Jake called over his shoulder.

"I just talked to her. She said Nina's in the hospital, and we need to get back right away." She was jogging now to keep up with them as the man led Jake out of the house.

"Well, she just reported that I kidnapped you."

Amanda stopped, almost tumbling into the perfectly mown centipede grass lawn.

"What!"

The black man stopped and turned as they reached the van. "Ma'am, I'm going to have to ask you to back away while we coordinate with our headquarters and prepare the suspect for transport."

"This is bullshit, NCBI man." Her argument was useless. The man had already turned away from her and was ushering Jake into the side door of a cargo van. The blond agent sped past her and planted himself in between her and the vehicle.

"Ma'am, our mission is to ensure your safety. You're a minor and you have been reported as being kidnapped."

"Well, it's a lie. I came here because my father was just killed in Afghanistan, and he wanted me to see some things. His name is Colonel Zachary Garrett, maybe you've heard of him." She was being a smart-ass, she knew, but her shock had given way to anger. Then she noticed something. There was a flicker of recognition in the man's eyes. The other agent stopped and turned around also.

"Say again, ma'am. You said your father is Colonel Garrett . . . and he's dead?"

The concern and sincerity in the man's voice caught Amanda off guard. Her mind flashed back to a few days ago when the two soldiers had come to her mother's house to inform her about her father's death. The major had openly wept. She was getting a sense of her father's gravitas outside of her mother's orbit.

"Yes. I was notified about a week ago. He wanted me to come here to his house. *Our* house. It's in his will. Jake drove me."

The two officers exchanged a pained glance.

JAKE'S CUFFS HAD been removed, and the four of them had gone back into the house. They sat in the family room on the sofa and two leather chairs.

"What is NCBI?" asked Amanda.

"North Carolina Bureau of Investigation. Sort of like the FBI, but for the state," Agent Rogers said. He was the tall, blond one. The other had introduced himself as Agent Landers.

"How do you know my father?"

Landers spoke up first. "I was in Special Operations with him a while back, but everyone around Fort Bragg knows your dad . . . excuse me, knew him, anyway."

"When is his funeral, if I may ask?" This from Rogers.

"They haven't told me yet."

Landers paused a second, seemed uncomfortable, and then began speaking. "Why would your mother report you as kidnapped, if you weren't?"

Amanda hesitated, looked at Jake a moment, then back at Landers. "I don't exactly know. Maybe she really thought I was."

The two agents gave her a discerning look. She could tell that they knew she was hedging, protecting her mother from a counterclaim by the government of filing a false charge. It was second nature to her to defend her mother. Hell, it was her responsibility.

"We understand."

They sat in the room for a few minutes before Amanda bolted upright and said, "I almost forgot. We've got to get back now. Nina's in the hospital, and Mom says she might not make it."

The two agents looked at each other, and then Rogers said, "We have to file a report, but we will write it up as a misunderstanding. Everything should be okay. But we can't leave you in the house. We'll need the key you used to get in, and we can't let you travel back with Jake. Or it'll be our ass."

"I hope you understand," Landers said. "We will put you on a plane to Spartanburg, Miss Garrett, and Jake can drive back in his truck."

Amanda protested but saw the futility. Jake turned over the key to the agents and then kissed Amanda good-bye. He told her that he would probably beat her home.

He pulled out of the driveway, waved to the agents, winked at Amanda, and then began to retrace his route out of the neighborhood.

The two NCBI agents dropped her at the Raleigh-Durham Airport, which was on the other side of town.

"Why don't you guys just drive me the extra ten miles to Spartanburg," she quipped.

Agent Rogers smiled and pulled a card from his jacket pocket, handing it to Amanda. "Call us when you know about the funeral. We're sorry about your loss."

As she was boarding the airplane, it dawned on her that they had not retrieved a single item from the house. The wicker rocking chair, the paperwork, the DVD, everything, were all still there. She would return, perhaps, on her way to Virginia for the funeral.

Yes, she determined that's exactly what she would do.

Finding her seat in the front row of the Canada Air Regional Jet, she glanced back through the cabin at the usual assortment of travelers. Several were chatting away on their cell phones. A few were pecking on Blackberry palm digital assistants with heads bowed as if in worship.

She buckled herself into her seat, hoping that Jake would be okay on the long drive alone. With time to think, she began to wonder about the emotions beginning to rustle inside her like the wisps of wind against the sea oats that precede a not too distant hurricane.

★ ★ ★

JAKE WATCHED FROM the side parking lot of the Texaco as the NCBI van passed him on Ramsey Street. He waited another two minutes, inhaling a microwave cheeseburger and downing a Classic Coke from the stained bench and table provided next to the lotto kiosk inside the food mart. Several Central Carolina Community College students drifted through the venue, most grabbing snacks on their way to their dorms, he figured. Once he was certain that the van was committed on its path to the airport, he doubled back into the neighborhood and pulled into the driveway of Colonel Garrett's house.

After trying the front door and the breezeway entrance with no luck, he walked around the house to the backyard. Pushing on the back door proved futile as well. He stood on the stoop, looking at the ground, noticing a gravel drainage area where the gutter downspout terminated. On a whim, he reached behind the downspout and was amazed to learn that the colonel kept a magnetized spare key box hidden.

He let himself in and walked around the two-car garage, admiring the colonel's Denali SUV and sturdy workbench. He handled a couple of the items, a hammer and screwdriver, on the workbench for no particular reason, then replaced them. He opened the breezeway door from the garage and then tried the key into the kitchen. It worked.

And it was obvious to him what he needed to do.

DEL DANGURS WATCHED it all from his excellent automobile and found the entire scene quite fascinating. He wanted to get into the house to dig for more insider information on Colonel Garrett and his Pulitzer prize winning series on the paradox between those in combat and those on the home front. After all, it had been his call to Nina that had prompted the whole NCBI idea. He was truly brilliant.

Now, he needed the football player out of the house and then the possibilities were endless. Perhaps even go find Julie Nguyen and soil the good Colonel's bed sheets. Sweetness.

He watched the football player enter from the rear and then come running out of the house quickly, looking over his shoulder, as if being chased.

CHAPTER 29
BAGRAM AIR BASE, AFGHANISTAN

SATURDAY

Mary Ann Singlaub, military correspondent for the *Charlotte Observer*, tossed her Greenbeans Coffee cup into the trash receptacle, blew her bangs away from her forehead and grabbed her steno pad. There was a story brewing. She could feel it, and it wasn't at the Big Army end of the base here in Afghanistan.

The shooting down of the MH-47 was the big news, but that story was out. She had been able to get a couple of exclusives with some of the recovery team who had cycled back from the crash site, which was some damn good journalistic work, if she did say so herself.

On her third tour in a combat zone, Mary Ann had become expert at using her best asset to her advantage. At the end of the day, it was all very simple. She was a strikingly beautiful woman who, with those deep brown eyes and chestnut hair, could make even the most hardened Special Operations soldier blush. She always chose her attire carefully, definitely LL Bean and Northface, which allowed her to blend in. But some days required a size 2 instead of a size 4 in order to set the hook, get them looking.

Today was a size-2 kind of day.

With just two days remaining until she jumped on an airplane to head back to Charlotte, she wanted the juice one last time. Always in a constant battle with her editor, Mary Ann refused to write a story that was in any way negative or inflammatory. She wrote human interest stories that somehow always seemed to work. In her view, there were enough journalistic predators out there digging for the nefarious deeds, and she was quite comfortable that all that was bad would be sufficiently reported. No, her perspective, her niche, was to bring home the good news. She sought the uplifting news about heroism and triumph over tragedy.

She stood from the bench as she spied her mark. He was a young soldier she knew had driven for Colonel Zach Garrett, the fabled and revered Special Operations commander killed in the helicopter crash. The news was devastating to this small military compound in Afghanistan. Every soldier killed in action was an individual tragedy of immense human proportions. Because of his stature, the Special Forces commander's death sent huge shock waves across this base and, she figured, around the world within this closely stitched community. The number of lives he must have touched, she thought almost out loud. That would be her angle.

Though he did not wear a name tag, none of these guys did, she recognized the driver's face from the one time she had seen Colonel Garrett going to the Big Army side of the base for a meeting. This soldier had been driving the SUV that had pulled up directly in front of the headquarters building and from which Colonel Garrett had stepped. She had walked up to the window of the SUV, which this soldier had rolled down for her.

"I'm sorry, I'm trying to find the PX," she'd said. "I'm new here."

He had been gracious, speaking with a slight Southern drawl and pointing her in the right direction. "Don't sell much other than toothpaste and razor blades, ma'am," he'd said.

"I'm not much older than you, big guy, so watch it with that 'ma'am' stuff." She had playfully punched him in the arm.

So now, she strode toward him, intercepting him as he walked toward the small store that sold the basic essentials that Sergeant Eversoll had mentioned to her.

"I found it," she said, waving her arms at him.

It was a bright morning, and he was wearing Wiley X protective sunglasses. Sergeant Eversoll paused for a moment, and she could tell he was processing where he knew her from, if indeed he remembered her at all.

"Excuse me?"

"The PX. I found it, thanks to your great directions." They were standing on the gravel parking lot outside of a small trailer the size of a mobile home. The sun was set against a pristine blue sky, and the temperature was the perfect balance between cool and warm. Say what you will about Afghanistan, she mused, the weather in the spring was as good as it gets.

"Yesss, the reporter," Eversoll said with time-delayed recognition. "So, you bought some toothpaste and razor blades?"

She rubbed her face with an open hand. "Closest shave I've ever had."

He didn't smile, but acknowledged her joke with a nod. She could see that he was not in a mood to chitchat, if he ever was. She took in his broad shoulders and round face. He was handsome in a country boy way.

"Mary Ann Singlaub," she said, holding out her hand.

"Sergeant Eversoll." His firm grip nearly crushed her slender fingers.

Removing her hand from the vise and shaking it gingerly, she smiled at him.

"Sorry," he muttered, and began to step away. "Just gotta pick up a couple of things. So, nice to meet you, ma'am."

"It's Mary Ann, and could I ask you one question?"

She watched him pause, could see he was uncomfortable. "Like, where's the PX, or, like, what happened the other night so I can print it in my newspaper?"

"Well, I've found the PX, thanks to you. What I wanted to ask you about was Colonel Garrett. He seemed like such a wonderful man and had touched so many lives. I wanted to do a feature piece on him."

Mary Ann suddenly felt like a bug underneath a kid's magnifying glass as Sergeant Eversoll stared at her. Was it the soldier's standard distrust of the media, or was it something deeper, as if she were violating a bond? Had she gone too far?

"You were his driver, correct?" she prodded carefully.

"No comment."

"I do human interest stories on soldiers and their families, Sergeant. I've never written a single story with a negative overtone. The research I've done on Colonel Garrett, and what others have told me, indicates he was a great man. I doubt there's anyone who could tell his story better than you."

More of the magnifying glass.

"He is a great man. Now if you'll excuse me, I need to get moving."

With that, Sergeant Eversoll left Mary Ann Singlaub standing in the gravel parking lot. She wanted to scream after him, "You mean, *was* a great man." Unless he was trying to tell her something. She dropped her arms to her side with a flapping motion. Wishful thinking, she scoffed. There's no pony in that stable, as her dad had always said when a situation lacked substance or possibility.

"He *is* a great man," she whispered to herself, unable to let go of the connotation.

Then she had an idea.

CHAPTER 30
KARACHI, PAKISTAN

SATURDAY

Mansur had debated what to do about Kamil. Finally, as they had arrived at the port of Karachi, he took Kamil into the dockside warehouse where they would wait for a truck back to Peshawar. They had made the trip in under two days so far and Mansur hated flying the leaky propeller airplanes of Pakistan Airlines.

"What's your better idea, brother, Mansur?" Kamil asked.

The warehouse was quiet, the occasional sound of a rat scratching along a rafter, the close boom of a tug pushing up channel, or the wind pushing against the corrugated metal roof. They stood next to two partially dis-assembled Tata Motors trucks from India, their notorious transmission problems apparently having sidelined both vehicles.

"We need to keep half the money," Mansur said. "With $500,000 we can live good lives in some country like India or Indonesia. Start a business."

Kamil regarded his childhood friend closely.

"Not possible." He shook his head sullenly.

"Think about it. We leave now—"

"And Rahman kills our families. I have two children, you have one! How can you suggest such a thing?"

"Rahman will not kill the children and we can find new wives. As Muslims we are allowed four, no?"

"How can you joke around at a time like this? Rahman was expecting two million and we only have one million and now you are talking about giving him nothing?"

"Did you see what we gave the man in Dubai?"

"Of course not. Did you?"

Mansur smiled, holding up the pocket sized Coby Ultra DVD player he had purchased for $25 at a local bazaar on the way to Dubai.

"We are forbidden. They have ways of determining whether it has been viewed."

"They let us go, no?"

Kamil fidgeted for a second. Mansur could see that he was curious.

"It is a video of an American special operations colonel denouncing the war and giving very detailed American withdrawal plans to Mullah Rahman. He said the Americans were tired of the war and were pulling out of their base camps along the border so that Afghan forces could get in there and defend their own country. And he described how Al Qaeda could effectively attack Bagram Air Base."

Kamil grimaced, as if knowing made him complicit in Mansur's scheme.

"I cannot know of this. Do not include me in your ill deeds," Kamil said, turning away.

"How long have we known each other?" Mansur asked.

"Since we were able to know our names," Kamil said. "Since Khagozi."

Khagozi was a small village to the northeast of Chitral, toward the sliver of Afghanistan that led into China, where the two men grew up together herding sheep. Now, they were carrying a million dollars in two bags.

"Can we not dream of another life far away from here?"

"And leave our families like cowards?"

"No, we can get our families, if you insist. I will say you were killed on the boat, lost at sea along with your money, and then I will go back, to be beaten assuredly, but you can fly, get there first, get your family and move quickly, maybe even get my family. Take $250,000 and leave it for Rahman."

"Your plan is full of holes. Mullah Rahman is too smart for these games. You know he keeps guards on our families until we return," Kamil said.

Mansur could see that Kamil was not going to participate in his scheme and so reluctantly shifted gears.

"I bought something else in the market when you were speaking with the ship captain," Mansur said.

He brandished a small knife, wickedly sharp, that he thrust into his friends abdomen before either of them had a chance to think about it. He pulled his friend close and whispered, "Since you won't join me in a new life, I will send you to another."

Ratcheting the knife up toward his sternum, Mansur felt Kamil's weakened grip attempt to push him away, but it wasn't enough.

"Traitor," Kamil whispered, a bubble of blood aspirating out of his mouth.

Mansur dragged Kamil's body to the back of the warehouse, which opened to a pier. In the dark of the night, he wrapped loose chains around Kamil's body, secured them with his belt, and retrieved his bag of money before dumping Kamil to the bottom of the Baba Channel where the ebb would certainly drag him into the Arabian Sea.

Cleaning up, Mansur took the full million dollars and improvised a new plan.

CHAPTER 31
NORTHWEST FRONTIER PROVINCE, PAKISTAN

SUNDAY

Zachary Garrett looked up at his captor's thin, evil grin baring rotten teeth. In the dim light of the adobe hut, Zachary could see the man's long beard and traditional head dressing. He was pushing a bottle of water toward him.

"Drink." The word came out, "dink."

Zach lifted a heavy arm and took the water, twisted the cap with a bruised hand, and gladly poured the entire contents down his throat. He could feel the liquid burning cold throughout his upper torso. He was dehydrated.

"More?"

The man laughed. Though Zach thought it was doubtful if the terrorist understood English, he believed that the man understood his gesture. Regardless, the captor pulled a pair of flexible handcuffs from his robe and quickly zipped Zach's hands together behind his back. Zach tugged at his hands, straining his shoulders. He silently wished that the Al Qaeda operative had known that the front position for the zip cuffs was preferred because men could relieve themselves without assistance, among other things.

"Stay." The man pushed a large olive hand toward Zach's face as if he were a cop indicating for traffic to stop.

Zach watched him disappear beyond a small opening, and then began to survey his surroundings. He was lying on a dirt floor in an enclosed room, save the opening through which his captor had just departed. He determined that the structure was typical of the Afghan and Pakistani people, caked mud walls that had hardened over centuries of sun and rain and constant repair. Through his time in Afghanistan, he had learned that the adobe structure was as strong as any rebar-reinforced concrete building.

He faintly recalled the tunnel complex as he tried to familiarize himself with his new surroundings. There was a man that called himself the Scientist who had been forcing him to kneel in front of . . . bin Laden? He had heard distant explosions and then lost consciousness. How long he had been unconscious he didn't know. A day, maybe two? Then he awoke in this place.

He was still wearing his army combat uniform. Thankfully, he had two layers of polypro underwear. He was surprised his captors had not stripped him. It was the only thing keeping him from freezing to death. May in the Hindu Kush Mountains could sometimes bring forth a beautiful spring that would pull forth the grapes in the vineyards and the apples from the orchards scattered through the valleys. More often than not, though, the long reach of a reluctantly departing winter would sweep its frigid hand through the higher altitudes. The temperature was probably close to thirty degrees. Inside the adobe home, it was more like forty, maybe. At least he was out of the wind.

He laid his head against the hard floor, trying his best to find a position that wasn't supremely uncomfortable. Finally, he decided that the best thing he could do was to lie flat on his stomach, removing the weight from his shoulders. As he nestled into the floor, he felt the searing pain of the knife cut to his neck and the two bullet wounds to his legs that he had suffered when he was rescuing Jergens.

Jergens. The rest of his men. What had happened to them? On the landing zone the last thing he remembered was a wild-eyed man leaping over him onto the ramp of the MH-47. Then everything had gone blank.

He felt his face grow cold against the bare floor as he shifted. He wanted to pray. He wanted to be able to place his hands together and pray to God for his men, that they were okay, that they had made it back to the base safely. He also thought of his brother, Matt, and Riley, his soul mate. Were they aware that he was alive? Were they suffering believing he was dead? Was anyone looking for him or was he presumed dead?

He did the best he could do and laced his fingers behind his back. He went deep into that place in his mind he had carved out long ago, before this or the Ballantine mission or any of the tight spots he had encountered. His silent prayer floated from his mind like a leaf blowing in the autumn wind.

Then, landing like a feather atop a gentle stream, the prayer carried on.

CHAPTER 32
CHARLOTTE, NORTH CAROLINA

SUNDAY EVENING

Riley Dwyer looked at herself with a mixture of despair and amusement in the mirror of the master bathroom of her Dilworth home. The house was just off Tryon Street in a swank row, maybe about a mile from her Charlotte office. The location was ideal, especially for a single woman. Tryon Estates was near all the trendy eateries, and Southpark Mall was twenty minutes away.

"You're getting old, Dwyer." She ran two slender hands along smooth cheeks, noticed her freckles, as prominent as ever, and sighed. She was being dramatic. She knew deep inside that she was pretty by even modest standards; most men considered her beautiful. Her mid-thirties were agreeing with her from a health standpoint, but these last few days were impossibly difficult.

She grabbed a scrunchie, knotted her thick hair into a ponytail, and then leaned over to tighten up her running shoes. Though it was getting dark, she really needed to burn some energy to clear her mind. There was still no word on Zach's funeral. No one seemed to know where Matt was, so she had called Karen, his sister. She was equally unaware of Matt's location or when Zach's remains would be ready for the family. She hated that word "remains." It begged the question, how much of him was really left?

She shuddered as she visualized the helicopter exploding and burning, imagining the fear and terror he must have felt along with that of his men.

Where do we find such heroes, she wondered? So many men lost, so many families torn apart, so few who truly understand the sacrifice. She didn't pretend to know the trials of a soldier, though she understood full well the anxiety of loving one.

Riley walked into her foyer, where she paused in front of her small print replica of Thomas Cole's *Voyage of Life*. She had all four paintings, arrayed from childhood to youth to adulthood to old age. She pondered her own life, visualizing herself in the boat with the broken till about to tip nose first into the rapids spiked with knife-edged rocks.

She sat down on the padded hall bench beneath the painting, wondering if she had the energy. Beneath the Cole print was a photo of her and Zach hiking in the low mountains near Lake Jocassee, South Carolina. She was wearing a funny gray Clemson sweatshirt that said, "Athletic Department— Yeah, right!" He was wearing his signature blue-and-orange University of Virginia hooded pullover.

She remembered that Zach had placed the camera on a rock, set the timer, and run toward her. The flash caught them laughing as he nearly knocked them both over the ledge. Behind them the world fell away to the east, toward Charlotte, and what she saw in the photo was two people as happy as they had ever been.

That was their first weekend together. Zach had rented a small, Spartan cabin in Jocassee after nervously asking her out. They had been on many dates for dinner and a movie, concerts in Charlotte, and any variety of other entertaining venues. Some of these dates were squeezed in after he had made an attempt to visit Amanda. That weekend had served, now that she really thought about it, as the turning point for Zach, where he decided to give Amanda her space; not to let go, but to maintain a respectful distance with a watchful eye.

Once they had returned from the hike, Zach and she had prepared a meal together in the kitchenette of the small cottage. He'd opened a bottle of dry white wine and they drank while they broke hard spaghetti and tossed it into the boiling pot.

"Hard to screw this up," she'd said.

"Watch me." Zach smiled.

"Oh, I can do that all day long." She winked at him.

"That's about how long this spaghetti needs to cook, right?"

"Uh, yeah, right, mister chef."

She leaned into him and smelled the fresh outdoor air on his sweatshirt. Holding her wineglass in one hand, she slipped her arm around him as he wrapped her up with his arms. Nuzzling into his neck, feeling the wine giving her a bit of courage, she lightly kissed behind his ear and whispered, "We can burn a little bit of energy first, if you'd like."

He reached over and placed his wineglass on the countertop and pulled her face to his, both of his hands framing her cheeks. Pressing his lips to hers, he ran his hands through her knotted, flowing hair all the way down to her back. He gently pulled her closer. Moving away briefly, he looked into her eyes so deeply that she wondered how they could have waited so long for this to happen. However, she knew that their relationship needed to develop at its own pace, and this moment was the perfect one.

Looking into his eyes, she registered that there was a purity mixed into those green irises that would not betray her . . . or anyone. Her thin hands pulled at his sweatshirt, lifting it over his head, revealing a white T-shirt that was a bit damp with the cool remnants of sweat. She had that off in record time as well.

Somehow they had managed to find the bed as they walked, kissed, groped, and discarded clothing, leaving a trail the same way a novice skier attempting a double diamond run marks his fall with a hundred-meter-long yard sale.

"I only want to do this if you're ready, Riley," Zach said, pulling away for a moment.

She looked at him with a fixed stare. "Ready? Zach, I've been ready for you for the last year. The question is, are you ready?"

Without answering, he began kissing her softly on the lips, moving to her neck, then to her shoulder, and back to her neck. He whispered, "What do you think?"

She looked into his eyes and then down below his waist and smiled.

"Can't be any more ready than that."

Two hours later, the spaghetti was a dried heap at the bottom of the pot.

"Told you I'd destroy the chow."

"Well, I'm letting you cook all the time," she chuckled. She wrapped her bare leg across his and pulled herself on top of him about three quarters of the way. She smiled at the confirmation of his tenderness. While strong and powerful, he was loving and gentle. She propped her chin on his chest and looked into his face.

"Thinking?" she asked.

"I'm thinking we fit together pretty good there, Riles."

"No question about that."

"I'm also thinking that you're the smartest woman I know. You've given me time and space to deal with Amanda while at the same time loving me and supporting me. I mean, wow, it just dawned on me how much I love you."

"You're totally worth it. Every bit of it," she whispered.

"Hey, come here." He pulled her on top of him completely. "I know another way we fit together."

"Oh, my, so you do."

Riley totally gave herself to him, handed him her heart as they softly loved each other that night.

"Promise you won't break my heart," she whispered.

"Never."

RILEY SNAPPED OUT of her flashback with a jolt.

"Never," she whispered to herself.

Yes, she needed to go for a good, long run. Moving the endorphins through the human circulatory system was a proven technique for stimulating brain activity, releasing stress, and reducing lactic acid buildup. She tucked her house key into the Velcro pouch on her running shorts and leaned against her front door to stretch each of her calf muscles. Then, swinging the door open, Riley found herself staring into the distorted face of

Amanda Garrett.

For a moment she could not find any words that would move from her brain to her mouth and make sense. To transition from the beautiful memory of her first lovemaking moment with Zach to the outstretched hand of his daughter was discomfiting, to make an understatement.

"Amanda, what are you doing here?" Not great, but the best she could do.

After a pregnant pause, Amanda looked up at Riley.

"I'm sorry about what I said to you."

An apology? This would be a classic breakthrough if it was sincere.

"How did you find my house? How did you get here?"

"Can I come in?" Amanda's voice was solemn. "I'd rather talk to you in the house."

Though she had never had a client in her home, she figured it would be harmless.

"Sure, come on in. Where are my manners?" Riley was still trying to find her footing here. She led Amanda through the foyer, past her study, and into the family room with its vaulted ceiling and stone fireplace. "Please, sit down. Can I get you something to drink?"

"I'm fine. I need to ask you a few questions," Amanda said emphatically. Riley thought she could hear the whisper of the words, ". . . while I still have the courage."

"Okay, sport, it's your dime," Riley said, more to herself now. Riley's radar had reengaged. Something seemed out of place.

"I went to Sanford Friday. I went to see my dad's house. You know, how this will thing tells me to, just like I have to see you. That was one of the requirements."

"Go on."

"Jake drove me, and he used the key you gave him. We were in there for about an hour, maybe, and then I guess my mom called the NCBI or something because some people showed up and arrested Jake for kidnapping."

"What!" Riley's hand came to her mouth. "Where is he now?"

"They released him, but made me fly back here because he's eighteen and

I'm seventeen. They couldn't let him drive me back. I kind of freaked, so I've been hanging at Brianna's house all weekend. My best friend. Mom, everybody's kind of freaked out, you know?"

Riley shifted in her chair and leaned forward. "So where is Jake now?"

"I haven't seen him since he got back. I even texted him that I was coming over here and it would be cool if he met us so we could, you know, talk. That's not what I wanted to talk to you about though."

"Let me ask you, what made the NCBI release him so quickly?"

"*That's* part of what I need to talk to you about. I'm afraid I'm seeing how screwed up in the head I am. I need to talk to you."

"We're talking, Amanda. It's going to be okay. And you're not screwed up."

"I . . . I don't remember things . . . about my dad. Well, sometimes I do, like today." Her words were coming out fast now. "When we were driving up the hill to his house I thought I was traveling back in time. I saw myself wrecking my bike, and I had absolutely no memory of that. Then . . . then we got into the house, and all these memories came rushing back like someone was playing a DVD in my head, you know?"

Riley watched Amanda speak, tears sneaking their way down her face.

"The images were so real. I was reading on the chair. I was listening to a bedtime story. I was asking him not to go to work. What's wrong with me?" she demanded, reaching out with her hands in frustration.

Riley grabbed Amanda's hands and held them. "Let me show you something, Amanda."

Riley guided her up the stairs and into what was obviously a guest bedroom. On the bed were several scrapbooks.

"Just for the record, Amanda, it's important for you to know that your father met me at the courthouse as he was leaving the hearing for the divorce. The marriage was over by the time we began our relationship."

Amanda didn't respond initially. Then she said, "No one wants to think of their parents apart, you know. But I've never thought of my parents even together. I just couldn't figure out why he was never there."

"But you have to know, he was there. Look here. Your dad and I put these photo albums together. Several are of him and me, but you're probably not interested in that," she said, opening one of the albums. There were several pictures of Amanda swimming, as if taken from the corner of the gymnasium. She flipped a few pages, and Amanda saw photos of the senior class production of *Gone With the Wind*, in which she'd played Scarlett O'Hara. "Your dad was with you, but the conflict was so damaging to you that he pulled away. He couldn't let you go. He had no intention of ever doing that. He just wanted you to have your space, to let you figure things out on your own. If that was possible."

"Why wouldn't it be possible?" Amanda asked, flipping through the photos.

"I mentioned to you the last time we were together a thing called parental alienation syndrome, do you remember?"

"I dunno, maybe, I guess."

"It's where one parent, usually the parent the child lives with most of the time, uses a child to hurt the other parent. It's also called malicious mother syndrome."

Riley eyed Amanda closely, watching for a defensive reaction regarding her mother. To her surprise, Amanda continued flipping through the book and looked up at her. "I'm listening."

"The incident, for example, that you describe about being locked in the back of a car while your mother demanded money from your father is classic manipulation of the child and the noncustodial parent, who was your father, in this case. It could be argued," she continued gingerly, "that your mother used you as a prop to compel your father to pay money to see you."

"What if he really owed her that money?"

"Doesn't make it right, honey," Riley quickly said. "Putting a child in that kind of situation is, in my mind, criminal."

"That's pretty strong, don't you think?"

"No, I don't, actually."

Amanda put down the photo album, walked over to the window, and stared into the darkness. Riley saw her look down and notice a book on the end table.

"What's this? This is you?" Amanda asked, distracted.

"Yes, that's me. My book, rather. The courts have a lot to learn about this sort of thing."

Riley walked over and took it from her.

"It's great that you're published."

"I think I'm one million five hundred thousand on the Amazon bestsellers list. Awesome." She smiled. Riley was being exceptionally modest. Her book had done well and had been chosen as a text at several universities. She wished to move past the book quickly, though. This was about Amanda, not her.

Riley did smile inwardly as she remembered Zach poring over the pages, saying, *"You have to attack this thing like a military problem. You have an enemy who has outer defenses, and they are holding someone hostage. What is your shaping operation? What are your interim objectives? How do you create the conditions for a successful attack while not harming the hostage? What is your defeat mechanism, that one thing that will assure you victory?"*

After a while, it had all became perfectly logical to her, though it was never in her nature to ponder the complexities of warfare. Psychology according to Sun Tzu. Wonderful.

"Can't you see this is exactly what they're doing? They are fighting a war, and Amanda is their point man. She makes first contact on their behalf. Then they develop the situation. She is trained as spy and infantryman rolled into one." Zach's words, now more than ever, seemed terribly poignant as she had begun to dismantle the first surface layer of Amanda Garrett's psyche. *Amanda is their point man. She makes first contact. . . .*

"Well, I'd like to be published one day."

"Really?"

"I know, it's not cool, but I like to write. Mom tells me it's for losers."

Riley stared at her a moment, noticing how much of Zachary she saw in her face. Strong cheekbones and the eyes, she felt as though Zachary were staring directly at her. Flint green specks burned brilliantly in what could only be called jade irises.

"What?"

"First of all, it's totally cool. Just look at me. Secondly, you look so much like your father. He was such a beautiful man. And I know, Amanda, that you have his heart, too. Your father was a writer. He helped with this book." She patted the hard cover of her opus. "And he wrote some other things, too."

Amanda looked down at the carpet. "I'm just so confused, you know. I need to go back to the house, I guess, and spend some more time there maybe. It was, I don't know, so good to be . . . home. I felt at peace."

Riley felt the sting of tears forming but managed to hold them back. "He always wanted you there, and I think you could see how much he carried you in his heart."

Amanda wiped her eyes and then dried her hands on her jeans. "Does this make me a worse person than I already am? That I abandoned my father?"

"Honey, you never abandoned your dad. You never had a chance. But what you can do, now that you understand more, is honor him the way that he honored you."

"How can I do that? He's dead. Gone."

"You'd be surprised at how much more in your life he could be, even now, Amanda. I'd say, if you have even one half the character of your father, which you do, then you'll find a way to keep him with you. Just because he's gone doesn't mean you can't have a relationship with him."

"Like he did with me? I was gone, really, but from what it looks like, he tried to keep the memories close."

"Something like that." Riley smiled tightly. She was straining under the pressure. She wasn't sure she could convince herself of the truth of her own words, much less carry the burden of helping Amanda to restore her relationship with her dead father. Riley knew that she needed to grieve but was sacrificing her own healing for Amanda's.

Just as she had promised.

CHAPTER 33
NORTHWEST FRONTIER PROVINCE, PAKISTAN

EARLY MONDAY MORNING

Mullah Rahman knew two things for certain.

The messengers had left Dubai a few days ago and should have returned by now. And the second layer of information contained on the flash drive, if true, was explosive. On it were the plans for a complete withdrawal of all of the border combat outposts that the Americans had built.

Operations Searing Gorge and Final Salute were the code names on the encrypted files. Rahman's information operations technician, Hasad Mohammed, had worked the flash drive and its contents for two days when he finally announced, "In Shallah."

As Hasad showed him the files, the more mundane sets of information included a variety of special operations policies and standard operating procedures that anyone could find on the Internet.

The gold mine had been hidden beneath a second encrypted layer of information, which at first blush appeared to be a special operations rifle range manual. However, Hasad had found maps and plans in Annex C of the Glossary.

Rahman asked himself two fundamental questions.

Are these plans accurate and why would a combatant be carrying them into battle?

He pieced together the information in the plan and matched it against the map hanging on his wall in a different home than where they had initially stopped. A few miles further east, they had moved at night and blended into an alternate command post.

The room in which Rahman stood was sparsely furnished with two chairs, a wooden table, a Dell laptop, a pewter water pitcher, and his sleeping roll on the floor next to his prayer mat. A generator hummed quietly outside, providing power to the weak lights and the computer. On the wall was a detailed map of the Northwest Frontier Province and Kunar and Nuristan Provinces of Afghanistan. His mission for the last two years had been to strike the Americans where he could, inflict maximum casualties as frequently as possible, and survive.

Now, with Habib's team already in the Naray area of Afghanistan digging for the Thorium, he apparently had captured an intelligence trove, because he saw phase one of the American operation was for two MH-47s to raid the mountain saddle which Rahman and his team had successfully defended. The plan called for an immediate follow on operation of the 101st Airborne to withdraw from the dozens of firebases up and down the border. This tracked closely with what the cowardly army colonel had mentioned after they beat him and with what the Americans had done previously in the Korengal Valley where Rahman's men had fought the Americans daily. After the Americans had suffered too many casualties, they had decided to abandon the post. It was that simple. So Rahman could see how his plan was working. Fight them hard. Cause casualties. Drive the wedge in the American public. And get them to leave

The documents contained detailed timelines beginning in the next 48 hours. All of this led Rahman to believe the information on the flash drive was authentic. The double encryption and the fact that the special operations soldiers were conducting a spoiling attack to allow for the withdrawal meant that they would have needed the sequential plan on hand, but secure, such as on a double encrypted flash drive.

So, Rahman looked at the computer, the flash drive still plugged into the USB port on the side, and scrolled through the images contained in a PowerPoint briefing. The first slide was phase zero, which included marshalling activities at Bagram Air Base north of Kabul. Rahman's sentries, which included two laundry workers on the base, confirmed that a large group of helicopters had been loaded the evening of the attack, taken off, and then returned to base sometime early that morning, after the fight at what the Americans appeared to be calling Objective 1422. The height of the mountain peak was 14,022 feet, and he assumed the Americans had shortened the number for convenience. This mountain also dominated the valley where the Thorium was located, so Rahman instantly understood the connection between the mineral locations and the invasion plan. If the Americans did not control the high ground in Pakistan, the Thorium mines would be vulnerable.

The second slide included the two-helicopter raid on Objective 1422, which was then going to serve as the pivot point for withdrawal operations up and down the valley to the east. The third slide showed significant helicopter movement of U.S. troops to Bagram. The fourth slide showed the Afghan National Army and Police moving into some of the abandoned bases.

Given the name of the operation, Rahman supposed that the Americans were going to retreat all of the way back to America.

Rahman's chest pumped up. He and his men had not only thwarted the raid and driven the Americans from the Korengal, but they also may have precipitated the full American withdrawal from Afghanistan. The new American president had agreed to a timeline and it appeared that even he was ahead of that timeline. For a long time Rahman's main fear had been whether the Americans would put fighters on the ground in Pakistan and attack them in their sanctuary. Indeed, he knew that his monthly stipends to the Pakistan Army officers in the region had secured his relative safety from the Pakistan military.

A plan came to mind. He could reinforce his efforts at capturing the Thorium mines and focus on attacking the Americans as they departed. He would push his chips all in.

Rahman's concentration was broken when he heard a knock on the door. "Come in," he said, activating his screen saver.

With Habib in Naray leading the miners, Aswan, a diminutive boyish Egyptian, poked his head around the door, and said, "Mullah Rahman, one of the messengers has returned."

"One?"

"I'm told we lost brother Kamil on the return trip."

Instantly suspicious, Rahman said, "Bring in Mansur."

Rahman retrieved his six-inch knife from his tactical vest that was hanging on a nail next to the map.

Aswan escorted Mansur into the dimly lit room and Rhaman's suspicions diminished, though they did not completely evaporate.

"What happened?" Rahman asked once Mansur stood upright. His face was bloodied, his hair matted with dried blood, and his arms raked with cuts, indicating defensive wounds. He was leaning on a tree branch, which he had fashioned as a crutch.

"Karachi. The truck driver took us to a warehouse where we were beaten. I escaped. Kamil was with me, but was shot."

"The money?" Rahman asked.

"As usual, we each carried half. Aswan has my $500,000."

"It should be a million," Rahman said, looking at Aswan, who extended the leather pouch full of money to his boss. Rahman snatched the purse and rifled through the stacks of bills.

"Dubai only gave us a million. They said the next million would be coming. They only had one million in cash on hand."

Rahman prided himself in controlling his emotions, but he was about to lose his temper. He turned and paced, then stopped, staring at the map. Five hundred thousand dollars would not pay for much of his retirement, especially after he paid sufficient bills to create the illusion that he was still in command. But with the new information on the flash drive, he could get the money he sought, if not from Dubai, then elsewhere, he was certain.

"Aswan, tell the guards to bring me Kamil's family."

Mansur immediately spoke, his words raspy with fear.

"Mullah Rahman I speak the truth. Please do not harm them."

"We have a deal. If the money or the messenger does not return, the family dies. It is well known. You both have been well compensated. So, your time for sacrifice has come."

"I beg you, please. We did our best."

Aswan disappeared and returned within minutes.

"The guards are bringing the family now."

Rahman turned toward Mansur and said, "Lock him up and kill the family."

"No!" Mansur screamed.

"Your family will be next if I hear another word from you, Mansur. I'm going to check out your story and then make my decision on your fate."

Rahman nodded at Aswan, who ushered Mansur from the house.

Rahman sat back at his computer, typed in the password to deactivate the screen saver, and then logged onto his satellite Internet service for the first time since they shot down the helicopters.

Which was when the flash drive finally began to do what it had been programmed for.

CHAPTER 34
BAGRAM AIR BASE, AFGHANISTAN

MONDAY

Matt Garrett sat in a metal chair inside Major General Jack Rampert's office at the south end of Bagram Airfield. Rampert had four maps on display, one on each wall. There was a world map behind his desk. To Matt's left was a map covering the Central Command area of operations from the Horn of Africa across the Arabian Peninsula to Pakistan. To Matt's right was a map of Afghanistan and Pakistan, and behind him was the big blow up of Afghanistan.

"We heard anything yet?" Matt asked.

Rampert shook his head, stood from his squeaky chair, and walked to the map on Matt's right, the Afghanistan-Pakistan relief.

"We raided right there," Rampert said, pointing at a dashed line on the map where the latest survey placed the actual border between the two countries, though on the ground it would be impossible to determine without a GPS. "And we're expecting something to pop up right there."

Matt stood and walked to the map and looked at Rampert's cracked, dry fingernail slightly to the right, or east, of the border and near a town called Chitral.

"Your guys approved this plan, Matt," Rampert said, warily.

"Don't get defensive, General. It doesn't suit you."

Standing next to Rampert, Matt was conflicted. Four years ago Rampert had pulled Zach off the battlefield in the Philippines and saved his life. Two years ago he had sent Zach into Canada on a suicide mission to kill or capture former Iraqi general Jacques Ballantine. Now, it appeared that Rampert had given Zach another high-risk mission, as if his brother was entirely expendable. But then again, weren't they all?

"Not defensive," Rampert said. "Just making sure you understand what's going on here."

"And what is going on?"

Rampert squared up to Matt. The two men were close in height, though Matt edged the general by an inch or two. The general's army combat uniform hung snugly on his fit frame. Matt looked powerful in his cargo pants and Under Armor shirt.

"We may never hear anything or the world could light up for us. You know the mission was a risk. We've got a bead, but our man's not communicating so far."

"I didn't know Zach was delivering the goods, General, so let's get off that point."

Matt worked his jaw a bit, clenching, unclenching, like he used to do as a college shortstop, watching the pitcher release the ball, expecting, hoping that the batter would drill a hard grounder to his side of the field.

The general's door opened and Van Dreeves stuck his head inside saying, "Sir, you gotta see this shit."

Matt looked at Van Dreeves' shaggy blonde head disappearing behind the door then back at Rampert.

"Let's hope the world is lighting up."

The two men moved quickly to Van Dreeves' technical center where he had two powerful computers and a server with a satellite shot to the National Security Agency's top secret Carnivore bird.

Matt stared over Van Dreeves' shoulder.

"It worked."

On the computer screen there was a flashing green light transposed on the map, which was displaying the Chitral and Northwest Frontier Province terrain of Pakistan.

"Son of a bitch," Rampert muttered.

"If Zach's alive, that's where he is," Matt said.

"If," Rampert reiterated.

Matt stared at Rampert, suppressing the comeback.

"Here's the deal," Van Dreeves said. "The flash drive put the Trojan onto the computer and it's been a few days now, so this is the first time this guy has gone onto the net. He's communicating with two people via a private message board that holds the message until the recipient has read it. Then it disappears."

"How can we see it?" Rampert asked.

"NSA built a screen shot program into the Trojan. Once a communication goes out, the software does a screen shot of the message whether it's a chat or an email or a webpage and stores it for us," Van Dreeves explained.

"So what's it saying?" Matt said.

"Mullah Rahman, our number three high value target for Al Qaeda is selling the plan for $5 million."

"Who's he talking to?"

"For the withdrawal plan, he's talking to someone in Dubai and someone in Yemen. For the Thorium, he's only communicating with Yemen. Tells me that Dubai is finance and Yemen is operations. We're working the back trails on those messages. These guys are pretty computer savvy, which is why I'm surprised Rahman put the flash drive in his computer. This is pretty basic."

"Maybe to someone like you, VD," Matt said. "But you find some intel on the battlefield like that, it's hard to resist."

"So what are we thinking?" Rampert asked, looking at Matt.

Matt considered the general for a moment and said, "You're not yourself, sir. Normally you'd just tell me what the hell we're doing."

Rampert smiled. "I'm seeing if you agree with me."

"We let Rahman work the computer. Make the two recipients. I agree with VD, one has to be a chief financier, the other a chief operative, if not *the* chief operative. Meanwhile, we go find Zach," Matt said.

"Great minds think alike. VD get a predator watching that area best you can. Let's see what we've got," Rampert ordered.

Matt nodded, walked out of the command center, and found his bunk. He laid his Sig Sauer on the bed, stripped it, cleaned and oiled it, and put it back together. Then he ran his knife against a whetstone a few times and speed loaded his magazines. Then he disassembled his pistol, cleaned it, oiled, and reassembled it.

All the while he was thinking Zach had to be alive. Everyone else doubted it, save Eversoll, but he knew it. He retrieved Zach's wallet with Amanda's photo and the Saint Michael medal. Turning it in his hands, he considered Zach's two great loves, his daughter and his mission. Maybe throw Riley Dwyer in there, too, he wasn't sure. His brother had risked his life and half of his team had been killed delivering the smallest payload ever to Al Qaeda, a two ounce thumb drive full of information. Those two ounces could ultimately do more damage than a 500-pound bomb. Way more damage.

Would it be worth the death of all the great men who were killed in the helicopter shoot down? That was a hard call to make. Matt knew that he would trade places with any of those men to have been on that sensitive and strategic mission. And he also knew that those men knew that any mission, especially this one, could result in their final trip home in a flag draped coffin.

Was it worth the death of his brother?

Matt decided that was a rhetorical question, because in his gut he knew Zach was not dead.

And he also knew that he had not told General Rampert the entire plan.

CHAPTER 35
SPARTANBURG, SOUTH CAROLINA

SUNDAY EVENING (EASTERN TIME ZONE)

Melanie Garrett nosed her Mercedes into the garage, stopping just in front of the riding lawn mower. Walking into the kitchen through the connecting door from the garage, she punched the dimly lit button to lower the garage door.

She hooked her car keys on a wooden plaque shaped like a lighthouse and dropped her purse on the barstool near the kitchen island. Retrieving her cell phone, she listened to the message again.

"Hey, Mom, it's me. Guess you figured out I was in North Carolina. Sorry about not telling you, but it's something I have to do to get the money, so I figured it was okay. Better to beg forgiveness, right? I'm doing it for us, though, so don't worry. I texted you all of this but just in case you are techno illiterate still, Bree picked me up from the airport and I've just needed some time to myself so have been hanging at her place this weekend. Love, Amanda."

Bree picked me up? What the hell was she thinking? And didn't Amanda sound a bit too *controlled?* Not her usual spontaneous self, that was for sure.

She walked absently into the family room, with its Hancock and Moore burgundy leather tufted sofa and matching love seat. She had opted for handmade furniture from North Carolina instead of something more exotic, say DeSede from Europe, but who was to say that she might not go more modern in the new house? But would that really fit, she wondered? A

Jeffersonian mansion with chic, hip furniture? She wrinkled her lips in disapproval, but did not totally dismiss the thought. There would be a need to have something unique, she considered, because everyone who lived up there had an angle, a distinction that set them apart.

Her mind wandered in the direction of her house-warming party at the mansion on Lake Keowee, visualizing who might attend and what they might expect to see. Bank of America's CEO walking through her house assessing her possessions, nodding in approval. Senior executives from Lowe's and Clemson standing in the backyard smoking cigars and drinking scotch, wondering if they might be able to clandestinely secure her affections. Perhaps, she didn't know. It depended on what they had to offer.

Maybe local television personalities would attend. People had always told her she should be on TV. For a moment Melanie actually saw one of the top news anchors running a gracious hand along the exposed wood of the hand-carved chair that sat across from the love seat. She could see her noticing the chunk of oddly shaped South Carolina granite fashioned as a coffee table in the center of the rectangular array of furniture.

"Beautiful," she would say.

"And let me tell you about it. . . ." Melanie actually did say.

She walked to the entertainment center, a handcrafted piece of rich cherry wood with shelves and sliding doors that retracted to allow full access to the plasma-screen television with built-in Internet, DVD, and stereo. She petted the piece as if she were caressing a loved pet.

She eventually wandered into the hallway and up the stairs that emptied onto the landing directly in front of Amanda's room. Without hesitation, as if pulled, her momentum carried her into her daughter's room. The sleigh bed to her right had been a stretch for a young girl, but it was so beautiful with its oak wood and hand carvings. The veneer of the room had all the trappings of a high school teenager getting ready to graduate. There were books scattered atop the oak desk with some loose papers next to the computer monitor. A few clothes were tossed clumsily atop the overstuffed mauve fabric chair. That had been a good find, she remembered. It was a $2,000 handcrafted chair that they purchased for $400.

Melanie smiled, as she always knew the asking price and the purchase price. That was the key, she had always said. The bigger the gap you could drive between the two prices, well, that was success.

Absently pulling open a drawer on the far side nightstand next to the bed, she looked down and saw a variety of knick-knacks. There were a few pens, some loose papers with random notes and doodles, as if Amanda would be scribbling while talking on the phone.

The edge of a picture frame at the bottom of the drawer caught her eye. She lifted it from beneath the pile of debris and gasped as she recognized the photo.

It was a picture of her and Zachary on their honeymoon. They had rented a beach house in Litchfield Beach, South Carolina for a week. Zach was wearing swim trunks and she had on a bikini. They were standing in the golden sand of the South Carolina Low Country with the deep blue aura of the Atlantic Ocean behind them.

She remembered the photo as if it had just been snapped by the tourist couple that had been passing them on a beach walk. She was hugging Zach around his waist, his muscles cut and chiseled even back then. His well-toned arm was pulling her into his side. They fit together nicely and no one would have ever predicted the sad course of their lives based upon the broad and loving smiles radiating from the photo.

Her hand came to her mouth quickly, as if to suppress something, as she sat on the edge of Amanda's bed. She remembered meeting Zachary at the beach of Lake Murray. He was there with some Army buddies and she was just out of University. He was headed to Fort Jackson for some military training and she was just chilling out with some girl friends. Their conversation had fallen into a natural rhythm quickly, reflecting their many commonalities.

She had been a cheerleader for the Gamecocks. He had been a star athlete and leader in scholastics. The surface connections were certainly there. Their courtship had been both quick and passionate, enduring a year of heart-wrenching breakups and equally emotional reunions. Zach's orders to be reassigned to Fort Lewis, Washington, had created an artificial catalyst of sorts, demanding that they determine what they were going to do with their relationship.

They'd decided on marriage and this honeymoon. Honestly, she told herself in this private moment, she had been happy and wishful. They were moving to Fort Lewis, Washington, and while living on the West Coast was part of the allure, she thought the distance might . . . help her. She remembered struggling to view Zach, though, through any prism but the one chiseled by her youth, where people in the military were those that could not find jobs elsewhere.

She had dated wealthy college students, for crying out loud, most of whom were lawyers and doctors. What was she doing with an Army guy? She was married to a second lieutenant making one-tenth the salary of . . . *any* doctor.

But there was that twinge in her heart as she looked at the picture. Maybe you only get one shot, she figured. Or maybe there's no shot to be had, as her mother had trained her. There is only what you can take in this world.

Their life, though, had been polarized until Amanda came along while they were stationed in Fort Lewis. She had been their unifying force until Zach's deployments increased, and his missions became more dangerous. And Nina's long reach began to exert that gravitational pull.

"Why should you stay out there if he's just going to leave you all by yourself? He can decide which deployment he goes on, and it seems to me he's deciding to go on all of them."

Ultimately, the stress and tension had become too much, and she began searching for the negatives. Instead of a unifying force now, Amanda had become the reason she needed to move back "home."

Turning the photo in her hands, she began to wonder why Amanda would keep this in her drawer and where she had found it. She carefully placed it beneath the papers, their disorganization assuredly masking the fact that it was not precisely returned.

Melanie looked up, her eyes searching the darkness beyond the bay window. In the nook, she noticed the oak trunk she had found at an antique store and loved because it matched the furniture in Amanda's room. She stood and walked to the antique, kneeling before it, and rubbing its rough-hewn finish with her hand.

She leaned over and hugged it, placing her head atop the lid that was ribbed with flat wrought-iron runners from front to back.

Lightly stroking the wood, she coddled the chest as if it were alive.

CHAPTER 36
CHARLOTTE, NORTH CAROLINA

SUNDAY EVENING

"I'm wiped out," Amanda said, sitting in a tiger-striped chaise lounge that was surrounded by spider and rubber plants along the back and sides. She swiveled her head, taking in the leafy environs, and settled her gaze on a small plant on the cherry Elizabethan coffee table with knobby feet.

Riley smiled, sitting across from her in a green leather chair with brass rivets. She had long ago given up on the idea of running. This was a major breakthrough if she could help sustain it, like pulling Amanda up over a ledge. Help her to higher ground where the view was better.

"Your dad gave that to me. It's called a ponytail bonsai tree."

"Cute."

They had moved from the bedroom into the living room after a brief stop in the kitchen for some water. Amanda had toyed with departing, but realized she didn't have a car. Miss Dwyer had promised her a ride if she would just talk for a short while, like two friends staying up late on a school night.

"All I'm asking is that we just talk, Amanda." Riley paused a moment and then said, "You're young. You probably know something about this." She shifted on the chair and used her hands to animate her speaking. "You know how when you delete something from your computer, you don't actually delete the file or the photo or the whatever?"

Amanda shrugged, "Sure. Everyone knows that. You're really just writing over the old file with the new one. The old one's still on the hard drive. Everything's still there, but there's only so much space."

Riley winked and pointed at her. "Think about that one. You've talked about these memories, and why some you can remember and others you can't."

Amanda, clearly uncomfortable with the topic, looked down at the tiger striping on the chaise. She ran her hand along the smooth fabric. "So, what's with the safari theme?"

"I change it about every two years. Your dad had been deployed to the Philippines, so I went native with him." Riley decided not to push the computer point. She thought it registered with Amanda and saw no purpose in pursuing it for now.

Amanda paused. "You really loved him, didn't you?"

"I really loved him."

A long moment of silence passed between them.

"Why?"

"There was a lot to love about him, Amanda." Riley looked into the distance, not so much within her physical space, but into a world which she had developed. It was that special province of someone who loved a soldier, a place where she could go with safely stored memories, just in case. Amanda nodded, ceding something to Riley; she wasn't sure what.

"The computer thing. Is that why I can't remember anything?"

"But you do remember. Sometimes."

"Sometimes, but then it goes away."

"Okay, then do this. Tell me about your mother."

Amanda paused and ran her hand through her hair, noticing it was becoming a bit greasy from all of the activity of the day. Did she really have the mental energy for all of this? Was it really worth it to go through all of these gyrations to get a half a million dollars? Did she really care about that anymore?

She figured that she could answer no to at least two of those questions, but pressed ahead anyway.

"My mother? What's she got to do with this?"

"I don't know, but you've got to have memories of her, right? Or is your entire mind, like, so totally blacked out, man, you know?" Riley waved her arms around as if she were a windmill.

"Don't go getting all goofy on me again, okay?"

"Okayyy, man," she said, getting goofy anyway. "Answer the question."

After a significant pause, Amanda sat up and said, "Okay. You just want me to free associate, right? Think out loud?"

"Oooh, free associate. I like it. But you know, dear, I'm a shrink . . . and nothing's free."

"Trust me, I know." Amanda raised her hands as if she were pushing away.

"So free associate away."

Amanda leaned forward, resting her elbows on her knees, then pushed back and laid her head against the arm of the chaise, the proverbial client to psychiatrist pose.

"My mom and grandmother raised me. They were always there. You name it, school, sports, cheerleading. Driving me to swim meets. Paying for absolutely everything. My dad just wasn't a factor."

"Let me interrupt you for just a sec, hon'. You're not giving me memories. You're giving me the party line, talking points. Give me a memory."

Amanda turned her head and looked at Riley. Then she turned away and looked up at the ceiling. She noticed the swirling patterns that the craftsman must have carved in the plaster using his trowel. She rested her mind and felt it swirling a bit, as if she might fall asleep. She was bone tired from the stress and the few hours of true sleep she had experienced since the day the Army officers had appeared on her doorstep. As she closed her eyes, she went to her own special place, a trapdoor in the back of her mind. Opening it slowly, she sensed something escaping; a butterfly taking flight from its cocoon. Then she started talking.

"We used to always go driving around Lake Keowee, looking at homes. Mama wanted to buy one of those big houses, you know? She always said, 'If your daddy would just pay child support, maybe we could be in one of these.' I remember one weekend when I was about nine or ten, my mother said he was supposed to be picking me up, but he never showed. So to make me feel better, we went out with some friends on Lake Keowee Jet Skiing, that kind of thing. There were lots of weekends like that. You know, when he wouldn't show up. I can remember when I was younger we'd play hide and seek sometimes when he was supposed to come over. He'd be knocking on the door and my mama or grandma, you know Nina, she would hold her finger up to her mouth for everyone to be quiet, and then we'd be real still. All the lights would be off in the house, and he would just be knocking away. It was the funniest thing. Then of course sometimes we would travel away when he was supposed to come over. I remember one time he drove over to Spartanburg, and we had gone to Myrtle Beach for the weekend. I got bit by a crab. Made me scared to go into the ocean anymore. Then there were all the times when Mama would say, 'If you don't do what I tell you, you're going to have to go live with your dad.' That scared the shit out of me. She might as well have been telling me I was going straight to hell, you know? And then there was that time when I was fourteen, and he was trying to make me come up to Fort Bragg for some stupid ceremony. My mom always made him come and pick me up. She wouldn't even let me fly alone, at least not to go see him. She'd tell him that I was too scared to fly. Of course, it was all bullshit, you know, but she was doing it to protect me. She's a really good person. Anyway, we couldn't escape this time, and he comes to get me at the house. So I'm like on my cell phone the entire way up to North Carolina, and he gets all mad at me, saying I should be talking to him, you know? So when we get to Fort Bragg I tell him I need to go into the ladies room at a gas station there. So I call my mama, but Nina picks up. I tell Nina what's going on, you know, and she tells me she's really worried about me, and so I should just call 911 as fast as I can. So I did. The cops came and it was only because he had some pull that he got out of it."

Riley had seen borderline personality disorder and even a few multiple personality disorders in her practice. However, she had never before witnessed a client go into such a trancelike stream of consciousness. Clearly Amanda did not intend to reveal these secrets so openly, but a combination of her depleted mental state, fatigue, and her most recent experience at her father's house perhaps had opened a seam in her psyche. Like water through a burst dam, the thoughts continued flowing.

"Anyway, I only lied about sexual abuse once or twice. I've got friends who have done that far more times than me. So that's not so bad, you know? But the times we got him best were when he was going overseas, you know, to fight, or something like that. I think it was two times he called to ask Mama if he could see me before he left. Initially she was, like, no way, but she never said that to him. Then, this was the first time, she and Nina had talked, and suddenly she was all bright and cheery with him on the phone, saying stuff like, 'Of course you can see her if you're going to be away for a while.' So, get this, she still makes him come all the way to the house and pick me up, but you know we live in a gated community, of course, and so she has a cop waiting for him at the front gate to serve him with a summons for an increase in child support. He doesn't have an attorney or any of that, so he has to spend all his time getting an attorney instead of being with me. Then, you know . . ." Amanda paused briefly, something catching in her voice.

"Go ahead, dear."

She spoke much slower now. "Then you know there was the second time when he got there late at night and Mama refused to let me go with him, but she said he could come in and read me a bedtime story. I was maybe ten. So he starts telling me one of his stories. I'm lying in bed, and he's sort of lying on the covers at the foot of the bed looking up at me. He told the best stories, you know. All of a sudden there's a cop in the house, and they pull him out of the bedroom. I go running out into the kitchen and see they've got him handcuffed and are taking him into the front yard. I remember . . ."

"You remember what, Amanda?"

"I remember seeing the front door had been damaged, like someone used a crowbar to open it. Then I heard Nina and Mama talking afterward, saying stuff like, "I can't believe he'd just break in like that.""

"But he didn't break in, right? You said that they had invited him in."

"That's what I thought, but obviously that's not what happened. He must've broken in, because the charges stuck."

"What do you mean, the charges stuck?"

"Well, he went to court and lost."

"Were you excited that he was coming to see you?"

"I don't know. I was confused back then. It's just like I can't explain it to you how I remember my mama letting him in the house, and how it was later explained to me that he had broken into the house."

"What did you see? Where were you?"

"I was in my room. It was springtime, I remember that. My window was open, and it looks onto the front yard. I saw his pickup truck out there, and I heard him ring the doorbell. I was pretty sure I heard Mama invite him in, but I guess I was wrong. I was only ten."

"What else did you hear? Think about the time your father was telling you the story."

Amanda sighed. "He was the best storyteller, so I guess I was just listening to him, you know? The story was all about how me and a bunch of my friends were saving some famous piece of artwork in a cave in New Mexico to help the Native Americans there."

"Pretty good memory of your dad there, sport."

Amanda ignored the comment and continued talking.

"So I don't remember much, though I think I heard a door slam out front. Maybe the front door or the car door. Or both."

Amanda seemed to pause, considering the possibilities.

"Is it possible that your dad was set up?"

"Anything's possible, but by who, and why?"

"I'm sure you can think that one through, Amanda. Tell me more about the story."

Amanda felt a smile come on, which she slightly repressed. "I don't know, I guess I've told you now like a hundred times that he told the best stories. He had so many. And I didn't know this until the other day, but he would go back and write them down after we fell asleep."

"Why do you think he did that?"

"Because that was his time? Because he loved me?"

Amanda felt tears begin to build in the back of her eyes. One escaped and carved a path along her left cheek.

"Because he loved me."

CHAPTER 37
NORTHWEST FRONTIER PROVINCE, PAKISTAN

MONDAY MORNING

Zachary barely slept, passing in and out of a light dream state, then woke, sitting upright. He had heard screaming most of the night from one room over. He hoped it was not an American prisoner of war, and had actually heard the name Mansur screamed a few times. Zach figured that perhaps an interpreter had been captured and was being held in the same prison as him.

He shifted himself back and forth until his back was up against the mud wall. His right arm was numb from sleeping on it. He tried rotating his shoulder, to little effect, and then opened and closed his hand, trying to get some feeling back.

As he moved his hand, something registered in his mind. It took him a second, but it seemed that the binding was less secure. He figured it was his imagination, so he tried it again. True enough, the base of his right hand slipped into the loop of the zip-tie handcuff. He could not dare to force it, not yet. His mind wanted to savor just the thought of the possibility of escape before having the notion crushed at his next movement. Assuredly it would confirm his fate, his doom, that this blossoming hope was merely a mirage, an illusion.

He gently slid his hand forward, away from the zip-tie loop, feeling the plastic ribbing rest on his wrist. Just a few days without proper nutrition and the body would begin to shrink, to deflate. His cheeks felt sunken, and his stomach was concave. Had his hand and wrist diminished enough to allow for his escape? Unlikely.

He looked for any sign of life, but there was none. His space was completely blacked out save a glimmer of dull light that provided no clue other than the location of the door.

Back to his hands, he thought to himself. The moment was an enjoyable one, the idea of escaping, of loosened binds. Let's end the party and go about thinking how to really get out of this predicament.

He took the thumb on his right hand and pushed it toward his small finger, forming a cup of sorts, trying to minimize the breadth of his hand. Slowly, he pulled his hand toward the zip-tie loop. He could feel the plastic scraping along the top of his wrist. Eventually he felt the binding begin to graze the outer portions of his right hand. He nearly gasped when he met no firm resistance until he reached the knuckles. How could this be?

Hope gathered momentum now. Slowly, he pulled and felt the plastic begin to squeeze against the skin on either side of his hand near the knuckles, knowing that if he could just get past that point, he would be out of the binding. The sharp-edged plastic was digging into his skin now. The inside portion of the loop was hung up on the knuckle of his index finger. He tried moving the finger toward the inside, again trying to decrease the width of his hand. It helped fractionally, primarily by decreasing the pain, removing the knife edge out of his knuckle.

He was bleeding now. He could feel the stiff plastic that remained between him and his freedom—at least the freedom of his hands—slipping on the blood.

A noise came from outside the door. Footfalls, followed by a voice, echoed ever so slightly in the structure. One voice, then another. Two people. Deep voices.

Now or never, was the thought that ricocheted through his mind. *Now or never!* He pulled down with his left hand and up with his right hand, feeling skin tearing off his knuckles for sure.

He held his hands up in front of his face in disbelief. Black hands against the blackness. He touched his face, felt his cold, sunken cheeks and rough, unshaven jaw. They were there. His hands were free. He had done it. He felt the warm blood seeping down his wrist. His own plasma had provided the lubricant.

This was step one. Now to deal with the voices, which were growing louder. More distinct. They were speaking Pashtu. During his time in Afghanistan he had come to learn the difference between the two major languages, Pashtu and Dari. Dari was a derivative of Farsi, spoken primarily in Iran. These men were definitely speaking Pashtu, which meant two things to him.

They were locals of some sort—either Pakistani or Afghan—which meant that he had a window of opportunity. It was small, almost negligible, but it was there. Al Qaeda were ruthless and very careful. Local tribesmen, even the hostile ones, however, were often careless. If his captors had left him in the temporary watch of two local Pashtuns, then perhaps he had a chance.

He fumbled with the zip-tie handcuff, removing it from his left hand as well by turning the jagged edges sideways and pushing them through the opening, like a trash bag tie. He swiftly lay back down, his hands behind his back, as he heard the men approaching the door.

"Garrett," the voice called. It sounded more like "Garreeett." "Garreeett," again came the voice. He heard the door opening, feet falling toward him. He saw two men, the lead man carrying a candle in one hand, and amazingly, protecting it against the wind with the other. He had no weapon. Before he could get too excited, though, he noticed the man's partner was carrying an AK-47 at the ready. Both men wore the traditional headdresses common to any number of indigenous tribes. They moved like silent ghosts in their flowing robes.

He lay still until the man with the candle knelt down next to him, the flame licking at the dark night, burning up the oxygen in his small room. The man's face was half lit, half dark, like a theater mask. He saw his beard flowing a few inches from his chin and dark eyes that looked as friendly as burning coals.

"What now?" Zach asked, sounding sleepy and groaning just a bit. "Let me sleep."

"Time to die."

He wasn't sure what he was expecting, but certainly he was not excited to hear this man utter those words in almost perfect English.

He surprised himself, though, with the quickness with which he moved. He accelerated off the floor, drove the candle up, ramming it into the hot coal that was the man's left eye. Pushing him upward and toward the man's backup, Zach used him as a shield, feeling him both scream at the burning candle in his eye and at the AK-47 rounds now punching into his back.

He released candle man, who was now simply dead weight, and lunged over his body to slip the zip-tie cuffs around the neck of the rifle-bearing man. Pulling back on the wrist holes, he surged and crisscrossed his arms, feeling the man's neck snap.

He picked up the AK-47, checking the magazine. He felt around each man for more ammunition, finding none, but securing a six-inch knife.

He moved through the door into another dark room and slid silently toward the corner. He waited a few seconds. When he heard nothing, he moved toward the outside door. Opening it, he looked through a small crack, enough to tell him morning was no more than an hour away. To the East, the slightest hint of light was beginning to crest the massive mountain peaks, leaving in its wake a cloak of darkness, for the time being, to the West.

He had to risk it. He had to move now. It was his only option.

He went back into the room in which he had been held and removed the robe from the man whose neck he'd snapped. He took the turban as well.

Dressed the part, he moved back into the front room. Minutes had passed. Gunfire would have been heard from miles away along the narrow valleys of . . . wherever the hell he was. The thought stopped him momentarily. Which way should he flee? Regardless, he needed to move.

He stepped from the mud hut, looked to his right, and saw nothing but mountains climbing into the black sky. To his left he saw a stream about one hundred meters away, knifing its way through a valley that was more akin to a fjord. Jagged spires of rock shot upward, denying any movement anywhere but along the valley floor.

To his rear he heard voices. Excited voices. Speaking Arabic.

He fled west, toward the decreasing light. Walking at first, he picked up the pace as he moved toward a small footbridge that spanned a creek about forty yards wide. Clear water spilled and tumbled across the rocky bottom, rushing toward his left. If he was in Pakistan, he would be moving toward Afghanistan. If he was in Afghanistan, he would be moving toward some coalition military base eventually.

Crossing the bridge, he could sense others watching. Nothing happened in these remote tribal villages without someone, if not everyone, noticing. Not unlike Small Town America, there was little chance of Zachary escaping his predicament without interruption.

The footbridge swayed and the water rushed beneath him. Taller than most of the local inhabitants, he was sure he would not go unnoticed. Bounding onto the rocky far bank of the creek, he spied a trail that led toward the westward peak. The trail followed a gorge with water sliding down the middle of the crevice, melting snow from the top of the mountain that fed into the rushing creek.

Zachary grabbed at a large boulder, pulling himself up onto the trail. His robe and headdress all might have bought him a minute or two, but the sandals he took from the rifleman, while uncomfortable, were helping him scale the slippery incline.

Just get moving on the trail, he kept reminding himself.

He was about one hundred yards into the steep draw, the village opening to his back, the trail narrowing to his front. Away from the sounds of the rushing water, he could again hear the pitch of voices, more excited. Then one voice above all others seemed to focus the group.

Zachary had not looked back. Never look back, the famous motto. Now was a time to live by that credo. Focused, he pulled again at rocks and scraggly trees sticking out from the massif. The only thing that gave him mild comfort was the AK-47 strapped across his back beneath his flowing robe.

The focused voice began screaming. Shots rang out, but not near him. Darkness began to encompass him.

He was two hundred yards up the valley now and moving more quickly. Three hundred yards up, the climbing got tougher. Hand over hand in some areas.

A quarter mile, he guessed. Still the gunfire, but nothing close. Were they executing the other tribal members responsible for watching him? His breathing was labored, but only because he lacked food, energy. His adrenaline kicked in, though, and supplied the glycogen to his muscles to keep him moving.

An hour later he was cresting the ridge of the mountain. He had to be ten thousand feet high, he figured. He paused, resting, breathing hard, and looked back at the trail he had just climbed.

Unbelievable. From his vantage, it appeared that he had scaled a cliff. Perhaps he had.

Looking west, with the sun now creeping over the mountains, he could see for miles. What he saw was jagged mountain ridgelines, capped with white snow, lined up as far as he could see, like a set of waves coming in off the north shore of Hawaii, massive, white tipped, forbidding.

He pulled the robe around him, glad that he had it for the extra bit of warmth it would provide tonight. He watched his breath crystallize in a fine mist. For the first time he allowed his mind to unlock from the task at hand.

Amanda. His men. His family. Riley. What else in life was there? For a few minutes he savored his relationships with his warriors. The bond they had formed over so many years, so many missions. Living a life in pursuit of nobility, the cause, the righteousness of what they did for a living. It was a good way to live . . . and to die. Hell, it was the only way he could live. His life had to have meaning beyond the paycheck. He had to feel like he was saving the world. That's how he'd operated ever since coming back into the service.

Then there was Amanda. His heart ached for her, not because of his loss, but because of hers. He had tucked away the injustice of it all so many years ago. The burden was too difficult to carry exposed, too heavy. Watching his relationship with Amanda morph from doting father and daughter to manipulative and destructive player and pawn caught him so off guard that for a couple of years he couldn't fathom it.

But now, his heart reached out to Amanda, as it always had. It opened full blossom. He would make a stand, again. And in the interim, he knew in his heart that Matt and Riley would do all they could.

Zachary scanned the incredibly beautiful mountains that surrounded him. He closed his eyes, clasped his hands together.

Lord, thank you for this opportunity. Thank you for everything that you have given me. Please watch over my men, wherever they may be, and please, please, watch over Amanda for me until I can return to her.

Right now, right here, he decided, again, he would reclaim his child, and his life.

When he looked over his shoulder, he noticed the flashlights moving up the trail.

CHAPTER 38
CHARLOTTE, NORTH CAROLINA

SUNDAY EVENING (EASTERN TIME)

Jake Devereaux had made the return trip from Sanford to Spartanburg after the brush up with the NC Bureau of Investigation. For a full day he dawdled around his house thinking about all that had transpired.

He was reluctant to call or text Amanda, fearing what her mother and grandmother might do or allege, not to mention that he felt someone had been keeping tabs on him since he left North Carolina. Neither did he want to discuss the situation with his father, an attorney, or his mother, who would worry.

It was Sunday evening and normally he would be taking Amanda to a movie or hanging with some of the other football players. He sat in his room wondering what he should do next and whom he might be able to talk to about *everything*.

His Droid phone suddenly moaned that he had a message. He had seen two others from Amanda telling him she was going to Dwyer's house. The sending phone was listed as private. His instructions were:

Pick me up at Dwyers house. 112 Tryon St. Luv u.

He figured Amanda's battery must have gone dead and she had texted him from Miss Dwyer's phone. This would be a decent opportunity to talk to Amanda away from her mother and grandmother, but with a neutral third party present.

He bounced down the steps of his house, fired up his truck, and sped away. He followed his GPS, turned off I-77 and missed Tryon on the first pass, as it was on a cul-de-sac off the main road. Doubling back, he found the home, a nice two-story narrow brick house. It looked like a row home, only it wasn't attached to another structure. It was free standing.

He parked in front of the house. Traffic whipped by on the main street just fifty yards behind him. There were ten homes he could see elegantly crammed into the semicircle. He didn't know much about real estate, but he did figure that these homes, as small as they seemed, probably sold for close to a half million dollars. She must be doing okay, he thought.

The house seemed quiet. A dim light shone through the window that appeared to come from well into the back of the home. He walked along the sidewalk, which was lit by a single wrought-iron gas lamp.

Approaching the door, Jake sensed that the house was empty. There were no indications of movement that typically provided clues that the occupants were indeed present. No television flickering, no radio, no computer monitor.

He rang the doorbell, which sounded characteristically suburban, a double chime in reverse octaves. After a few moments, he pressed the dimly lit button again with his thumb. Lastly, he knocked on the heavy oak door, which surprisingly gave way and drifted open.

Jake looked down at the floor and then up as the door continued to open as if welcoming him on its own. A leafy plant was just inside the foyer to his right as he stepped through the threshold and into the wide foyer.

"Miss Dwyer? Anybody home?"

His voice sounded alien to him inside someone else's home.

Jake looked at his watch. The time was just past 10 p.m. He had received the text message no more than forty-five minutes ago. Amanda should still be here.

"Amanda?" He spoke louder this time. "Amanda!"

The quiet house was eerie. The narrow rooms that funneled toward the rear were all dark and foreboding. He dared not venture any farther.

Turning, he placed his hand on the doorknob and immediately recoiled, as if bitten by a snake. The brass handle was slick with a dark substance that looked like paint, maybe.

Stepping back onto the porch, he pulled the door shut, trying to avoid the grease or paint he had touched. He realized that if Miss Dwyer had gone out jogging or something, he might have just locked her out. He nearly tripped over the gas lamp as he sniffed his hand.

He opened his truck door, turning on the dome light, and in the weak glow he saw red smeared across his palm and fingers. A sickening thought occurred to him as he was reaching into the glove box for the Purell hand sanitizer that Amanda always kept in there. That was when he saw the flashing lights behind his truck.

CHAPTER 39
SPARTANBURG, SOUTH CAROLINA

SUNDAY EVENING

Amanda slowly pulled into her mother's driveway. It was nearly midnight on a Sunday. She had ignored what seemed like a thousand calls from her mother and grandmother over the weekend, staving them off with a text and a voicemail to the home phone. Now she worried about the wrath she might incur for having hidden out at Brianna's for the weekend.

She saw her mom's twin Mercedes in the driveway as she shut the lights and quietly slipped from the car.

Spending the night with Brianna had been weird. Her best friend had seemed distant, but they were all getting ready to graduate, so she chalked the oddness up to nervousness about the upcoming life change.

Amanda slipped quietly into the house, snuck up the steps, entered her room and locked the door. She leaned back against the door and shut her eyes, sighing heavily.

Shower. She needed a good, hot shower. She stripped off her clothes and turned on the shower, letting the steam build up. As the forceful flow beat against her skin, she replayed the sessions with Riley Dwyer in her mind over and over again, confused about what she was thinking. More troubling, though, was what she was feeling. Her emotions had ranged widely since receiving notification of her father's death. Initially she was as emotionally responsive as a flatlined heart monitor on a victim of cardiac arrest.

As she was exposed to the terrain and physical surroundings where positive actions had actually occurred with her father, memories came rushing back to her. The recurrences were like a silent train emerging from a dark tunnel at breakneck speed. The tracks followed the wild zenith and nadir of an unpredictable sinusoidal wave. Amanda's emotions chattered along as if on a roller coaster, at first plunging toward the depths of her anger and hatred for a man she was convinced was a deadbeat, only to be rocketed upward toward the peaks of what could only be described as complete and unmitigated love for a father she adored.

The memories only came to her, though, when prompted, as a stopped heart may only begin beating again when the electric paddles are applied. She still did not know what to make of Riley Dwyer. It was unsettling to follow her through the labyrinth of her father's life. Yet, the memories of her father were but snapshots in time. The movie of her life, it seemed, was here in Spartanburg, devoid of her father and any connections to him. She had always believed that was intentional on his part.

She brushed her hair a hundred times, or close to it anyway, before dimming the light and sliding into bed. She pulled the Hammacher down comforter up to her chin as she nestled into her one-thousand-count Egyptian cotton sheets. She was worn by the swinging emotions and the back and forth travel. This was what happened, she thought to herself. The travel, the emotions, it was all too much. It was a rare moment of insight, perhaps ignited by a receding consciousness and prevailing set of facts.

HER MIND SWIRLED as if a small twister were forming on the Kansas plains. Suddenly she *was* in Kansas, but without Toto. Instead, she had a Beagle named Floppy for the hue of his nearly bare belly as a young pup out of his mother's womb. She had been four or five, she remembered, and there were three baby Beagles lying in straw at the bottom of a box. "That one, the floppy one," she had said, pointing. So Floppy was jumping at the door in this vision, and Captain Zach Garrett was standing up from the breakfast table.

Amanda was playing with her spoon, dipping it into and out of her Fruit Loops and milk with a devilish grin on her face.

"What?" her father asked, smiling.

Her big green eyes batted at him. "Nuffin', Daddy."

Floppy was jumping at the door, which meant one thing. Zach's car pool ride was in the driveway.

"Gotta head on out of here, baby girl. Kite flying at 3 p.m.? Can you work me into your schedule?"

Amanda giggled. "I've got a 'pointment at free p.m."

"Yeah, what's that?" Zach was standing now, smiling.

"Kite flying with Daddy, silly."

He bent down to give her a kiss

She took his face in her hands. "Later, alligator." Then she kissed him on the cheek. "Love you, Daddy."

"Love you, too, BG."

Suddenly she was walking through the forest following the giant paw prints of an unknown animal.

"That way," she said, pointing and looking at her father. She was maybe ten years old now. It was a cool day in the Blue Ridge Mountains of Virginia, and Amanda was dressed accordingly in her blue Gore-Tex Northface jacket and faded light blue dungarees. Supple brown hiking boots left cloverleaf imprints as she walked through the sandy soil along the creek bed.

Zachary was following behind, letting her lead. He was close though, as the paw print might *really* be a bear or a mountain lion. He was quite certain it was the large Saint Bernard that the Shiffletts owned.

"Okay, let's go that way, then," her father whispered, as if the hunters might at any second become the hunted if they gave away their position. Amanda held a stern look on her face, using her hands to brush away the low-hanging branches of pine saplings.

"This trail is what the wild animals use to come to the stream to drink water. Animals are just like humans in that they need to drink a lot of water. And if big animals are here, what else is probably here?"

Amanda looked at him intently. This was no game in her book. They might as well have been on an African safari stalking a lion's den. Her mind raced, searching for the right answer. She so wanted to please him by knowing. She wanted to show how smart she could be. Big, he had emphasized the word "big." He was talking about how animals needed water. What else would they need? Food? She had it.

"Smaller animals? For food?"

Her father smiled, and she knew she had it right. Pride surged through her, and she tried to hold back a smile, but couldn't resist. He was smiling, too.

"That's right, baby girl. This is the chow hall."

She could hear the South River churning to the east. Mist escaped her mouth as she breathed. She could sense her father right there behind her. His presence was comforting and reassuring . . . and necessary.

Her father saw it first, which is why he placed his hand on her shoulder and deftly stepped in front of her.

"Don't move," he whispered. He moved a step to her front and a bit to the right, it seemed, so that she could see. Drinking from the stream was what looked like a big tabby house cat. She had owned several that had either run away or died in some accident or another. She always had pets and remembered a tan Manx cat she had when she was much younger.

"Mountain lion," he mouthed as he looked at her while placing his index finger over his lips, indicating for her to be quiet. She stared at the animal, its back to them, oblivious to their presence. A combination of a north wind and the rushing water most likely masked their approach to the typically alert feline. Then she looked at her father's face, strong and rugged, without a trace of fear. He looked confident and assured.

She lowered to one knee, edging a shade closer to her father, resting a hand on his shoulder. They waited and watched this cat drink water, occasionally look to its left and right, and then go back to lapping at the stream.

For fifteen minutes they became lost in a trance, connecting with nature. The sun broke through for a moment and a sliver of yellow light spotlighted the animal's silken gold coat. Then, as if the sunbeam was its cue, the mountain lion lifted itself off its rear haunches and loped harmlessly along the river bank to the east.

Now she was on the tennis court in maybe one-hundred-degree heat on a searing North Carolina July afternoon. The coach had just made the tennis camp team run four laps around the entire complex. Unsure if she could continue, she noticed someone move to her periphery and whisper in the coach's ear.

Wiping away the sweat that was stinging her eyes, she raised herself up from resting her hands on her knees and looked toward the coach, who was nodding at her father. She saw her dad dressed in his army uniform. She wasn't sure what all of the symbols and decorations meant, but she did know that it was her father and that he would make it all okay.

He walked away into the officers' club which was adjacent to the tennis courts. The coach blew the whistle with a loud, ear-piercing blare and screamed, "Okay everybody, bring it in."

Twenty girls and boys came limping over to the coach, all drenched with sweat, some seemingly on the verge of dehydration, as indicated by their vacant stares. Amanda tried to see beyond the throng now gathering, looking for her dad.

"Good job, everybody. I want you to take the rest of the day off." A chorus of cheers erupted. "Okay, okay. Hit the locker room."

As the tennis camp crowd entered the clubhouse and its inviting cold air, she looked up in amazement. Her father was standing in the middle of the pro shop wearing a T-shirt that said "Lifeguard" and a geeky pair of swim trunks with a mixture of red, white, and blue colors fashioned in a swirling pattern. On his feet were flip-flops, and in his hand was a sheet of paper.

"Gather around, team," he called out, waving his arms toward the aspiring racquet masters. With some energy, they began to huddle around. Amanda was up front. This was her daddy. She stared up at him with adoring eyes. "Here's what we're going to do. There's coolers of Gatorade in your locker rooms. You are all going to go drink an entire bottle and then put on your bathing suits and meet me at the swimming pool."

A collective scream sounded from the small crowd. Amanda hugged her dad's leg, looking up at him through her salty face, and then turned to her friends.

"That's *my* daddy," she proclaimed just like a parent might proudly say, "That's my girl," when she rips a line drive in a Little League game.

She was sitting now in a library in Spartanburg with her father across the table. Construction paper and photos were scattered like a magazine editor's workplace.

"The name of this place is Wanda?" Amanda asked, eyes innocent and wide.

"That's close, baby girl, but it's Ra-wanda. Just try saying Rah, like you're doing a cheer, followed by Wanda."

"Rah-Wanda."

"Very good."

"It seems so sad," she commented, looking at the pictures of young children with distended stomachs, well over one hundred of them, standing naked, staring at the camera, eyes wide with fear. She could make out flies crawling across the children's eyes as if their eyelids could not function. Their stares were catatonic, envisioning some distant land or faint hope that they would die a quick death. They were all standing in a muddy opening, and there wasn't an adult in sight. "Did you go there to fight them?"

"No, honey, we went there to help them. To protect them. Always remember that wherever I go, my purpose is to help the good guys."

"I know that, because you're one of the good guys."

"And sometimes good guys need help."

"Am I helping by doing this school project? By letting other people know about it?"

"Exactly. Even little things can make a big difference."

"Maybe one day, you know, I can make a difference like you do."

"That's all I ever want for you, baby girl."

Bright images raced through her mind like butterflies escaping from captivity as she recognized now the rock face she was climbing.

They were scaling a steep bluff along Lake Hartwell just south of

Clemson, South Carolina. The engineers had created a series of canals and dams on the Savannah River a hundred and fifty years ago to provide power for textile mills and other manufacturing.

"Be careful, honey. It gets slippery." Her father was directly behind her, as he always seemed to be.

"I know, Daddy. I'm being careful." Amanda rolled her eyes just a bit, smiling, as she was approaching that age where young girls began to develop emotionally and physically.

The rock face was about a forty-five-degree angle, so if she kept all four points of contact, both feet and both hands, on the rock face most of the time, she would be okay. There was a steeper part, but a two-foot-wide ledge that angled upward allowed them to handrail along the lip and then climb up when they reached the summit.

They were breathing hard when they sat down, their feet dangling over the ledge. It was a sublime autumn Saturday afternoon. While most people in this region were watching the USC Gamecocks play the Clemson Tigers in football, Amanda and her father were doing their thing, being together.

"Beautiful day," he said.

"I guess."

He blinked in the sun, and looked down at his little girl. "What's up?"

"Nothin'."

"Nothin' nothin'? or nothin' somethin'?"

She fidgeted, absently splitting a blade of grass. "I'm scared, Daddy."

"What are you scared of, baby girl?"

"Of it not always being this way."

CHAPTER 40
SPARTANBURG, SOUTH CAROLINA

MONDAY MORNING

Amanda bolted awake and grimaced as the sun shot through the mini-blinds in knifelike shards. Sitting up, she ran her hands through her hair. Her face was slick with a film of sweat.

"That was so real." She sat motionless for a long minute, her hands pressed firmly into the sheets. Some dreams she could remember, most she forgot, but these were vivid, as if she were watching a DVD. The words, the movements, the actions were all lifelike and logical. These dreams made sense. Why? Why did they seem to flow logically?

She remained motionless in her bed, staring blankly at the screensaver scrolling across her computer screen. "No Dad. No Dad. No Dad. No Dad." Her mother had helped her with the poem and had suggested she make the screensaver the title to give her inspiration.

She had settled nicely into her comfortable life with her Mercedes, the beautiful home, and the affections of her mother and grandmother. Now this foundation, it seemed, had been shaken to the core. Everything she had come to accept and believe—that her father was a no-good deadbeat and that her mother and grandmother were her saviors—was now being challenged.

Slowly she regained her composure by doing the only thing she knew to do. She looked at her right hand and said, "Okay, my dad leaves me five hundred thousand dollars."

She stuck one finger out, as if keeping score.

"I've got at least four, no, make that five good memories of him."

Two fingers out now.

"The house has all of those things he wanted me to see. Riley Dwyer's photo albums. They all tell me that he loved me." Then she placed her hand to her heart. "And I can feel it."

Four fingers were out.

She was crying now. For another five minutes she cried and wiped the tears away, then cried again until finally she ran out of tears. She felt an image fluttering in the back of her mind. It was the substance of memory. Inexplicably, she stepped into her walk-in closet. In the closet was a small half door that led to an unfinished part of the home. It was essentially a storage area. Loose sheets of plywood were arranged atop the two-by-eight beams so that someone could walk across gaps that were filled with pink insulation. A few boxes were scattered on the plywood.

She tugged on a single chain that lit a naked bulb. She opened one box that had mostly old clothes in it. She saw a set of pajamas with Barney the purple dinosaur on them, and a few stuffed animals. These were all that remained in her possession from her time with her father. Haphazardly stuffed into these boxes, the items were molding and needed to be discarded, really.

Opening the next box, she saw a few photo albums and books. One of the books was *Charlotte's Web*. She now remembered reading that with her father when she was little. She knelt onto the hard plywood and lifted the book, thumbing through its yellowed pages. She set it atop one of the boxes she had not yet opened. She pulled two more books out, thumbed through them, and placed them atop *Charlotte's Web*.

She found herself staring at a blue album that looked like any other photo book. On the front she could see where she had written in her best second-grade handwriting:

The Invisible Children of Africa by Amanda Garrett.

With two hands she carefully lifted the album from the box, brushing a dead silverfish from its top. She blew some dust away as if she was excavating a ruins site. Carefully, she opened the book. If nothing else, the images she saw confirmed to her that while she was sleeping, those were memories that had come rushing from the wellspring of her mind, not dreams. She saw the picture that she now clearly remembered. The eyes of the children were staring up at the camera, which her father had told her he had held. There were no adults in any of the photos. As she flipped through the pages of their project, she placed her hand over her mouth as she got to the last page. There was a photo of her father surrounded by scores of naked children as he passed out food. She could see his face so clearly.

She lightly pawed the photo, as if to touch her father. She flipped the last page and saw her handwriting again: *It is my goal to one day help the invisible children of Africa. They are invisible because they have no parents . . . and nobody cares, except me and my daddy. Amanda Garrett.*

She closed the book and placed it back in the box, aware of what might occur if her mother caught her with it. Perhaps to distract herself, she picked up her cell phone to check it for messages. To her dismay, the battery was dead, and she had forgotten to plug in the charger. She leaned over and connected the black cable to her Razr.

Amanda walked to the bathroom in her pink flannel pajamas. She stared at herself in the mirror, rubbing her reddened eyes and wiping away the stains of her tears. She ran a stream of toothpaste onto her toothbrush and started brushing her teeth as she walked back into the bedroom. Absently, she picked up the phone with her free hand. She had no messages, which she thought was odd. For two days now she hadn't heard from Jake, but the North Carolina cops had put the fear of God in both of them, so she cut him some slack.

Now it was Monday morning and with the full realization that Jake might still be in North Carolina, she freaked.

She realized that she had stopped brushing her teeth, the toothbrush dripping saliva and paste onto the carpet. She stared straight ahead at the window that opened onto her front yard.

She tried Jake's cell, which went straight to voicemail. Dialing his home number Jake's father answered.

"Amanda, we're going to have to ask you not to contact Jake anymore," he said.

"Huh?" she said, dumbfounded. "I don't understand. What's happened? Where's Jake?"

"Jake's in jail and is charged with burning down your father's house and the attempted murder of Ms. Riley Dwyer, your psychiatrist."

"Burning down my father's house?" Amanda said. "It's not burned! He did none of those things."

"This is a legal matter now and we can't have you discussing any of this with Jake. Thank you for your cooperation, Amanda."

Jake's father, the lawyer, hung up the phone. She stared at her cell phone blankly for several moments as the gravity of his words settled over her.

She could feel the vivid memories in her mind beginning to recede as if someone had picked up the remote of her life and punched reverse. It was as if she was the patrol leader, and her team behind her was being picked off one by one.

Then, in a moment of pure realization, when she realized what she had done, she screamed.

CHAPTER 41
BAGRAM AIR BASE, AFGHANISTAN

MONDAY EVENING

Mary Ann Singlaub sat at her computer terminal in the small cubbyhole of the public affairs office known as the RLB, or re-locatable building. Amongst the twenty some journalists that had to elbow through it's narrow spaces each day, it was, more affectionately known as "Really Lousy Bull-shit."

It was a basic four-walled structure with plywood shelves tacked into the walls at waist level, like chair molding, and held up by two-by-fours hammered at an angle from the outer edge of the plywood to the wall. About thirty computers were perched precariously along this makeshift workspace. An Internet drop was the only perk, and once a Web site loaded, a task that sometimes afforded one the time to retrieve coffee, use the latrine, and take a smoke break, it would work reasonably well. She typed in her password and pulled up the Google Web site. Typing in "Colonel Zachary Garrett," she hit Return and watched 72,116 hits appear.

"Wow," she said to herself, and hit the News tab, which narrowed the search considerably to 127 articles.

She blew a small tuft of hair away from her forehead as if it were a fly bothering her, swatting at it as well. She scrolled through the articles, most having been posted within a few days, naming him as the senior U.S. officer killed in the War on Terror. Scrolling and scanning, Mary Ann zeroed in on an article that mentioned the colonel was survived by a daughter in

Spartanburg, South Carolina. Bingo. Another potential source.

She quickly Googled "Amanda Garrett" both in a Web search and a news search, which turned up a trove of swimming meet times. Deep into the search of the 237,124 hits on Amanda Garrett, Mary Ann found two court documents. She printed those out and continued to scan until she found her address and home phone number. She then went back to Zachary Garrett in the news.

She froze on an article released only hours ago on the Associated Press wire and published in the *Charlotte Observer* by a freelance journalist named Del Dangurs. While it was possible that he was new, she found it curious that she had never heard of him, especially since he was reporting within a military domain, her area of expertise.

Her curiosity at who the reporter might be was replaced by shock at the content of the article.

Colonel With Spartanburg Ties Dies In Afghanistan
Leaves Behind Questionable Legacy
By Del Dangurs

Colonel Zachary Garrett was killed in a helicopter crash last week in Afghanistan in the U.S. military's continued failed attempts to find any of the leaders of the 9-11 attacks on America. A review of the officer's life raises important questions about his death and the suitability of the senior officers we have fighting the War on Terror today.

Court records show that Colonel Garrett was divorced, estranged from his daughter, and had twice been summoned to defend himself against breaking-and-entering and child-abuse charges.

But today's revelation that Colonel Garrett allegedly provided Al Qaeda reams of top secret documents detailing the U.S. military intentions to withdraw from

Afghanistan on a more rapid timetable have shattered the revered commander's reputation and perhaps set back the war on terror by years. He is also implicated in the massive leak of classified operational documents to the Wiki-Leaks website. This is a developing story and the *Charlotte Observer* has exclusive inside sources providing up to date information.

With a senior leader such as Colonel Garrett living a life of familial abuse and abandonment, and potentially even guilty of treason, is it any wonder we are not further along in the so-called Global War on Terror?

It is true that Garrett played some nominal role in defeating the Ballantine attacks last year. Yet conspiracy theorists make much of the fact that he actually captured Ballantine in the first Gulf War, arguing that their relationship might have actually strengthened over the years and led to a role in the attacks for Colonel Garrett. After all, they ask, how did he mysteriously wind up in Lake Moncrief, the terrorists' den? The explosive treason charges against Colonel Garrett seem to strengthen the critics that argue Garrett was in collusion with Ballantine.

According to a Defense Department official, selection of military commanders is conducted by a group of officers, picked at random every year. . . .

"No way." Mary Ann went back and read the first part of the article again, her jaw agape.

She knew all of the sayings about what goes on behind closed doors, but also had spent a considerable amount of time at Fort Bragg, in Iraq, and in Afghanistan. Few officers were accorded the respect that Colonel Garrett received from the Special Operations community. There were none that she knew of that maintained the respect of everyone at Fort Bragg the way Colonel Garrett did.

So, either the good colonel lived a double life or someone was doing a hatchet job on him. Having never heard of the reporter, she had her guesses.

As she was printing the article, she heard a commotion near the front door. There was some jostling, and someone shouted, "Hey, where are you going?"

As Mary Ann Singlaub stood and turned, she found Sergeant Lance Eversoll staring her in the face.

"This your idea of a human interest story, bitch?"

Stunned, she looked at the piece of paper in his hand. The story was being broadcast all over the Web to millions of people. MSNBC, CNN, FoxNews, and all the dot coms were publishing the story.

"I had nothing to do with that story, Sergeant, and if you call me bitch again I will throw this coffee in your face and kick you in the nuts. Do we understand each other?"

She had been raised in the South, too.

They squared off, the public affairs office a tense set of bystanders in Dodge City, Kansas, waiting to see who would draw first.

"I'm pissed off, too. I've never heard of this reporter. Even if it were true, which I don't believe it is, it would be wrong to publish this bullshit. Now is there somewhere we can talk?"

She followed him out of the newsroom, leaving behind a whirling vortex in their wake.

MATT GARRETT PACED the floor of the Special Operations joint operations center, or JOC. He would stand at the large plasma-screen television that was displaying the Predator satellite feed and then break away, walk across the room, and stare at a map that included Afghanistan and Pakistan.

"You see that bullshit article on Zach?" Matt fumed.

"That's the point. It's bullshit. Settle down," Rampert said.

"Easy for you to say, General. Not your brother."

"Not your solider. So, it affects both of us. I'm going to have some pasty white inspector general over here seizing all of our computers and investigating us probably by sundown."

Matt stared at Rampert and nodded, ceding the point.

"We think Rahman leaked it, but we can't be sure. I mean, why the *Charlotte Observer?*"

"North Carolina maybe? Make it seem more homespun kind of thing. It's already gone viral," Matt said.

"Or you've got a mole in the CIA that knows about Searing Gorge."

"Always a possibility," Matt said. "Also you may have a mole here. No matter how much it pisses me off, though, the story helps in a way, you know? I'm sure some of this is already leaking out from AQ central"

Van Dreeves interrupted, pulling them to the map.

"Matt, we've got about twenty AQ with flashlights moving up this ridge here." Van Dreeves was talking to him at the map, pointing with a stick at the exact location. To Matt, on the map it looked less than a few inches. So close, yet so far. "It's about five miles into Pakistan from the border of Kunar Province. We're violating all kinds of shit by looking over there."

"Who gives a rat's ass?" Matt paced back to the Predator feed.

"Sir, see that right there, that's enemy looking for something," Hobart said, pointing at the screen.

"Maybe they're just infiltrating, you know, coming this way," Matt countered, not wanting any hope to blossom too soon.

"Too far away," Van Dreeves chimed in. "Bastards usually take an SUV up to the border area, some small village, get their weapons, and cross into the country in tough terrain."

"Okay, so what are we going to do?"

Rampert turned away from studying the map and walked over to the group. "Let's see if we can get closer with that Predator."

"No way, sir. Paks will shoot it down. I'm flying over the Afghan border and angling in." Matt knew that the Predator operator was actually at an air force base in the United States. Van Dreeves was on the phone telling the guy what to do. The wonders of technology.

"Can we look ahead of the group to see if they really are chasing someone?"

"We can try. I've already done one scan, but it's hard to find just one.

I'm not sure we would have found the twenty if they didn't have flashlights."

The group listened to Van Dreeves give a "Move to the left, okay, that's it, now up some" to the operator over the secure phone. They watched the camera slide to the left of the screen and then toward the top where it was obvious, even in the darkness, that a trail led up the mountain.

The camera rotated back and forth between hot white and hot black, showing anything that had a heat signature—an animal, a warm vehicle engine, or even a rock retaining the sun's heat—as white or black respectively. Switching between the two helped the observers determine living from inanimate objects.

"What's that?" Hobart was pointing at the mountain ridge. The anonymous operator at the unknown air force base in the United States had selected hot white as his heat signature of preference.

All eyes focused on a white spot. Really, that was all Matt could make out. It was moving slowly, carefully along the spine of the mountain ridge.

"Could be a sheep, camel, anything," Rampert said.

Matt was holding his thoughts closely. He wanted to be circumspect here amongst these warriors with whom he had so far shared two battlefields. Having personally saved Rampert, Hobart, and Van Dreeves during the Ballantine action in Canada, his stock was as high as it could possibly be within this clandestine community. He did not want to abuse what really amounted to authority. Though these men did not work for him or even in the same organization as he did, he knew that if he gave the order, as he had done last time, "Let's go," they would grab their weapons and say, "Where to?"

They continued to watch the white figure slide across the screen, moving now perpendicular to the axis of advance of the flashlights. They could clearly see about fifteen to twenty white spots moving up the trail. The lone white figure was moving toward the bottom of the screen, toward the Predator flying over the Afghan border.

"The one by itself looks similar to the ones moving up the mountain. I think it's him." Matt's words hung in the air, reverberating like a gunshot echo. He had pointed out the most obvious thing of all. If they believed the twenty figures moving up the valley were people, then the one moving by itself along the ridge must be a person also.

"Good point," Rampert noted. He ran a leathery paw across his gray crew cut and turned to Hobart. "What's the grid?"

There was a tone of resignation in his voice. He did not relish doing two unauthorized missions across the border into Pakistan in less than a week, but he would. He had a soldier on the ground, and it was his responsibility to bring him home alive.

"Grid's actually about eight kilometers east of the border, right here." Hobart handed a map to Rampert while Matt looked over his shoulder. Matt could see that the white heat signatures were on a ridge, about two kilometers away from where they had done their previous raid.

"We know the flight route most of the way. We can use the same crew. We're going to need Van Dreeves to stay here and talk us through the Predator feed." Matt's words came out rapid-fire, machinelike.

"Roger. We'll take Eversoll in Van Dreeves's place," Rampert added. "VD, why don't you go find Eversoll? Tell him to be ready in fifteen. Hobart, give the pilots a call, let them know we need blades turning in ten."

"That's fine. I'm broke dick anyway," Van Dreeves responded. "As much as I hate to miss the action."

"Are you monitoring Rahman and our two friends in Yeman and Dubai?" Rampert asked.

"Roger that, sir. Rahman's not come up on the computer. I'm guessing he's involved in this hunt, at least from a command and control perspective."

"Let me know if something breaks there," Rampert directed.

"We're pissing away time, General, let's go," Matt barked. "Once VD gets a bead on Yemen and Dubai then we'll focus on that, but until then my brother is the priority."

The team began moving quickly around the joint operations center. Matt stood motionless, watching them. He looked over his shoulder as Eversoll came in, slinging his packed gear over his back. Matt nodded, thinking that it didn't take Van Dreeves too long to find Eversoll, who he surmised was most likely waiting directly outside the JOC in anticipation of this exact mission.

"We ready, sir?" Eversoll's voice was firm.

"Think so. Think we've got him pegged."

"Count me in."

"Wouldn't have it any other way."

Soon Van Dreeves and Hobart reappeared. Rampert walked in the door with his M4 in his hand. Matt looked over at his weapon and rucksack.

"Let's go get my brother."

CHAPTER 42
SPARTANBURG, SOUTH CAROLINA

MONDAY MORNING (EASTERN TIME)

Melanie Garrett put down the phone and sat at the kitchen table nibbling at breakfast. Amanda would be down soon and off to school, but this was an interesting conversation, she thought to herself. She began to thoughtlessly twirl a Hermes silk scarf through her hand. Memorial Day was approaching, so she decided she'd go with a flashy pattern of red, white, and blue for her matching linen jumpsuit.

She pulled the material through one hand and then retraced the route through the other while staring absently through the sliding glass door and across the recently stained deck. A steaming cup of coffee sat next to her elbow. She was looking at nothing in particular, just lost in thought.

"Who was that on the phone?" Nina asked.

"Principal Rugsdale. He just got back from some Southeast principals' convention in Raleigh. He was extending his condolences about Zach. Why are you here so early on a Monday morning?"

Nina stared at her a moment. "Needed an update. Lot's going on. Dan Rugsdale? What's he care?"

"Not sure he does. Maybe he was just being nice."

"Is that all?"

"What else could there be?" Melanie's eyes remained fixed on the horizon.

"Sounded like you were on longer with him, that's all."

"You worry too much."

Changing the topic, Nina said, "I checked out last night when you said Amanda probably wasn't going to come by. No point in paying for an extra day."

"Bree picked her up."

"Bree? That slut?"

"Don't ask. She got in last night after spending the night with her Saturday. She's acting strange."

Nina considered the comment and asked, "How much time do we have left?" She was leaning against the center island of the kitchen holding a dish towel in her hand.

"You know as well as I do when Amanda's birthday is, Mama. We've got less than a week."

"That's not going be a problem, is it?"

"Depends on how everything plays out."

Nina sat next to her daughter in an adjacent chair, resting her wrinkled arm on the reflective sheen of the recently polished kitchen table. She was wearing a sleeveless chartreuse top with bone-white Capri pants and matching straw sandals. She stared at her arm, then covered it quickly with her hand. If only there was plastic surgery for arms.

"Well, this is what it's all about. You know what they say. 'When the going gets tough, the tough get going.' The question is, are you tough enough? Can you look her in the eyes and do what you need to do?"

"I haven't had any problems so far, Mama."

"That was child's play, literally. You remember what they said to Herschel Walker when he finally joined a real football team? 'Welcome to the NFL.' You've got a half a million dollars from that worthless son of a bitch sitting out there. He made it hard on you in life, and now he's making it hard on you when he's dead."

"Amanda has gone to this shrink. Then she went up to the house. She was required to do those things, and she's done them. I'll talk to her before she goes to school this morning, and we'll get the Army guys back over here to sign all the paperwork."

"Before her birthday?"

"Before her birthday."

Nina leaned back into her chair and nodded in approval. Over the years she had nudged and cajoled when necessary. Other times she had intervened and been more direct, more forthright, like she did at Riley Dwyer's office. She was raised in the same swamps in which Francis Marion had earned his "Swamp Fox" moniker during a time when blacks weren't slaves, but they might as well have been. Real men beat their wives, screwed the "help," and sometimes slept with their daughters. The tough girls escaped, some with the scars, some without.

Nina Hastings could be someone's best friend and an instant later be working a serrated edge into their back. A vacuous narcissism dominated her psyche, and some of her theatrics were Oscar-worthy. Over time she had developed the street fighter's knack of recognizing a threat and either establishing an alliance or swiftly cutting its throat. Some of her instinct was primal, as if she'd been raised in a jungle of beasts that wanted to take what she had gathered. All that mattered to Nina Hastings was that she got hers, and she kept it.

Agile enough to socialize and win key acquaintances to her fold, her veneer would shed as quickly as snakeskin when a threat presented itself. Moreover, she could seize an opportunity better than any battlefield general, exploiting her daughter and granddaughter like infantrymen sent as fodder to enemy trenches, to achieve her victory.

"Hey, Mom," Amanda said, sitting down to the table with her book bag over her shoulder. Her hair was still wet from the shower.

This was Nina's cue to melt away. Never be near the conflict, if it was to develop. Amanda glanced at her grandmother's visage disappearing into the dining room. Amanda grabbed two pieces of toast from a plate on the table and took ample bites.

"Good morning, Amanda." Her mother hesitated. "Are we going to talk about this weekend?"

She swallowed hard and said with a partially full mouth, "Well, Jake's in jail, and I'm kinda freaked out right now."

"Jail? Why would Jake be in jail?"

"Something happened to Miss Dwyer and to Dad's house—"

"Who's house?"

"My dad's house, Mom. You know, your ex-husband?"

Amanda had rarely used the term "Dad" in the presence of her mother or grandmother because of the reaction the utterance would create. *He may be your biological father, but he's no Dad.*

"Don't talk to me that way, Amanda. We've got something more important to talk about right now."

"Wait a second." Amanda held her hands up as if warding off an attacker. "My boyfriend's in jail and my father's house burned down, maybe, and there's something more important?"

"What can you do about the house, if indeed it burned?"

"I can find out what happened, first of all. There was a lot of important . . ."

"What? There was a lot of important what? What was in that bastard's house that you want?"

"What is up with you? The man's dead and you don't have the decency to talk about him with any respect whatsoever?"

"Where is this coming from? What about the poem you wrote? What about all the crap for the past ten years?"

"You wrote that poem, Mom. I submitted it."

"That's not true."

Mother and daughter squared off across the kitchen table. Nina's presence permeated the house. This was the classic showdown. The moment of truth had come. Whose side was Amanda on? Was she in the fold or straying from the flock? This may not have been the sordid backfield of a Moncks Corner farm, where nefarious deeds occurred out of sight and out of memory, but it was the same essence—primary greed being advanced at all costs.

Amanda slumped in her chair. "Okay, whatever. Can you just help me with Jake?"

"You need to get to school. Your little excursion last week isn't helping matters, but we'll talk about that later."

"What matters?"

"Principal Rugsdale called me this morning. He's wondering what's up with you."

"I'm cool with him, Mom."

Melanie paused a moment, considering the comment. She decided to leave it alone. "I'll call Jake's mother and see what's going on."

"Thank you."

"That's more like it. Now we need to get those papers signed that the Army men brought by."

"What's the rush?" Amanda asked, shifting from one line of thought suddenly to another. A distant alarm rang in her mind, perhaps indicating the acorn indeed does not drop too far from the tree.

"They just want it signed. You've done everything you need to do. You've met the requirements."

"I'm supposed to see Miss Dwyer a couple more times."

"You are trying my patience, Amanda. You've gone to her three times, and you've been to your father's house. Now, when you get back from school today, I'm going to have the Army people here, and you will sign those papers."

Amanda opened her mouth to speak, but stopped herself. She processed a myriad of thoughts faster than any computer chip might and decided to bite her tongue.

"I'll see you after school then," she said, breaking into a slight smile.

"That's more like it."

Amanda stood, twirled on her feet, and walked into the foyer.

"Amanda?"

"Yes, Mother?" She looked over her shoulder, noticing Nina's shadow reaching from the dining room into the kitchen, cast by the rising sun blaring through the eight-foot east-facing glass in the bay window.

"Are you going to be okay?" The question was totally devoid of emotion, concern. It was more the stuff of a back alley pimp wearing a purple velvet fedora making nice with one of his girls.

Amanda cocked her head, pursed her lips and said, "Yeah, Mom. I'm good to go."

CHAPTER 43
SPARTANBURG, SOUTH CAROLINA

The morning sun glared through his window as he swirled his coffee cup. He leaned back in the faux leather chair of his makeshift home office and thought about the nom de plume, Del Dangurs. What did it mean to him? Who was he in relation to this name? Why was he at odds with himself over it? Was he his own Javert to the Valjean that resided within? So many questions wrestled in the mind of a writer, he mused.

He scrolled through the article destroying Colonel Zach Garrett's reputation. He had to admit it was brilliant, if he did say so himself. If they wanted to seal the public image of this man in a nefarious light, he had to agree that the mission was accomplished.

How far should he take this, he wondered? To what end? And what would be the next move? That was his primary question.

As he thought about next moves, Amanda Garrett came to his mind. An image of her hovered in his daydream, looking just how he had last seen her.

Pitching forward, he suddenly stood, then abruptly sat down again. He was anxious, and he knew why. He ran his slender fingers along the worn seam of the chair's armrest.

"I've tried so hard to resist," he whispered. He traced the outline of his face with his hand, feeling its smooth contours. Was he becoming obsessed with Amanda? It seemed as though she was being offered to him.

The paranoia reminded him of the electric charge he had felt when he'd been caught with Emily Wilkinson in college. He had been careful since then and had narrowly escaped being registered.

The case had been handled discreetly. Given his age at the time and the fact that Emily's parents had wished to hide the event as much as he wanted to get beyond it, the mediator was able to reach an out-of-court settlement.

She *had* been drinking, after all, and she *had* willingly returned to his dorm room, the argument went. There were multiple eyewitnesses that could place her as the aggressor at the party. While the college had forced the issue to court, her parents chose to settle and keep the record sealed. Ultimately, there had been no charges brought against him for having sex with the under-aged girl.

He clicked his mouse and pulled up the Photoshop program. Two more clicks, and he found her face staring at him. He had conducted a Google search on her and then found her page on Classmembers.com. Though considerably older now, she was his first. And this was how he liked to remember her. Her blonde hair was parted down the middle, and her head was tilted to the side just a bit in typical yearbook fashion.

"So beautiful," he whispered. "And so young."

He smiled as he recalled Matthew McConaughey's character's line from the movie *Dazed and Confused*. "I love high school girls. I keep getting older, and they keep staying the same age."

He had been careful to avoid obvious targets. With the broad reach of the Internet, his hunt had not been deterred. There were legions of young girls looking for adventure, especially from experienced men. For every twenty he "worked" through e-mails and chats, he might choose one.

Paranoia had to reign supreme. He knew about the stings the television programs were doing and how active undercover agents were patrolling the Net.

No, he was like a stockbroker who, if a stock doesn't feel right to him immediately, he unloads it. And so it was with the girls. There were plenty that really did want to be with older men, especially one who would be famous one day.

His passion, aside from young girls, was his short stories. He fancied himself to be something of a modern-day Edgar Allen Poe, though he couldn't portray that persona in public. This double life was fitting for a Gemini, born in June, he thought to himself.

Instantly his mood darkened as his eyes caught the cork bulletin boards he had posted around the spare bedroom. He had converted it into his author's den. Viking, Random House, Pocket, Doubleday—all had rejected him, many times.

"Thank you for your submission, but we only take solicited manuscripts. . . ."

"While your writing is interesting, it's not right for us at this moment. . . ."

Others were less kind, containing only the submitted manuscript and a form letter, usually unsigned.

Lately his short stories had taken on a more macabre tone, his real essence, with titles such as "The Knife." It was about a married couple who learns each of them is cheating on the other. They scream at one another across the kitchen island, which has a solitary butcher's knife poised in the middle.

Then there was "Seductive Fire" about a woman who bedded as many men as possible and burned them in their sleep.

"Nectar of Darkness" was perhaps his most disturbing, and most Poe-like, he believed. He had submitted it to an agent and was only waiting for the word that it had been sold. This was the one.

As he usually did, though, he was toying with the ending again. The narrator was contemplating whether to kill himself after falling in love with a young girl, or whether he should kill her because the laws prevented her from being his. Naturally he could not let anyone else have her.

Yes, "Nectar of Darkness" would be the one. If not, he didn't know what he might do. But in part, his addiction to teenage girls was like a research project for his writing. He rationalized that if tapping into that prohibited wellspring of inspiration was required to catalyze his genius, then it was worth the risk. Society would thank him.

He thought that with some effort, he might be able to have it all at once—the writing, the girl, the reputation. It was all possible. He had desperately tried so many times to abstain from his weakness, but he could not. And he kept crossing the line. Like the marijuana user migrates to crack cocaine, it was to be expected, he told himself. He had considered waiting until she was eighteen, but that would be . . . not improper. And therefore less exciting.

And so, Amanda Garrett would be his . . . soon.

His computer beeped as an e-mail hit his inbox. He recognized the name and decided that it was time for more inspiration.

He read the e-mail and grabbed his car keys. Del Dangurs would have to wait, he decided. Though he was close, he knew, there would be no more research or writing today.

In fact, he would make a brief appearance and then pursue his new conquest.

CHAPTER 44
SPARTANBURG, SOUTH CAROLINA

"Why'd you leave yesterday? Thought you were hanging with me?" Brianna Simpson asked Amanda as they waited for Mister Dagus to appear for their fourth-period journalism class.

"Long story," Amanda sighed as she slumped in her desk seat.

"Lenard is late. Talk to me, bitch."

Amanda grimaced, not able to control the fury that raged in her mind like a wind-whipped ocean. She extracted her cell phone from her purse and checked it. No messages.

"Jake's in jail," she whispered.

"*No way!*" Brianna's voice was not so much loud as it was emphatic. Sitting at the back of the classroom, each was convinced their conversation could not be overheard.

"I just found out. And I'm going nuts here thinking about it. Mom made me come to school. You know the deal, missing two days of school before graduation can get you pulled from the ceremony." Amanda fidgeted for a second with her pencil, a mechanical number two from Jamaica advertising "Fun In The Sun!" along its beveled edges. "Not that I care about a graduation ceremony."

"What happened? Why's he in jail?" Brianna managed to hide her enthusiasm with a fair degree of furrow-browed concern—a kind of "I'm so sorry, but can you get on with the good stuff" approach. Inherent in a seventeen-year-old girl's psychological repertoire was exactly this kind of duality. One hand was reaching out with consolation while the other was placed firmly around the throat, pumping for more information.

Amanda slumped even farther in her chair. "I don't know. I haven't seen him all weekend and I haven't been able to talk to him."

"You told me you two had a fight?"

"I didn't tell you the truth. Friday. We went up to North Carolina. To my dad's place."

"You did *what?*" Brianna had been with Amanda during the peak of her hatefulness toward her father. What little Brianna "knew" about Amanda's father was from the last four years. Now it seemed that there might be a difference between what she had been led to believe and what might actually be true—not an easy distinction for a seventeen-year-old young lady.

"It's part of the insurance thing. I had to go," Amanda said, rolling her eyes out of habit. It sufficiently offset Brianna's shock, making perfect sense to her shallow friend, she was certain.

"Still, you guys risked a lot by going up there, graduation being so close and all."

The class had been gurgling with the loud murmur of several similar conversations, yet Amanda was certain that none of them centered on a half a million dollars, a burned-down house, a possibly murdered woman, and a jailed boyfriend. Though knowing some of her classmates, she couldn't be sure.

Abruptly, as if intercepting her thoughts, the entire class stopped talking and turned their heads toward Amanda and Brianna.

Someone knew.

Somehow, someone had become privy to the information, and now the tidbit was like the faint red tip of a cigarette tossed into a windswept Montana forest. Its fire and ravenous energy was spreading quickly across the student population, consuming Amanda's life. The captain of the girls' swim team and the captain of the football team were soon to be locked in scandal.

"Is it true that Jake was boffing some old bitch and then killed her?" The voice was from a student whom she barely knew. She was a heavyset girl with oily brown hair and pimples across the bridge of her nose.

Amanda grabbed her book bag and purse and ran from the classroom. As she was approaching the door, she plowed squarely into Mister Dagus, who reacted by hugging her, wrapping his arm around her. She could feel her breasts pressing into his firm chest, her face against the bare skin exposed by the open collar.

He pushed her out to arm's length, holding her by the shoulders.

"Whoah, Nellie. Amanda, are you okay?"

"I—I'm fine, Mister Dagus." She looked away from him, embarrassed. She was drawn to something, though she couldn't identify it. All she knew was that she needed to leave, and now. She felt herself starting to crack. She couldn't take any more.

"I was just coming in to release the class. Some other things have come up for me today," Dagus said.

Amanda ran. As her mind tried to catch up with her instinct to run, like Lassie chasing Timmy, turning and barking as if he had missed something important, she felt a gnawing at the back of her mind. She *had* missed something important. Amidst the chatter of laughter emitting from the open door at her back, she fought the urge to stop and think.

It would soon come to her, but now she needed to run. Graduation be damned.

CHAPTER 45
PAKISTAN

TUESDAY MORNING (HOURS OF DARKNESS)

Zachary Garrett tumbled hard down the steep incline. Scraping his knees and arms, he spun into some gravel, then stood, resting momentarily. He could hear them in the background. They were coming for him. He had traveled two, maybe three miles since his escape. The black night provided no sense of relief. He knew that his captors could travel the trails of the Hindu Kush blindfolded if necessary.

He could hear the faint gurgle of a river or creek to his west. West would take him toward Afghanistan if his guess was right that he was in Pakistan. He cut through a deep ravine, sheer rock walls reaching upward like spires on either side. He was limping now, the fall having taken a toll. He touched his face, and felt blood. Water would be good. He needed to drink. He was becoming dehydrated again.

The moon sneered at him as he slid on his hindquarters down an embankment that stopped on a dirt road paralleling the water. The gurgle he had heard, however, was now a bold roar. Zach's assessment was that the water was about a hundred yards wide and moving fiercely. He didn't think it was fordable at this location, but with a road nearby, maybe there was a chance.

He chose to move south, to his left, anticipating that perhaps the river widened and lowered to the point where he might find a ford site.

He could hear more voices now, coming down the same way he had. The road was even and littered with potholes, standard for this part of the world, yet sufficient for moving wagonloads of poppy resin to the market.

Breathing heavily, working against his injuries, lack of sleep, and lack of water and food, Zachary needed to get across this river and buy himself some time. He could see in the distance, about a hundred meters away, where the road dipped to the right, toward the water. Could it be a crossing?

Shots now. Zipping over his head like angry hornets, these were AK-47 rounds. Maybe they were warnings. Maybe the shooters simply had bad aim. Either way, he needed to get on the other side of this river. If this was the Kunar, it would mean he had made it all the way back into Afghanistan. Instinctively he didn't believe it was. However, the thought gave him a glimmer of hope, enough to get his adrenaline going.

He found the spot where the road turned into the river. It didn't seem like much, but it was all he had. He waded into the tumbling water and immediately sank to his waist. Farther out, he pushed against the raging current. Now he was up to his chest and slipping deeper. He thought he could sense the *puck-puck* of bullets smacking the water near him. He was sure of it.

Suddenly something slapped him in the back, and he was down, rolling, gulping in water, and speeding with the current, the water whipping him around and banging him into jagged rocks that defined the path of the river.

Zachary Garrett retreated into himself, bundled up not unlike a paratrooper going through the door. *One-thousand, two-thousand, three-thousand, four-thousand . . . waiting for the opening shock.*

He was no longer in control, if he ever had been, and determined to let go of everything. His mind quit assessing the tactical situation, quit running through the different permutations of what might play out. Tumbling through the savage current of this Pakistani tributary, Zachary Garrett focused on his daughter Amanda.

Her beautiful face hovered in his mind like that of an angel's.

Her sweet voiced asking, "Daddy, are we good to go?"

"We're good to go, baby girl."

CHAPTER 46
SPARTANBURG, SOUTH CAROLINA

MONDAY AFTERNOON (EASTERN TIME)

Amanda stopped by the principal's office on the way out. Dan Rugsdale looked up from his desk as she lightly rapped on his open door.

"Do you have a second, sir?"

He put down his pencil and flipped over the typewritten pages on which he had been working. "Sure, Amanda, how can I help you? You're lucky you caught me. I'm only in the office a few minutes today."

"I'm just stressing about my father's death and really need a couple of days."

"You can take some time, Amanda. I understand," Principal Rugsdale said to her. She sagged visibly. "I knew you'd understand."

"Do you know when the funeral is?"

"No, they haven't said anything about a funeral yet. He was Special Forces, you know. But I will let you know, if you're interested."

Rugsdale stood and walked toward her. He was a big man, more broad than tall. He put a large hand on her shoulder and looked in her eyes.

"I'm here if you need to talk to someone. I know this is a tough time for you."

Amanda looked at his hand on her shoulder and then back at Rugsdale's eyes. She saw a dark cloud pass across them like the anvil head of a summer thunderstorm.

"Thank you, sir." She stepped away, feeling his hand refusing to give initially. Finally, she was free and moving out of the door.

Dan Rugsdale watched her leave and then turned toward his window. He pulled up the blind and he observed her walk quickly to her car.

Again, the touch. Like the high five last week, he sensed danger.

AMANDA ARRIVED AT the police station and parked diagonally in an Authorized Vehicles Only spot, cutting across the line. The cops would have to walk off some of that donut fat, she thought to herself. She stormed through the glass-and-chrome door that led to the desk sergeant.

"May I help you, ma'am?"

"I'm here to see Jake Devereaux. He's in here somewhere. Now tell me where he is," she demanded.

"Listen, little lady, you come in here like that we might just lock you up with him, you hear me?" The police officer had a crew cut, his hair appearing like the stiff bristles of a gray brush. His uniform was impeccable and creased vertically along each breast. He had half-lidded eyes that indicated he was mostly a man of composure, a gatherer.

"I'm sorry, officer. I'm just sort of freaked out, you know? My dad died and my boyfriend was arrested—"

"He's not here."

"—and I know he didn't do anything and I haven't—Did you say he's not here?"

"I did. He made bail today. Surprised the hell out of all of us to see him in here in the first place."

"How long ago?" Amanda chewed on a fingernail. "Who got him out?" She became hopeful that her mother or grandmother had paid the bail, which would help her figure out some other things as well.

The officer wrinkled his forehead and said, "Oh, I'd say about an hour ago, maybe less. His daddy came down madder than hell. Nothing like a damn big-shot attorney having to bail out his own son."

Amanda felt a stab of pain in her heart. He hadn't called her. That would have been her first call had their roles been reversed.

"Was he charged with anything?"

"Damn straight. Breaking and entering, assault and battery, attempted homicide, and North Carolina's got him on arson charges. Apparently he burned some house up there clear to the ground. Nothing but ashes left."

Another slice of pain carved through her. Gone, everything she was supposed to remember was gone. All the evidence her father had gathered had gone up in smoke, embers floating meaninglessly through time, evaporating into the ether.

Without proof, there was no hope. Without hope, there was no reason to fight. Without a fight, there was no reason to try.

That had been her mantra. She realized it just now, standing in the foyer of the Dilworth Police Department. She had one foot tapping the floor, one fingernail chewed to the quick. No hope, no fight, no purpose.

Then it struck her. The officer had said assault and battery not murder. We all find our own silver linings, she figured. This was one.

"Where is the victim, Miss Riley Dwyer?"

"They've still got her over at Carolinas Medical Center, where I think she'll be for a while. Your beau there did a real number on her."

AMANDA WAS IN her car, actions outpacing her thoughts, as if she was carrying something so fragile and time sensitive that if she did not receive some reassurance she would lose this opportunity. She was not quite certain what opportunity she was considering, but she could sense that a door had opened for her. "Life is about chances and choices," her father had once said to her.

Chances and choices.

Presently she was taking a chance, a risk perhaps, to find Riley Dwyer. Maybe she could tell her something that would make sense. She maintained an image in her mind of a trail of gunpowder being poured out behind her, the beginning having already been lit. Could she move more quickly than the cordite would burn? Or would it capture her, resulting in combustion of some sort?

Skidding into the parking lot at Carolinas Medical Center, she raced to the information booth. Having learned her lesson at the police station, she composed herself, wiping her wet palms on her blue jeans.

"Ma'am, will you please tell me the room number of Miss Riley Dwyer?"

Works every time, she considered as she jogged to the elevators, punched in the number four and impatiently waited for the door to open.

Once out of the elevator she followed the provided directions to room 412. The door was closed. She looked over both shoulders to determine if anyone was going to stop her, then she turned the door handle and let herself in without knocking.

The room was large, with a runner along the ceiling where a curtain could divide the space into two patient areas. There was no one in the first bed.

She cautiously stepped around the curtain and froze as she saw the battered visage of Riley Dwyer, tubes sticking into her face and chest. Her eyes were closed, and she did not appear to be breathing.

She looked dead. No machines were beeping. No lights flashing. There were none of the indicators of life that would normally accompany a recovering patient. The television was not on, there were no visitors, and there was no respirator forcing air into her lungs.

Then she looked at the steady green line tracing across the black background of the heart monitor. . . .

She ran so fast down the hallway of the hospital that she never heard the nurse screaming at her to stop.

THE SURREAL IMAGES of the past few days were racing through Amanda's mind like Formula One cars all speeding in different directions unbound by a track or railings. The thought of speeding made her glance at her speedometer, where she noticed the red needle twitching past the one hundred mph mark.

"Get a hold of yourself, girl."

Where was she? She had blacked out. It would not be the first time. Her memory lapses relative to her relationship with her father were minor when compared to some of the bouts of amnesia with which she had struggled. One moment she would be in class, the next she would be in her car in the student parking lot staring through the windshield, an hour having elapsed.

For some unexplained reason she began thinking about the day Jake and she had visited her father's home.

As the NCBI agents began to depart for the second time, she had excused herself for one last restroom break before going to the airport. In the home alone, she walked directly to the downstairs half lavatory situated beneath the stairs, as if pulled by a magnet.

You know what you need to do, Amanda. *The voice in her head was not hers, but she owned it now, she knew that much. Do it quickly, so no one will know. She stood in the small bathroom with a toilet and pedestal sink. There was a candle atop the toilet lid, one of those giant Yankee candles, cinnamon, or apple crisp, something she would want to eat rather than burn.*

Burn it. Do it now. Destroy the memories.

The voice resonated so loudly she was certain that the others might hear from outside of the home. She stood in the bathroom, staring at the mirror, her face contorted—not beautiful, but wicked. She saw Nina and then her mother and then herself. The blended images seemed to be cinematic, but in fact were real. She could see her matriarchal lineage so clearly. These images guided her hand to her purse, where she removed a lighter.

With a simple flip of the wrist she turned and stared at the Yankee candle. It was probably some kind of spice, she determined. She looked above the deep red wax and blackened wick at the low-hanging set of towels. With her free hand she tugged the towel to within an inch of the wick, repositioning the candle only fractionally backward toward the wall.

She moved the lighter toward the candle.

Burn down this place, Amanda. Destroy your father.

The beeping horn brought her back to I-85 and the driver in the next lane gave her the finger as she swerved and nearly clipped his car.

"Sorry," she said, unsure to whom she was responding.

Similar to awaking from a dream, she could not reconnect with the series of events that had been replaying in her mind. She was not entirely keen on doing so, but it was important to her, because she truly could not remember. How, or why, this memory suddenly flashed back to her, she was not certain.

She found herself pulling into Jake Devereaux's driveway, where she removed her cell phone from her purse and pressed speed dial number one. While the phone was ringing, she put her head into her hands and began weeping.

Then the thought of what had happened at Riley Dwyer's home last night came rushing to her.

THE PLANS

CHAPTER 47
KUNAR PROVINCE, AFGHANISTAN

TUESDAY MORNING (HOURS OF DARKNESS)

Matt Garrett looked at Major General Rampert in the dim light of the MH-47 helicopter. He felt the lift and churn of the dual blades chopping their way through the thin night air. They were flying through a narrow corridor at about ten thousand feet above sea level, yet only about fifty feet above ground level. One fractional mistake and the aircraft would splinter apart and create a debris field about a mile long.

"Hey, Doug, we're getting the word to turn around. It's coming in from Van Dreeves," Rampert said into his headset to the pilot.

"Wilco, sir," Doug responded. No questions, just execute the assigned mission.

"What's going on, General?" Matt asked through his headset.

"Central Command commander said to stand down the mission."

"Didn't know he knew about it."

"Me neither. Must have a spy somewhere back at headquarters. Not unheard of."

"What's Van Dreeves saying about Zach?"

"Stand by."

Rampert flipped a switch on the communications platform in the back of the aircraft so that the entire crew could hear Van Dreeves's situation report.

". . . thirty-three followed him to a river, a tributary to the Kunar along the border near Naray and that old mine. He was taking fire from a group of about twenty enemy personnel. He tried wading across the river and then was swept away. Being springtime, those rivers are over the banks and faster than hell with all the snow melt and rain."

Van Dreeves paused.

"Then I lost him. He moved too fast or went under; I'm not sure. I've been scanning up and down the banks ever since. Sorry, Matt."

"Not your fault, VD. Listen, Zach used to surf, so those rapids will be nothing for him. We'll find him."

Matt's optimistic words did not match the burning hole in his gut. He felt the aircraft bank hard, back toward their starting point. Matt watched Eversoll drop his head in disgust, shaking it wildly.

"Can we fly the Kunar? We can't be that far."

Rampert looked at Matt, who had just asked him to disobey a four-star general's order. "Why the hell not; we're already in over our heads." He flipped a switch so he could talk to the pilots. Matt watched him mouth some words into the microphone, felt the aircraft bank again.

"Actually, this is a good idea," Rampert said. "It's on the way back and maybe we can kill some of the enemy."

"Roger that," Eversoll barked into his headset.

The tail door gunner got up and walked toward the ramp of the aircraft. He was wearing a crewman's helmet with a clear visor that made him look a bit futuristic. The ramp lowered so that it was even with the floor of the aircraft. The gaping hole opened to the Afghanistan night, always pitch black. They could determine an occasional jagged cliff they had just passed over as the pilots flew nap of the earth. The tail gunner hooked himself into a long strap called a 'monkey harness' that allowed him to move about the aircraft with the ramp down without fear of falling to his death. If he fell outside of the aircraft, he would at least be dangling by twenty feet of nylon cord. Of course, the pilots weren't flying much higher than that above ground level.

The door gunners made some more room for an extra gunner each on either side of the aircraft so that they could each take up observation and firing positions.

Matt hooked into a monkey harness and laid down on the tail ramp. He figured this would give him more observation capability and better fields of fire, though he might miss something going on in the front of the aircraft.

Hobart and Eversoll each positioned themselves in opposite doors. Each man locked and loaded their M4 carbines then snapped their night-vision goggles onto their helmets. There were two M240G machine guns at each crew chief station as well as the tail gunner. The 240 was a superb weapon for providing heavy suppressive fire. The crew chief completely turned off the dim LCD light that was providing some glow in the rear of the aircraft.

In the headset Matt heard one of the pilots say, "Large group of personnel moving south along the eastern bank of the river."

"Roger, I called the conventional forces, and they have confirmed they have no friendly forces operating in this area. Prepare to engage." Rampert's voice was crisp and sure.

"We're taking fire. We've got tracers coming at us," the pilot calmly announced. Matt felt the aircraft bank, do a quick zigzag in the air, and suddenly he saw a heavy volume of tracer fire screaming across the field of his night-vision goggles.

Everyone with a weapon in the helicopter returned fire at the enemy.

"General, don't you think we'd be better off on the ground fighting these bastards?" Matt asked.

"Can't risk it. I'm calling for air support right now."

"General, if they've captured Zach again, we might be firing into him. Maybe we should back off."

A moment of silence passed.

"Okay, I've told the pilots to break contact and asked Van Dreeves to get the Predator over these guys."

The aircraft suddenly listed to the right and bolted skyward on its hour-long flight back to the air base.

BACK IN THE headquarters they linked up with Van Dreeves. Walking from the flight line to the headquarters, they all let out a few expletives at not being able to find Colonel Garrett, but mostly at having some general eight thousand miles away cancel a mission. The "eight-thousand-mile screwdriver," as Rampert termed it.

"Looks like you killed a few of them, sir," he said to General Rampert.

"Good."

"See this bunch here?" Van Dreeves said, pointing at the large video display. "They are treating wounded and trying to drag bodies." He punched a button and another screen came up on the display. "These guys here are still moving along the Kunar to the south. Looks like they're still looking for Colonel Garrett."

"Still the right call to wave off. There was no way to tell," Eversoll said. "At least we killed some of them."

"Roger," Rampert said. "Matt, let's think things over for a minute."

Matt followed Rampert into his office.

"Coffee?"

"No thanks. Got enough adrenaline in the system right now."

They each sat down in hard wooden chairs. There were no luxuries here in a combat zone.

"What do you think?"

"I think he's alive, and he's still on the run."

"I agree," Rampert said.

"We'll find him."

"If we all still have jobs in the morning."

"That, too."

Rampert paused, taking a sip of coffee from a cup that said "**KILL THE ENEMY**" in big block letters.

"You ever sometimes think all this shit ain't worth it?"

"Worth what?" Matt countered.

"You know, we've got your brother out there running for his life, we've had I don't know how many soldiers killed lately, and all these dumb-ass politicians and appointees just spanking the monkey."

Matt looked away. He didn't like to think about the worthiness of what they were doing. There were too many questions, too many decisions that didn't pass the common sense test.

"I never really think about all that. I'm afraid if I ever stopped to really consider it, I'd be too disgusted."

"And then who would do this," Rampert said, waving his hand.

Van Dreeves poked his head in the door. "We're getting some special intelligence here, sir. Listen to this."

Van Dreeves played with a small box that looked like a radio but was actually a highly classified signals intelligence platform. He was able to intercept certain types of communications.

"This is the man we call the Scientist. It's Mullah Rahman, the one who has the flash drive." The voice was ranting a continuous stream of Arabic, interrupted occasionally by another voice that was distinctly different, yet still in Arabic. Van Dreeves, fluent in the language, was writing furiously. They listened to the diatribe for close to five minutes when the voices stopped.

They gave Van Dreeves a minute to finish writing. He ran his hand through his blond hair and said, "Holy shit."

"What?" Matt asked.

Van Dreeves looked at Matt and then at Rampert. The calm operator was more excited than usual. He began speaking, using his hands to emphasize certain points.

"The Colonel escaped and killed at least two of their men. They lost him around the Kunar River."

"That was them."

"Wait. They just put a five-million-dollar price on Colonel Garrett's head." He paused. "Around the world. A *Fatwah*."

Matt looked at Rampert. The team fell silent, considering the ramifications. Al Qaeda was a global operation with unlimited funding. Even if they got Zach back alive, they would have to be very circumspect. Maybe even hide him for a while. But first things first.

"We've got to find him," Matt said.

"Roger."

"Wait, there's more," Van Dreeves said, finishing some scribbling. "Something about a suicide mission on military bases. He gave guidance to stand up the network."

Rampert scratched his chin. "That could be anything, anywhere. We've got to make sure we tighten up our gate guard checks and other procedures. We've got a hell of a lot of local nationals that work on this base."

"Well, the first priority is to find Zach, so we've got to get our network going also," Matt emphasized.

"Consider it done," Rampert said. "VD, get me the team. We're going to full alert here."

"What are we hearing from Yemen and Dubai, VD?" Matt asked.

"The message board is active. Almost like a chat. Rahman's telling Yemen and Dubai that Colonel Garrett escaped. Dubai asked if that compromises anything. Yemen wants to know if he's seeing anything else with the master plan to withdraw from the border region. Dubai is the one who said that Rahman needs to produce Garrett to get his money. There's your five-million-dollar Fatwah," Van Dreeves said.

"General I recommend we do three things. First, we move the 101st Airborne to the border to see if they can find Zach. Second, let's get Predators over Dubai and Yemen and see what we can find out and destroy those targets. Third, we need to get our asses back into the fight. So either drop my ass from an airplane into the middle of this thing or let's get another helicopter moving."

Rampert looked at Matt then at Hobart and Van Dreeves.

"You heard the man, let's get moving. VD tell CENTCOM we need Predators over the two grids for Yemen and Dubai. Hobart let's get the Nightstalkers turning now. I'll call Art Griffin, the commander of the 101st and tell him what we need," Rampert said. "If we put the Screaming Eagles on the border, all the helicopters flying around will feed into the deception plan that we're attacking, too."

Matt stared at Rampert. The time had come for full disclosure.

"Here's the breaking news. Who said anything about deception?"

The command center went quiet.

"What are you saying?" Rampert asked Matt.

"I'm saying that General Griffin with the 101 already has orders to do a major air assault into Pakistan. The plan on the flash drive was more than an illusion. The best deception feeds into what the enemy already believes. We've got this stupid withdraw timeline. We've got the closed base from the Korengal. The enemy is seeking nukes. So we wrapped that all together to get them moving toward the border, which we see is happening. Now we are going to put massive boots on the ground in Northwest Frontier Province and Waziristan behind them while we seal the fake mine we sent their fighters into. This is the moment of truth for this war."

It was Rampert's turn to stare at Matt.

"You son of a bitch," Rampert barked. "You frigging used us? JSOC? Your own brother?"

"I didn't use anyone, General. This is a major opportunity. The president recognizes it. Pull your head out of your myopic ass for a second and think about it. We've got the main AQ operative in Pakistan unglued and we know where he is. We've got the financier in Dubai and a mystery operator in Yemen. We've not had an opportunity like this to disable Al Qaeda since just after 9-11 when Tommy Franks couldn't find his ass from a hole in the ground and didn't have the stones to put a hellfire missile on bin Laden. Now we're wasting time, so let's get moving."

Matt had always believed in the dictum, "When in charge, be in charge." He knew that he didn't have actual command authority over Rampert or any of the military in Afghanistan, but he had the legitimacy and the extended authorization from the National Command Authority.

"I think, VD, you'll find that we've had Global Hawk over both Yemen and Dubai for a couple of days now. The financier is none other than a respected Dubai citizen, Jamal Mohammed, whom AQ calls the Technician. He is going to die very soon. Probably his family, too. We've had a more difficult time identifying our friend in Yemen. He's got medical problems apparently, because a van arrives everyday at nightfall and two men get out of the van carrying assorted medical equipment. One day it was a doctor's bag, another day it's a dialysis machine. So who knows?"

Again the command center fell silent.

"But that son of bitch is going to die soon also. And we're going to wait until the medical personnel are there so that we know he's in there. So they'll die too. All of that is in the works. I've got two teams prepared to do night jumps to extract and confirm the bodies when we decide to pull the trigger. Could be tonight, could be next week. I will provide the best recommendation to the president on when and how to do this. If you're nice to me, maybe the five of us can jump in and go get this guy. And now my first priority is to go get my brother, who risked his life to make all this possible."

Without waiting for an answer, Matt turned and walked out of the headquarters.

CHAPTER 48
SPARTANBURG, SOUTH CAROLINA

MONDAY (EASTERN TIME ZONE)

Melanie Garrett walked through her dining room, running a moisturized hand along the reflective sheen of the wood. Nina Hastings leaned her aging but agile frame against the portico that separated the foyer from the dining room.

"Whatcha gonna do?" the mother asked with a toying smile. The relationship was too complex to be characterized as mother-daughter, teacher-student, or squad leader-soldier. Co-dependent was too simple a phrase that failed to capture the multiple linkages and twisted interrelationships between the two. These women were sociopaths who carved out their own niche in this world, this survival of the fittest existence.

They acted without conscience and without mercy. The ends *always* justified the means.

"I'm thinking things are going just about right, Mama."

"Well, you need that paperwork signed."

"Amanda will sign it tonight. She has to be scared. Everything but us has gone to hell in her life."

"Heard Dwyer died."

"No, unfortunately. They forgot to hook up her machines or something, but she's as good as dead as far as we're concerned."

"So, what next?" Nina Hastings, dropping bread crumbs along the path she wanted her daughter to follow, smiled at her own manipulation.

"Amanda comes home, we call the military, and they process the paper-work."

"How you going to do that without Dwyer's signature?"

"Oh, I've got that already."

Nina raised a pencil-marked eyebrow. Had the warrior outdone the general? Melanie smiled. She had forged enough insurance checks to buy a new car, just a little bit at a time so no one would get alarmed. And, she had forged Zach's signature on so many checks and documents that she had been able to, without concentrating, imitate his signature at will.

"Practice makes perfect." She showed her mother the document, which she had retrieved from Amanda's room.

"Gonna tell her that Dwyer signed it at the hospital?"

"Yep. Went over there today, spoke with her briefly, and she agreed. Unfortunately, she fell unconscious after that, but thank God that we can move on."

"Gotcha."

They turned their heads when they heard the car door slam in the drive-way.

"Let me handle this, Mama. I've got it under control."

AMANDA PULLED INTO her mother's driveway after having left Jake's house. She stopped the car and sighed heavily. She leaned over, pulling at her hair, banging her forehead on the upper leathered portion of the steering wheel.

"What is wrong with me?" she screamed inside her nearly soundproof Mercedes. The advertisements championing the heavy doors and airtight fit were all true. An outside observer would see her moving her mouth, but be unable to hear anything unless they were directly beside the vehicle.

She pulled herself together and walked through the front door entryway, seeing Nina leaning against the doorjamb as if she were hanging out at the soda fountain, twirling a toothpick in her mouth. Next she saw her mother standing in the dining room. What were they thinking?

"Hey, baby, how are you?" Nina Hastings was instantly upon her. While

Melanie's need was money, Nina's was attention, manufactured or not.

"Fine, Nina. I mean, not really. There's some stuff that's happened."

"Want to tell me what you've been up to?" her mother chirped from the dining room.

Yes, Melanie Garrett to Nina Hastings was daughter to mother as Goebbels was to Hitler. Who was more evil? Hard to tell. Each was capable of independently operating for her own purposes, but they were so much better together. The whole *was* greater than the sum of the parts.

She wasn't sure when she had reached this conclusion, but Amanda stared at her mother and grandmother, debating with herself the course of action she had entertained on the drive back from Jake's. Their visit had been brief, the electronic bracelet around his ankle a visible reminder of what they faced together. Nonetheless, her thinking had crystallized after their short conversation. It was all starting to make sense, and she had a plan. *The apple doesn't fall far from the tree.*

"Well, Mom, you know it has just been one of those weeks. You-know-who is dead. Jake's in jail. There's a half million dollars out there for the taking. So, you know, cut me some slack, please."

Melanie Garrett tapped her foot, covered in an Italian leather pump, then softened considerably. Be tough, then loving; keep her off balance. Never be predictable. These were her operating credos. Amanda was beginning to see through the smoke screen that was intentionally laid in front of her.

"Speaking of the money, Amanda, we need to talk."

Amanda held up her hands. "Mom, it has already been a long day. I know what you want me to do, and I will do it. The problem is that the original that was signed by you-know-who is still with Miss Dwyer."

Melanie paused and decided to let Amanda continue. The copy she had made from the version Amanda kept in her lockbox was nearly perfect. Yet, the raised seal was not present; not that she couldn't fix that in a hurry.

"So, let me go see Dwyer tomorrow at the hospital, if she wakes up, and we'll get this done." Jake had received the news that Riley Dwyer was still alive and had passed that much on to Amanda. Amanda knew she needed to start taking responsibility for her actions—an alien concept to her—but she thought she might know how to begin.

"I'm told she's in a coma, almost died," Nina said, speaking up for the first time.

"Well, can we just deal with it tomorrow? I want that money just as much as anyone. I know it will do us some good. I'm on the team, so don't sweat it."

The two older women stared at their protégé.

"Okay, then, but first I want you to take a drive with me," her mother said.

"Mom, please—"

"Amanda, you've been out of it the past few days, both mentally and physically, and I need to show you something."

Amanda recognized this as her "no negotiation" voice. Some days she was bewildered by the way her mother and grandmother would seem to be out of synch, one nice, the other mean as hell. She loved them, for sure, but at times she could swear that they were almost *working* her.

"Amanda, why don't you do what your mother says," Nina urged sweetly. "You haven't had much time with her, and I think this whole ordeal has been harder on both of you than either of you realize. If there were ever a good moment for some mother-daughter time, this is it." Open the steam valve just a bit, release some pressure from the situation. She was a master.

Sighing, as if to vent, Amanda muttered, "All right, but I need to catch up with some schoolwork."

CHAPTER 49
THE CLIFFS AT KEOWEE, SOUTH CAROLINA

She found herself completely disconnected from reality as she sailed along in the passenger seat of her mother's Mercedes, top down, on this beautiful spring day. Quickly she saw that they were on South Carolina Highway 11, and she knew intuitively that they were heading toward Lake Keowee. Her mother had been obsessed with buying a home in that area for years, as if it was what she lived for.

Her hair whipping in the Cabriolet's slipstream, she tried to use the time to sort out the colliding emotions, thoughts, and actions of the last week. She had just a few days until her eighteenth birthday and her emancipation as an adult. Memories of her father, long forgotten or erased or suppressed, she wasn't sure which, had come crashing back into her life with the force of a battering ram against a secured medieval castle door.

They traveled mostly in silence, her mother appearing lost in thought as well. Amanda's infrequent glance was a mere turn of the eyes as she rested her head against her hand, elbow propped against the passenger door. Her jade and copper flecked eyes carried a scorn deep within that somehow she could not control.

In short, she was going out of her mind trapped in the car with her mother. She'd had momentum. She'd had an idea and the energy to follow through, which was now being stifled by her mother's banal diversion.

Keeping me off balance.

The thought circled through her mind like a hawk seeking purchase atop a mountain peak. Bad thoughts about her mother did not come to

her naturally, if ever. The same held true for her grandmother. Speaking
of which . . .

"Mom, I thought Nina was sick."

"Doctor released her. She is sick, but they need to do more tests, and you
know how expensive those damn hospitals can be."

"She looked fine to me."

There comes a time in every young woman's life where she begins to see
herself apart from how she was raised. More to the point, she begins to
analyze the rearing process. She begins to transform from girl to gatherer. It
is mostly an instinctual progression, natural that is, as she begins to intuit
that one day she will have children of her own; and thus she is moved to
review her own upbringing.

What had she missed? A week ago, she would have blithely responded to
herself, if she had even thought of the question, with a straightforward,
"Nothing." Her father's will, which caused her to examine at least a portion
of her relationship with him, had put a chink in the armor that her mother
and grandmother had wrapped around her.

Her mother eyed her, causing the car to awkwardly negotiate a tight
corner as they rolled through the countryside.

"Don't get smart with me, Amanda. I'm trying here. The least you could
do is meet me half way."

Amanda looked at her mother with a full turn of her head. She wanted to
say something, but she refrained.

Suddenly the car pulled over into a gravel section beside the highway. For
a brief moment, Amanda thought her mother was stopping to scold her, not
wanting to perform two challenging tasks simultaneously.

"There." Her mother nodded with her head past the passenger side of the
car. Amanda looked to her right and saw the long driveway and split-rail
fence framing the perfectly tended lawn that fed at least a quarter mile up to
the beautiful Jeffersonian mansion.

Jefferson. Monticello. The memory was immediate and visible. Her father
had taken her to Charlottesville when she was nine. They had toured Thomas
Jefferson's home, with the perpetual motion calendar, the vineyards, and the

beautiful rotunda. She remembered it so vividly that she began shaking.

"What's going on, Amanda?"

Her mother's voice was shrill, fingernails on a blackboard, against the serene images of her walking hand in hand with her father through Jefferson's immaculately designed boxwood hedgerows and vineyards. She remembered him putting her on his shoulders so she could see over the rows of grapes and their symmetrical beauty.

"Amanda!"

She had begun crying. "Nothing, Mom. It's beautiful. I think it's beautiful, and I'm just so happy for you, because I know that with the five hundred thousand dollars we'll be able to afford this house."

Amanda felt her mother's icy eyes upon her, cold and hard, but quickly giving way to warmth and love.

"I'm just happy for us, you know, Mom."

Her mother reached across the polished mahogany gear shift and hugged Amanda, awkward as it was. "I knew you'd understand."

"Of course I understand, Mama. Why do you think I'm going through all this bullshit?"

"Well, I don't like that word, but I do like your attitude."

"We're a team, Mom. The three musketeers, remember?"

"All for one . . ."

"And one for all."

"I just need you to be really sure, you know, committed here on this one."

"I'll be there for you, Mom."

THEY HAD REMAINED silent the entire trip back. Cycling through Amanda's mind were the images of the African children from the photos, lost and forgotten in a world that cared more about Tiffany jewelry than human suffering. The thirty-minute drive back to the house gave her time to process her thoughts. Still dominant was her disbelief that her father had been dead for less than two weeks, yet her mother had already picked out a million-dollar home.

Pulling into the driveway of the house, Amanda decided to ask her mother a question. "Can we really afford that house, Mom?"

"Well, if we all pitch in, we can. We already have a buyer for our house here."

"Really, when did this happen?"

"Well, homes around here sell quickly premarket. We'll get about four hundred thousand for it. Plus, with your five hundred thousand, we'll be able to take out a three-hundred-thousand-dollar mortgage."

"What's Nina doing?"

"All her money is tied up in long-term CDs. She'd pay a huge penalty right now if she cashed out, but she'll be there for us, as always."

"Well, I'm glad all of this is working out for us."

Her mother smiled warmly and placed her hand on Amanda's shoulder. "Why don't you head on up to your room and we'll talk more about this later."

Amanda walked mindlessly up to her room, passing through the foyer. Nina still stood against the doorjamb as if she'd never moved. She lifted a hand in the direction of her grandmother, as if to say Hi.

As she closed and locked her door, she heard Nina say, "So, how'd it go?"

Setting down her book bag next to her computer, she logged on and changed all of her security passwords and defaults. Likewise, she changed her screen saver from "No Dad" to "Good to Go," which scrolled slowly across the monitor during periods of inactivity.

She began to feel her energy return. Something was stirring inside her. A magnetic pull, as if from far away, was directing her. She closed her eyes and saw the image of her father in his army uniform, weapon at his side, crooked grin and bright eyes smiling at her.

Putting her head into her hands, she took a deep breath and exhaled heavily. Then she sat straight up, energy restored, momentum turning after the diversionary road trip with her mother. It was uncanny, she thought to herself, how every time she began reconnecting or thinking or even remembering something good about her father her mother or Nina was right there to sweep it away. There was always a bigger toy for Christmas, a better trip for vacation, or a tighter hug following a crisis.

It was time, however, to begin to gather—to review her own life through her own lens. There were things that didn't make sense, but they were gaining clarity. That much was certain.

From her purse, she pulled a thumb drive that Jake's father had handed to her when she'd gone to his house. While she had spoken to Jake just the one time, his father, ever the lawyer, had moderated the exchange of the flash drive, ensuring she received it and that Jake had delivered it. Apparently, Jake had gone back into her dad's house after the NCBI agents had taken her to the airport, to retrieve the portable memory device. He had seen it on the desk in the guest bedroom. She stared at it for a long time, wondering what it might contain. Taped on it was the inscription:

Amanda: Just in case . . . I Love You, Dad

CHAPTER 50
SPARTANBURG, SOUTH CAROLINA

TUESDAY MORNING

Amanda woke up with an impossible migraine. With time of the essence, though, last night she had mapped out her plan.

She quickly dressed in a pair of jeans and a tight green T-shirt that said "SMILE" across the front. It was the first thing available. Style was less important than speed. She slipped on some clogs and moved quickly to her car before her mom or Nina could stop her momentum. She heard them call over her shoulder, but continued on, waving over her back as she had done before. She was making a munching motion with her hand, like a gator mouth yapping.

In the Mercedes now, she sped to the Charlotte Hospital, found a parking spot and was knocking on Riley Dwyer's room when a nurse came up to her.

"Can I help you, dear?"

"Yes, ma'am, I'm a friend of Miss Dwyer's. I need to just make sure she's okay."

"Well, she's feeling better. Let me see if she's taking visitors."

Momentarily the nurse reappeared and held the door open for Amanda.

She stood about ten feet from the bed; her jaw would have hung to the floor had the mandible allowed such an extension. Riley Dwyer was purple throughout her face and neck, her right arm was in a cast, and her eyelids appeared shut.

"Com'ere, kiddo," is what Amanda thought she heard Riley say.

She moved closer to Riley, almost fearful that moving too close might hurt her. Though the idea was illogical, it seemed possible given the nature of her injuries.

"Well, you look . . . better." She didn't know what to say.

"Fanks for comin'." Again, almost unintelligible.

"You're welcome, Miss Dwyer." She fidgeted for a moment, picking at her fingernail.

"Whasson yer mind." The words came out tinny and hollow, not fully pronounced, but recognizable nonetheless.

"Riley, I mean, Miss Dwyer, I need a lawyer. Do you know a good one?"

Riley lay still for a moment, not that she had much choice in the matter. Her beautiful auburn hair was splayed across the back of the pillow like a translucent orange fan growing from a coral reef.

"Write," she mumbled and tried to make a writing motion with her hand, but winced in pain.

Amanda retrieved a pen and paper from her small book bag.

"Harlan Woxworth."

She shook her head. "*Woxworth. Woxworth.*"

"That's what I said."

Riley shook her head again and sighed in frustration.

"Oh, *F*oxworth?"

She shot Amanda a thumbs-up with her left hand. Then she pointed to the counter.

"What? You want me to get something?"

Riley nodded.

"I don't see—oh, gotcha," Amanda replied. She stood and grabbed Riley's purse. She fished a day planner out of it. Thumbing through the address portion, she found the phone number.

"Okay, now more importantly, did Jake do this to you?"

She shook her head.

Amanda sighed. "I knew it. Can you tell me who did this? A clue? Anything?"

Riley was drifting off to sleep as the nurse came in and touched her arm, indicating it was time for her to leave. As they reached the door, she heard a muffled word: "Write."

Amanda looked back over her shoulder. "What did you say? Did you say, 'write'?"

Riley nodded and made a writing motion with her left hand.

"Okay, okay, what do you want me to write?"

Riley was unresponsive, though her hand was pointing at the newspaper at the foot of the bed.

CHAPTER 51
CHARLOTTE, NORTH CAROLINA

The nurse pulled her away, and Amanda found herself heading back toward her car. She punched in Mr. Foxworth's phone number, got a young-sounding assistant, and asked if he could see her on short notice regarding the death of Colonel Zachary Garrett.

A minute passed to two as she negotiated her car out of the parking lot in the direction of North Carolina on I-85, where she would find the attorney's office.

"This is Harlan," came a strong, authoritative voice.

"Mr. Foxworth, my name is Amanda Garrett, and my father's been killed in Afghanistan. He left me a will with some complicating issues, and I need someone I can trust. My father's girlfriend, Riley Dwyer, who is lying in a hospital right now with her face beat to a pulp, told me to call you."

"I'm sorry about your father. What about Riley? Is she okay?" Genuine concern shrouded his words.

"I think she's going to recover, but right now she's not okay. Can you see me today? Now?"

"Have you had breakfast?"

"No. I'm starving."

"Meet me at Starbucks off Piedmont."

After a twenty-minute drive, she nosed into an empty space at Starbucks. As she stepped through the doorway she scanned left and right, then picked out her mark. He looked nice enough, bespectacled and probably in his mid-forties. He had a round, friendly face and a receding crop of dark hair. He was hunched over a newspaper.

"Mr. Foxworth?" Amanda asked, tentatively.

"Yes, please have a seat," he replied, looking up at the teenager.

Amanda sat in the metal chair opposite him. He looked down at his paper and up at her. "Have you seen this?"

For the next five minutes Amanda read with horror the story in the *Charlotte Observer*. She read it several times over and then put her head into her hands.

"Is this true?" His voice was somehow comforting, as if he didn't believe any of it. He was probing what she might think.

"Who knows? I don't know. I mean, no. How could it be?"

She watched him take a bite of a muffin and place it back onto the napkin.

"Want something? Coffee?"

"No, thanks. Suddenly lost my appetite."

She checked the byline of the story. "Who the hell is Del Dangurs?" she asked.

"I've seen some articles by him in the past and have never been very impressed. He does book reviews and some commentary on other light-weight trivia like the dating scene and so forth. This is a bit out of his lane."

"Out of his league."

She watched him study her as he held a half of a blueberry muffin in his hand. He turned the paper around and looked at it again. "Well, how can I help you? Other than the obvious."

She finally decided to eat something. She ordered an egg sandwich. As soon as it arrived, she realized how hungry she really was. She was still stumped about where to begin. With just a few days to go until her eighteenth birthday, she knew she needed to move quickly if she was going to pull it all off. Her plan involved more than simply getting the money. Her realization of what had been taken from her spawned new goals that she fully intended to achieve.

In between bites, they discussed what had transpired and what Amanda had in mind.

"I think I might be able to help you," the attorney said after listening to her story. "Let me make some phone calls and I will be in touch with you. Cell number? I'm assuming you don't want me calling your home phone?"

He handed her a Mont Blanc pen from his shirt pocket, which she used to scribble her phone number on a napkin. Folding it, she handed both the napkin and the pen back to him. "Just the cell. The quicker the better."

"I'll be in touch shortly."

AMANDA WAS LATE for school, and the parking lot was nearly full.

She walked through the main hallway, lockers standing erect like a cordon of soldiers welcoming her arrival. She was beginning to piece everything together now and hoped over the next few days she would be able to resolve the final few issues that still confounded her. Her departure from Riley Dwyer's hospital room, however, still tugged at the back of her mind. *Write. Newspaper.*

And then it occurred to her that the article Foxworth had shown her might bear some relation to Riley's attack. But what?

"Hey, Garrett, you got a second?"

Amanda stopped and turned. The hallway was empty save the phalanx of wall lockers and Principal Dan Rugsdale. She noticed he did not look happy and cautiously approached him. He remained motionless beneath the fluorescent lights. Though she had not thought much about the principal in the past, she noticed his determined stare.

"Yes, sir?" she asked sheepishly.

"You want to tell me what's going on?" Her principal's request hung in the air. His eyes were unflinching black marbles.

"Sir, I'm—" she began, only to be interrupted.

"Hi, Dan. I thought you were in North Carolina at that convention." It was Mr. Dagus to the rescue. Then, before Mr. Rugsdale could answer, he went on, "Amanda, do you have that project I asked you to work on at home the last few days?"

Thinking quickly, she broke the icy staring contest with Rugsdale and looked at Dagus, summoning the best acting skills she could muster.

"I do. That's why I was late this morning. I appreciate so very much both of you giving me this time to grieve the loss of my father and to finish up my high school experience."

"Len, I'd like to talk to you when you're done with Miss Garrett," Rugsdale said with an irritated edge.

"Sure."

Dagus or Rugsdale had given her that break because her father had died. She knew she was close to validation, but had never believed she was quite there. Regardless, the majority of the students who had not been so lucky raced to classrooms for the next final exams. Conversely, Amanda's big chore today was to finish the final layout copy of the Venture.

Rugsdale turned and walked toward the administrative offices. Once he had reentered the glass door, Amanda wilted and leaned into her teacher. "Thanks for saving me."

Dagus caught her and then held her away quickly, as if sizing her up. "No sweat. I know it's been tough for you lately."

Amanda stepped back. It was actually good to see him. He had been such a reliable friend and mentor over the past couple of years. She sighed, the stress still overwhelming her. They walked into the classroom together, she following his lead. He sat at his desk and simultaneously pulled down his laptop screen as he crossed his legs. She noticed a small digital camera connected to his laptop.

Amanda sat in the chair across from his desk, laying her book bag on the floor.

"So, how are you managing?"

"Wiped out, you know?" She leaned into her hands with her elbows propped on the desk. Sunlight blared through the open windows, casting huge rectangles on the floor. "You were right. This sort of caught up on me."

"By 'this,' you mean your father's death?"

She nodded as she stared at him.

"Well, I hope what I said didn't make it any harder."

"Please. It sort of woke me up. You're, like, the only sane person in the entire drama."

He nodded at her approvingly. "Is there anything you'd like to talk about?"

Amanda couldn't stop staring at him as she tried to figure out what it was that was bothering her.

"Amanda?"

"Oh, I'm sorry. I'm just a space cadet right now. Anyway, looks like someone's been out in the sun."

Dagus ran his long fingers across his face.

"Played some hooky and went to the lake. Finals are all done, you know."

"Fun." She paused then said, "Can I just go ahead and finish that edit job?"

He smiled at her. "Well, you know where the editing room is, and you know where I'll be when you're done. How long do you think it will take you?"

"I don't know. Couple of hours? You want to check it out when I'm done?"

"I'll be free about six tonight. You can either leave it on my desk or meet me here, whichever you prefer."

She pursed her lips, which was her thinking pose. "I'll just call you." She paused a second and then said, "By the way, do you mind if I don't publish that poem about my dad?"

He stared at her a moment, rubbing his chin. "I think that's a wise move, Amanda. I understood the emotion with which you wrote the piece, but think it makes eminent sense not to publish it in light of what has happened."

"Thank you."

He coughed into his hand and then replaced it on his knee. "You know, you've matured this past week in many ways. This is just one."

"You have no idea." Her words came out louder than she desired, but she was so satisfied that someone had noticed. Maybe she was even glad it was him. "Finally, someone is taking me seriously." She noticed, not for the first time, his copper-colored eyes that remained fixed on her. They were . . . consoling.

"I've always taken you seriously, Amanda. What are you talking about?"

"You know, just teenager stuff." She waved her hand dismissively. She needed to move quickly before she embarrassed herself.

She grabbed her backpack and walked into the adjoining room, filled with copy tables, computers, and printers. She shrugged her shoulders once and shook off whatever it was that had initially bothered her.

Suddenly she lifted her head and said to herself, "Rugsdale was in North Carolina?"

CHAPTER 52
BAGRAM AIR BASE, AFGHANISTAN

WEDNESDAY MORNING (HOURS OF DARKNESS)

"You had no right, Matt," Rampert said.

"Grow up, General. You've been using everyone your entire career. I've got your dossier. Don't think I don't know about your interrogation activities in the Persian Gulf or your shady dealings with Ballantine. You escaped all of that bullshit, I know, but you walk a fine line."

Rampert stared at Matt for a moment, his gray crew cut looking like a wire brush.

"You don't know shit, Garrett."

"Either we're on the same team or not. I couldn't give a rat's ass about what you've done in the past but we've got a few objectives here that we need to accomplish. I have no doubt that you believe every one of your ends justifies the means you use to accomplish them. So, first, get my brother back. Second, invade Pakistan. Third, kill Dubai and Yemen."

They had begun calling the two Al Qaeda operatives by the names of the countries they were based in for simplicity.

Rampert's cheap circular wall clock ticked away. Matt stared at the general, keeping his momentum. He had to keep moving. If he stopped, he would decelerate, which was never good.

"You know I'm in, you asshole, but I don't like it. Pakistan is our domain and I don't like giving up turf."

"We're going to put more boots on the ground in there than you could ever muster and we'll be flushing bad guys like rabbits from the bush. So give me a good plan to get over top of these guys with the Predators and your special intelligence and let's see what we can get."

Rampert nodded.

Changing tack, Matt said, "I've got to call Amanda, Zach's daughter." Maps still decorated the walls of Rampert's makeshift office like badly hung wallpaper, all different sizes with unique scales. Rampert sat down and crossed his feet so that they were resting on the tip of a steel-grey desk. With the apparent truce, Matt sat down and began running a toothpick through his teeth, leaning back into an uncomfortable wooden chair.

"There's a brilliant idea. Give the plan away to a teenager who hates her dad."

"Well, it's the right thing to do, regardless of it being a good or bad idea."

"We don't know anything for certain, do we? If he's dead or alive. We think we may have been following him, but we can't be sure."

"We're sure." Matt stopped with the toothpick and looked at Rampert with hollow eyes.

"Yeah, you're right." Rampert withdrew his feet from the desk and leaned forward, sighing. "But it could compromise our efforts to find him."

"I know. I'm just thinking about that little girl. Well, she's almost eighteen now. But she's been through hell."

"You mean the whole Ballantine thing?"

Matt scoffed. "Ballantine was amateur hour compared to the bullshit her mother and grandmother have put her through. Zach made me promise that if anything ever happened to him, that I'd take care of it."

"She's eighteen, not much you can do anymore."

"I remember her standing there at Zach's funeral. Unbeknownst to me at the time, we buried Winslow Boudreaux next to my mother on the farm while you had Zach down at Fort Bragg recuperating. You had officially listed him as killed in action."

"We've been through this, Matt."

"Amanda was at that funeral and later found out her father was alive.

Zach was the only decent thing she had going for her, even if she refused to acknowledge it."

The two men stared at one another. It was clear to Matt that Rampert accepted his responsibility in the matter. He had deceived the government and the families involved. It was the stuff of the "dark side." Why not develop a truly covert operator? It was difficult to become more covert than to be presumed killed in action. And so Rampert had evacuated Zach Garrett from a Philippine jungle, switched identification tags with an operator who had been essentially vaporized by an enemy weapon, and reported Zach as killed in action.

All is forgivable if a happy ending is to be found, which of course it had been. Zach was used in a covert manner in the Ballantine mission, and the nation was spared the death and devastation of a nuclear attack by retrofitted unmanned aerial drones launched from a Chinese merchant ship. The post 9-11 world not only excused such excesses, it demanded them. Nonetheless, the hardened men who toiled at the sharpened edges of this global war separated themselves from their enemies by having a conscience. Morality was, after all, the fuel that burned the cleanest when you were driving a machine bent on destroying your enemies.

"How can I help?"

Matt looked at the floor, spinning the toothpick in his hands, and seemed to consider his shoelaces. "By finding her father."

"You know I'm doing all I can. And when we put this Airborne division in there, it could help or it could hurt."

"I've thought of that. You're just pissed we're bringing in conventional soldiers to do a special ops job," Matt said.

"Not really. I'm glad we're going into Pakistan. Been needing to do it for a long time. Like you say, it will flush some of the bad guys. Plus we've got Dubai and Yemen we're still looking at.

"There's that."

They sat quietly.

"You gonna call her?"

"I think I'm going to call her and maybe just confuse her a little bit."

"Don't you think that'd be worse than just lying to her?"

"I'm trying to balance what we need to do to find Zach against her best interests. There's a middle ground somewhere. She's a smart girl, but she has been her mother's spy and personal suicide bomber for the last half of her life. These madrassas in Pakistan have nothing on the brainwashing techniques of her mother and grandmother."

"Sounds like a couple of real sweethearts. Now you know why I spend so much time over here fighting these bastards."

"Why's that?"

"It's easier than fighting a woman with sharp fangs and poison in her veins. Remember what Rod Stewart said? 'Next time I tell you I want to get married, just make me buy a house for a woman I hate and leave it at that.' Something like that."

Van Dreeves came barreling into the general's office holding a piece of paper in his hand. "Sir, we've got something. We had a walk-in. Reliability undetermined, but he claims an American serviceman is being held in a house in Asadabad in Kunar Province."

"Held?"

"Roger. A local family is protecting him. AQ has been negotiating to buy him back, but they refuse. This is Pashtun-Wali at its purest. The informant doesn't know how long it will last."

Pashtun-Wali was the code of honor and protection to which the Pashtun tribe adhered. Difficult for most Westerners to understand, the code was more powerful than law enforced by police and judges. Most of all, a Pashtun who is obligated with the protection of someone who has helped the tribe will defend him to the death.

"Let's get some eyes on this place and get a plan together. I don't want to miss this time." Rampert's orders were clear.

Van Dreeves moved quickly into the adjacent operations center to begin to steer the Predator to the location they had been provided. Matt wandered into the operations center, which was now buzzing with activity. Hobart was at the map plotting with a compass and pencil. Even Eversoll was repacking his rucksack, conducting pre-combat inspections of his gear.

Matt walked up to the large map that covered practically the entire wall. With his finger, he traced the Kunar River from the Pakistan border south where it wound its way to the populated town of Asadabad. They had been right. It was him.

Zach was alive.

"And here," Van Dreeves said. "I found the group of enemy we fought on the raid to get Colonel Garrett."

Matt and Rampert watched the Predator feed zoom in on a group of about twenty fighters, plus what looked like some locals with picks and shovels.

"They took the Thorium bait. That's the exact location of the primary Thorium mine on the bogus map we planted on the flash drive."

"They're going into the mine," Van Dreeves said.

"What do we have flying?"

"A B-1, two A-10s and the Predator."

"Put a JDAM on the mouth of the mine once they're all in there," Matt said.

Rampert looked at him. "They're some villagers in that crowd."

"They know what they're doing, General."

"Last man is in the mine," Van Dreeves called.

"Put the biggest thing you got on it, then drop whatever the A-10s have in there, put a hellfire from the Predator on top, and then have some troops go check it out to make sure."

"You're not messing around."

"If Rahman thought there was Thorium in there, he would have sent his A-Team. It's time to close the mine and attack into Pakistan."

"Shit, I'm getting a woodie," Van Dreeves said.

"Save it for the sheep, VD. Just order the strike," Matt said. "General?"

"Do it."

Five minutes later, the B-1 had repositioned and punched in the geo-location of the mine. He gave instructions as Matt had articulated.

A few minutes later, the front hillock that formed the mouth of the mine exploded, whiting out the screen until the dust settled and then the A-10s put 500 pound bombs a bit deeper into the mine.

"No need to waste the hellfire. Save it for squirters if there are any," Matt said.

"Ain't nothing squirting out of that," Van Dreeves said.

"This is how we win," Matt said and then walked out of the command center.

CHAPTER 53
SPARTANBURG, SOUTH CAROLINA

TUESDAY EVENING (EASTERN TIME)

Having completed the layout for the magazine, Amanda had rushed from
the high school back to her home. As she pulled into her driveway, she saw
Brianna Simpson through the windshield of her car standing on her front
porch talking, rather arguing, with her mother. Amanda lowered her window to listen, but she was still too far away.

As they noticed her pulling in, Brianna raced from the porch through
the front yard. She did not acknowledge Amanda as she climbed into her
mother's old VW bug.

Amanda jumped from her seat, only to watch Brianna speed away. She
stood there for a moment, looking over the top of her Mercedes at the
empty front porch. She was pretty sure it was her mother, but it could have
been Nina, who had been talking to Brianna. Sometimes it was hard to tell
them apart. She wasn't certain if her grandmother looked young or her
mother looked old.

Determining that she would catch up with Brianna later, she refocused,
feeling energized now. She had taken Harlan's *Charlotte Observer* and now
she glanced at the article trashing her father, sitting face up in the passenger
seat. Somehow, it motivated her. She had begun to crack the puzzle.

And she was juiced.

She bounded up the steps and plugged her charger into her cell phone,
laying it on her nightstand. She stretched, raising her arms and bowing her

back like a cat might.

She sat on her bed and thought for a moment. The best way she could describe what was happening was that two parallel universes were colliding with utter force. In the past, it had been no big deal. Her mother's universe—which she now understood to be comprised of deception and lies—had always dwarfed whatever straightforward purpose her father would come bearing.

Those collisions often produced sparks and tension well beyond the average human interaction. And through all of her observations, Amanda was coming to the conclusion that both her mother and grandmother enjoyed the manipulations and the mind games. It was as if Lake Moultrie's dirty secrets and poisonous ethos had found better packaging and marketing up here in Spartanburg. Thus, in Amanda's young view, simple and straightforward had always lost out to manipulative and ill-purposed. Hell, that had been the pattern of her life.

How could so many good memories just fade away, as if they had never existed at all? What secrets of power did her mother and Nina know that others did not? They always seemed to be getting their way. Were people really just means to whatever ends you sought, she wondered?

She pulled the thumb drive out of her backpack and plugged it into the computer. After a series of commands, she finished storing all of the digital media inside her computer and then looked at the thumb drive. It had a long lace that was intended to be used as a lanyard so she could carry the portable drive around her neck without fear of losing it.

She laced the cord around her neck, pulling her hair back to allow the necklace to rest against her skin. She opened the file on her computer and clicked on the "Grandmother Letters" file that her father had created. There were only a few documents in the file, all of which had been scanned. She opened the first one, marked, "The Beginning."

". . . instead of divorcing Zach right away, you should get pregnant first. A baby will provide you with a steady source of income and will be more influential with a judge when you finally do leave him. You'll get child support for at least eighteen years and a kid will give you a better shot at getting alimony for life."

Shaking her head slowly and whispering to herself, she skipped to the next letter labeled Divorce.

". . . I'm not sure what you are waiting for. It's about time you divorced Zach and moved back to South Carolina. I'm tired of you moving around and am ready for you to be home. When you file, make sure to be as aggressive as possible: kick him out of the house, antagonize him with the hopes that he hits you, try to get a neighbor to stand up for you. Your main thing should be to threaten his career. Once you do that, he will probably give you anything you want.

"Break your locks, hide some valuables and call the police. Make sure when you do this that he has no one who can account for his time. You will need to make four or five charges against him for one or two to stick. That has been my experience. If he doesn't respond to that immediately, then think about how you can say he 'does' stuff to Amanda. She's only three and is easily influenced to say whatever you want her to say, though she is very close with Zach, and you will need to be careful there. You may need to do some prep work yourself if you choose to use this scare method.

"Remember, Amanda is your ace in the hole; prepare to use it at the right time.

"Love, Nina."

Amanda leaned back in her chair and sighed with such force that her breath blew her bangs up, separating them. Her grandmother, the Wizard of Oz, she thought to herself, pulling the levers behind the scenes. Had her mother ever stood a chance?

After a moment of thinking, she determined that her mother did have a choice. She could have decided to ignore the long reach of Nina Hastings's icy fingers. Nina, it turned out, needed her mother and herself within her fold for her own selfish purposes. She figured that it wasn't so much the money as it was the love, the attention, and the avoidance of loneliness.

She felt nauseous. She pushed away from the desk, descended the steps and pushed through the front door just as the UPS man was preparing to knock.

"Perfect timing," he said. "Are you Amanda?"

"That's me."

"This box is for you. Just need you to sign right here." Amanda grabbed the pen, scribbled something that looked like a signature and retrieved the small box from his outstretched hand.

The man stood there for a second, as if he had another package.

Preparing to continue her quest for oxygen, she looked up at him, a young man in his mid to late twenties.

"Is there something else?"

He shuffled his feet a second and then said, "I'm sorry about your father. I served with him in the Airborne. He was a great man."

Amanda paused, then stepped toward him and wrapped her arms around his big shoulders. He hugged her back.

"Sorry," he said. "We've lost so many. I just never thought he would be one of them, you know?"

"Thank you. I really appreciate it. Please, never forget him."

"That, ma'am, would be impossible." He turned and walked back to his boxy brown truck, backed away, and waved good-bye.

Amanda motioned back with a slight wave of her hand. She walked down the steps and then onto the bench in the garden toward the end of the porch. The bench was a wrought-iron flowered design painted totally white. Set against the azaleas and dogwoods, it was a peaceful respite. Using her good fingernail, she sliced open the package, which was about the size of a cigar box.

Inside the clumsily wrapped package was thin wrapping paper balled up around a dirty Velcro wallet. Through the clear plastic cover she could plainly see her photo from several years ago. She was surprised by her reaction. She didn't cringe at the fact that she had no makeup on or that her hair was not highlighted. The angle of the camera had not even captured her good side. She didn't care.

This was clearly her father's wallet. She opened it and saw the Saint Michael's medal, silver and worn. She removed it from the pocket and held it between her fingers.

"Protect us," she whispered, and looked up into the sky. "Please?"

She saw a small note inside the wallet. Opening it, she read:

Amanda, This is your dad's. Never lose hope.

I'll be in touch.

Love, Uncle Matt.

She began crying uncontrollably. Hope? How can I lose something I don't have, she wanted to scream. She shook and bent over her knees, screaming voicelessly into the garden. For the first time she felt entirely alone. Fear was an invisible finger tracing up her spine to her neck, which began to constrict. Her breaths became rapid and shallow, the onset of panic. Guilt was a tightening noose around her throat.

Forgive me. Please.

CHAPTER 54
AFGHANISTAN

WEDNESDAY MORNING (HOURS OF DARKNESS)

Colonel Garrett's mind drifted into and out of consciousness as if he were looking through a dusty Coke bottle from the inside. Distorted shapes and sounds formed around him. He registered a shadow bending over him, then pulling away. Something was touching him; he wasn't sure what. Voices were sometimes loud, other times soft, and frequently absent altogether.

His hands and legs did not appear to be bound, but it was a passing thought. He was uncertain of his status. Dead or alive? Captured or free? The energy it required simply to think about it drained him. His mind began to swoon again. It occurred to him that he may have been drugged. Lightheaded and peaceful, he succumbed to the welcoming respite.

His mind played on themes from his youth, with Matt and Karen on the farm, and the happy times with Melanie and Amanda and Riley. They were a welcome distraction from the pain and fatigue his body was suffering on the cold, hard ground.

He awoke to the sound of metal sliding along the dusty floor.

"Eat."

Having no motor control over his limbs, he couldn't move his body to perform the simple task of nourishing himself. His body was aching for energy, yet he was unable to translate the urge into action.

Soon he found his mouth being stuffed with something. It was some type of meat, which he readily devoured. He gnawed at the rubbery substance and swallowed. His mind registered that it might be lamb. At least he hoped that was the case. More of the meat came and was followed by a tin cup to his lips. He drank the water like a man with a mouthful of anesthesia after a day of dental work, the liquid spilling across his face.

The apparition vanished as soon as its feeding chore was done. He found a soft spot on the blanket for his head and rested again, his mind swimming and taking him back to an even less pleasant time.

Zach was about to deploy to the Philippines; 9-11 was still a fresh wound, and he had rapidly signed up for any mission that would get him into the fight. Like many soldiers, he knew combat and its difficulties, but he also knew that the country and its soldiers needed the best leadership it could muster to win this war against the nation's enemies.

Amanda had been ten at the time, and he had called Melanie to orchestrate a visit prior to his departure overseas. Having driven the five hours from Fort Bragg to pick up his daughter, he had an uneasy feeling that something was amiss.

He had learned to expect the unexpected in almost all facets of life, but the one realm that continued to catch him off guard was the new tack that had begun with Amanda. It was part disbelief and part debilitating love. His mind could perceive, yet never understand, some of the actions that had taken place at the hands of Amanda's mother and grandmother. Yet, his heart refused to believe that anyone could be so cruel, especially to their own flesh and blood. Which was why he was continually surprised.

At the exit off I-85, he pulled into a RaceTrac gas station to get his wits about him. Normally he would call Amanda and chat the remaining fifteen minutes to the house. She had been distant on the first call and then had not answered his two subsequent attempts.

Driving always gave him time to think. Sometimes he would listen to a book on tape. Other times he would drone along, staring at the white passing stripes, and try to understand where it had all gone wrong.

His discussions with Riley had given him enough insight into the idea that a child who was once close with her father, if sufficiently manipulated by the mother, could develop a split personality, of sorts. Nothing clinical, she had told him, but the child would develop an outward ability to 'handle' the noncustodial parent—the father typically—while remaining loyal to the custodial parent, the mother in most cases. Further, Riley had pointed out, in a case like Amanda's, her pre-existing love for her father, though muted, was expressed in the form of not wanting to hurt him.

As he pulled up to the guard shack at the gated community on the outer reaches of Spartanburg, the guard stepped forward.

He rolled down his truck window and said, "Hi, I'm here to pick up Amanda Garrett, please."

The guard was a hefty female wearing a white shirt with a sewn-in patch that said "RONCO Security." She was a block of a woman, no shape or pattern to her. Her face was oval, and she looked mad at the world.

"Just a second," she muttered. Walking to the far side of the shack, she waved at someone. A uniformed police officer for the city of Spartanburg appeared while Zach was idling in his truck at the shack. The gate was a standard wooden arm with a cantilever that lifted the barrier when block woman pressed a button. He was trapped.

"Sorry to do this, Mr. Garrett, but I have a summons to issue you to appear in court next week."

This couldn't be happening. Then it occurred to him, of course, that this was the famous baited ambush. Amanda was the bait, and he was the target. The attack could not have been performed better by Sun Tzu himself. Naturally, he had to deploy in three days and could not appear in court the following week. He had no attorney and was only hoping to spend a couple of days, perhaps his last days ever, with his daughter before heading off to combat.

"Well, I'm heading overseas Monday, can't this wait?"

"I'm sorry, it can't. My orders are that I have to issue this to you if I can find you. And here you are."

Zach took the document and signed the police officer's paper on the wooden clipboard. He opened the document and began to read it, but block woman raised her voice. "Come on, buster, you're holding up traffic."

The arm lifted and his spirits sank, but he pushed forward anyway. He heard the woman mutter, "Deadbeat," as he was moving past the gate.

He pulled into the parking lot of the country club and did what not many Airborne Ranger captains would readily admit to—he cried. He processed the last three years of pain through his system, weeping at his own ignorance. But he grieved mostly for Amanda. He had failed her.

His overriding thought was that if Amanda's mother was capable of doing this to him at this time, what on earth had she been doing to Amanda?

He was horrified at the thought.

He rolled on the dusty floor again, still inside the Coke bottle, but somehow less so. Pain was coursing through his body as if along fiber-optic lines, unimpeded. He surmised he had been given some kind of painkiller earlier because presently he was awake and fully aware that he had some broken bones and serious lacerations.

He ran his tongue across dry, chapped lips that were cracked and bleeding. He felt the stubble of days of beard across his upper lip. Again he was surprised that he was not bound or gagged. Perhaps his captors understood his injuries to be so severe that he was immobile, which certainly seemed to be the case.

There was always the possibility that he was dead and simply hovering above his physical being prior to departing for eternal peace. He had so much unfinished business, though, with Amanda that he was skeptical of the notion. Plus, the sheer pain was an indication that he was still residing in the confines of his mortal tabernacle.

His focus shifted and he became alert as he heard voices. Hanging onto the prayer that all of this was worth something, he shuddered as he saw men with weapons come into the room.

CHAPTER 55
SPARTANBURG, SOUTH CAROLINA

TUESDAY EVENING (EASTERN TIME)

Nina's wrinkled hand separated the miniblinds so that she could see Amanda sitting in the garden crying.

She watched Amanda open a box and extract something from it, though she couldn't determine what the object might be. Her narrow eyes tried to squint in an effort to see better, but were unsuccessful because the Botox had frozen her face muscles in place.

Amanda's plight plucked no particular string in her heart other than to cause her to worry about the pending $500,000 in insurance money and whether the child might waffle on her commitment. Nina knew that she and Melanie could not close the deal on the mansion without the half million dollars. A child mourning her father was no big deal. A new house on the lake would soothe that wound, and soon there would be no memory, no pain.

And so as she watched Amanda in the garden, she felt no emotion whatsoever. Amanda's father might have been a decent guy. It didn't matter. With a soul as dry and dusty as a Kansas prairie, Nina Hastings had no sympathy.

The blinds flapped closed with a shattering sound as she turned and walked into her daughter's bedroom. "Melanie, I think you've got problems."

Melanie was staring in the mirror, applying the last touches of lipstick.

She smacked her lips and looked at her mother. "Nope, mama, we've got the Army coming over right now, and then the real estate agent is bringing the paperwork. Amanda told me she wanted to knock it all out today."

Though it didn't square with what she had just seen, Nina accepted it.

"You sure?" she replied curiously.

"What's not to be sure about? Her father's dead, his house burned down, her boyfriend's under house arrest, and her shrink's comatose in the hospital. What else could this be but the capitulation? She's got nowhere else to go."

"Well, something doesn't feel right."

Ever the skeptic, Nina walked from the room and answered the front door as the chimes rang.

The Army major and the chaplain entered. They produced the paperwork as pleasantries were exchanged.

"Amanda has to be the signatory on all of these documents," Major Blair said to the two women staring at him. "I hope you understand."

"They understand," Amanda called from behind the group. "Let's go into the dining room."

As the group began to move from the foyer into the dining room Amanda said, "Mom, Nina, I've got this."

The two women stopped briefly and then continued on.

"Amanda, you're not even eighteen. As your guardian, I need to ensure what you are doing is legal and proper," her mother said.

Amanda was unrelenting. "Major, is there somewhere else we can go?"

Major Blair stopped and replied, "Certainly."

"What are you doing, Amanda?" Nina inquired.

The five of them stood in a circle like a football huddle. Amanda was in the unfamiliar position of calling the plays. She was looking at the line of scrimmage, reading the defense, and calling an audible.

"Do we need the money or not?" Amanda asked. Neither her mother nor Nina responded. "If you can't trust me to do the right thing, then what good is any of this?" This play was a calculated risk, but in a sense she needed to be hiding in plain sight. "Besides, I've always trusted both of you."

After a long pause, Melanie said, "Okay, we'll be in the kitchen."

Amanda saw Nina snap her head toward her mother, uncharacteristically showing a hole card.

"Thank you."

Amanda sat at the dining room table facing the door opening to the kitchen. She motioned to the two Army officers, indicating for the tall and broad-shouldered Major Blair to sit across from her with his back to the door, to block their view. Major Blair reached into his briefcase as he was sitting.

"Just sign right here, Amanda," he said, pointing at the two documents he spread on the table. He only made his comment once, though. He looked at her as he did so.

She nodded in recognition. Harlan had mentioned the other document would be presented to her. She quickly signed her name to both documents. The chaplain leaned over from the head of the table with a notary stamp and pressed the seal into each signed document. Then the major and chaplain signed as witnesses.

The major smiled at her and nodded, then grabbed her hand with both of his. "It's going to be fine."

"I pray that it is."

He started collecting all of the paperwork, saying, in a voice calculated to carry, "I know it's getting close to supper time, so let me get these copies to you in a couple of days."

Standing, Amanda said, "That's fine." She noticed her mother and grandmother returning from the kitchen.

Amanda walked the two officers to the door and bid them farewell.

"You didn't even get to keep a copy?" Nina squawked.

"They'll get it to us," Amanda said. "I'm just so glad it's over, you know?"

She continued to stare through the open front door as the men drove away.

As Amanda closed the door, she noticed a Lexus SUV pull into the driveway. Not recognizing the vehicle, she turned to her mother, who was standing behind her and announced, "I think you have company."

Her mother stepped onto the porch and waved hello to Tad Johnson, her real estate agent. Tad climbed the steps with an accordion folder tucked under his arm. Melanie introduced him to Amanda and Nina.

"Let's have a seat," she said.

They discussed the asking price of the mansion. One point four million dollars.

"I thought it was one point two million," Melanie said.

"There's another offer coming," Tad replied. "It's for one point three. The owners said they'll sell it to you for one point four if you decide today and close by Wednesday."

Melanie leaned back in her chair, despondent.

"It's okay, Mama," Amanda said, reaching out to her mother. "I just signed away the entire five hundred thousand, and I think with this house sold you've still got the money." Amanda chose her words carefully as she spoke.

"Well, we've only got two hundred thousand in equity in this house. I think Mama's talking about providing two hundred thousand."

"All I've got," Nina Hastings muttered.

"Yes, but it's still a four hundred and seventy thousand dollar mortgage. At these rates it's going to be about three thousand a month in mortgage payments."

"Well, maybe I can get a job, you know, instead of going to college right away. That would help, wouldn't it?" After making them go into the kitchen while she signed the insurance paperwork, she needed to reel them back in quickly. Forgoing her college career for her mother and grandmother was an indicator she was willing to sacrifice for them.

Nina and Melanie exchanged glances. If nothing else, it told Amanda that she was back in the fold. They trusted her. She felt the constant allure of their twisted affection. Much like battered women return to an abusive husband, Amanda could sense the ease with which she might come back to the only thing she knew, submissive capitulation to the whims of her matriarch. She struggled with these feelings as she objectively tried to set the conditions for her plan.

"I think we can work something out," Melanie said, triumphantly.

"Okay, well, let's sign the paperwork and get an earnest check. They need one hundred thousand dollars by tomorrow," Tad thumped cheerfully.

Melanie pondered the thought, looked at her mother and then turned to Amanda.

"How soon did those Army guys say you can get that money?"

"It won't be tomorrow," Amanda responded. "You probably want to close on the house first."

"This is all happening so fast." Melanie leaned back in her chair again.

Tad, ever the salesman and smelling 3 percent of $1.4 million, quickly summarized. "The nature of this market, Melanie, is that you either act immediately or not at all. I had two houses sell yesterday in the same neighborhood. One went for 1.7 million and the other for 2.5 million. This market is sizzling. In a year you can probably turn around and sell this house for anywhere from a five hundred thousand to one million dollar gain. It's a no-brainer. We're doing these quick closings all the time. Banks prefer them, actually. Saves all the hassle. I can have an inspector at the house tomorrow. He'll give you a punch list that we attach to the contract, and you've got a fail safe.

"I do have to advise you that this sale is final. There is a clause on the contract, as all of them are stating nowadays, that affirms the contract. It is not revocable once you sign. Both homes I sold yesterday were the same way. So there's no way that your buyers can back out and leave you hanging. We can get all the paperwork done in less than three days, and then it's up to you to get the movers rolling you into your dream home. That house is a gold mine." Perry Mason had never made a better closing argument.

"Please, Mom? Can we just do this before any of us changes our minds?" Amanda's emerald eyes were pleading as she leaned forward and placed her hand on her mother's arm.

Tad leaned back in his chair, letting Amanda do the work. A good salesman, as Tad was, knew that when a family member began to do his job, rule number one was to not get in the way.

"It's a lot of money for a house," Nina chirped. "But if we can make some money on it, I'm in. Amanda will probably have to work, though. Are you sure you want that?" She was talking to both Melanie and Amanda, eyeing each of them with her blackened marbles.

"It's just a year, Mom. It would be so cool for all of us to live up there." Again with the pleading emeralds. She had known coming into this discussion that she would need to be the counterpoint to every obstacle Nina established.

"Okay," she sighed, leaning forward. "I must be crazy, but where do I sign?"

Tad produced the paperwork quicker than David Copperfield could pull a rabbit from his hat. As Melanie was reading, he went back into his closer role.

"Now, Melanie, if you or Nina have a checkbook handy, I can take the down payment check tonight. We can get a day's head start on this."

After an uncomfortable pause, Nina uncharacteristically came forward and remarked, "I've got a checkbook. Let me write it, and we can just get this over with. If it keeps Amanda here another year, well, then it's worth a hundred thousand."

"A hundred and forty thousand," Melanie corrected.

"Whatever, once you get over five thousand I lose track. Why don't you go get us some water, Melanie?"

Needing a quick break, Melanie walked into the kitchen. As she returned, her mother was handing Tad the check. He folded the parchment and placed it in his shirt pocket.

"Again, this document," Tad joined in as he watched Melanie sit and lift the pen, "is irrevocable once you sign it. The house becomes yours."

Amanda watched with satisfaction as her mother closed her eyes and signed, the sharp edge of the Mont Blanc cartridge pen sounding like a scratching claw.

CHAPTER 56
KUNAR PROVINCE, AFGHANISTAN

WEDNESDAY EVENING

Matt felt the MH-47 helicopter settle onto the rocky landing zone along the Kunar River in the province that bore the same name. Asadabad was a waypoint along this ancient trading route at the mouth of the Hindu Kush Mountains. To the west and north, spires of granite angled upward, touching altitudes of fifteen thousand feet like randomly constructed temples of nature. Here, shepherds and traders could lay tithe or prayer. Certainly such raw beauty and perfection must have been personally carved by God. As if to counter the point, jagged edges jutted upward and outward from sheer cliffs. Boulders and slabs of rock crouched menacingly in the crevices, ready to avalanche on call as if evil was prepared to offset the cleansing power so clearly resident in these mountains.

Exiting through a sandy dust field created by the whirring dual blades of the MH-47, behind Matt were Major General Jack Rampert, Van Dreeves, Hobart, and Sergeant Eversoll. They all ducked and then took a knee, waiting for the whirling dervish to lift away and in its wake leave behind an alternate form of solitude. The utterly chaotic, but controlled noise of the hulking machine was dominant. Its giant rotors spun against one another, creating the lift necessary to carry forty-thousand pounds of machine, people, and cargo. Instantly this chaos was replaced by the sounds of the wind through the temple spires above. On the valley floor, the insertion team was only at five thousand feet above sea level; the abrupt rise of the mountains seemed all the more stark and aggressive.

Rampert looked at Matt and pulled out his map. "We're right here, about two miles from the village. I think our preplanned route is a good one. There's enemy in between us and Zach, but we've got a Predator flying overhead and an AC-130 as long as we've got the cover of darkness."

A thin gray film of light was evident from the west, but fading rapidly. End of evening nautical twilight, which occurred well after sunset, was nearly complete and here in the shadows of the Hindu Kush, it was all but gone. Slices of gray hovered around the mountaintops like windward clouds on an ocean island, held in place as if snagged, and providing no light on the landing zone.

"Moon will be up in a couple of hours, so I suggest we get moving. You know we're being watched." Matt talked in a low whisper as he tugged at a knee-pad, repositioning the device to place the hard-shell surface between his kneecap and the rocky ground.

They stood in unison, Sergeant Eversoll taking point. Through his night-vision goggles, Matt saw Eversoll's hand rotate a few times and then point to the north, toward Asadabad.

They followed in single file down a steep draw and then found a decent trail that paralleled the river. Matt could hear the rumble of the water as it shot through rapids and rushed over steep drop-offs. They were maybe fifty meters from the river on its west side. He thought of Bernouli's equation, the old math formula that described volume as it moved through a constricted space and how its acceleration increased the smaller the space became. Force equals mass times acceleration, he thought to himself. The impulse momentum that resulted from applied force and constrained space was captured in the velocity of the current as the river narrowed against rocky intrusions. Why these thoughts on the properties of physics were coming forward now, he wasn't sure. Perhaps he needed grounding in reality, in facts and equations, prior to rescuing his brother. Such thoughts may keep in check the blossoming hope that always accompanied, and clouded, such missions. *Momentum*, he thought to himself. *We have the momentum.*

AFTER AN HOUR of walking they had reached the outskirts of a small village. They took a knee behind a mud wall that was certainly part of some family's *qalat*, or walled-in compound. Rampert and Matt huddled while the other three faced outward, providing security against detection or enemy fire. While the town of Asadabad was largely pro-government, and supported the Coalition Forces that were fighting the terrorists resident in their country, the metropolis was infested with indigenous scouts, some armed, some not. These zephyrs provided early warning to the enemy that typically enjoyed sanctuary in the upper reaches of the villages where backdoors led to escape routes into impossibly difficult terrain.

"The GPS shows we are less than two hundred meters from the grid coordinates for the target compound." Rampert spoke in hushed tones, his voice barely audible.

"Soft knock or hard knock?" Matt's question was one they had discussed earlier. Did they quite literally knock on the door and wait to be invited in? Or did they breach the door with explosives or by a well-practiced battle drill?

"The guide should be here any moment. That orchard over there next to the river is our line-up point." Rampert pointed at a grove of fig trees that was barely noticeable in the blackness. The moon was cresting above the eastern mountain range, whose massif ran parallel to the north-south flowing Kunar and whose peaks were the meaningless indicator of the Pakistan-Afghanistan border. "The issue is that AQ are here, too. They know he's being protected, but the village elder refuses to give him up. Pashtun-wali. I give it a few more hours before they decide to take him by force."

In the scant moonlight Matt saw a figure emerge from the fig orchard, as if on cue. The man walked toward them holding his hands high so that the Special Forces team could see that he was unarmed.

"Do you have any figs for us?" Matt asked in Pashto.

"I have only one fig." The man knelt down and held out a small fig in his right hand, completing the bona fides and confirming he was the contact.

"This way," the man said as he led them toward the front of the compound. "He is inside."

CHAPTER 57
KUNAR PROVINCE, AFGHANISTAN

WEDNESDAY EVENING

Zach Garrett figured his time had come. He had been bewildered by the fact that his hands had not been shackled nor his feet bound—bewildered, but nonetheless grateful. He was equally mystified by the apparent care that he was receiving in captivity. The armed men had brought him food, real food. Lamb and rice. He had eaten ravenously. They'd given him water and nursed his wounds.

He had awakened this evening with two insistent thoughts competing for his attention, like children tugging at his leg. The first siren in his mind was that he had to escape, and now. Despite the seemingly good care he was receiving, he could reasonably conclude it would not continue. Even more, he determined that they, the enemy, were either fattening him up for a television or video appearance or perhaps an International Red Cross visitor to confirm his prisoner of war status.

The second alarm ringing in his mind was that Amanda was in trouble. He didn't know why or how, but he could sense her distress the same way an animal tastes distant fear. His dreams had been vivid and true. She was perhaps not calling out to him so much as she needed him. Nine time zones away, he could sense the chaos awakening in her life again. She needed him, and that was all the motivation he required.

The two instincts were intricately linked, of course. He needed to escape in order to get back to Amanda.

With that thought, he slowly stood. His left leg screamed with the sharp pain of a break in his lower calf area, probably the fibula. He was able to sustain some weight on the leg, especially if he leaned inward. The fibula was designed to protect its larger mate in the lower leg, the tibia. He determined that with some effort, he would be able to endure the pain. He steadied himself against the wall.

He noticed a rectangular section of dim light beaming onto the floor. He followed the ray to a high window that he surmised to be about two feet wide in both directions. Reaching with his hand, he took hold of the ledge and pulled himself upward. His ribs—broken, he was sure—came alive with searing heat. Despite the pain, he was able to lift his good leg onto the ledge and work his body into the sill. Moving with more deliberation now, he slowly pulled his left leg through the opening so that both legs were suspended outside of the home. Again his ribs hurt, as they rubbed against the outer ledge of the window, the pain nearly unbearable. He looked beneath his feet as he dangled a few feet off the ground. If someone were to happen upon him now, they might just as easily consider that he was breaking into the home as he was fleeing.

He let go and dropped mercifully onto his good leg, a one-legged parachute landing fall, which you are never supposed to do, he reminded himself. Nevertheless, he had absorbed the fall with no consequence.

Immediately he was leaning against the wall, calculating his surroundings. The moon was rising above the mountains in the east. His last memory outside of this building was that of falling into the river. Now he could hear the whisper of the rapids in the distance that perhaps carried him to safety or had nearly drowned him. It all depended on how he considered his fate. In life there was always such a thin margin between luck and skill, winning and losing, good and evil, redeemer and taker.

As he moved toward the gate in the high mud wall, he felt the sharp sting of the broken fibula with each abbreviated step of his left leg. It was as if someone struck the same spot on his leg with a ball-peen hammer the moment pressure was applied. Once he passed through the gate, he noticed a fig orchard to his right, toward the river. Outside the high walls of the compound, the river spoke more loudly. He felt its presence—perhaps calling him or maybe warning him, he was not sure.

He limped between two rows of fig trees, wanting to move as quickly away from his previous confines as possible.

Now the river roared with life. The sound of the water's rush dominated his environment. Loud and overwhelming, the water actually appeared less menacing than it sounded. He stood awkwardly upon the bank, fig orchard to his back, rising moon to his front.

The boat lying on its side in the rocks looked like a wooden canoe. Poplar or ash planks ran horizontally like a tongue-in-groove hardwood floor held together by black resin or henna along the seams. This gift that appeared at his feet seemed Heaven sent, and he was thankful. Carefully, he edged his way onto the rocky bank. His left leg was unable to negotiate the loose stones as well as he'd hoped. He slipped once, which caused a brief loss of breath as his ribs pinched him like a vise. Positioning himself behind the canoe, he was able to pull it into the water about a third of the distance.

Suddenly, the boat began to spin, sucked into the raging current. Out of position, he had to leap from his left leg into the boat, banging the injured bone against the lip of the rail as he slipped into the now-speeding craft.

Nursing his leg momentarily, he grabbed the one oar that had been positioned in the vessel and began a futile effort of attempting to steer. He remembered Riley's Thomas Cole painting and thought that he was most certainly entering raging waters to an unknown destination with little more than a makeshift paddle. He was essentially without ability to govern his speed or direction. A better allegory to Cole's idea, he had not seen.

So, with little ability to assist in the process of steering through the rapids, he used the paddle as a crutch as he knelt. While upright, he spread his arms wide as if he were a preacher in the pulpit and screamed his daughter's name against the thunderous and omnipotent roar of the river.

"Amanda!"

He desperately wanted her to know that he would not let her down this time.

Wisely, he lowered himself into the vessel as it went churning through the narrow defiles. After several minutes of scrambling through rapids, he felt something strike the craft. These sensations were followed by barely audible sounds above the din of the water. A few more of these sensations followed. He felt splintering chips of wood strike his face.

As he recognized what was happening, he noticed the water appeared to pool to his front, perhaps slowing as the banks widened. Jagged mountains on either side of the river reached into the black night with sharp triangular peaks still capped with snow.

He came to his knees as the boat slowed. Though it was too late, his mind was screaming at him to hide below the upper rim of the canoe. His tactician's mind had reengaged and realized that the slow water and the high cliffs were the perfect ambush location.

The fusillade of machine-gun fire tearing through the night air, popping above his head and into the swirling water, came from both sides. The sounds were now more audible as he emerged from the rapids.

He dove into the water to his left and held his breath for almost a minute. He counted the seconds as he used to do as a child so that he would know how far he could go without breathing. Ninety seconds had been his record.

Approaching that number he realized that his right arm was stinging with pain, feeling for the moment much worse than the broken leg.

Ninety seconds passed, and he knew that he was going to have to surface. He prayed he was far enough away from the canoe to avoid detection while still being able to get back to it if necessary.

He floated toward the surface, pressing his face against the meniscus of the water. As his mouth and nose protruded, he could see the stars, bright pinpricks in the black curtain of night. He noticed some of the towering peaks on either side of the river as if through a thin layer of film.

Another gulp of air, and he was back under. As he allowed his body to drift with the flow of the water downstream, he wondered why the ambush had been established at that location. Further, he wondered why they would randomly shoot at him.

The U.S. forces operated under the notion of positive identification, meaning before shooting at someone the soldier had to determine hostile intent and make sure that collateral damage would be minimized if not eliminated.

Clearly, the enemy operated under no such limitation.

Strangely, he had drifted back to the boat as he came up for a second breath of air and nearly impaled his face on the stern. He reached up with his left arm and held onto the rim and then floated.

His world began to fade as weakness overcame him. He was cold. His mind spiraled, registering that there were several places on his body that hurt worse than his broken leg.

CHAPTER 58
SPARTANBURG, SOUTH CAROLINA

WEDNESDAY MORNING (EASTERN TIME)

Amanda awoke with the single-minded purpose of talking to the one man she felt she could trust aside from Jake. While talking to Riley Dwyer had been helpful, she needed an objective, neutral opinion. After all, Riley was an advocate of her father. And Jake's parents had kindly asked her to refrain from talking to him until the legal matters were resolved. So that left Mr. Dagus. She decided to approach him. At school, though, she was informed that he had taken the day off.

Instead, she spent the day cleaning out her locker and school supplies. She accepted a few sympathy greetings from friends and then went home. She was thankful, too, that she had not seen Rugsdale today. He was beginning to creep her out. Coming and going, she had not seen his car in the parking lot.

The day seemed to pass quickly as she loaded her things into her car. As she looked at the growing pile in her backseat, she wondered how the heck all of that had fit into the skinny wall locker. There were five sets of swim goggles she had forgotten about.

As she arrived back home, she caught her mother in the driveway returning from work. She was dressed in a taupe pantsuit with a silk white blouse. Not her best color, but Amanda remembered her saying something about seeing a "conservative" client today.

"Hey, Mom." She saw her mother wait for her to park. She was growing anxious and wished to avoid a conversation with her mother. At the same time, she didn't want to alarm her either.

"How was school? Getting wrapped up?"

"Good. You know, just cleaning things out. I wanted to talk to Mr. Dagus today, but he wasn't in." They walked onto the porch together.

"About what?"

"You know, stuff. Sometimes it just helps me to talk to him."

"Well, just give him a call, why don't you? Or maybe talk to Gus, if you're looking for a man's opinion."

Amanda looked at her mother. Why was she suddenly being reasonable? "Okay. I might do that."

"They're both pretty level-headed about things."

She was right about that.

"By the way, have you seen him today?" her mother asked.

"Gus? Not my day to keep up with him. Why?"

"We were supposed to have lunch. I called his office at the magazine, and they said he wasn't in. Strange."

"Ain't seen him."

As the day wore on, Amanda became more anxious. A feeling of intense loneliness encapsulated her. She was emotionally isolated. While she was deciding what to do, she ate a quick dinner of frozen pizza and diet Coke and then spent an hour in her room. She made a couple of phone calls to Dagus, but to no avail. She thought about calling Jake, but decided to respect his parents' request. She liked them and didn't want to lose their trust.

Finally, growing impatient, she jumped into her car and drove toward the town of Alpharetta. She had been to Dagus's house twice before for journalism class parties, which he held annually. Her nerves were overwhelming her. They were moving into a million-dollar house. Her life as she knew it was a charade. Finally, loneliness gave way to fear.

She called his home phone twice more, but both times got the answering machine. Undeterred, she pressed on, taking all the shortcuts she knew. She whipped through residential neighborhoods, rolled through stop signs and generally broke every driving law in the code.

She found a parking spot about four houses down from Dagus's town-house, which was an end unit. She walked through the mild night air toward the home with a brick veneer Victorian elevation. It was a bit too Norman Bates-ish for her; nonetheless, she remembered from the journalism parties that it was a spacious home. She pressed the dimly lit button and listened to the chime.

She rang it again.

She crossed her arms as if to hug herself, wondering if Norman was peering down on her from the third-floor dormer. But then she found herself ignoring that notion and nearly praying that she would hear the telltale sound of footsteps moving in the house.

One more ring.

Nothing.

Please, please, I need to talk to you.

Chewing on her fingernail, she remembered that his backyard was easily accessible from the street. He had a screened porch where she might be able to wait.

She opened the back gate by reaching over the picket fence and lifting the latch. As if she lived there, she continued with purpose toward the porch. This time, luck was on her side. It was unlocked. She went inside and walked deliberately past the hunter-green patio furniture and a few sprawling palms toward the back door to the house. She knocked several times, each time calling out, "Mr. Dagus?"

She checked the doorknob out of curiosity. Fortune failed her this time, as the door was locked, but a moment later she was back outside kneeling in the garden where the fake rock with the key was located. She had seen Dagus open the house using this key when, during the backyard party, someone using the restroom had accidentally locked them out. He had vowed in front of her to find a new hiding spot, but old habits were apparently hard to break.

"I must be crazy," she whispered to herself. She extracted the key, unlocked the door, replaced the key in the rock, returned the rock to its garden spot, and then entered the house. She moved in fluid motions so that her courage could not wane with inaction.

She stood in the dark kitchen for a few moments gaining acuity.

"Mr. Dagus?"

Her voice echoed eerily.

"Mr. Dagus!" This time louder. She didn't know why she was suddenly frightened.

She remembered her father had always taught her to remain motionless for a short while when she was entering an animal's domain. *Listen, watch, get your senses on a par with the animal. In the forest, you are in their living room. They probably know when you're there, so get your instincts in tune with them.*

She was about to be, literally, in Dagus's living room. She jumped as she felt her cell phone vibrate in her pocket. Lifting it, she saw that it was Dagus's cell phone number.

"Amanda, it's Len Dagus. I see you called a few times. What's up?"

She felt a huge sigh of relief and physically sagged, leaning against the kitchen counter. "I'm at your house, actually. Outside," she lied. "I just needed to talk."

His pause made her feel as though she had been too collegial with him. He was, after all, still a teacher.

"Okay, I can't be there for an hour, but if you can hang around, I'm happy to listen. I'm sort of pursuing something here."

"Okay, I can hang."

"Listen. If you remember where the key is in the back, just use it and let yourself in. Turn on the tube and make yourself at home."

Well, actually . . .

"I think I can find it. Out back by the screen porch, right?"

"That's it. Make yourself at home. Just relax."

"You're awesome, Mr. Dagus."

"Don't mention it. As Shakespeare had Claudio say, 'Friendship is constant in all things. . . .'"

CHAPTER 59
SPARTANBURG, SOUTH CAROLINA

WEDNESDAY EVENING (EASTERN TIME)

She hung up the phone and swallowed hard. ". . . save in the office and affairs of love," she murmured, recalling the quote from *Much Ado About Nothing.*

She stood still in the kitchen. Why did she hesitate? Her instincts were telling her to leave. Yet, she stood fast. She trusted this man as much as any other, save Jake.

She took a tentative step. Another step, she was passing the kitchen island now, and moving into the dining room to her right. The dining room had a dark wood table with a matching hutch and buffet. She peeked around the corner into the living room, which connected on the far side, and saw a sofa, plasma television, and two chairs. A coffee-table and end tables were situated between the sofa and the fireplace. She backed out of there and retraced her route through the dining room, into the kitchen, and then into the foyer hallway that led to the front door. Still, no lights were on anywhere on the bottom floor, and she thought to compliment Dagus on his energy-conservation measures.

From the foyer, she noticed a light blue light flickering at the top of the stairs. She heard voices from the second floor.

"Mr. Dagus?"

She placed her hand lightly on the oak banister that guarded the stairway, and began ascending toward the upper floor. She stopped when she heard a scratching sound that sounded like it might be coming from a window to her rear, perhaps the front door. Frozen, she checked over her shoulder to determine whether she was high enough that someone could not look in the small windows on either side of the door. To be sure, she moved two steps higher, silently. Again, she waited, her instincts sharpening and pulling in the specific sounds of this lion's den. A scratch here, a creak there; what did they mean? House noises, she comforted herself, and continued up.

The voices grew louder as she crested the last step. To her immediate right on the landing was a closed door. To her left front was an open door to the bathroom. To the left were two doors, both open. Okay, she thought, master bedroom on the right, guest bedroom and computer room to the far left. She looked into the computer room, where the blue light was shining.

She could see the large plasma computer screen emanating its blue background. She noticed a media player was playing a continuous loop of Lenard Dagus appearing on CNN discussing the need for verifiable sources.

". . . but don't you think that would unnecessarily restrict journalists in pursuing the truth?" A blonde-haired reporter was seated on a barstool in a CNN studio asking him questions. He was sitting across from her on a matching stool and wearing a button-down polo shirt open at the neck with his sleeves rolled up just beneath his elbow. It was a classic reporter's pose she guessed he was attempting to emulate. She could see the dark hair on his arms and even some on his chest protruding at the V in the neck.

"No. What has been proven is that verified sources provide the most accurate and compelling stories. It is when you don't hold journalists accountable that we get into trouble. Just look at—"

She reached up with her hand and paused the media player, which served to mute the voices and freeze Dagus' image on the screen. She had heard it all before.

Then she stopped as a detail that had been nagging at her suddenly resurfaced. She quickly maximized the screen again, focusing on the hair. She thought back to running into him as she had fled the classroom, embarrassed over Jake's confinement. His chest had been bare, and his arms. Not a single hair, for the first time since she had known him. What she had assumed was bad sunburn, though she had never seen him with it before . . .

She could barely believe that she was thinking it—but were these signs of a badly managed arson job?

Has Dagus been following me? Dad's house? Riley? She placed her hand to her mouth, holding back a scream. Her first instinct was to run.

She minimized the YouTube display again, irrationally believing that if she hid the image the reality would also vanish.

As she minimized the window, his Comcast homepage began blinking at her with scrolling images of the day's latest news, each accompanied by a photo of some sort: *Julia Roberts Gets More Collagen . . . Brangelina have another child . . . Stock market bubble again? . . . Colonel in Afghanistan leaves dubious legacy . . . President vows to remove troops from Iraq . . .*

Grabbing the mouse, she scrolled back to the Afghanistan story, fear already boiling in her stomach. She looked over her shoulder as she clicked on the link to the article.

The Web site appeared along with a full facial photo of her father looking very handsome. His hair was cropped closely to the sides of his scalp while a thick tuft was present on top. He looked simultaneously mean and compassionate, with deep-set green eyes, high cheekbones, and an unsmiling face. But the eyes, she thought, they were hers. Or hers were his. It didn't matter. And with those eyes staring at her, she heard his voice. It was a whisper creasing the stagnant air of the house. *It's okay, baby girl. Just follow your instincts. I'm so proud of you.*

That's all she had ever wanted, she thought to herself, her father's pride. "I love you, Daddy," she whispered aloud, then refocused on her new mission.

Her mind was moving quickly now. She forged ahead. If Dagus was the one responsible for the horrible events of the last week, then surely there would be evidence on his computer. An hour. He had said he would be there in an hour. Looking at her watch, she figured ten minutes had already passed.

She rapidly went to work opening his My Documents folder and began scanning the subfolders. There were several marked Journalism 101—2006, 2007, 2008, 2009, and so on. She opened the 2010 folder and scanned the documents, recognizing all of the homework assignments. Ruling out the remainder, she continued scrolling through the subfolders: Assignments, Bill's Wedding, Bank Information, DD, MediaHunt, PTA, Dagus Family, Videos. There were the usual program files mixed in, but she locked onto MediaHunt. Knowing about Dagus' extracurricular watchdog group, Amanda wondered, *what might be in there?*

As she opened the subfolder, she saw several other subfolders, including one labeled CO. *Charlotte Observer?* The same paper that had originally printed the story about her father. She clicked on the subfolder, which showed several JPEG images listed. Clicking on one, she saw an article written and published in the *Charlotte Observer* two years ago about the musical *Les Miserables*, the headline claiming it to be passé. The byline, though, was more interesting to her. Del Dangurs. She clicked on another icon, again a musical review, this time *Miss Saigon*, again by Del Dangurs. She continued clicking, hoping that maybe he had collected all of these articles from Del Dangurs. Maybe he was a personal fan of the writer or perhaps he liked the shows or the reviews.

She skipped ahead to the DD subfolder. Here she found more portable document files of articles written by Del Dangurs. As she scrolled through the documents, she lighted upon one marked Garrett, with a date of three days ago.

"Unbelievable," she muttered. She clicked on the icon and up popped the text, almost verbatim, of the article she had recently read in the *Constitution*.

She pushed back in the chair and ran her hands through her hair. "Del Dangurs," she muttered aloud. Grabbing a pencil from the desk drawer and yanking a piece of paper from the printer, she began playing with the name. It took her three tries to contrive "Lenard Dagus" from the letters of "Del Dangurs."

"Dangurs is Dagus? Dagus is Dangurs?"

Again the scratching noise appeared in the front. She stood and walked to the window, her heart pounding like a war drum. Pulling apart the curtain slightly, she peered below into the front yard of the townhome. Nothing.

"Why would he write that article about my father?"

Sitting back in the chair, she looked at her watch. She had been in the house now about thirty-five minutes and figured she had ten minutes to go, if she was lucky.

Pressing on, she pulled up Dagus's e-mail and opened a new message. She attached the article and the Adobe file from his subfolders and forwarded them to her personal e-mail account. Then she went into his Sent folder and deleted the e-mail, followed by going into the Deleted folder and permanently deleting the e-mail.

She backed out of the folders, closing them all, and then began scanning his e-mail. There was the usual assortment of advertisements to make his penis larger and sell him Viagra. She noticed an e-mail from an address: househunter2010@hotmail.com. Opening it, she read the contents:

"Dan, I just wanted to make sure we still had a deal. I'm sure you will be happy with the new arrangement."

That was it. There was nothing more. She closed the e-mail and then clicked on SENDER so that all of the emails would align by sender. There were two others from househunter.

"Dan, glad we finally reached an agreement. Just wanted to confirm we are all set."

Again, very cryptic and very carefully worded. The third, which was the original that she could find, read: "Dan, we need to talk. I think you will want to reconsider. Call me."

She forwarded all three to her e-mail address and then repeated her deleting process. On a whim she pulled up Internet Explorer and typed in Mapquest. The Web page opened quickly, and she found the Address History box. She clicked on the drop-down menu that would reflect any addresses he might have looked up lately.

McClellan Drive, Sanford, NC 28311.

She gasped and backed away from the computer as if it might hurt her. She quickly printed that page, unsure what good it might do.

Looking at her watch she knew she had far outstayed her time, but she had one more folder she wanted to open. *Pushing your luck, Garrett.*

She grabbed everything she had printed out, closed anything that she had opened, and then reopened the subfolders, found *Videos*, and clicked on the icon. Each of the files was listed with a date, so she just picked the most recent one. It was dated two days ago. The computer paused a second, then Windows Media Player popped up on the screen. A few seconds later she was watching a grainy black-and-white video of Dagus having sex with someone in his bedroom.

"Gross," she muttered, but she was transfixed. The girl's face was indistinguishable at first, but after a few minutes of Dagus slipping around and grunting, she could see Brianna Simpson wiggling beneath his tall frame.

"Oh my—"

She was cut off by the low hum of the garage door opening.

DAGUS NOSED HIS BMW convertible 330i into his driveway. Getting the call from Amanda Garrett had been a pleasant surprise. He thought he had noticed her Mercedes in one of the general parking spots available to guests. He was glad that she had chosen to wait for him. He pulled into the garage and punched the button to send the door back down.

He switched off the ignition of the car, but let the radio continue to play. The Eagles were belting out "Witchy Woman," a personal favorite of his. He drummed his fingers on the steering wheel as he contemplated his dilemma.

He was curious how the desire built in him so quickly knowing Amanda was waiting for him. After receiving her phone call he had thought, given his activities of the day, that he would be able to resist the urge. His simple rule had been to never allow his weakness to affect any of his students. He had reconciled in his mind that if he never touched a student of his, well then, it was all okay. Jimmy Buffett's "Sixteen Will Get You Twenty" played in his mind. Somehow, that thought had never deterred him.

On the other hand, he believed in certain principles, was committed to a higher cause. He had been careful for so long, he considered. What was one more dalliance now? *It is right there in front of me every day, and I never partake.*

What should he do? Amanda needed his help, but who was she? There were others that needed his help, his love, as well. What was that old commercial about the potato chip? You can't have just one?

"I guess not," he whispered to himself as he pulled his key from the ignition.

CHAPTER 60
KUNAR PROVINCE, AFGHANISTAN

THURSDAY MORNING (HOURS OF DARKNESS)

Matt Garrett led the team into the compound, moving quickly. He pushed open the door, using the small Magnum flashlight affixed to the barrel of his M4 carbine to sweep the room. Van Dreeves and Hobart moved into the open space behind him, whispering into their wireless communications gear.

"Two up."

"Three up."

"Roger, one up. No contact."

Rampert and Eversoll were rear security, positioned immediately to the front of the door, kneeling and covering against any intrusion from that direction.

Into the next room they went, first Matt, followed by Van Dreeves and Hobart. Popping up from a floor mat were two individuals. Matt shone the flashlight on them moving it quickly between their frightened faces. Both were Afghans and neither were armed. Van Dreeves moved left, and Hobart moved to the right. There was an adjoining room, and Hobart, on the right, called out, "Room!"

Matt and Van Dreeves cleared to the left to ensure there were no openings or doors while Hobart kept his flashlight on the dark opening in front of him. As Matt turned, he heard Hobart say loudly, not really a scream, just an authoritative "Halt!" While it was doubtful that the elderly man in a white bed dress understood the command, he no doubt comprehended the muzzle of the weapon staring him in the face.

Confused, Matt moved quickly to Hobart's side and said in Pashto, the man's native tongue, "Do you have a captive here? An American?" The man had a long, graying beard and thin strands of hair on his head. Matt could visualize him in his traditional headdress looking much more authoritative.

Quickly the man nodded, as if to say yes. He then began waving his arms for them to follow. Cautiously the three men trailed behind the man in the white robe and began to gather hope, the worst of all emotions.

Instantly, as they entered the room, Matt knew that something was wrong. He could see the spot where his brother should have been. A mat and blanket were lying on the floor as if they'd been recently used. Two water bottles were tipped over, empty, against the mud wall.

The man was screaming now, "Taliban! Taliban!"

Matt placed his hand on the man's shoulder, calming him. Again, in his native language, Matt said, "Time?"

The elder muttered something he did not understand, but the body language indicated that he had just seen him only minutes ago. He was pointing at himself and then back at the mat. He walked over and picked up a water bottle and then pointed at himself again, followed by emphatically demonstrating how he had just provided a bottle of water to his guest.

Matt quickly walked through the other rooms until he found himself back with the others. Van Dreeves was standing next to a window about seven feet above the dirt floor.

"Look at this shit," Van Dreeves said, running his hand along the wall. "He went out here. Climbed out, or someone dragged him out."

"Damnit!" Matt and the others raced through the front door and around the back toward the fig orchard.

"Footprints, sort of," Hobart barked, shining his flashlight on the ground. "You can see one leg is dragging a little bit."

Matt knelt onto the moon dust to examine the tracks identified by Hobart. He ran a gloved hand across the imprint, as if to touch his brother's soul. He looked over his shoulder at the nervous old man whose home they had just raided in search of Zach.

"Where was he hurt?" Matt asked in Pashto. The man immediately began touching his left leg.

By now Sergeant Eversoll was kneeling next to Matt.

"He can't be far, sir."

"Far enough."

"What don't you see?" the sergeant asked.

"Other footprints."

"That's right. He thought he was escaping. That's our Code of Conduct. Always try to escape."

Matt hung his head for just a moment. So close, yet Zach was nowhere to be found. He was like a zephyr.

"The river. He probably moved toward the river knowing it would flow south. Hell, he probably thinks he's in Pakistan." Sergeant Eversoll was visualizing what he would have done.

The team covered the ground to the river in short order, each searching in an opposite direction. Matt looked to the south, his eyes searching desperately for his brother.

His gaze was met only by the discomfiting beauty of the mountain range angling sharply into the narrow valley through which the river and its rapids ran. He was reminded for a brief moment of his time with Zach in the Blue Ridge Mountains of Virginia. Often, they would raft or canoe along the rocky banks of the South River.

"Call the pilots and have them fly the river from south to north as they come in to get us. He'll be on the river."

Matt felt a trickle of confidence fight his despair. They were close and would soon locate Zach.

The first shot struck Sergeant Eversoll in the chest, knocking him backward into the rock jetties that bordered the rushing water.

Suddenly a fusillade of rocket-propelled grenades and Russian-made PKM machine-gun fire enveloped them from the far bank.

Matt dove for cover near Eversoll and returned fire. Van Dreeves opened his first-aid kit and ripped away Eversoll's body armor and outer tactical gear.

"Hang on, buddy, we're right on top of you."

As Matt was returning fire, the thought occurred to him that the closer you approached your goal, the tougher your path generally became. The end of a race, preparation for a final exam, or closing in on the enemy leader all shared the same ingredient. The challenge increased as one neared the objective. He could not remember how many Stratego games, the object of which was to capture your opponent's flag, he and Zach had played as kids. But he had learned an axiom in life after being defeated by Zach's bombs and swift game-board tactics: the enemy always gets a vote and usually has a different idea than you.

Eversoll's breathing labored as Van Dreeves worked feverishly to find the wound. Rampert called on the radio to the helicopters. Matt and Hobart returned fire with well-aimed precision.

COLONEL ZACH GARRETT crawled to the shore, pulling the boat with one hand behind him. He settled onto a sandy outcropping as he noticed a few dim city lights in the distance. Having operated in Afghanistan for several months, he thought he recognized the terrain and was visualizing where he might be located on a map. Generally an optimist, Zach resisted believing what his instincts, even memory, were telling him.

The river broadened and slowed considerably. Bernouli's equation was at work again, where the same volume of water through a less constrained space had reduced velocity.

As he struggled to secure the craft between two rocks, he noticed the pain in his leg had gone mostly numb. About two miles downstream from where he had put in, machine-gun fire had echoed along the valley floor, tracers poking through his craft, leaving small smoking holes. Only now did he realize that he had been struck at least once. He limped weakly as he attempted to move to cover.

Grabbing some washed-up poplar tree limbs and straw, he shrouded the boat as best he could. He needed time to think before venturing into the city, where assuredly he would be detected. For the most part, if it was Jalalabad, he should be safe, but there was no guarantee. More often than not, it was Al Qaeda and the Taliban who were prowling the streets late at night, intimidating citizens and flaunting the chronic lack of government authority.

Shivering on the bank of the river, he watched an MH-47 cargo helicopter and AH-64 Apache gunship suddenly appear in the mouth of the valley to his south. He tried to stand, leaning against two rocks in the sandy bank. He stared into the black night at the familiar sounds of the welcome aircraft as they raced overhead at what he believed were speeds in excess of one hundred and fifty miles an hour. The helicopters were visible only briefly as they flew low and fast along the river, weaving with each curve of the valley.

Always amazed at the skill with which these pilots flew, he was suddenly mad at himself for pausing in his solitary journey. While the aircraft were most likely responding to a fight somewhere, he believed that if he had been in the middle of the water, they would have at least reported that fact to the headquarters as a matter of routine.

More importantly, the presence of U.S. aircraft flying freely in the area indicated to him that he was in Afghanistan, not Pakistan, and that his instincts were proving correct. He was essentially paralleling the Pakistan border about a mile or two to his east. Zach looked at the snowcapped mountain ridge etching its way along the black night as if to illuminate with a highlighter the Pakistan border.

The two helicopters were only visible to him for a couple of seconds and then had vanished. Where they were headed he could not determine; however, he believed that they would have to follow the same route on their egress. This would afford him the opportunity to signal, somehow, the crews in the aircraft. He had no lighter or matches to ignite a fire, nor did he have any means of signaling. The enemy, over the last week of his capture and subsequent escape, had stripped him of every usable means of signal, including the infrared patches that were attached to his uniform.

Faint with cold and fatigue, he slid down against the rocks, watching the Kunar wander past him toward Jalalabad. His sense of Amanda's need was the most palpable he had ever felt. How, from a world away, he wondered, could he see the image of his daughter so clearly and feel her calling, feel her need for protection. Something horribly wrong was occurring not only to her, but within her.

"Come on, Amanda, talk to me," he whispered to the flowing current, which soaked in his words and carried them downstream.

He closed his eyes, feeling light-headed, the pain returning to his leg, but not to the exclusion of the rest of his body. He was reeling now, swooning as if to sleep. He consciously knew that he was suffering from the pain, which was causing his body to shut down.

He dreamt, or was offered a vision, he wasn't sure which. Perhaps it was their two parallel universes colliding. Amanda was sitting at her home, crying into her hands, silken strands of light-brown hair cascading over her slender fingers, which were perched against her forehead as if in an awkward salute. A bluish light bathed her face. Through her eyes, he could see the documents scrolling along the computer monitor. Each was so intently focused on the area it was possible for both to believe that they were in a sense channeling with their target.

Zach *saw* her. First she was flipping through official-looking documents. Next she was reading letters he had written to Melanie asking if Amanda could stay with him long enough to reestablish their relationship. She would read, weep, and scroll. He saw her as clearly as if he were in her room. Then, again through her eyes, he saw his house in North Carolina, in a heap of black ashes looking like ruins amongst the tall, charred pines, and Riley's battered image floated into his mind as if she were lying in a hospital bed. He was twinning now with Amanda, in synch, siphoning her thoughts, or more appropriately, splicing into them, as if reading over her shoulder. He visualized placing an arm around her, telling her it was going to be okay, that she just needed to be strong.

Emotions raged inside her like small vessels in a violent storm off the coast of Cape Hatteras, tides clashing, winds whipping, and ships sinking. Springing from the well of her energy, he saw something emerge for which he was unprepared, but which he should have expected. He saw Amanda's countenance shift from peaceful and loving to calculating and . . . vengeful? She was, after all, her mother's daughter. What would she do with the newfound potency, he wondered? Like a sorcerer's apprentice, the powers could be wildly devastating.

Suddenly, he felt hands upon him, lifting him. He heard voices, familiar ones. "Yes, that's him. Be careful. Okay, easy now, he's bleeding."

He was surprised that he hadn't heard the helicopters, but was glad to be in the arms of a friend.

He felt a blanket pass over his face as he was loaded onto the aircraft. He tried to remove the cloth they had pulled over his head, but his arms wouldn't move. He spoke, but there was no sound.

And suddenly it was clear to Zach why he had pulled over the boat, and why he had been able to so easily enter Amanda's universe, watching her. It would be okay, he thought to himself, if it stays this way. *Just give me unfettered access to Amanda, Lord, to guide her, be her angel. That's my only request.*

Zach figured it might be an acceptable one, for he wasn't asking for a last cigarette or a steak and shrimp dinner. He just wanted to take up spiritual residence closest to Amanda.

He could think of no greater glory for a dead father to do for his abused daughter. With that, he thought of a saying: *Perfect speed is being there.*

So get me there, perfectly.

CHAPTER 61
SPARTANBURG, SOUTH CAROLINA

WEDNESDAY EVENING

Amanda closed the video file and did the only thing she knew to do, which was send it as an attachment to her e-mail address. Of course, the file being so big, the hourglass continued to pour out sand as if she were playing Scrabble and had two minutes to come up with a word.

Finally, the Sending Message prompt disappeared and she quickly repeated the signature deleting process. Confident the computer was relatively in the same configuration as she'd found it, she bolted out the door. Instead of going down the steps, she hooked a left into the guest bedroom, dodged the bed and bureau and found the window, which was sealed shut.

She flipped the brass latch at the top, lifted the inside frame, and popped the screen off the bottom hinge. She looked below and saw that she could make the screened porch roof if she was good.

She slithered through the bottom of the screen and turned to pull the window down. She would not be able to lock the brass latch, but figured that was a chance she would have to take.

Standing on Dagus's sloped roof, she eyed the more gently sloping surface of the screened porch ten feet away. In her hand she held the pages that she had printed from his computer and the notes she'd scribbled as she undid his anagram. She looked over her shoulder and noticed a dim light flick on through the window.

Without hesitation she jumped, landed with a thud, and rolled to the edge of the screened-porch roof. She was staring down directly onto the rock where she had retrieved his key. Knowing that he would have heard the noise, she scrambled to her feet and leapt the remaining ten feet into the grass, rolling into the side of the fence. She stood and ran to the gate. She unlatched it, bolted through, and darted across the parking lot to her car.

She pulled her keys from her pants pocket, fumbled with the fob, and then opened the driver's door. She didn't notice the commotion behind her as she backed out and sped away until, in her rearview mirror, she saw some-one moving in the backyard.

When she got what she thought was a safe distance away, she checked her messages, only to have it vibrate immediately with a number she didn't recognize.

"Hello?"

"Amanda, this is your Uncle Matt. I need you to come to Arlington National Cemetery Friday."

The rest of her trip home was simply a blur.

DAGUS HAD COME into the house through the garage door. "Amanda," he'd called out in a pleasant voice, nerves and anticipation building inside. How much easier could it get? He'd wondered. She was feeling alone and afraid, and she'd come to him looking for comfort.

"Amanda? Where are you?" He made a motion to look in the kitchen when he heard a sound on the roof. Initially confused, he jogged upstairs to find the unsecured window latch. He slammed the window shut and ran downstairs and out into the backyard in time to see Amanda's Mercedes speed out of the parking lot. He immediately went back inside and made a phone call.

"I need you."

"I—I can't. I have to—"

"Now! I need you here, now!"

An hour later, he looked at Brianna Simpson standing in his foyer. Her thin blonde hair was falling softly on her shoulders. Her wide blue eyes showed confusion, perhaps fear.

"This is the last time?" she asked.

"I promise," he replied, as he had so many times before. Dagus rubbed his chin, thinking.

"I don't know, Len. . . ."

He frowned at Brianna and said, "I really do care about you. I can't help myself."

Brianna made as if to continue resisting.

Then she relented, giving in to his physical presence and the deal she had struck.

CHAPTER 62
C-17 TRANSPORT FROM BAGRAM, AFGHANISTAN

THURSDAY

Matt Garrett, his mission completed, sat in the back of the C-17 Globe-master aircraft. He was tired, having been without sleep for what seemed like weeks. He drifted in and out of consciousness, unable to believe what had transpired and what had to come next.

So close, yet so far. The thoughts shot across his mind's eye like burning arrows slung from an archer's bow, the words leaving a smoking trail. The attack across the Afghanistan border. Watching Zach on the Predator feed run from the enemy. The attack into Kunar Province. And then the linkup with the guide where they had come so close.

He stared at the flag-draped coffin shackled to the center of the large cargo bay. No one should die alone, he thought to himself. Yet, the coffin was a solitaire, and perhaps rightfully so. Singularity sometimes accords the appropriate attention.

As the C-17 glided through the night sky over some part of the world in between Afghanistan and the United States, Matt couldn't help but wonder about the price of it all. The cost, in human terms, of this war. These wars. Could you separate them, Iraq and Afghanistan, he wondered?

His singular actions two years before had helped save the nation and his brother, and now he felt powerless and impotent. He disagreed with so much, so many, yet continued to soldier on in an effort to make a difference from within, as so many heroes do. He had tried talking to the director about his concerns, but his insights had fallen on deaf ears. Presently, his just rage was muted against the Globemaster's droning engines.

He thought of Amanda Garrett, his niece, and all that she had been through. He had received an update prior to his departure. A friend had passed him a note that his brother's house had been burned to the ground. Insult to injury. But that was their way, he knew.

Then the newspaper article questioning Zach's integrity. He shook his head, staring absently at the black, granular no-slip pads spaced evenly along the silver metal flooring of the C-17.

Matt remembered a passage from Sun Tzu which he had always kept in the back of his mind: The wise general cannot be manipulated. He may withdraw, but when he does, moves so swiftly that he cannot be overtaken. His retirements are designed to entice the enemy, to unbalance him, and to create a situation favorable for a decisive counterstroke.

Poor Amanda had been kept off balance her entire seventeen years, Matt thought. The women that surrounded her were generals in their own battle-space. They directed Amanda around like a pawn, a foot soldier, in their private war to destroy. What had his brother done to deserve such treatment? What *could* he have done? More importantly, especially now, what had Amanda done to be so abused, to have her memories of her father be tarnished or erased?

Justice? Matt's wandering mind tapped on all of the world's issues, large and small, in the long airplane ride. Where is the justice in the soldier killed on the battlefield where incompetent generals applied insufficient force, and inept intelligence analysts missed all of the signals? Where is the justice in the Marine killed in a war whose causus belli is now proven a myth, a ghost that never was? Where is the justice in a young girl used as a weapon against her father? Millions of children, abused in such a fashion, he guessed, without so much as the hope of a chance for something better. Left to fight for themselves, yet seduced by the luxuries of the high mass-consuming society of today. Most, he presumed, chose not to fight, and simply followed the path of least resistance. In their wake, they left behind the charred remains of a father's dignity or a soldier's idealism.

Better yet, Matt steamed, where is the outrage? Where are those that would stand up for these heroes, the soldiers and the children, sometimes one and the same, who, with immature wisdom, trust our leaders? As in love, he considered, in life we all look for heroes. We overlook obvious faults or flaws. The old saying, "You want it bad, you get it bad," came to his mind. We all knew intuitively, he simmered, that invading Iraq before finishing the fight in Afghanistan was wrong. Now America's treasure was just trying to keep pace. He mused that serfs and peasants could rarely influence public policy, but they sure as hell could go die for the same. Life in a kingdom, not a republic.

He stared at the patterns of rivets in the fuselage, wondering why those politicians who most avoided war in their youth sought it with such vigor in their political careers. In this era of Rostovian High Mass Consumption, the Secular Spiritual Stagnation that has followed not only rots at the collective soul of the nation, but also erodes the individual's morality, Matt thought.

He thought about Department of Defense policymakers who were most responsible for the Iraq invasion and scoffed. Morons who don't know the cost of war. This stagnation creates a disembodiment with our most senior public leaders that manifests itself in a form of irony. Because they have nothing vested, they seem to think they have everything to gain.

Where was the finesse that should have followed 9-11? Pursue the legitimate war in Afghanistan with enough force to block the egresses into Pakistan. Jump the 82nd Airborne Division into Khowst and Jalalabad while you air assault the 101st Airborne Division into the mountain passes in Kunar, Nangahar, and Paktika. Use Special Forces to embed with the Pakistan military along the border. *Then* attack with the Northern Alliance from Mazir e Sharif to the south to destroy Al Qaeda first, followed by the Taliban. Contain Iraq and further strangulate that country through diplomatic initiatives with Syria and Iran. *The enemy of my enemy is my friend.*

Instead, Matt fumed, we limped into Afghanistan the one time the American public has asked for, and deserved, a head on a platter. Flawed from the start, the plan had allowed nearly all of the Al Qaeda senior leadership to escape while Taliban cannon fodder held at bay the meager forces that were attacking. Inexplicably, the focus was already shifting to Iraq, where we had led with the chin of the American soldier and Marine. He shook his head in disgust and looked across the casket.

Joining Matt on this journey home was Mary Ann Singlaub, a reporter from Charlotte. She had her story, he guessed, and she was done. Sitting across from him, he saw in her beautiful face the anguish that only true caring could bring. The coffin was situated between them like a barrier. Singlaub was openly weeping as she stared at the flag tucked securely around the metal container. Strangely, her agony helped ease his.

How much more are we going to take? What is the end state? How much longer can we go on without mobilizing the country? It seemed odd to Matt that Americans were enjoying a peacetime standard of living while their all-volunteer force fought in Iraq and Afghanistan. Eversoll had said to him, "Sir, the military is at war. The nation is at the mall."

Yet, neither were they mobilized internally, he reflected, as he began to think about Amanda again. That a child could be so manipulated in plain view only underscored his point.

The coffin fastened down in the middle of the C-17 would remain an unmistakable reminder of the cost of war, so close and so personal.

Matt thought about what they had just done—the raid, the fight, the dying, the destruction, and the ultimate personal sacrifice sitting before him. What had it achieved? He wasn't sure he could answer that question, and that bothered him. Were they fighting now just simply because they could? Was this the modern equivalent to Grant having the Union troops build the cutoff canal across from Vicksburg, not because he ever intended to use it, but because it kept his soldiers busy until they had received all of their supplies? Where was all of this heading?

They stopped briefly at Ramstein Air Base where he made a short trip to the military hospital at Landstuhl, Germany, conducted his business, and made sure all of the paperwork was in order. It was hard to get back on the plane, but he rejoined the crew for the long flight home. He would be back soon. His mind wandered, searching for purpose perhaps, but randomly pinging against emotions that he knew were useless: anger, fear, frustration. The pinball in his mind rolled to a stop, lodged on a thought.

Soldiers deserve competent leaders just as children deserve competent parents. He looked at the coffin and thought of Zach, watching him singularly elude Al Qaeda on the full-motion video only to meet a fate he was certain his nation might only marginally notice. His nation had asked him to do this. He was a loyal servant, achieving state ends.

Likewise with Amanda, and her suffering at the feet of her mother and grandmother with the help of a court system blinded by political activism. Point man, spy, and infantryman in her mother's fight against her father, Amanda's youth had been drafted by a field general equal to Rommel in achieving her own goals and end states within the system. But like Zachary, where did that leave Amanda, and what did she get for her sacrifice?

The parallel was so obvious to him. It was not the individual. Their efforts were almost always heroic. The vacuous soul of a nation—aloof Pentagon policymakers, or a parent, separated from their moorings—created the conditions for both the soldier and the child to ultimately face their destinies. The good soldier, as well as the good child, will find the chance, the opportunity to break free from the ill-conceived plans and fix things from the ground up. An engineer may be able to design a car, but rarely can he fix it once it breaks. And it always breaks.

Nation to soldier. Mother to daughter. With that thought, Matt began to worry about the predicament that he had learned confronted Amanda. Perhaps there was something to be gained. Matt knew her to be her father's daughter despite the trials of the past. Would she be able to access those forgotten and repressed memories and instincts? If so, she had a chance.

The good soldier. The good daughter. Father and child.

CHAPTER 63
CHARLOTTE, NORTH CAROLINA

FRIDAY (EASTERN TIME)

The early-morning drive to the Charlotte airport was miserable for Amanda for several reasons. They were plowing through a thunderstorm and the resultant flooded streets. Her mother was giving her instructions on what to say and not say, do and not do, be and not be. And she really missed talking to Jake. She needed him, especially now that she had uncovered that Dagus, the one man she'd thought she could trust, was actually Del Dangurs and was working against her.

On the airplane, though, she chased away her dark thoughts of Dagus by reflecting on what she had learned last night from her Uncle Matt. How her father was a hero, and the effort they had expended searching for him. They had finally found him lying on the bank of the Kunar River after an Al Qaeda ambush. It was something no daughter should ever have to hear, but something she desperately wanted to know.

The flight from Charlotte to Washington Reagan Airport was mercifully quick. She deplaned, found her luggage, and began to call Matt when she saw him leaning against the wall, smiling. His head was cocked to the side and she could tell he was measuring her. It had been almost two years since they'd last seen one another. For a moment, she believed she had seen the ghost of her father standing there, they looked so much alike.

"Hey, Matt," she waved.

"Darling, how are you?" He came over and grabbed her luggage out of her hand while he simultaneously hugged her hard.

"Okay, considering, you know?"

"I know it's been hard. This is just something I needed you to do, for your dad."

"I'm here, Matt. You know, maybe a month ago I wouldn't have cared about any of this. But . . ."

"Things have changed."

"They've changed," she acknowledged.

They found Matt's old Porsche 944 in the parking garage, managed to fit her duffel bag in the back and then found their way to the Embassy Suites in Crystal City.

"I got us a couple of rooms at the Suites. We'll attend the funeral in the morning, and then I'll drop you back at the airport."

"Thanks for the ticket, by the way. No way Mom would have paid for it."

She noticed Matt did not acknowledge her comment. Too much class or perhaps too much anger for all the discontent her mother had created, she now saw. But really, what did it matter anymore? she wondered.

They had adjacent rooms. Matt helped Amanda get settled, and then they walked to dinner at Champs in Pentagon City. It was a loud sports bar that had over twenty televisions playing at least ten different games. Music blared from one corner. A healthy mixture of young professionals and urban dwellers mingled comfortably. Matt found them a small table outside in an area staked off with a black wrought-iron fence. The spring air was relaxing, and she was glad she had worn jeans and a lightweight blue Northface windbreaker over her white knit blouse. She downed a full dinner of salmon and mixed vegetables and was having a nice conversation with Matt when he said, "There's someone I want you to meet."

Amanda paused. "Okay, who?"

"Her name is Mary Ann Singlaub, and she's doing a big story on your dad. She'd like to talk to you."

She looked at Matt a moment. His brown hair was full and soft, tossed from side to side yet not appearing unkempt. He had her father's face, square jaw and high cheekbones. They could be twins. She knew Matt was younger but had always been impressed with his maturity and love for his older brother.

"I don't know, Matt. All this is way too early, too raw. Plus, didn't you see that hatchet job Del Dangurs did on him?"

"Just meet her tonight, and then you can decide later. She's flying back to Charlotte with you. I think you'll like her."

"I'll meet her. No promises."

Matt paused, studying his niece.

"You okay, really?"

Amanda looked away, thinking.

"I'm doing better," she said. "I'm talking to someone . . . and that's helping."

"Riley?"

"Yes, Riley. She's in the hospital or she'd be here, I'm sure."

"I'm sure. What kinds of things are you talking about?"

Amanda fidgeted with her fork, put it down.

"Things like why I treated him so badly. Why I don't remember the good stuff."

"Lots of good stuff."

Matt watched Amanda struggle with the conversation. As an interested, but somewhat objective observer, Matt had seen the manipulation wrack Amanda.

"Remember Faith Hill at Fort Bragg?"

Matt smiled. "How could I forget? You sat on my shoulders the entire time. I'm two inches shorter because of you."

She giggled, displayed what Matt thought was her first genuine smile.

"But I had no memory of that, Matt, until I went to Dad's house, our house."

Matt cocked his head. "Really?"

"Riley says it's all because of the hard drive. The database in my head. Like with a computer, when you delete something you just write over it. The information doesn't really go away. The database is always there."

Matt stopped and put his fork down. His mind was reeling and apparently his face gave away his shock.

"What?" Amanda asked, nervous.

"Nothing. Nothing," Matt repeated. "That's true. The database is always there."

Matt composed himself, paid the bill and they walked the mile back to the Embassy Suites. In the downstairs lobby she spotted a lone woman surrounded by four men with short haircuts. She looked decidedly uncomfortable.

"I think I see your friend, Matt," Amanda pointed out.

"Sharks circling. Let's save her, what do you say?"

They approached, and two of the men eyed Amanda until they saw Matt's steel gaze. Mary Ann was thrilled to see them, as indicated by the way she lunged from her chair the moment they were within eyesight.

"Nice guys?"

"The best," she quipped.

Matt steered them to some low back chairs in a more private part of the lounge.

"Mary Ann, this is Amanda Garrett."

Amanda studied the woman for a brief moment. She was very pretty. Even striking, but not in a severe way. Her beauty was balanced by compassionate eyes. She was wearing a blue blazer atop a cream silk shirt with a matching blue skirt. Amanda reached her hand out only to be bypassed with a hug from Mary Ann.

"You've been through so much, honey."

Amanda surprised herself and returned the hug, saying, "Thank you."

They sat in the chairs and began talking about Afghanistan and everything that had happened there.

At that moment, Amanda knew that she would talk to Mary Ann.

The woman would be a big help to her plan.

CHAPTER 64
ARLINGTON, CEMETERY VIRGINIA

SATURDAY

Amanda tuned out much of the funeral, as it was a challenge to absorb everything that had occurred in the last two weeks. She was wearing her black outfit that her mother had selected for her. "You must look the part, Amanda, so don't let on that you don't give a damn, okay?" she'd chimed as she dumped her at the Charlotte airport Delta Airlines baggage skycap.

She stood in the cool spring morning of Arlington National Cemetery, surrounded by hundreds of people, some in uniform, others not. She knew so few of the attendees that she clung closely to Matt, the one person with whom she was not totally uncomfortable. There was a church service at the old brick church that stood atop the hill at Fort Myers, and that was followed by a procession led by a horse-drawn carriage that carried the flag-draped casket to an open hole in the ground. Freshly tilled earth sat beside the rectangular hole in an orange and brown heap in contrast to the crisp maneuvers of the military funeral detail and the perfectly aligned rows of white crosses.

So many crosses, she thought to herself. Her mind was wrestling with issues that were so narrowly defined by her own existence that she had a hard time understanding why so many could have sacrificed so much.

But she was beginning to get the picture. The conversation with Matt and Mary Ann last night had filled in many gaps in her mind. Her sleep had been restless, though, with so many conflicting ideas and emotions. The gravitational pulls on her from multiple directions were enormous. Her mother, her grandmother, Dagus, Brianna, Matt, and now this Mary Ann were competing for her attention and energy. She had a plan, and she needed to stick to her chosen course of action no matter what.

Standing graveside, watching the funeral, she slipped into an alternate space as she recited in her mind the words to Jessi Alexander's soothing "This World is Crazy."

I'm a part of you; you're a part of me, too.

Take refuge in me, 'cause this world is crazy.

Crazy is right, she thought. In the last two weeks her world had literally been transformed when the major and chaplain had arrived at her house that Sunday morning. Now, the words had *meaning*. She had an angel watching over her, feeling her joys and sorrows, guiding her through her darkest fears and helping her confront her strongest demons.

Before she could comprehend what was happening, someone handed her something, which was quickly secured by Matt, and the casket was lowered into the rectangular hole with the awkward pile of dirt. Having only attended one previous funeral in her life, Amanda was not prepared for the emotion connected with this event. The outpouring of support and the strong, almost familial bonds evident between the soldiers and the others were contagious. She could feel the love and understand now the cama-raderie of which her father had always spoken.

She recalled with ease now a time her father had pulled over on the side of the road and picked up a soldier walking upon the shoulder. His car had broken down, but he really didn't need a ride, especially from a major. Despite the protests, her father had driven the soldier to the auto shop, back to the car, and helped him fix the problem. Amanda and he were still able to go to the mall in Raleigh and enjoy a day of hanging out, her arm linked casually through his as they sauntered along talking about nothing much . . . and everything.

There were so many other times, and she could see it now so clearly, that he had gone out of his way to help another soldier or a family member. And now she could remember clearly admiring her father's spirit and the purity of his motives, understanding this even as a young child growing up amidst divorce. Her time with her father, she now remembered, had been a refuge for her. *Take refuge in me.* Shelter from the storm.

Eventually, though, the storm must have washed the shelter onto the rocky shores that had shattered so many dreams and hopes. She remembered the transition from admiration to ambivalence and finally to outright hatred, though she'd never felt that the migration had been natural or right. In fact, she believed it to be wrong. In the end, though, the seduction had been all too effective. So clear now, the wizardry then had been invisible to the naked eye, better than a practiced magician's sleight of hand. At times the techniques had been blunt, locked in the back of the car. Other times they'd been more subtle, a weekend away when he was scheduled to visit.

Yet she had been just a child. How was she supposed to figure out what the hell was going on? She clenched her fists in anger. Tensing as people passed by her, she let go, as she could not hold back any longer. The pressure against the dam of her soul was too powerful. She acknowledged, and she cried, as her face wrinkled into a tortured mask.

She wept now, openly, her hand to her face. Matt's arm slid around her back, pulling her close. She leaned into him, heaving, sobbing, completely out of control.

"Why?" she managed in between near shrieks. "Why did he have to die?"

"It's okay, honey."

More sobbing into Matt's dark suit, staining his rep tie. Her carefully coifed hair was now no more arranged than bedding straw tossed to the ground.

She managed to gain a bit of composure. She would be strong, she determined. She had to be, for her father, if for no one else.

"I have to do something," she said, wiping her nose and looking up at her uncle. "Sorry." She noticed the giant damp circle on his gray shirt. The circle was darkened with the mean streaks of mascara and foundation.

"It's okay, Amanda."

She patted Matt on his chest and pulled his suit jacket lapels from either side in a vain attempt to hide the stain she'd created. "Sorry," she said again.

"I have more shirts, Amanda."

Truthfully she was just stalling, as she knew what she needed to do. Mustering her courage, she walked over to the end of the row of seats and knelt next to the man and woman who were still seated. Most of the crowd had shifted toward the road that led to the chapel.

With her knee pressing into the lawn, she could feel the dampness in the mown grass as her stocking soaked in the morning dew. She looked up at the man and woman, people whom she had only recently come to know.

The woman was wearing a modest black dress with shoes that matched but somehow seemed less elegant than the occasion demanded. The man wore an off-the-rack dark suit that fit, but was perhaps a shade too tight, as if he had purchased it years ago. Amanda noticed the woman had a clear countenance in her round face, as if God was escorting her through this time and space. The man's wrinkles and weathered skin revealed a life of working outside with his hands.

Placing a hand on the woman's knee, Amanda paused until Mrs. Eversoll looked at her. Amanda noticed Mr. Eversoll turn and look at her as she knelt in front of the dead soldier's mother.

Amanda looked at the American flag sitting in Sergeant Eversoll's mother's lap in a perfect triangle.

"I'm so sorry your son died fighting to help my father," Amanda said through tears that were sliding freely down her cheeks. "I promise I will never forget the sacrifice he made."

Mrs. Eversoll looked at Amanda with the clear-eyed confidence of a woman who believed so entirely in God, whose faith was so strong, that she knew her son was in a better place.

"Your father was the best thing that ever happened to Lance."

Those words, spoken by the parent of a dead soldier, were perhaps the most profound words she would ever hear. Their son had died in combat trying to save her father. Their son was in the casket behind them.

She finally understood that life was about more than serving materialistic desires and hedonistic pursuits. No, serving a cause larger than herself would be her calling. Even if her father could not be present, he would be a part of it, forever.

She stood, leaning over to hug the Eversolls.

"Thank you, Amanda, for coming. This has meant more than anything else, your being here."

They hugged for longer than she could remember, the three of them, bonded as one forever by this most unlikely of events.

I'm a part of you; you're a part of me too.

CHAPTER 65
CHARLOTTE, NORTH CAROLINA

SATURDAY AFTERNOON

She had bid farewell to Matt. There would be more news about arrangements for her father, Matt assured her as he climbed in a black SUV headed to Andrews Air Force Base where he would board a Gulfstream G5 and fly directly to Bagram Air Base in Afghanistan.

Mary Ann Singlaub had proved a good companion for the return trip. She had helped catch Amanda up on some of the details that had been missing, and, in turn, Amanda had given her some good background on her father. All positive.

After landing at the Charlotte airport on an earlier flight, they had taken a cab together to her office at the *Charlotte Observer*, where Amanda had arranged for the attorney, Harlan, to meet them.

They chatted briefly in Mary Ann's cubicle, which was as unkempt as a college professor's office.

"Need to do some spring cleaning, lady."

"Don't get sassy with me," Mary Ann shot back, picking up a stack of *The Economist* magazines and moving them out of a chair, "or I'll make you read these."

Amanda glanced down and smiled. "I'll be quiet, trust me."

Mary Ann's phone beeped, and a mechanical female voice announced, "Visitor."

They walked to the front desk and met Harlan. Amanda waved from a distance as they approached, but she noticed that he did not return her gesture. For a moment fear struck in her belly that perhaps something had gone wrong.

Her concern melted when her teenage girl instincts reengaged and she noticed that Mary Ann's and Harlan's eyes were securely locked in the type of stare usually reserved for high school kids who recognize love at first sight. Amanda could have fallen through a trapdoor and they would not have noticed, she thought, smiling. They were smitten with each other.

As she watched them introduce themselves, she began to think about all the positive emotions and encouragement that she had been able to experience since her father's death. The two NCBI agents had altered their course because they knew him. The UPS guy had hugged her and grieved with her. Even Harlan had said he knew of him. Where had these positive reinforcements been in the past? Now she could feel his strength and positive energy. Karma, perhaps.

"Hey, guys?" Amanda said and smiled, waving her hand at the pair.

"Yes, Amanda, how are you?" Harlan acknowledged, pulling a business card from his wallet. He looked back at Mary Ann, handed her the card, and said, "In case I forget."

"Like I would let you," she replied.

"Oh, please, I've heard better lines in my school plays," Amanda interjected. "Now let's go before my mom gets suspicious."

They entered the conference room, which was dominated by a large dark wood rectangular meeting table surrounded by high-backed black leather chairs like the Praetorian Guard standing watch.

They each took a chair, Amanda at the head of the table and Harlan and Mary Ann facing one another on either side of her. She figured they had engineered this seating arrangement quickly so that they could continue looking at one another while she tried to understand all of the paperwork in front of her.

Instead, Harlan immediately began. "Amanda, I've checked all of the documents, and they are in order. You are completely protected in every sense of the word. I've talked to Major Ramsey, the casualty assistance officer who's been working with you. He gave me all of the paperwork, and I am representing you on this matter."

Amanda looked down uncomfortably. "How do I pay you?"

"We'll discuss that later, but don't worry about it now."

"But what if I can't afford it?"

"That sounds remarkably like worry."

"Amanda," Mary Ann interrupted, placing a hand on her arm while looking at Harlan. "Trust us, okay?"

Us? Since when were these two an "us"? she wondered.

"Not a real strong suit of mine, this whole trust thing. I found out one of my teachers is the guy who burned Dad's house down. For all I know, he probably beat up Riley."

"Your uncle called me last night after you told him. We've got his name, Amanda. I think the police will watch him for a day or two and then move in," Harlan said.

"Okay, but don't wait too long."

"They know what they're doing. And, you know, you might as well find out now that you cannot count on yourself to do everything that has to be done in life."

She turned toward Harlan as he spoke.

"You have to learn to trust people. The primary issue is learning which people to trust. You've been double-crossed as a young girl, and so your foundation is shaken. You don't know what to believe, or more importantly, who. Now here you are with two nearly complete strangers, and we are asking you to do something that you at this moment are not able to do with your parents. So, I understand it's a challenge, but one you have to rise to over the next couple of days. The closer the Americans came to Germany, the tougher the Germans fought."

Amanda furrowed her brow. "I was following you until the whole German thing."

"I think what he's saying, Amanda, is that the closer you get to your goal, the more resistance you will face," Mary Ann explained.

"Oh, why didn't he just say that?"

"He's a man. It's mandatory that he use war or sports analogies when speaking. They're taught that in guy camp."

"That was a joke, right?"

"Exactly."

"Okay, so what's next?" she asked.

Harlan took over again.

"I've talked to Tad Johnson, and the contract on the house in which you currently live is now closed and owned by another family. The closing for the mansion your mother bought is set for this afternoon. Inspection is already done. There are no issues with the house. I've reviewed the contract, and it is clean. Your mother has one task left to complete regarding the house. None of your money will be involved. And the contract is binding. So, you have achieved your effect. Your mother is trapped. She will have about half the capital for the house yet will not be able to afford the mortgage that she will be required to obtain. She will have to immediately resell at a significantly lower price, unless of course someone loans her the money. Perhaps your grandmother. Your only obligation is to now stay out of the way. Can you do that?"

"Sometimes the way finds me," Amanda responded.

"Then hide. Stay in your room," Harlan emphasized.

"What did she forget?"

"I'll discuss that with you tomorrow, for your own safety."

Amanda paused. "Just tell me?"

"It seems amongst everything going on she has yet to insure the new house."

"Oh, well, she'll get that resolved fast enough, trust me on that." She looked at Harlan, who stared at her until she broke the gaze. A thought came into her mind, and then she changed the subject. "What about Jake?"

"I've hired a private investigator, who is in North Carolina now doing some interviews of neighbors and talking to your buddies at the NCBI. With Dagus's name we should be able to move quickly. Someone should be able to recognize him," Harlan said.

"Right."

"Once we have more information, we should be able to get Jake cleared and charge the appropriate person."

"Well, I'll give you everything I've got on him. What about Miss Dwyer?"

"Riley's doing fine. She went home today, a bit banged up, but she'll survive, which apparently she wasn't supposed to based upon some other things we've already found."

"You're joking."

"Afraid not. So, I come back to 'stay out of the way'." He emphasized the last five words by shaking his finger at her. "This is dangerous. And being the student of human behavior that I am, I fear you might be in jeopardy."

"How so?"

"Well, here's the way I see it. If the one person who has been orchestrating all of this catches wind of what you have been up to, you could become the victim of a preemptive strike."

Amanda nodded.

"And, second, once we execute the plan, there is the off chance that you may be associated with some of what has transpired. Some people will be angry with you."

"I can handle angry," Amanda said.

"Can you handle a murderous rage?"

"Probably not."

"Then, again, stay out of the way."

Mary Ann dropped Amanda back at the Charlotte airport thirty minutes prior to the time her mother was scheduled to arrive.

"Remember—"

"I know, stay out of the way, right?" Amanda interrupted.

"No," Mary Ann countered. They were standing on the curb as a policeman was walking toward them, assuredly prepared to tell them to move along. "I want to help you any way that I can. I think we've got a good, *safe* plan, Amanda. So, just stay in touch, okay?"

Amanda sized up Mary Ann. Dark hair tossed across her smooth face. Her clear countenance exuded both confidence and warmth. Why had she not had a female role model such as this, she wondered?

"Thank you. I'll be in touch."

They hugged tightly. Mary Ann waved off the cop, hugged her again, and then said, "Okay, homie, be careful."

Amanda nodded, grabbed her duffle bag, and then walked inside the terminal. A few minutes later she appeared outside farther down the arrivals section, as if she had just arrived on her originally scheduled flight.

She never saw the individual who had been waiting on her all along.

CHAPTER 66
SPARTANBURG, SOUTH CAROLINA

For Amanda, the drive to Spartanburg was another torturous journey. Her mother was relentless, probing her for information at every turn.

"So, tell me about the funeral, Amanda."

"Mom, there's nothing to tell. I was there with Matt and some others. It's over."

"We're talking about your father, right?"

She shook her head violently and emphasized, "Enough! Stop with the questions, Mother. What is it with you? Are you so damn self-centered that you can't see past yourself?"

"Don't talk to me that way, Amanda. Who do you think you are?"

"I'm sorry," she demurred. "I'm just emotional. Can we just agree not to talk about it? I mean, I've got a few days until graduation. I turn eighteen soon. Trust me, I'm stressed." She touched her mother's arm. "Sorry. Can we talk about something else, you know? Like how's the closing coming on the house?"

Melanie Garrett paused and then patted Amanda on her leg. "We went ahead and did it today. The sellers gave us a fifty thousand dollar discount for doing so. We were preapproved for the loan once you agreed to join us in the business venture."

"All of that sounds good."

"Well, we don't have to make a payment until the first of July, so the bank has loaned us the money and then we just dump the insurance money against the mortgage and pay it down. So we'll be borrowing about a million dollars, so these Army guys better come through."

"They promised me it's all going to be okay, Mom. Don't worry about it. You'll probably pay down the mortgage before the first payment is due. And this is great. It's your dream house."

She watched her mother, pale-blue eyes fixed to the road. She seemed lost in another world, perhaps envisioning how she would move her Ethan Allen maple dining room table into the new mansion or how she would decorate for the house-warming party. A slight smile turned up at the corner of her mother's mouth while her eyes sparkled.

"Yes. My dream house." The words were ushered from her mouth as if in a sigh. It was a swooning declaration. She was finally going to arrive. She *had* arrived! The years of plying away and trying to scrape her way into the upper crust had finally borne fruit. It would all be hers. "You've done well."

At that moment, Amanda did not know to whom her mother was speaking. It was creepy, she thought, the trance she had slipped into. How she could drive and be visualizing another scene was scary enough.

They continued driving in the eerie silence, her mother rearranging furniture in her daydream, most likely. Or maybe she was entertaining Ted Turner and some of the CNN anchors she always seemed to criticize. "She's ugly." "Who dressed her?" "That's a terrible tie." Amanda laid her head back against the stiff leather headrest and closed her eyes.

Eventually she felt her mother's hand on her knee. "Better off he's gone, you know? No more hassle. Turns out he was worth more dead than alive."

Amanda squeezed her mother's hand, but kept her eyes closed, then turned her head toward the window. She stared through the passenger-side window to her right, watching the traffic ebb and flow around her. An old lady driving a large Buick crawled along, inviting mild road rage from those trying to pass. Amanda stared into the sideview mirror with the cautionary words about objects being larger than they appear. Her blank gaze migrated to one of curiosity as she thought she recognized a vehicle trapped in the web of cars and trucks behind her mother's Mercedes.

Soon they were speeding along at seventy-five miles an hour, though, and the image was lost. Perhaps she was right about what, and who, she had seen. If so, what did it mean? Probably nothing, she determined, as red mustangs were free to move about Charlotte's highways just like any other cars.

The thought prompted her to check her cell phone. No new messages. Interesting. Then she had an idea. "Hey, Mom, so what's the status of the house? You got everything covered?"

"Well, I just got the paperwork back from the agent today, so we should be all set. I've got an appointment Monday morning at State Farm, and then when you get home from school Monday, we'll head out to our new home. I didn't really think we could move this fast on either house, but the market is crazy right now, and this is the norm."

Amanda chewed on her fingernail, thinking. Ideas were circling through her mind like race cars around a track.

"Monday sounds good. You've got your thing in the morning, and I have missed some classes, though Rugsdale said I've already technically graduated."

"It's a deal then."

They trudged through the rush-hour traffic in silence, the palpable tension easing a bit. Amanda guessed the questioning would resume at some point, if not by her mother then from Nina. As they drove she went through everything that Matt had told her yesterday and that which she had covered with Harlan and Mary Ann only recently.

Their plan was decent, she figured, but hers was better, especially now. A Cheshire grin crept out of the right side of her mouth, unnoticed by her mother. It must be true; the acorn really doesn't drop far from the tree. Her Machiavellian scheme had hatched in her mind when she least expected something so elaborate or wicked to reveal itself.

I-26 ticked by as they sped along I-85, approached the Spartanburg exit, and soon found their home. To her surprise, Nina's car was not there, though she knew it would not be long before she arrived. Her grandmother would want the scoop as well, no question.

"Thanks for picking me up, Mom."

She popped the trunk, grabbed her duffel bag, and maneuvered it upstairs quickly, locking her door behind her. She charged her cell phone, unpacked, and booted up her computer. She filed all of the e-mails she had forwarded herself from Dagus's computer, conjured a password for that file and hid it in a systems folder to further conceal its location. Then she mailed the entire folder to Harlan. Lastly, she copied all of the e-mails and attachments onto the thumb drive Jake had given her and debated whether to take the next step. Staring at her computer screen, she decided that only one other person could know about *her* plan, and even then, she wasn't sure. Her finger hovered over the mouse with the cursor arrow blinking above the send button.

She heard a car pull into the driveway and continued to debate what to do. With no further thought, she did what she felt was the right thing, closed the program, and then walked to the window.

Nina. She had been right about many things lately, and Amanda wondered about how to further refine her plan to make it all the more encapsulating. She wanted not just her freedom, but total victory. The competitive gene sparked like the pilot light of a furnace whose thermostat had reached ignition temperature. She had been ignited, no question.

She checked her computer once more, activated the right program, and made sure all the passwords were still in effect. She checked the microphone to see that it was on. She watched the volume bar exhibit several green bars as she repeated the word "testing" several times. She adjusted the volume so that it was more sensitive and then backed away into the center of the room and tried it again. She locked her computer but left the program running beneath the screensaver.

Once satisfied, Amanda quickly changed into a pair of stone-washed jeans and a dark blue hoodie with short sleeves and a kangaroo pocket. She slowly opened her door, peeked around the corner, and could hear her mother and grandmother in the kitchen talking in hushed voices. She needed to move now.

She gingerly walked across the landing into her mother's bedroom. Moving with purpose, she navigated to the far nightstand and opened the top drawer. In plain view was a Colt Peacemaker pistol. She retrieved it, checked the cylinder to ensure bullets were loaded, and stuffed it into her hoodie pocket. She turned and quickly moved back to her room. Though she didn't hear their voices, she was relieved as she closed her door behind her and locked it.

She stuffed the pistol into her backpack. Slinging the pack over her shoulder, she noticed the weight difference. No problem, though, she determined. Then she grabbed her cell phone and keys, and bounded cheerily down the stairs.

"Hey, Nina!" she said with enthusiasm as she leapt down the steps.

"Well, aren't you enthused for having just gotten back from your father's funeral?"

Amanda stopped her momentum briefly, but made it clear she was leaving by resting her hand on the front doorknob. Her other hand held her backpack strap across her shoulder. "I'm just glad it's over, you know? Well, almost. But it's going to be peaceful around here soon, you know? Anyway, you look nice. Gotta run."

"You just got here."

"I know. I've missed lots of school. Going to the library to catch up."

"You can't go anywhere dressed like that!"

Amanda paused a moment, taking notice of something that was out of synch. Her grandmother was standing there wearing a charcoal pantsuit with a brilliant pearl necklace. It wasn't her attire, though. Always skeptical and cynical, Nina now seemed more so, if that was even possible. Amanda's warning radar began to alert with a fine buzzing in her ears.

"Gotta run, Nina. Love you."

As she drove along the highway, Harlan's warning resonated in her mind like the lone flashing stoplight of a small country town.

Stay out of the way.

THE DATABASE

CHAPTER 67
AFGHANISTAN

SUNDAY EVENING

Major General Griffin, the commander of the 101st Airborne Division, sat in his command and control UH-60 Blackhawk, staring at the barely lit screen of a map-board to his front. He was in the rear center seat with his fire support officer and operations officer huddled tightly on either side. The intelligence officer and Matt Garrett were conferring over their headsets on the rearward facing seats across from Griffin.

"The landing zones look good so far," Matt said. "I was on these two the other day and we can get in there."

"That's in Pakistan," Lieutenant Colonel Becky Jabonski said through the mouthpiece of her headset.

"No shit," Matt said. Matt was strung out and short tempered, having immediately departed from Andrews Air Force Base in Maryland on a C-17 after the funeral and conducted two in-flight refuelings before landing at Bagram and almost immediately transitioning to Griffin's command and control helicopter. All the while he was thinking, *The Database is Always There.*

"Team, in case you haven't noticed, we're inserting two battalions, about fifteen hundred troopers on the ground in the Northwest Frontier Province," Griffin said. The interior cabin of the Blackhawk was dark as they flew from Bagram Air Base toward Jalalabad where they would refuel and then continue east into Pakistan.

"Mr. Garrett here is the agency representative on the ground that is going to ensure we have the right intelligence, get on the ground in the right areas, and attack the correct compounds. The mission is to disrupt Al Qaeda and Taliban sanctuaries sufficiently for them to either fight back or relocate. Either way, we've got them."

"Would have been nice to know about this sooner," Jabonski said, her voice tight with anxiety.

"Your CG has known and a few others. Now you know. You can either help or get out of the way," Matt said.

"Mr. Garrett, she works for me. I'll deal with her," Griffin said. "She's on board."

"As we reach Jalalabad, we'll have 20 Chinook helicopters moving one battalion north through the Kunar Valley and then they will cut over the ridge into the Chitral area, releasing 600 troops with supplies. From there they'll have multiple objectives to rapidly seize to secure the operating base. Likewise, we've got another 30 Blackhawks flying with seats out putting 600 troops into the Miram Shah area. These are simultaneous hits and we will stay for the duration until we kill enough bad guys," Matt said through the headset mouthpiece.

The operations officer, Colonel Dave Simmons said, "We're all set, though I think we've telegraphed this thing a bit."

"That's true, we have," Matt said. "But there was no avoiding that. You can't move all these helicopters and not have the enemy wonder what's going on."

"What about the Pak military, Matt?" Griffin asked.

"They don't know. They're going to be in a dilemma. Either they shoot at us and we crush them or they let us pass and bitch about it. I'm thinking they're going for option two."

"Pretty risky," Griffin said.

"Well, we'll be the biggest target, because we're going to be circling in their airspace," Matt said.

"Thought we were going to stay behind the ridge in Afghanistan?"

"Initially yes, but once the troops are on the ground, we've got to get over top of them and make sure they have what they need. Then we head back to J-Bad, refuel, cross over Tora Bora and head into Miram Shah."

"You with us the whole time?" Jabonski asked, clearly displeased.

"I might get off in Chitral, depending on what we find out," Matt said flatly. "Dave has the entire execution checklist."

"All 34 pages of it," Simmons said.

"Well, it's detailed. Our guys worked it and your aviation team has been rehearsing, though they didn't know what for. It was the only way to pull this off."

The command and control helicopter sliced its way through narrow, snowcapped defiles as it passed through the Lagman Province area en route to Nangahar Province. In truth, Matt knew that the entire 101st Airborne had been rehearsing these attacks back at Fort Campbell. When Matt had convinced the National Command Authority that the only way to succeed in Afghanistan was to get boots on the ground in Pakistan, then the 101st Airborne began receiving cryptic orders to deploy their units not to Fort Polk in Louisiana or Fort Irwin in California for training, but to Camp Hale, Colorado, the original home of the 10th Mountain Division. There the unit established its own forward operating base in the freezing cold February temperatures and conducted raids into sanitized objectives. While Matt and a few others knew that the objectives were intended to be in Pakistan, the troops on the ground were simply rehearsing the fundamentals. Get on the helicopter, get off the helicopter, follow the squad leader, kill the bad guys, find intelligence, protect your buddies, get back on the helicopter, eat chow when you can and sleep when you can.

They popped out of the defile seeing the lights of Jalalabad to their southeast. Through his night-vision goggles Matt could also see the hulking forms of CH-47 helicopters flying in formations of four, the configuration chosen to match the number of formations to the number of refuel points at Jalalabad Airfield.

As they flew, the Chinooks dipped into the airfield, sucked as much fuel as they could, and took off rapidly. As the last formation departed, the command and control helicopter refueled along with two flights of three Apache gunships, also along for the insertion. The first three immediately sped like angry wasps up to the lead of the Chinook formation, covering its flanks and prepared to conduct preparatory fires. Matt knew that overhead were two AC-130s on the northern series of landing zones along with two F-15s. The southern insertion package had the same air cover, to include two Predator unmanned aerial vehicles.

As they juked north up through the Kunar valley, Matt thought of Zachary and his fate in this forbidden land. At least he had been there for him, as Zach had for Matt in the Philippines.

As the first of the Apaches and Chinooks turned east out of Kunar, the headsets lit up with chatter.

"This is Monster 16, Approaching LZ Thunder, negative contact."

"This is Monster 26, Approaching LZ Lightning, negative contact."

Matt registered the good news with caution, knowing that in an instant it could change.

Looking at the mountain peaks—like church spires he thought—he again thought of Zachary and said to himself, "This is where I need to be."

The excited chatter of Monster 36 came across the net, "We are in a huge ambush in LZ Squall. 360 machinegun and RPG fire! Troops almost off the birds!"

Matt turned and looked at MG Griffin.

"Put me and my commo guys down in LZ Squall, General. That's where we're going."

For a moment no one spoke, but he could feel Jabonski's eyes on him and knew that her distaste had given way to respect, tinged with perhaps a bit of fear for herself as she realized what he was taking them into.

"Roger," Griffin said.

The UH-60 lifted across the mountains that separated Pakistan and Afghanistan and suddenly the United States was fully invading the sovereign territory of another nation in the post 9-11 world.

And to Matt Garrett, it felt good, because he finally figured it out.

Al Qaeda. Literally, The Base or the Database.

The Database is Always There.

CHAPTER 68
CHARLOTTE, NORTH CAROLINA

SUNDAY AFTERNOON

Amanda had spent Saturday night at Brianna's house and had long discussions with both Brianna and her mother. Brianna's mother was key to the plan and was quickly a convert after watching with outrage the CD of Len Dagus having sex with her daughter.

She made a few key phone calls with her Droid, turned on the GPS tracking device inherent in the phone, and then grabbed a disposable cell phone she had purchased.

She then bid Brianna and her mother farewell and drove to see Ms. Dwyer.

"Hey," Amanda said in a low, sweet voice to Dwyer.

"Hey, yourself." Much of the swelling on Riley's face had gone down. Stitches etched their way across her left cheek like a fossilized caterpillar. Her left arm was broken just below the elbow, a defensive injury. She reported that there were a few cracked ribs also. The decisive blow was a twenty-seven-stitch wound on the back of her head that had come from the baseball bat.

"I don't remember what happened, really. I remember you being here and then waking up in the hospital."

"You have to know, Miss Dwyer—"

"Riley, please."

"—that I, okay, Riley. That I did not do this."

"I know you didn't do this, Amanda. You're not capable of such a thing. You may have had some things deleted from your hard drive, but they're still there. They're coming back." Riley pointed at her own head when she spoke.

Amanda paused as she absorbed the image that was lying before her on the sofa. Little did Riley know, Amanda thought. She flicked at a fingernail, looking down.

"Can I trust you with something, Riley?"

"Of course you can. I might have been your stepmother one day, you know, so just look at me like that." They both paused and then giggled, Riley as best she could through the swollen lips and jaw. "Well, maybe not such a good idea," Riley added. She placed a hand on Amanda's knee. "Tell me."

"I'm getting ready to go do something that might be a bit risky, you know, and I'm sort of scared."

"Plenty scary stuff's been happening already, girlfriend. Can't you just let it alone?"

"You're just like Harlan; he's been telling me to stay out of the way."

"Why do you think I told you about him?"

Amanda sighed. She stuffed her hands into her hoodie pocket and looked around the living room, noticing for the first time there were some pictures of her father on the mantle above the fireplace. She could see that in one of the pictures he and Riley were standing atop what looked like Stone Mountain. She was hugging him with her head on his chest, her reddish hair spilling across her face. He was holding her against his side with an indistinguishable look on his face—not overly enthusiastic, not unhappy. Amanda casually walked over to the picture and lifted it off the mantle, studying her father's face.

"Looks like when I was about thirteen or fourteen?"

"Bout that."

"I hated him then, you know."

"Not really. You just thought you did. Remember, computer hard drive?"

"Right." Amanda stared at the picture. It came to her that there was a deep-set sadness in his eyes. She was neither psychologist nor mind reader, but it occurred to her that she was looking at a wounded man, struggling, she figured, with the encompassing rejection promulgated by her. Not so much the way a wine connoisseur embraces the aroma of the settled tannins in a fine Chardonnay, but more the manner in which an apprentice marvels at the work of the tradesman, she understood what she saw in her father's face. Never before had she really cared or wanted to know what he'd felt, but now it was so obvious.

"Then why did I do all those horrible things?"

She really did want to know. Not that there was much she could do about it now. Amanda sat next to Riley on the sofa, sliding her hips backward until she was touching Riley's legs, which were beneath a lightweight blanket. She looked at the photo in her hand and then at Riley. She noticed some color coming back into Riley's face. She was very pretty, as well as loving and compassionate. She could see why her father would have loved her. She would have made a great stepmother.

"What is it that you're getting ready to do that is so scary?"

"I have to fix things."

Riley sat up and was awkwardly placing the unbroken arm around her. "You've already gone a long way toward that, but some things aren't fixable."

"Maybe so," Amanda said, smiling weakly. "But I'm going to fix what I can, and I just needed to talk to you. I've got the courage to do this now. So, thank you."

"You're scaring me, Amanda," Riley said. "Don't make me bop you with this cast."

Amanda leaned over and kissed Riley on the forehead. "Get you anything before I go?"

"Why don't you stay with me tonight?"

Amanda walked toward the door, as if pulled. "I told you, I have to go fix things."

As she pulled onto the freeway, Amanda never noticed the vehicle that had been waiting in the shadows of the tall elms just past Riley Dwyer's house.

CHAPTER 69
THE CLIFFS AT KEOWEE, SOUTH CAROLINA

SPEEDING ALONG I-85, she checked out her new, disposable cell phone. She had left her Droid at Brianna's house with its GPS tracker switched on.

She punched her address book in the disposable cell, pulled up one of the few numbers she had added, and dialed. "Hey, Mister Dagus. I really need to talk to someone tonight. My mom bought this new house. I was wondering if you could meet me there." She provided him the prestigious address at The Cliffs and then said, "Sorry I missed you the other night, but I had waited and had to rush out. Call me, please."

After an hour, including two stops, she had finally reached the winding road that led to her mother's recently purchased mansion in The Cliffs at Keowee. She reached the long gravel drive just as the sun was dipping below the hills to the west and gripped the steering wheel with tense anticipation. Could she pull it off?

She noticed that Tad had been so efficient that he had already placed a SOLD sign on the lawn.

Checking her watch as she parked in a noticeable position in the front, she thought once more about the car. It should be okay, she reassured herself. Looking at her watch, she figured she had an hour before Dagus showed up, if he got the message. She still registered shock when she thought about the video with Brianna, but his weakness would serve as her bait.

While she didn't know to what degree Dagus was complicit with her mother, Amanda did know that he had written the article trashing her father. He had most likely beaten Riley Dwyer and had also likely burned her father's house.

Amanda pulled a small duffle bag out of the trunk of her car. She tried not to think about her plan as the reality of execution began to set in. Too much thought, she figured, might lead to inaction. She needed action.

She placed the bag on the brick porch with a clunking sound. The real estate agent's lockbox was behind a fern hanging from the porch ceiling. She spun the combination and got lucky on the second try. Extracting the key, she opened the door and was taken aback a moment by the beauty of the foyer.

Large oak plank tongue-in-groove slats shone pristinely beneath her feet. Tad had mentioned that they had just been freshly lacquered. The staircase to the left was directly out of the movie *Gone with the Wind* and, she considered, may even have been the actual version used in the movie. Her mother had told her the house was beautiful, but this was breathtaking. She walked straight through the foyer, across a luxurious authentic Persian rug that absorbed her feet, and into a large family room studded with floor-to-ceiling windows across its rear-facing wall. The view spread from the deck onto the crisply mown sloping lawn to a boathouse that looked like the main residence. She could see the moonlit shimmering waters of Lake Keowee beyond the pier.

"Like mini-me," she giggled, noticing how the boathouse was brick with a white rotunda. The reflection of an ascending moon was a broadening yellow stripe as it skidded across the water's still surface. Taking in the view, she got down to business.

She took the *Gone With the Wind* steps two at a time and was pleasantly surprised to find a large den at the top of the staircase. A maroon-felt pool table was situated in the center of the room, which opened onto the landing at the top of the stairs. Someone playing a ball from the near end of the table would be visible from the front door. This same pool player, if he looked up from a shot, would be staring at a six-foot-square plasma television screen deeper into the room.

"Perfect."

On that notion, she unzipped the duffle bag and placed the revolver in the middle of the pool table.

LENARD DAGUS STEERED his car along the winding road, fumbling with his cell phone. Finally able to retrieve his last call, he punched SEND and let the phone ring.

"Yesss?" He heard the suggestion in her voice.

"Amanda, it's Lenard Dagus. I'm on my way. Are you there?"

"Sorry about last night. I waited, but you never showed. I *really* wanted to talk."

"I'll be there in about ten minutes."

"Okay."

"See you in a few."

Dagus felt himself stir at the thought of what he might do to Amanda Garrett. He would try not to hurt her too much. He could make no promises, though. That scab had been picked. He knew that he was no longer in control. He was someone else now. Besides, she was playing with him. He was smart enough to detect the tease in her voice.

He raced the engine and negotiated the winding curves like a Formula One race car driver.

AMANDA STARED AT the pistol and then turned as she searched for the entertainment center's remote control. Amanda ran a light hand across the dials and buttons of the DVD player. "Come to Mama."

She pressed the eject button and slipped a disk into the player. Punching the remote, she watched as the television screen appeared. The DVD player came on immediately, to her surprise, when she punched the TV/DVD button.

"Bingo." The image she wanted was on the screen. She pressed the off button and slid the remote into her hoodie pocket.

She was ready.

CHAPTER 70
NORTHWEST FRONTIER PROVINCE, PAKISTAN

MONDAY MORNING (HOURS OF DARKNESS)

The UH-60 command and control Blackhawk settled with a hard rocking motion in the uneven terrain. Matt was out of his safety strap as were Hobart and Van Dreeves, the two "commo guys" he had brought along.

"Thanks for the ride, General. We'll be in touch," Matt said into the headset mouthpiece. The interior of the aircraft cabin was dark save the spotted red and green lenses of staff officers' flashlights. The crew chief opened the door so that the three men could exit.

"Good luck, son," General Griffin said.

"Luck, sir, has little to do with what we're going after, but thank you."

With that, Matt and his team leapt from the aircraft, took a knee and then laid flat on the ground as the helicopter powered up, spitting rocks and debris upon their backs. Once away, the Blackhawk shifted direction toward the west, lifted and flew back into Afghanistan and safer territory.

"Let's move," Matt said.

He turned on his GPS, which put him two miles from the target location where the flash drive had originally sent out the beacon. On his radio he heard the occasional spot report of troops in contact. Intermittent machine-gun fire and mortar explosions signified the metered pace of the Screaming Eagle advance through the Northwest Frontier Province. They had inserted along multiple landing zones and by now hundreds of air assault troopers were scampering through the hostile villages of this Al Qaeda stronghold in heavy handed fashion. This was no peacekeeping mission.

Rather, this was a raid that was intended to produce at least one pearl of intelligence, whether it be weapons of mass destruction, Al Qaeda or Taliban leadership, or indicators of nation-state support to the enemy. They needed to come back with something, Matt knew, or they were screwed. Pakistan would go ape shit and America would have to hasten its withdrawal from the region. But now seemed as good a time as any to put on the full court press, which is what Matt had argued for with the National Command Authority and he was glad that Houghton had backed his recommendation.

"One and a half miles men. We need to get there before any of the Airborne guys," Matt said.

"Their objectives are in the two opposite directions," Hobart said. "I made sure of that."

"These guys can get lost. We need that computer and we need to docex that bitch," Matt said.

"I've got that covered," Van Dreeves said.

They climbed from 12,000 feet to 15,000 feet and back down to somewhere around 14,000 feet. They quietly bypassed goat herders and kids running around in the middle of the night with all of the commotion. To the best of their knowledge they had not been compromised.

As they approached the valley that led to the village, which was the object of their advance, Matt halted. They were standing in ankle deep snow, a cool breeze rifling through the v-shaped notch in the mountain pass. He saw a few dotted lights below in the valley and knew that they had found their mark. The satellite and Predator reconnaissance missions they had performed matched closely the sparse layout of the *qalats* spread through the kilometer-long valley, which was protected by knifelike ridges on three sides. Snowcapped, they looked positively impassable. How Zach had ever escaped from this location, Matt would perhaps never know.

"This one's for Zach," Matt whispered.

"Roger that," Van Dreeves and Hobart chimed in unison over their cordless voice microphones.

"Hobart, give me some overwatch as Van Dreeves and I snake down this trail. It's the only way in and we'll need a sniper shot, I'm sure."

"Roger." Hobart moved about twenty meters up the ridge, extended the bipod on his M24, sighted in, and reported, "Two guards on the number three."

They had mapped the 12 homes in the village and given each one a number so that they could easily reference where they were and where they needed to go. Number three was the target home.

"Anything overwatching the pass?"

"Hang on."

Matt waited as Hobart scanned for likely shooter locations. Small hilltops, caves, crevices, rooftops, and the like.

"Got a warm body on the western side of the ledge about 200 meters above number two."

"Anything else?" Matt asked.

"I've got something on the east side, looks like it's aiming at the switch-back we'll have to go down," Van Dreeves whispered. He was looking through his thermal scope.

"Hang on," Hobart said. After a pause. "Yeah. I've got him. The pussy is all wrapped up in a blanket, but he's got a DSHK machinegun. Looks functional."

"Any comms on him?" Matt asked.

"Looks like a small personal mobile radio."

"Okay, when I say we're moving, shoot him between the eyes, then focus on the far side guy. We'll take his PMR as we pass by. All set?"

"Roger," Hobart said.

"Roger," Van Dreeves agreed.

"Moving," Matt reported. He stepped through the snow onto the trail, his boots gaining purchase in the thick packed snowfall. He heard the audible click of Hobart's weapon firing and continued moving, not waiting for the report. Hobart was good and odds were he killed the guy on the first shot.

"He's dead," Hobart reported. "No further movement."

Matt and Van Dreeves moved quickly nearly a quarter mile, switching back through the mountain defile, lowering and slipping into the valley until they found the ledge upon which the doomed machinegun position was perched.

"Good spot," Van Dreeves said.

"For us," Matt said. "Search him quickly." Matt had his flashlight out and they scanned the machinegun, then the body, quickly determining that the personal mobile radio was the only thing of value. "Leave the machinegun alone. We may need it getting out of here."

"We're moving," Matt reported to Hobart, who came back quickly.

"Our friend near number two is up and looking. He's onto something," Hobart said.

"Kill him," Matt replied.

"Roger."

A few seconds passed when Hobart said, "He's dead."

"Okay, the two guys near number three?"

"Still there. Not moving other than kicking goat shit."

"We're going to hold up at number one and then make our move on number three."

"Roger. I have clear shots on both guards on number three," Hobart said.

"Once I give the word, take those shots and then come down to number one, we'll consolidate there."

"Roger."

Matt and Van Dreeves dove into a small ditch and waded through thigh-deep snow toward a remote house separated by a couple hundred meters from the rest of the village. They exited the ditch, stumbling on the rocks and snow as they crossed to the high walled compound.

"You getting any activity on one?" Matt asked Hobart.

"Nothing. No sign of life."

"Okay, we're going in and if we find anyone, we'll bind and gag. Then we'll gather here and move to three as a team."

Something at the back of Matt's mind was telling him that this was too easy, but he pressed on. He had set a few baited ambushes himself where he had lured his prey into an untenable situation, but now he was at least semi-confident that the massive raid with the 101st Airborne had put the inner security ring for Mullah Rahman on the move. How good they were was anyone's guess, but he suspected they were not bad.

He led Van Dreeves through the gate of the walled compound and turned right, calling, "Clear right," as Van Dreeves called, "Clear left." Matt sighted down his weapon using his night-vision monocle and saw a couple of goats wandering aimlessly. He looked at the window of the house for movement and saw none. He covered the twenty meters to the house with Van Dreeves to his left rear. They stacked along the wall opposite the doorknob. With Van Dreeves looking to the rear, Matt ducked, tugged slightly on the knob. Too stiff. Maybe rigged. He backed off, moving his hand across his throat to indicate to Van Dreeves that he didn't like the front entrance.

They moved as a team to the north side of the home and found a low window, maybe five feet high. It was big enough for a man to climb through. Matt stuck his head around the corner and turned on his infrared flashlight, which illuminated the room in invisible light that only his night-vision technology could see. It was an empty room with a door that opened toward the front of the house.

"I'm in first, then you follow," Matt whispered.

"Roger. Hobart just made it to the front gate."

"Hobart, cover the front door in case anyone comes out. We're entering from the north window."

"Roger," Hobart replied, his breathing heavy from the run through the snow.

The wind picked up and howled across the barren terrain, reminding them of their vulnerability to the elements.

Matt climbed in and quickly went to one knee, his goggles scanning left and right, looking for the trap. Van Dreeves was surprisingly quick, landing like a cat to his left.

"Let's move," Matt said.

They stacked against the open doorway then Matt spun inward toward the back of the house while Van Dreeves turned toward the front door.

"IED," Van Dreeves said quietly. "Don't move."

Matt froze. He had read about the "House-borne Improvised Explosive Devices." Essentially the house could be remotely detonated to implode.

"What is it?" Matt asked.

"Wait, looks like it's triggered by the front door," Van Dreeves said.

"Any kind of remote device?"

"Still looking."

Van Dreeves was on one knee bravely using his flashlight around the device. Matt stole a look and saw a cooking pot with wires sticking out of it, one of which led to the front door. He saw the telltale playing card clamped between to drawing pins pressed into the inward edges of a wooden clothes pin. If the door were to open, the wire would undoubtedly remove the playing card from the clothespin and the two metal contacts would close a circuit powered by the battery next to the cooking pot, which Matt was sure was filled with ammonia nitrate, the most lethal nonmilitary explosive in country.

"Can you cut the wire?" Matt asked.

"Rather not mess with it, you know. Not sure about anti-handling. Right now we're okay. Let's see what they're protecting and get the hell out of here."

"Agree," Matt said. "Let's move to the back. Hobart, you monitor all? Do not go near the front door?"

"Roger all."

By Matt's estimation there were two more rooms to inspect. They entered the first and it was a sparsely furnished room with a sleeping roll, prayer mat, and table.

"No joy."

They moved to the second room and Matt switched on his flashlight, bringing his Sig Sauer up quickly against a figure chained to the wall, his head hanging limply. Then he caught Van Dreeves's flashlight out of the corner of his eye on a body on the floor covered in a blue sheet of some type.

"Help," came a low moan from the man on the wall.

Matt moved his flashlight to the man's face, badly beaten and bleeding.

"Help me."

Van Dreeves was on one knee, his hand on the neck of the woman on the floor.

"She's dead. Probably earlier in the day, at least."

Matt recognized now it was a burqa covering the woman.

They quickly removed the man from the wall and Matt found a tin cup on the floor, opened his Camelbak, filled it and let the man drink.

"Hobart. One dead woman and one severely beaten man inside. We'll need to cuff him and take him with us when it's time."

"Roger."

Once the man was on the floor Matt gave him a few minutes, precious time he didn't have, but if the man was a local he might be able to provide precise intelligence. So he thought it was worth the tradeoff in time.

"Name?" Matt asked in Pashtu.

The man lifted his head, but turned away from the light, holding up a scarred hand.

"Please, no light. Eyes."

Matt shut the light and flipped on his infrared light, switching to his goggle.

"Name?"

"Mansur. I am a messenger."

"For who?"

"For the man you are looking for."

"Who am I looking for?"

"Rahman. Mullah Rahman."

"Why am I looking for him?" Matt pressed feeling the need to move.

"Must stop him," Mansur said. "Trying to escape."

"Where to?"

"Dubai. Maybe Yemen."

It all made sense now. Rahman was communicating with operatives in Dubai and Yemen and needed one last payday.

"He's got the plan. This plan," Mansur said.

"Where is he now?"

"Fighting. Not sure."

"Where is his house?"

"He has many. But here, two houses up the road."

Number three. They were on target.

"Why do we need to stop him?"

Mansur's head lolled back and forth, as if he were on acid swaying to a rhythmic Beatles song.

"Killed so many. So many to come."

"Matt, we need to bolt. I've got movement up on the ridge," Hobart reported.

"Okay, we'll come back for Mansur after we hit Rahman's house."

"I think we might have a fight on our hands," Hobart said.

The night opened into a brilliant display of fireworks as soon as Matt and Van Dreeves stepped to the window.

Hobart angled his sniper rifle out of the opening as a deluge of machine-gun fire rained down upon them.

CHAPTER 71
SPARTANBURG, SOUTH CAROLINA

SUNDAY EVENING (EASTERN TIME)

Melanie Garrett paced nervously in her kitchen, spiked heels echoing like gunshots off the parquet floor.

"Got your attention yet?" Nina Hastings leaned against the center island's gray marble top.

"Well, Mama, she's got something going on, that's for sure."

"I'll tell you exactly what she has going on. She's been commiserating with a journalist, an attorney, and that shrink, who is out of the hospital. Doesn't sound like a good combination. Still think you got it all under control?"

"Who? What—who has she been talking to? I mean an attorney? What's that all about? How do you know this?"

"Calm down, Melanie. I know this because I've been doing something besides being a greedy bitch. Like I always tell you, you get in this life what you take, and I've never gotten anything by standing around. Amanda is playing you for a fool. She got you to sign that big house contract, and you let yourself get pressured into doing it."

"Well, you agreed."

"My name isn't on that document anywhere is it?"

Melanie Garrett stopped her pacing and looked at her mother in stunned silence. In the seedy back lots of her Deep South youth, Nina Hastings had learned to play for keeps. She was, in fact, no different than the run of the mill terrorist, plotting the destruction and sending others to do her bidding. At the very core of her existence was a narcissistic drive fueled by a fear of unworthiness, but which manifested itself in the form of vitriolic subterfuge. She had to destroy everything around her to make herself feel worthy.

"What are you saying? We're in this together."

Nina stared at her daughter. Her emotions were not clashing. Rather, she viewed everything through a lens that reflected back onto herself. Her prism was indeed a mirror. Nina chuckled a patronizing tune.

"Of course, dear." She would just have to see how everything developed. Nina Hastings always kept her options open.

"Is Dagus still with us? He's not going to blow the cover, is he?" She was beginning to feel paranoid.

"What you don't know is that he got all moral and everything about this stupid media hunt group he's in. He started to back out. He said it was more important to expose the truth. The people have a right to know and all that happy horseshit."

"But the pedophile thing. We've got him on that."

"He called your bluff, Melanie. Only you weren't here. I took the call, and we met after school last week. Dagus knows the file is sealed, and it would take an act of Congress to open it."

"But still, just the implication—"

"And he sues your ass for a million dollars."

"So what did you do?"

"Let's just say I gave him some incentive."

Melanie looked at her mother warily. "Incentive?"

"I made a deal with him. He lives up to his end of the bargain, and I give him $10,000."

"You did what?"

"Don't you think I know what's going on around here? I knew the man was a pervert from the first day I met him. He *wanted* Amanda. I diverted his attention to that little slut Brianna instead." Nina waved her hand as if to swat a fly and turned away. She walked out of the kitchen and up the stairs. Melanie followed her mother into Amanda's room.

"Are you saying he wanted to have sex with Amanda?"

"Oh don't pretend to be so naïve, Melanie. You knew that from the beginning. And to protect your five hundred thousand dollars I'm sure you were considering it. I heard you in the driveway, urging Amanda to go see Dagus. And you knew! I saved you from yourself!"

Melanie crossed her arms and looked away at the oak chest she had cradled the other day.

"Go ahead, pretend it isn't true. I don't care." Nina drove the stake in a bit deeper.

"But—"

"No 'buts,' Melanie. Listen. I've seen the way Brianna looks at Dagus. So, she gets to experiment. Dagus gets a fix. He keeps his mouth shut for you. Brianna gets some money for her mom. Everybody wins."

"For me?"

The two women stared at one another for a few moments.

"Well, are we going to just stand here, or are we going to finish this thing? Is that keystroke software still working?" Nina asked, staring at Amanda's computer.

Melanie looked into the hallway, as if she was expecting Amanda to materialize, and then back at her mother. She did a quick visual tour of the room. The bright yellow-and-white patterned bedspread was made neatly. The mini-blinds were opened slightly. The street light painted muted yellow prison bars on the floor. Amanda's desk contained the usual smattering of notepaper and opened school books.

She sighed, as if to shake off the film of their nefarious deeds. "Of course. We've been using it for years. Why wouldn't it work now?"

And of course she picked up right where she left off. "Then let's see what our little girl has been up to."

Melanie sat down at the computer and pressed four keys at once, but instead of prompting her to activate the keystroke copy software she had installed on Amanda's computer, it stopped her screen saver and prompted a password.

"That's new." She tried again the four simultaneous keys required to activate the keystroke software saved on the root drive, with no result.

"Why would she change her password?" Melanie asked aloud.

"Why do you think? I thought I trained you better than that." Nina's voice drew a sharp edge. "She's hiding something."

Melanie tried several different combinations of passwords that she had retrieved from the keystroke and screenshots secretly saved to her hard drive. All were unsuccessful. There was even a function that recorded the information and sent blind e-mails to a designated account, essentially delivering everything the individual typed into the computer keyboard as well as screenshots every minute. The screenshot was particularly useful in seeing what others were sending Amanda or what she was viewing on the Internet. Melanie had rationalized the use of the software four years ago under the premise of protecting Amanda from Internet predators.

Nina sat on the edge of the bed as Melanie turned around to respond to her question. "What are you going to do?"

"Well, I need to find out what she's hiding from us. It's the only way to keep her under control."

"I'm aware of that, but if you can't get in, what can you do?"

"We've got to find her and stop whatever it is she has planned. There are too many people involved now, if what you say is true. A lawyer and a journalist to go along with this Dwyer bitch?"

"That's right."

"Who's the lawyer?"

"You don't want to know."

"Humor me."

"Foxworth."

Melanie let out a long sigh. Just about everyone in the Carolinas had heard the name of the promising young attorney whose litigation brilliance compelled adversaries to seek solutions outside of the courtroom. "He's the 'fathers' rights' guy?"

"Part of his portfolio."

Melanie chewed on her bottom lip for a minute and looked at her mother. "I've got to find Amanda now. Talking to her is the only way."

"Good luck."

As she stood, the home phone rang. Answering it, she heard what she thought was Amanda's voice screaming. "Mother, it's the new house! Come, quick!"

★ ★ ★

JAKE DEVEREAUX SPUN the ankle bracelet that the deputy sheriff had secured to his leg several days ago. "Fricking house arrest . . ."

He lay back on his bed and stared at the ceiling, absently tossing a football to see how close he could bring it to touching the plaster without actually making contact.

On his fifth try he nicked the ceiling and some white dust fell into his face. Spitting it out, he sat up, which was when he heard his computer buzz. He had been keeping connected to his Yahoo! instant messenger with voice, hoping Amanda would contact him.

He sat down at his desk, shifted the mouse to remove the screen saver and then listened as the two women talked. The voices were surprisingly clear, though one seemed closer to the microphone than the other.

"That's new."

"Why would she change her password?"

Jake scrambled for his cell phone. He had to call them before it was too late. He made the connection and began a long conversation.

CHAPTER 72
PAKISTAN

MONDAY MORNING (HOURS OF DARKNESS)

Mullah Rahman received the call from Bagram that "hundreds" of helicopters were taking off and flying to the east. Translated, that meant probably thirty or forty. His man inside in the Laundromat had spotted "thousands" of 101st Airborne Division soldiers boarding the helicopters which meant that the action was going to take place inside of Afghanistan as the conventional soldiers never pressed too far up against the border, much less crossed into Pakistan.

He posted his sentries along the ridge that separated Pakistan from Afghanistan along the Nuristan and Kunar Province borders so that they could report on the locations of the landing and then Rahman could use his rockets and mortars to harass the Americans all night long without fear of reprisal.

He had killed Kamil's wife and kept Mansur chained to the wall then rigged the house to explode the minute someone tried to enter. He still thought Kamil might return and the isolated qalat was always the initial link up location. Its tunnel complex beneath led to his house inside the village and to an escape route into the side of the mountains.

Initially, when he had heard the reports of hundreds of helicopters, crossing the jagged snowcapped ridge his first thought had been, "They're lost." This actually happened on occasion given that the borders were not marked with fences, or beacons, or anything other than indiscriminate shale and snowfall.

But when the soldiers began disembarking in valleys to his north and south, he thought about his flash drive and said, "They tricked me."

But something was off. The flash drive plan had a withdrawal plan. He had committed his fighters into Afghanistan and the Thorium mines based on that information. Plus, this was forbidden terrain and he had paid his contacts in the Pakistan military handsomely to provide him any information about impending attacks, which the American forces always coordinated with the hapless Pakistan military commanders.

While many believed that fighting for terrain and people was the primary focus of this war, Rahman knew that the true duel was about acquiring and protecting information.

And he starkly realized he had lost this particular contest, temporarily.

The wind stung his face as he knelt on the outskirts of his escape cave no more than 400 meters from his home. Through his night-vision goggles he could see the helicopters a few miles to the north and a few miles to the south, but nothing in his immediate area. His big problem now was that he could not communicate with any of his watchmen.

Suddenly, Aswan, who was huddled next to him, muttered, "Three Americans."

Rahman turned and peered through his goggles barely making out two men going into the window and another running through the snow and pressing himself against the wall of the qalat.

"What did you do with the computers?" Rahman asked his aide.

"They are in the basement, protected by a fake IED," Aswan said.

"Get to the DSHK and shoot at Mansur's house until you ignite the explosives. I'm going back for the hard drive. They get that, they get everything and I . . . we lose our advantage. Our just reward."

Rahman and Aswan gave each other the warrior hand-to-forearm clasp and departed in two separate directions. Aswan overland to the DSHK position and Rahman back into the dark tunnel that led to the basement of his house.

About half way through the labyrinth, Rahman heard the dull thump of the DSHK machinegun firing at the house where he had killed Kamil's wife and shackled Mansur.

He needed to grab the hard drive and the remainder of the $500,000 and escape into the next set of villages to the east. Always push east, further into Pakistan, away from the Americans.

Who had surprisingly attacked on his turf.

Reaching the outer door to the basement, he heard voices above.

CHAPTER 73
LAKE KEOWEE, SOUTH CAROLINA

SUNDAY EVENING (EASTERN TIME)

"Hi, Amanda," Dagus called from the foyer. "Wow. Nice. This the place your mother's buying?" Then after a moment. "Smells like somebody's getting ready to barbecue or something."

Amanda cocked her head from the balcony that looked down onto the atrium. She opened her mouth to say something, but then decided not to.

"So how are you, Amanda? Are you coming down? Want me to come up?" Dagus apparently wasn't going to wait for an invitation, moving toward the steps as he removed his jacket. She watched him ascend as if propelled. He was different, she thought. Did he know something? Had she left a clue behind at his house?

"Sure, Lenard, come on up."

Amanda moved away from the railing, turning to her right to watch him approach the top landing. She saw he was wearing a long-sleeve madras shirt with tan khaki pants and dock shoes. He had gelled his hair and his physical presence was preceded by a crisp, citrus scent.

"Lenard. I like you calling me that. It connotes a certain . . . intimacy."

Amanda gave no indication of her inner turmoil. The pressure she felt was enormous. He approached her as he stepped onto the landing. To his right was the railing that gave way to the foyer below.

"Or would you prefer I call you Del?"

Dagus stopped at the top step, one foot on the landing and the other on the next to last step. "Come again?"

"You know, Del Dangurs? Like Jimmy Olson, star reporter, who gets jealous of living in Superman's shadow?"

"Amanda, I've no idea what you're talking about." He went for a consoling voice that somehow made him seem more dangerous. Controlled rage. How long could someone bind fury, she wondered? And how many years had he lived behind this veil? The pressure *he* must be feeling at this moment.

Amanda wrinkled her nose as if to let him know that she wasn't buying his act. "Well, I read newspapers too, Del." She backed around the pool table, keeping her back to the entertainment center.

"Honestly, I have no idea what you are saying, Amanda." He paused a second; something seemed to register. "Were you in my computer, Amanda?"

"Why, sir, I've no idea what you're talking about," she mimicked in a syrupy sweet Southern drawl. Scarlett O'Hara had been her favorite role in the high school drama club.

"You came to me because you needed help, Amanda. I'm here to help you." Dagus stopped when he saw the pistol lying in the middle of the table. "What the hell is that?"

"What?" Amanda continued to look him in the eyes.

"That," he growled, pointing at the pistol.

"Oh, that," she chuckled. "Why, sir, I believe that's a Colt Peacemaker." She winked at him suggestively. "Wanna make some peace?"

If the moment were not so serious, the look on Dagus's face would have been priceless, but she didn't have the time to savor it.

His left hand reached toward the center of the pool table.

"You know, the police can prove that you burned down my dad's house in North Carolina."

A dull glaze covered his eyes—the sullen look of a man who was crossing into the irrational. She knew this would be the dangerous part, as her manipulations would be less effective and she would, therefore, have less control of the situation. But she had to know. She checked her watch, wondering what could be taking so long.

As she looked up, the pistol was in his hand. "Amanda, why is this here? What are you doing?"

"Come on, Del Dangurs, tell me about that article you wrote trashing my father. Why'd you write it, you son of a bitch?"

"I'm not Del Dangurs!" he screamed.

Backing slowly to the entertainment center, she lifted the remote out of her kangaroo pocket and pressed PLAY.

Dagus moved to the side of the table, holding the pistol in his hand. He stopped abruptly as the image of he and Brianna was projected across the giant screen.

"Gotta love these jumbotrons, you know. I thought this might help us sort some things out. Now why did you decide to meet me here tonight? Thought you were getting some of this action?"

"How'd you . . ."

"I thought a tall guy like you would, you know"—she looked at the screen and squinted—"have some size to you or something. I guess I was wrong." She shrugged.

The bound fury showed signs of loosening. His face was flush red, and sweat was beginning to seep onto his brow.

"Cat got your tongue, Del? Can't find a woman your age, so you have to hump my best friend?" Her guess had been that he was so controlled that once the fury was unleashed, the pendulum would swing completely in the opposite direction. Passivity would give way to action. Warmth would quickly blend into rage. Control would find its match in abandon.

The situation into which she was thrusting him, she hoped, would be overwhelming to him. She was banking on the belief that he would snap, once threatened with publication of the fact that he was molesting a minor, had burned down her father's house, and had written a smear article about him in the newspaper.

The loud moans from the video made the scene surreal. His composure was striking to her. He was remaining calm in the face of irrefutable evidence.

"She that good, Del?" she said, looking at the video and then turning from the hideous image.

Then it happened. He moved across that line, and she could see the rage burning in his eyes. "You die, all this dies with you. It will look like a suicide. The forlorn daughter kills herself after reading the article destroying her father's fabled reputation." The pistol was firm in his hand as he pointed it at her face from a distance of about five feet. She backed away, keeping the pool table between them. Worse, his voice was still measured and calm. Controlled and decisive.

"Not so, Lenard. My friend at the *Charlotte Observer* has all your videos and a bunch of other e-mails, too. Maybe you know her?"

"I don't believe you."

"You'll find out soon enough. You should know her from your work at the newspaper." She checked her watch again.

"Turn off the video, Amanda!" he screamed. There it was. He was losing control now. He continued moving toward her and she kept moving away from him, resulting in a ridiculous bit of circling the pool table. "What's so funny? I came here to help you!"

"Chill out, Del."

"Shut up!"

"Hey, just because you're having a bad day doesn't mean you have to project that onto me. I mean, you're probably only looking at thirty or forty years in prison. And the good part is"—she threw her hands out as if in a welcoming gesture—"you get to be someone's prison bitch."

He lunged at her across the table, swiping the pistol at her face.

She laughed. "You're supposed to use it to shoot people, not hit them with it, you coward. All this time pretending to be the good teacher, and now everyone will know you as the child molester. The arsonist. The attempted murderer. Thanks for burning down my dad's house, you son of a bitch. And then you try to kill an innocent woman?"

Amanda recounted the crimes visited upon her life in recent days. The destruction of her father's house and his carefully stored memories. The assault on Riley Dwyer. The framing of Jake. It was as if she was the point man in a combat patrol, and the enemy was silently disabling everyone around her so that when she turned around to get a head count, there was no one left. She was alone in her struggle. Her epiphany was that it had always been this way.

He stopped circling and stood still. A chill shot up her spine as if along an electrical current propelled through copper wires. Calm settled over him like a morning fog.

"What are you talking about, Amanda? I didn't do those things."

Amanda thought to herself that he sounded more like a mental patient calmly denying reality. It seemed he was trying to convince himself more than her. Why would he deny it?

The front door swung open, and Melanie Garrett entered the foyer.

CHAPTER 74
THE CLIFFS AT KEOWEE, SOUTH CAROLINA

"What are you doing, Amanda?"

Melanie Garrett walked carefully into the foyer, her steps pinging hollow against the strained noises of Dagus giving commands on the video upstairs. She watched her mother stop with one foot on the first step up from the foyer. She sniffed. "What's that smell?" But it was more a question to herself than one she was seeking an answer to at the moment.

Before Amanda had a chance to respond, her mother was at the mid-landing of the stairway, one hand atop the beveled handrail. As if pulled by a string, she continued until she was standing on the second floor, the steps immediately to her back, the railing with her hand still upon it to her right, and the drama of Dagus's shaking hand holding a pistol aimed at her only child directly to her front.

"Len, what are you doing? What are you doing with my gun?"

"Amanda seems to think that I've done some bad things, Melanie. Why don't you tell her what's really going on?"

"Lenard here wanted to come here and hook up with me for sex, Mama," Amanda whimpered and then changed the tone of her voice. "What do you know about all of that?" Her tenor was sharp and judgmental.

"What are you talking about Amanda? Now, Len, put down the pistol." Melanie's voice quivered as she spoke.

Amanda stared at her mother. She was wearing a cotton knit short-sleeve sweater with green and orange rain forest designs of palm trees, banana leaves, monkeys, and other animals stitched into the pattern. Bright orange Capri pants stopped a few inches above Bruno sandals. A pumpkin-colored sandstone necklace circled her neck like orange Chiclets. She had clipped her hair back, not her most flattering look. If the light hit her mother at certain angles, her plastic surgery scars, however faint, were visible.

"Mama, this crazy bastard had sex with Brianna. See," she said, pointing at the television. "He burned down my daddy's house, beat up Riley Dwyer, and then he went and wrote that terrible article about him."

"What are you talking about?" Her mother's question seemed sincere. "The house was an accident, Amanda. Your shrink was mugged. And the article is mostly true, and Brianna's a whore. So, why don't you tell me what you're doing here with your teacher?"

"What am I doing? He came here to rape me, and now he's got a gun on me. And you suggested I talk to him!"

"Shut up! Shut up, both of you!" Amanda had momentarily switched off Dagus, but now she became fully aware that he had escalated out of control.

"Okay, okay! Enough!" Melanie screamed. She saw Dagus flinch and tighten his grip on the pistol. His breathing was heavy and rapid, as if he were nearly hyperventilating.

"If you prick us, do we not bleed? If you tickle us, do we not laugh? If you poison us, do we not die? And if you wrong us, shall we not revenge?" His voice was tinny and awkward. His bizarre quoting of Shakespeare at this moment, and particularly a quote about death, was unnerving.

She saw her mother freeze. The severity of the situation had finally registered with her, it seemed. But Amanda remained cool and focused, just like her father would have.

I'm a part of you . . . you're a part of me too.

Her mother's face was in clear focus. The skin stretched taut against the cheekbones, eyebrows arched a bit too high, the nose sloped with a small lift at the end, freckles dotted either smooth, sanded cheek.

Disregarding Dagus's insanity for the moment, she zeroed in on her mother, and began saying what she had been waiting to say. "Well, I checked, Mama, through my attorney, and you forgot one thing. You of all people. And then you confirmed it in the car yesterday." She shook her head and made a "tsk, tsk" sound.

"Your attorney?" Melanie scoffed, and it came off as a high-pitched laugh.

The thunderous boom of the pistol deafened her for a brief moment, but she was surprised at how calm she remained. Where had he aimed the pistol?

"Now do I have your attention!"

"Lenard, you're losing it, baby." He was around the table and on her in a rapid movement that surprised even Amanda. She felt his sinewy arm crook around her neck and the cold steel of the Peacemaker against her temple. As he pulled her against his body, she reached into her hoodie pocket and retrieved her lighter. The movement was inconspicuous and therefore not noticed by her mother or Dagus, who were focused on one another.

"Shut your mouth, Amanda." She felt him fumble with the pistol a bit, as if the weight of it might be tiring his arm.

"Len," Melanie said carefully and slowly. "We can all get out of this. We can pretend nothing has happened. Just put the gun down."

Amanda was surprised at how calm her mother seemed, though she could hear the fear in her voice. But of what was she afraid? For whom was she scared? And why would she want to pretend that nothing was happening? A madman had a gun to her head! That was what hurt most of all at that moment, that her mother appeared not to care.

"Yeah, Lenard, just give her the pistol back, you coward. You won't use it anyway."

"Amanda Garrett! You let me handle this, young lady."

"Please, Mom, don't you think it's a bit late to be trying to discipline me?" She paused then leaned over her shoulder, separating the pistol from her temple. "You looking forward to taking it up the ass in prison, Lenard?"

She felt him clench against her. "I swear to God I will kill her, Melanie, if you try to take me down. I've got the goods on you two, you know." He started to shuffle her along the pool table toward the staircase. "Now move away. I'm taking her as insurance."

Insurance. There was that word.

"Ooh, sweet," Amanda said. "Insurance. Make you think of anything, Mom?" She spun the wheel once on the lighter and the flame jumped out brilliantly.

"This is out of control. What in the hell are you talking about?"

"What's with the lighter? Get rid of that!" Dagus challenged Amanda, lamely attempting to move the pistol from her head to ineffectively swat at the lighter, while retaining his grip on her neck.

She moved her arm and wrestled against Dagus as she flipped the small switch that would hold the butane aperture on the lighter open so that it would burn without the force of her thumb. Dagus had almost moved her to the top step that would lead them down the staircase.

"Wait, one second, Lenard." She was pronouncing the name in a way that she knew would upset him, piss him off. She was mocking him. "I need to say something to my mother before you take me to your place and try to do to me what you did to Brianna and any number of other underage girls."

She could feel him trembling against her. She sensed that he was confused, teetering on the brink of something, perhaps reaching a tipping point.

"That ought to add another twenty years to your sentence. Rape of a minor. Hey, I've got an idea, why don't you just put that pistol in your mouth and end your miserable life right now? What would you say? Some *Romeo and Juliet*? Parting is such sweet sorrow? Or how about some *Macbeth*? Those clamorous harbingers of blood and death?"

Feeling the momentum, she could sense that she was inside his thoughts staring at the confusion ripping his deranged mind apart like demons. "Go ahead, just do us all a favor, you shithead, and kill yourself. Stick it in your mouth now. Isn't that what you said to Brianna, 'Stick it in your mouth'? Go ahead, stick it in your mouth."

"Amanda, stop it!"

"You stop it, Mother! You show me what you love more, this house or me." She held the lighter high over her head as if at a rock concert.

"Get rid of that lighter!" her mother screamed, swatting at her hand. She connected with Amanda's and the lighter broke free, bounced once off the railing and then fell toward the foyer. The flame cast an eerie ball of light, which caused shadows to dance rapidly on the walls of the foyer below. Landing with a slight thud, flame erupted as the lighter fluid she had poured into the thick Persian rug accelerated the fire instantly across its twelve-foot expanse.

"Nooo!" Melanie Garrett leaned over the railing, her face a contorted death mask, haunting and pained.

"What are you thinking about, Mother?" she screamed above the roaring fire. "Did we forget to insure the house? Oh my, after years of making me go to the doctor so you can make a few bucks off Dad's insurance, how can you forget to do something as simple as insuring the house?"

Her mother stared at her with a palpable hate. Amanda could sense the poison filling the venom sacs.

"How could you do this to me?" Melanie ran past her and the man holding a pistol to her head. Amanda watched her leap down the steps and race toward the back of the house, only to have the fire, which had already begun licking at the freshly lacquered hardwood floors, push her back toward the front door. "Call the fire department!"

"How could you do the last seventeen years of my life to me, and to my dad?" she called over the banister. "It's your turn."

Then Amanda turned to Dagus, still holding her, but seemingly over-whelmed by the turn of events—perhaps in awe of her manipulation; she didn't know.

"Looks like we're screwed, Lenard. No way out of this now, you know. Don't worry, there's a copy of the video at the *The Observer*, too." His arm was pressed tight against her throat, causing her to thrust her words past her larynx and then gulp in air. "And Mama's going to lose about a million bucks. What a shame. Fire department comes, the cops come, and so on. They'll all be here, wild man."

She was surprised as it happened. So rarely in life does anything play out almost exactly as one envisions it. Blaming Dagus for the article defaming her father, for violating her best friend, and for all of the other horrible things she had seen on his computer, Amanda felt vindicated. Payback's a bitch.

And as far as her mother was concerned, Amanda felt little satisfaction, yet had accomplished her goal of finding out what she loved more: her or her possessions. Her mother did not love her. It was that simple. Painful, but she had needed to be sure.

"For in that sleep of death, what dreams may come . . ." Dagus began. He gently released her and then swiftly moved the pistol under his chin. The bullet kicked his head back with such force that his tall frame flipped against the railing and slid along the handrail until his momentum carried him over the banister and into the flame.

She stood on the balcony watching the fire lick at the steps. From this point on, everything would be hard, but also easy. Cutting against the grain of her upbringing would be hard, but her motivation would be pure. There would be no conflict. Up until now, she had been unsure, didn't know whom she could trust.

Amanda fled into the master bedroom and raced down its deck steps into the backyard. The moon had moved overhead and cast enough light to give her some depth perception.

As she rounded the side of the house, she saw her mother running back toward the front door. Flames were now visible through the windows of the rooms adjacent to the entrance. The fire was spreading and would consume the house, she thought.

As she approached her car, she stopped and turned to see her mother reaching for the brass-handled front doorknob. *Not a good idea, Mom*, she wanted to say as she slid into her driver's seat. She thought she heard the anguished wail of a damned soul above the din of her engine and the crunch of her tires as she rolled away.

Immediately she grabbed the cell phone and saw that it was off, as she had left it. The plan would not allow her to call for about thirty minutes, so she drove in silence, no iPod or radio, until she reached I-85.

She could feel it coming together. She had envisioned the plan and executed it. Worry continued to bite at her, preventing her from becoming too excited about the recent accomplishments. She had to hand it to Dagus, he had remained consistent in his denial.

"Out of the jaws of death," she whispered to herself. She looked at her hands upon the steering wheel. They were shaking terribly as she noticed her speed approach ninety miles an hour. *Slow down*, she told herself.

There was still much to do.

Once she was at the predetermined distance away from the mansion, she picked up the cell phone. She played around with it for a moment, learning the buttons, and called the number.

"It's done. Go ahead with it."

CHAPTER 75
NORTHWEST FRONTIER PROVINCE, PAKISTAN

MONDAY MORNING

The Database is Always There, Matt thought.

Huddled with Hobart and Van Dreeves in the room where Mansur was shackled to the wall, Matt calculated that someone had manned the DSHK machinegun and was pummeling the house in an attempt to ignite the IED. From a certain point of view, he considered this to be good news. It suggested, in simple terms, that the IED most likely had no remote detonation capability, which would buy them some time unless the .50-caliber rounds punched through the right spot and caught the cooking pot full of explosives.

"Hobart, can you get a shot on this dick?" Matt asked.

"Not sure what's on the other side waiting for us to come out, but I can try," Hobart said.

"Wait," Mansur coughed. "Tunnel."

The three Americans stared at the Pakistani and were immediately suspicious.

"Tunnel?"

The house suddenly shook from an explosion that rocked the foundation, caving in the southeast portion of the building, which would give the DSHK gunner a semi-clean shot at the IED. He wasted no time in gunning for it, and heavy lead began ricocheting all around the house in the vicinity of the pressure cooker.

"Where's the tunnel?" Matt asked Mansur.

"Unchain me, then I tell you."

Van Dreeves removed a set of small bolt cutters from his rucksack and snapped the chains around his wrists and ankles.

"This way," Mansur said, then stopped, falling backward. His head had exploded from a .50-caliber round that shrieked through the open window.

"Damnit!"

"He was going this way," Matt said. "Let's see what we can find. Pound on the floor. I give it another minute before this place explodes."

The cacophony of machinegun fire intensified as if to emphasize his point.

After about two minutes, Hobart called out, "Over here. Trap door beneath the sleep roll."

He had the sheet of dusty plywood off the spider hole and shone a flashlight into the darkness.

"Has to be it," he said.

"Let's go," Matt said, pulling his Glock as he snapped his Sig Sauer onto his outer tactical vest.

He shone the light through into the tunnel and saw darkness start where the light ended. Van Dreeves was in and as Hobart was coming over the edge, the DSHK gunner hit his mark with the entire house exploding into a giant fireball of debris, dust and flames. Hobart fell to the bottom of the six foot drop, immediately covered by falling debris. Matt and Van Dreeves dragged him into the tunnel as the entry hole continued to fill with falling detritus.

Matt surmised that there would be no going back out in that direction.

"Let's move. They'll inspect the house soon and when they just find Mansur they'll know we got in the tunnel."

They scampered along the surprisingly well constructed path. Every ten meters or so thick 4 x 4 logs supported the sides and the ceiling. After ten minutes of hunched walking-running in flash lighted darkness, they came to a fork.

"Go left," Van Dreeves said.

"That's it I think, gotta be to house number three," Matt said.

Matt continued to lead and found a small ladder another fifty meters in. He turned to Van Dreeves and Hobart and said, "I'll go up first and go straight. VD you're second and to my left. Hobart, you're third and to the right. Both of you need to check the rear also. If this is house number three, we grab the computer hard drive and go."

"Uh, Matt," Van Dreeves said.

"What?"

"I've got two computers right here. Laptops. Looking good. Maybe a year old, no more."

"You're shitting me."

"I shit you not. And a flash drive."

"Bull's-eye. Can you slide them in your ruck?"

"Wait a minute. These puppies are rigged with explosives. Looks like C4," Van Dreeves said.

"Dismantle it. If this is Rahman's house, the entire database may be in there."

The three warriors stared at each other, briefly contemplating the significance of finding The Base. Al Qaeda was Arabic for The Base and was simply the name of all Al Qaeda members, meticulously kept first in Jeddah as an anonymous database of Islamic Conference attendees. Over time, bin Laden hijacked the system as a way to keep a list of all supporters and fighters. This was what Matt had come for, the hard drive that kept the database of enemy fighters so they could systemically locate and kill this amorphous enemy.

"Okay same plan then, but we make a quicker sweep through the house and then move to checkpoint seven on the western ridge to link up with the 101st guys."

As Van Dreeves knelt to begin dissecting the bomb so he could load the two thin Dell Laptops into his rucksack, they heard a noise directly above them.

And then the trap door opened.

CHAPTER 76
SPARTANBURG, SOUTH CAROLINA

LATE SUNDAY EVENING (EASTERN TIME)

Amanda pulled to a stop in front of Brianna Simpson's home in one of the lower-income areas just inside Greenville, near Spartanburg. Low income was relative, with house prices soaring into the upper six figures, yet Brianna's mother had struggled to keep pace with the costs of raising a child as a single mother without support from Brianna's father.

The home was a modest brick and siding rambler. Without the address, someone who didn't know the area would struggle to find the house, because all of the homes were similar in appearance. Red brick and white siding on the frame of the house with moderately sloping roofs appeared on every home on the street in some variety. Some homes had chain-link fences in the backyard. She could still see where some of the fences had only recently been removed from the front yards in accordance with the new community standards.

Amanda pulled into the driveway and nosed the car all the way beneath the carport. Brianna's mother, Charlotte, had left her VW Bug on the street so that Amanda could quickly park.

The screen door made a metallic rattling sound as she knocked on the side door that led from the carport.

"Come on in, Amanda," Charlotte Simpson called from the kitchen. "Hurry."

Amanda opened the door while Charlotte walked briskly past her, holding her car keys in her hand. She was wearing a worn Adidas light blue workout suit atop a white T-shirt and had yanked her bleached hair back into a ponytail.

"Better watch the television, hon. Brianna's in the back. She's still a little shook up from everything Jake told her. He called as soon as he heard them talking on your computer."

Amanda walked through a small laundry room and into the kitchen, which was not much larger. On the small television stuffed onto the counter next to the microwave there was an image of a house in flames, with fire trucks spewing streams of water into it. The video was obviously being shot from a helicopter flying over the mansion. There were several cars stacked up along the long driveway, many with flashing blue and red lights. She squinted and could barely make out her mother's Mercedes, but it was still there.

The crawl at the bottom of the news feed began to spit out small factoids as they were being reported, no doubt by crack journalists on the scene.

. . . historic mansion destroyed by fire . . . flame believed to have been started by burglar . . . weapon and dead body found . . . deceased is male suspect . . . home recently purchased by Melanie Garrett of Spartanburg . . . ex-wife of Colonel Zachary Garrett, recently killed in Afghanistan . . .

The picture cut to a feed from a ground crew who apparently had recently arrived at the scene. On the screen was a plain-looking woman reporter who had obviously gotten the assignment because she lived nearby and could change out of her pajamas quickly. She wore a windbreaker over blue jeans and spoke rapidly as she held the microphone to her mouth. Behind her the flames in one part of the house were still roaring and appeared much larger from this vantage.

Oddly, Amanda was reminded of when her father had taken her to watch the reenactment of the burning of the Heidelberg Castle in Germany. Flames were licking from the windows like tortured demons wishing to escape hell.

"Bill, what we have here is a huge fire in a house that was sold only a couple

of days ago," she said against the jet engine roar of the fire behind her. *"Police are on the scene, and firefighters have subdued the flames at the entrance to the home, where they believe the fire began. These are only initial reports, but there is confirmation of one deceased male in the home, and authorities are telling me that they have found a small pistol on the scene. What that means they are unwilling to speculate, but the owner of the house, Mrs. Melanie Garrett of Spartanburg, is hysterical. She has been running up and down the front of the house yelling at the firemen, telling them to pour more water on the flames and to do it faster. From what I can see, Bill, these men are doing a fantastic job of just trying to save some part of this home. Let's see if we can't get a shot of the owner."*

The camera panned to two firemen holding a stiff hose that was spewing a solid stream of water into the right front of the house. Amanda could see that a charred, black hole was located where the dining room used to be. Suddenly, she saw her mother pushing the firemen and screaming, waving her arms toward the house. The camera panned onto her face, the same contorted mask she'd seen as her mother had knocked the lighter out of her hand and onto the Persian rug.

". . . bastards, get more trucks here! Save this house! Damnit, I've got no insurance! Damn you, save this house!"

Amanda dropped her eyes. No matter how despicable her mother had been, it was difficult to watch someone acting with such a lack of human dignity. And while Amanda had suspected that something of this nature might happen if the plan worked, actually watching it was challenging.

Then she thought that it was no more challenging than how she had watched her mother and grandmother emasculate her father on a daily basis until it became routine, commonplace. The notion that he was a deadbeat bastard had eased its way into their lexicon and become a staple of their lives. It was a notion that was so opposed to reality that in hindsight it seemed absolutely absurd to her that she had ever taken the bait.

"Looks like you got her good, hon."

Charlotte had returned her car to the driveway to help hide Amanda's

Mercedes and to provide a plausible explanation should any police arrive.

"What do you mean? I've been here with you and Brianna all night."

"You got that right."

CHAPTER 77
NORTHWEST FRONTIER PROVINCE, PAKISTAN

MONDAY MORNING

In the tunnel there was very little space for the three of them. One hand grenade would possibly kill them all. The scraping of the floorboard and the partial opening of the trap door into what they believed to be house number three made the next few seconds seem like an eternity.

Matt grabbed Van Dreeves, who was cutting wires on the bomb protecting the computers that potentially contained the database. It had to be somewhere and what the technicians from Langley had forwarded to Matt was a message that the flash drive's Trojan had piped back to them a partial file that looked like a list of names, phone numbers and addresses of fighters, financiers, logisticians, businessmen, all of whom were a part of the loose network of Al Qaeda.

In the modern era, such a list would be akin to finding the personnel roster of a nation's standing army. Matt knew that the Rosetta stone was not killing bin Laden, though he hoped to do that soon, but to get the list, the database, the Al Qaeda, and then systematically move down that list and kill or capture those on it. Only then could America tip the balance of fear away from its own shores and back towards those who wished to do her harm. Constantly updated, the list was rumored to be kept on two hard drives. Initially on the server in Jeddah, bin Laden determined to keep that list up and running as a decoy. Intelligence agencies spent years chasing the Jeddah server list, which was mostly made up of Muslims who wanted to travel to the conference on Islamic Affairs. True, there were some who ultimately joined bin Laden's organization and cause, but he transferred them to a different list.

Getting Van Dreeves to safety and protecting the computer and their hard drives was job one.

Surviving was job two.

"It's a fake," Van Dreeves said about the time Matt pushed him.

Matt's credo had always been that a good offense would eventually wear down a good defense. If you hit enough baseballs over the fence, you win. When in doubt, attack. In the nanosecond that flashed through Matt's mind as he grabbed Van Dreeves and shoved him past himself and Hobart, he turned to Hobart and said, "We're going up."

He stepped on the wooden ladder that led up to the trap door that was by now two-thirds of the way open and raised his rifle. He flipped on his flashlight and shined it right into the face of a startled man who was brandishing a weapon of some sort.

Matt shot him in the face, the bullets kicking the man backward. The trap door did not fall, which to Matt meant that there was someone on the backside of it holding it open. In the next nanosecond he put two rounds into the flooring that served as the trap door. In the yellow beam of his MagLite he saw the wood splinter and a penetration hole appear through the panel, which began to fall. He pushed his shoulder into the door and lunged upward from the top rail of the ladder in the direction of the hinge on the trapdoor.

The door snapped off its hinges and Matt tumbled onto the soft body of a moaning man. He scanned the body for weapons and saw an AK-74 about five feet away. He put his flashlight on the man's bearded face and saw that he was grimacing in pain. Thinking that he may want a prisoner, he decided to check fire.

"I'm up. One KIA, one WIA. Let's move," Matt said.

Soon Hobart was up and pushing across the dead man that Matt had shot first.

They were breathing heavily in the dark, letting the silence settle over them, making millisecond calculations as to what they should do next.

"VD, stay below until we've got this thing sorted out."

"Roger."

"And protect that precious cargo."

"Roger."

"I'm thinking if the other house was rigged, maybe this one is also," Matt said.

"Roger that."

They both heard a noise opposite of their location, what Matt presumed was the front of the house, though he had no way to determine precisely where he was in relation to the home's blueprint. Their preparation had not detected any tunnels and so he tried to calibrate what he did know about the home. Two back bedrooms, two other rooms and a front door that led to a walled compound. Pretty basic. Four squares within a larger square. Each room led to another room. They were against a wall and Matt slid his back along it until he reached a corner. Hobart had done the same thing, so that now they were in opposite corners aiming at the doorway.

"I'll take the door and then next room. You follow," Matt whispered into his voice activated communications device. "VD, act as rear guard against anyone coming from the tunnel."

"You got it."

"Shoot to wound. This is Rahman's place."

Matt moved silently to the door, which opened inward, so he took the opposite side and kicked it open, inviting a fusillade of automatic weapons fire in the general direction of Hobart.

"You ok?"

"Yeah, coming up your back," Hobart said.

With the door open, Matt and Hobart pushed back from the opening, both hearing the unmistakable click of a spoon popping from a hand grenade and seeing the equally unmistakable toss and whir and roll of the baseball sized object.

"Grenade!" Matt screamed. But he realized that they were not the intended targets. It had been a careful toss to roll toward the sloping hole where the trapdoor was open. Matt had thought to leave the door open to make Van Dreeves' route of egress from the tunnel easier. He had not calculated the enemy's use of the open door. He thought about Van Dreeves and he thought about the hard drives and the database that was always there. He wondered if Al Qaeda kept a back up of the database and he suspected that they didn't. Bin Laden had been anal retentive about using servers and anything the U.S. intelligence agencies could crack. Paper initially and then hard drives, which could be removed and stored and hidden, but were easier to manipulate and update than using paper and pencil.

He heard the crunching roll of the grenade as it slid across the gritty, dirt floor. Turning, he dove across the reignited wall of lead that the enemy had started pouring into the room again. Like the shortstop that he was he dove with an outstretched glove hand, his left hand, watching the grenade bounce along. This was nothing but a sharply hit ground ball into the hole. Backhand this baby and then rifle it to first base. His weapon slapped him in the face and he felt the weight of his body armor slow him down as his fingernails scraped against the grenade that was rolling slowly toward Van Dreeves and the database that would always be there.

His body was twisted and he was airborne as the grenade took a funny hop off the fuse straight up into the air, giving his body mass time to catch up and he clutched the round object with his left hand.

Matt had turned hundreds of double plays as a shortstop and fielded thousands of ground balls in little league, high school and college. The key was the quick transfer of the ball from glove hand to throwing hand. Sometimes he caught the ground ball or the second baseman's flip of the ball with his throwing hand and seamlessly, less than a second, could rocket the ball to wherever it needed to go. From the time a baseball would leave the bat, enter Matt's glove, and then be released, less than two seconds would have transpired.

The fuse on a standard M67 hand grenade lasted three to five seconds. If this was a three second fuse, Matt knew he was screwed. If five seconds, perhaps not. Matt calculated that already two seconds had transpired, as he wrapped his hand around the grenade and his body landed with a scraping thud on the dirt floor. He pictured the door directly behind him.

He had no alternative but to whip his left arm backward, releasing the grenade, as if he were glove tossing the ball to the second baseman, a trick he had mastered at the University of Virginia. While not left handed, he was nearly ambidextrous, and flicked his wrist toward the open door with the machinegun fire raining down upon them.

In those brief seconds, Matt heard the whirring of the hand grenade, the sound of machinegun fire, the screams of Hobart and Van Dreeves, and the chop of helicopter blades above the roof.

Then the world stopped for Matt Garrett when the hand grenade and its millions of metal splinters filled the house.

CHAPTER 78
SPARTANBURG, SOUTH CAROLINA

SUNDAY EVENING

Amanda found Brianna lying on the twin bed in her small bedroom. She was wearing a pink T-shirt with the word "GODDESS" in sparkling letters printed across the front, and white sweatpants. Amanda could see that she had been crying, though Brianna's face was turned away from her. A salty path stained her left cheek and was clearly visible. Amanda also noticed Brianna's old tennis racket in the corner of the room next to a pile of clothes. Two large posters of Britney Spears wearing next to nothing were hung on either side of the lone window. One of the posters was drooping from the top left-hand corner as the tape had dried and lost its adhesive properties.

"Hey," Amanda said as she slowly walked into the room.

Brianna turned her head and looked at her. "I'm so sorry."

"About what?" She stopped when she saw the bruises on Brianna's face and neck. She gasped. "He hit you?"

Brianna turned away and nodded.

Amanda placed her hand on Brianna's shoulder. "I'm the one who should be sorry. You're my best friend, and I never even cared enough about you to realize what was happening. I was just too wrapped up in me, you know?"

Amanda sat on the bed next to her and brushed back Brianna's hair. She thought to herself about maturity and how in the last two weeks she had transformed herself from an immature, selfish brat to a caring, concerned friend. She made a mental note that if the transition was this fast, then perhaps this might be who she really wanted to become, or even had been all along.

"You got a raw deal, bitch," Brianna said, wiping a tear from her eyes as she sat up in her bed. She pulled her knees up to her chest and clasped her arms around them, resting her chin on her knees as she turned her eyes toward Amanda.

"Not any worse than having to be with Dagus."

Brianna shuddered and closed her eyes so tight that wrinkles formed around her young face. "Is he really dead?"

"I watched him put a bullet in his head. Hard to get any deader than that."

Brianna put her forehead on her knees, and Amanda could tell she was crying, so she put her hand on her friend's back and made slow circling motions as she spoke. "It's okay, Bree. I never knew."

Brianna kept her forehead on her knees and shook it left to right as if to indicate "no."

"Come on, Bree. I know about almost everything. How much was she going to pay you?"

Brianna turned her head to look at Amanda and said weakly, "You don't know everything."

"Then tell me."

"What difference does it make, Amanda? You'll go on with your life. You've got your half million, and what have I got?"

"I'm not taking all of the money, Bree. I've decided to do something else with it. I can't say what, but just trust me on this, okay?"

Brianna seemed to consider Amanda's comment. She was now resting her head sideways on her knees, not looking at Amanda, but staring at no particular spot on the far wall.

"Nina made me do it. She promised me some of the insurance money. Ten thousand. Screw him five times. What's the big deal, you know? My mother has been struggling lately, and I thought some quick money would help. Plus, you know, we'd all wanted to be with Dagus at one point in time."

Amanda considered the comment and decided to ignore it. Though she had never made the transition to wanting to be with her teacher in that way, the very thought, particularly now, was especially revolting.

"That's why your mom agreed to help me so fast when I stopped by a little while ago?" It was a question phrased as a comment.

"That's right. She was really mad."

"Like I said, I'm sorry."

"Well, if I hadn't done this, maybe he would have never written that article."

"You can't blame yourself for that. You were just a down payment. They've been doing that to me for years. You know all those doctor appointments?"

"I always wondered about that. You sure went to the doctor a lot for being the healthiest person I know."

"Jake and I were in my dad's house, and we saw all these records of how my mom cheated three different insurance companies. She was making money on me by taking me to the doctor."

"Why didn't anyone do anything?"

"In his notes he talks about having tried, but it was only like twenty thousand dollars or something, and there were million-dollar corporate cases out there."

The two friends sat for a while on the bed without saying anything. Amanda continued to absently rub Brianna's back as she was now leaning into her, shoulder to shoulder.

"What about Nina? What are you going to do?"

"I've got a plan for her," Amanda replied. "But can I ask you why you didn't say no to her?" Amanda believed she understood why, but wanted to be sure.

Brianna rocked against her for a moment and said, "I think you know, but here goes." She paused, sniffed once, and continued. "Your grandmother, you know I don't even feel right calling her by that fake name, 'Nina,' anymore."

"I know what you mean."

"Anyway, two years ago when you were told your dad was dead the first time, she came to my mom one day asking if she could help out with any expenses. You know, mom had gotten laid off from her job, and, well, you know I've never really had a dad. We were hurting, and the swimming, well, that was all I really had."

"But you couldn't afford it anymore?"

"Anymore? Try ever. My mom even tried sleeping with the swimming coach, but that didn't work out for long."

"Jesus. I'm sorry, Bree."

"Don't be. But you know, your grandmother sees a lot, and I think she saw that. We were getting free lessons for a while, but that dried up when my mom and the coach broke up. All of this happened about the same time. So your grandmother either started paying the lessons or worked a connection. I think it was a connection, but I'm not sure. All I knew was, I got to keep swimming and to hang out with you."

"So you owed her one?"

"That's right. Thinking about it now, I think she was probably planning for something like this way back then. But then there was no insurance money, I heard."

"That's another thing; there was some money, and my mother got it. She lied to me."

Brianna slowly shook her head and then looked at her for the first time in awhile. "I'm so sorry, Amanda. All I ever wanted was for us to be best friends, you know."

Amanda wiped a tear from her own eyes and laughed. "We've got to quit saying 'I'm sorry,' you know?" Then she shoved her with her shoulder. "We came out okay, didn't we?"

"Yeah, I think so. I think we'll be okay."

Amanda prayed that they would be.

"I still can't believe Dagus burned down my dad's house. . . ."

"When did he do that?"

"Right after we were there the other day."

"The day you went to North Carolina? He couldn't have. He was at the lake with me. He got totally sunburned."

"But what about his arms and chest? The hair was gone. I just assumed he had burned himself."

Brianna looked down, embarrassed.

"He made me shave him. Amanda, he didn't burn down your dad's house. He wasn't there. He's a sick freak, but he didn't do that."

"If he didn't do it, then who did?"

A wave of panic rushed over her as she considered the possibilities.

CHAPTER 79
BAGRAM AIR BASE, AFGHANISTAN

MONDAY EVENING

"What's your deal, man?"

Matt was, at best, foggy on where he was and who was talking to him, though it sounded like Hobart. He sensed he was on his back and in a bed. The last thing he could remember was . . . well he wasn't sure.

The Database Is Always There.

The hard drives. Mullah Rahman's house. The hand grenade.

It was coming back to him slowly, like a vintage car driving a winding mountain road.

The hand grenade.

Since he generally had no feeling or sensation in any part of his body, he wondered if he had survived, and, if so, how well.

"I'm serious, dude. You backhanded that bitch like you were A-Rod or some shit."

Matt opened his eyes and saw Hobart standing over him, hair disheveled, face unshaven, uniform dirty.

"Van Dreeves?" The hard drives were all Matt could think about.

"He's fine," Hobart smiled.

Matt managed a weak smile and said, "The hard drives?"

Hobart nodded his head.

"The. Entire. Database."

"Can we crosscheck against Yemen and Dubai?"

"Already have."

"And?"

"And aren't you even remotely interested in your own condition?"

Matt coughed, felt a pain in his ribs. "Only if there's something worth going after."

"Listen, dude," Hobart began. He grabbed and held up both of Matt's hands. "You've got all your limbs. You can breathe. And you're going to be ok. That's what counts."

Matt nodded.

"What counts is starting with Yemen and Dubai and then going after the rest of that list."

"Mission for Dubai is tonight. We're sending a bunker buster in there. Going to explode it from the inside out," Hobart said.

"And Yemen?"

"We're watching it. Developing patterns of life." Hobart hesitated.

"And?"

"And maybe waiting for you to be ready."

Matt smiled.

"Was it a three second or five second fuse?"

Hobart laughed.

"Four. That bitch flew past my face, got into the other room and exploded, killing the dude shooting at us."

Van Dreeves came walking in.

"How's A-Rod?"

"Bite me, VD," Matt said. "Rahman?"

"Got away. That was his detachment left in contact. Son of a bitch is slicker than snot on a doorknob," Hobart said.

"But we've got a bead on him," Van Dreeves said. "That's why I'm here."

"Fatwa still out on Zach?"

"Five million."

"We've got to capture that dude, get him to retract it and then . . ."

"Right, and then . . ."

Matt sat up, stiff, and looked at himself in the mirror of his hospital room. His face was lacerated and bandaged in different areas. His hair was matted with what he figured to be blood. "Where the hell am I?"

"Bagram. Air Force had a new hospital built. It's like the Taj," Hobart said.

"Injuries?"

"Nah, we're okay," Hobart smiled.

"I'm talking about mine, dickweed."

"Just jacking with you. You took some shrapnel to the face, which improved things quite a bit, by the way. And then some in the legs."

"And you have no penis," Van Dreeves added.

For a brief moment Matt considered the possibility, as evidenced by the stricken look on his face, and then realized Van Dreeves was joking.

"Just kidding, dude. Still got that little thing."

Matt smiled and looked out of a small window that gave him a view of the Bagram runway. He could see the MH-47s huddled at the south end like hulking beasts, resting, awaiting their call. The heat waves made it seem almost as if the machines were breathing.

Next to them he saw a C-17 Globemaster aircraft.

"When do we go get Rahman?"

"We're working that now. We think we've got him pegged in Quetta in a small village. If we get a confirmation, we'll move."

Matt nodded. "C-17s don't usually park at the special ops end of the ramp."

Hobart looked at Van Dreeves.

"They do when we are about to jump into Yemen."

"So tell me. What precisely does the database say is in Yemen?"

"The top of the list."

CHAPTER 80
SPARTANBURG, SOUTH CAROLINA

MONDAY MORNING (EASTERN TIME)

Nina Hastings sat on the leather davenport in the den of her daughter's home, steaming coffee cup in one hand. The news played silently in the background as she wondered exactly where Melanie might be. Nina had watched the live reporting from last night, but lost track of time as she fell asleep on the sofa.

She had to admire how Amanda had engineered things. Though she did not know the particulars, she would soon find out. As Kryponite was to Superman, she chuckled, she was to Amanda.

Nina fashioned herself an expert at creating the insecurity and then filling that void with her own version of love and affection. Sometimes it even felt real. She had learned long ago that one got out of life what one took. Nobody gave you anything, and it was survival of the fittest. Her operating premise was to assume everyone was lying to her, question everything, and, above all, strike first, even if she wasn't certain. When she struck, she was convinced, it had to be hard and from a totally unpredictable direction.

This was usually done best by having better information than anyone else. Say what you would about Nina Hastings, there were few that had more tentacles in more places around the greater Charlotte metro area. She built bridges as fast as she burned them, maybe faster. Dr. Homer Jones and Judge Bart Holbrook were just two of her many sources.

Lenard Dagus was a perfect example. Within five minutes of meeting him she could see that he was a lecherous man. She had actually caught him staring at Amanda one time. Having taken notice, she had logged the information away where it might be useful one day.

When Nina had been dating Judge Holbrook in the Charlotte Circuit Court, he had with hesitation told her about the sealed Emily Wilkinson case, where Lenard Dagus had sex with a fourteen-year-old girl when he was nineteen. Nina and Melanie had thrown a Christmas party where both had been invited. Late in the evening, after the judge had spent a considerable amount of time talking to Dagus, he had asked Nina to have a word. He'd had a few drinks and so his judgment was impaired, yet the judge had pardoned his own ethical break by rationalizing that he was trying to protect Gabrielle's granddaughter. He was doing her a favor. That he did.

That pearl of intelligence had been her leverage to keep Dagus from going nationwide about having uncovered Del Dangurs' bogus article on Colonel Zach Garrett. He had come to them in earnest, telling Melanie and Nina that he had discovered who Del Dangurs really was and could expose him for using bogus sources and participating in yellow journalism. Sometimes things just worked out, Nina thought, and smiled to herself.

She looked over at Del Dangurs. He was lying on the sofa shirtless. His bare chest was smooth, hairless. His sandy brown hair was tossed haphazardly. Nina had been able to seduce him one final time.

"Well, Del Dangurs, I think you've done enough," she said with a wicked smile.

He was running a hand along his chest. He smiled at his lover. Though he was initially surprised that she had been good in bed, and that he enjoyed it, he now wondered if he could stop. At the spry age of fifty-nine, Nina Hastings had turned out to be quite masterful at the art of seduction.

"What do you mean? The house, the woman. I did all of that for you, Gabrielle," he protested. He had been her submissive slave both in the bedroom and outside. Her directions to him had been to burn the house and to kill the woman. Additionally, he was to try and frame Dagus or Jake, whichever was easier.

"One question," she asked. "How did you pin it on Dagus? The house,

I mean?"

"Well, when the cops show up at his house today, they will find a digital camera memory chip of the house, the interior, and the gas can. It's right there on his desk. But of course no one has helped us more than Amanda. I don't think I could have pulled a manipulation like that."

Nina nodded in approval, perhaps pride. This was all good. Very good.

"And you're sure no one saw you in Sanford?"

Del thought of the Asian, Julie Nguyen. Their hookup had been so quick. It had to be, as he had to return and take care of Riley Dwyer in time to make it look like Jake Devereaux had done the job. But Julie had been too much to resist.

"I'm sure, Gabrielle."

Nina stared at him a moment, and he shook his head. "None."

Nina nodded in approval.

Burning the house to destroy the physical memories had been phase one. Killing the psychiatrist to deny Amanda access to living memories had been phase two. There he had not succeeded, but had done well enough. Framing Jake for both the arson and the murder was the most they could do to separate Amanda from his strength of character. Lastly, offering Brianna to Dagus to not go public about Dangurs' fictional news article was a perfect fit. Brianna needed the money, and she knew Dagus would not be able to resist.

It was a simple fix. He gets Brianna, Brianna gets $10,000, and the article sealing the fate of Amanda's father endures for all eternity unchallenged. End of mission. And it was to be paid for with Zach's insurance money.

"We're done, Del. I told you that from the beginning. We all serve a purpose, and you've served yours. I'll pay you when we get things all sorted out."

She watched him pull his shirt over his muscular frame. There was a part of her that would miss the sex, but not a large part. He was okay, a means to an end.

The best part? Nina Hastings's fingerprints were nowhere on this thing except on the $100,000 check she had written out of her daughter's checkbook. Melanie had been so absorbed in the rapid closing of the house, she hadn't noticed Nina pull out her checkbook and sign her daughter's name. Melanie wasn't the only one who could forge a signature.

"I'll take my money now, if you don't mind," Del said, interrupting her train of thought.

"You'll get your money tomorrow, maybe later today. Like I said. I need to go to the bank. This all happened a day or two more quickly than I thought."

He stood in front of her, still seated on the sofa. She locked eyes with him and seemed to telepathically move him to the door. Transmitting her will through her gaze, he understood that he needed to leave now.

"I've got more to do today, Del. Thank you for your efforts." She was a businesswoman thanking a salesperson for spending some time with her. *Thank you and have a nice day. Next.*

She turned her head as she watched him leave. She felt no emotion. She would pay him to keep him quiet, not for the job he'd done. Besides, he had not completed the Dwyer job, now that she thought about it.

She turned her attention to the television. Flipping through all of the news channels with the remote, she took a sip of her coffee and placed the cup on the cherry wood end table. She kicked off her slippers as if she had just returned from a long day at work and tucked her feet underneath her on the sofa. Finding a station that seemed to have more video and less talk, she watched the video replay of the house burning over and over on different channels.

"Glad I didn't commit to that one," she whispered to herself. She smacked her lips at the strong coffee, all the while contemplating her next move. Melanie would be bankrupt because she was certain that she had not insured the house prior to signing the contract and closing. Amanda obviously had learned things from her father's house and the other people with whom she now consulted. But what else had she learned, and would it threaten their relationship?

On the contrary, with Melanie the clear instigator and manipulator in Amanda's eyes, this panned out about as she'd expected and hoped it would. As Amanda went to college or moved out of the house, she would have to divide her time between her mother and grandmother, making difficult choices about who to see and when. The life of a young adult revolved around her friends and immediate social network more than her family, Nina knew. When the child came back for the holidays, whom would she see, spend time with, show affection to? Those were the key issues that dominated Nina's thought process. Her goal was to make sure that Amanda tilted that balance in her favor.

Amanda's love for her had always been a mainstay, undeniable and irrevocable. She was confident that would remain steadfast. Like a true believer, Amanda would remain loyal to her, she was certain. After all, there was nothing in any chain of events that could be traced back to Nina.

In her mind, morality was a rationalization. The moral thing, the right thing, was always to take care of yourself, take what you could get. Scratch and claw for it if you had to, but best to learn the polished approach and make it seem like everyone else was fighting, and you were just trying to make peace, the innocent bystander. And why go to those lengths? Well, if the thread came undone on the newspaper article, she had decided, the entire scheme could unravel and expose not only their most recent antics, but possibly years of petty crimes.

Most importantly, if Amanda were led to believe she should love her father, then there would be less for her. That was the reality.

Watching replays of her daughter on television screaming at firemen made her look casually around her confines and smile. Amanda had survived the night but was assuredly sweating bullets somewhere. The scared and insecure little girl would soon come running home to Nina. She swirled her coffee cup in her hand and offered a silent toast to Amanda as if to notch one on the scoreboard for her.

Yes, Nina Hastings was doing just fine, thank you.

She looked at her watch when she heard the key enter the deadbolt on the front door.

"Right on time."

CHAPTER 81
SPARTANBURG, SOUTH CAROLINA

Amanda smoothed out her light green windbreaker, which she was wearing half zipped over a chartreuse short-sleeved sweater and blue jeans. She had changed and left her hoodie and other jeans at Brianna's house for Brianna's mother to wash. She rubbed her eyes again, then squeezed a few eye-drops into each, followed by a light tossing of her hair. The morning sun had crested and this Monday promised to be a turning point in her life. With graduation less than a week away, she was going to step into the big, bad world a new, wiser and stronger person.

Fumbling with the keys, Amanda burst through the front door, tripping in the foyer of her mother's house. As she did so, it occurred to her that they had actually sold the house. They intended to vacate it this weekend for the new owners.

"Nina! Nina! Are you here?"

Amanda darted into the dining room and the kitchen, but did not see her grandmother. Reversing course she entered the main hallway and shot straight back to the den, where she saw Nina standing with an expression of concern on her face. Amanda immediately ran to her and hugged her.

"Oh, Nina, it was so bad! Have you turned on the television? Did you see what happened?"

"What's going on, Amanda? You can tell Nina."

Amanda pressed her face into the silver silk blouse, feeling her grandmother flinch when she knew that Amanda's tears might stain the fabric. Having the good fortune of hindsight now, it occurred to Amanda that when her grandmother referred to herself in the third person as Nina, she was full of the conceit that served as her fuel.

"Mama, Dagus, it was all so bad last night. He was going to kill me, and then there was Mama. It was terrible." She heaved into her grandmother's bosom, holding her tight. She felt a little like Dorothy after she had returned to Kansas in *The Wizard of Oz*.

"It's okay, Amanda. It's okay. You know, it's just you and me now, and I'm going to make it okay for you like I always have."

She felt Nina embrace her, but it wasn't a loving embrace. The way that she could feel her grandmother's muscles flexing in her arms, Amanda sensed that she did not want so much to hold her close, but to prevent her from getting away. It was a clutch rather than a hug.

"Oh, Nina, I'm so sorry for all of this. I know that you have been the one there for me all this time. It's only you, Nina."

"It's okay, Amanda. I'm here for you."

Her conversation with Brianna had refined the path that she had finally chosen. She'd learned many lessons living within the confines of the psychological hell her grandmother and mother had created for her. Primarily though, she had discovered that everyone had a soft spot, a weakness.

For example, looking at Nina Hastings, the average person would believe she was a refined, cultured woman with a sense of humor and a tough edge. Her father's revelations to her, even in his death, however, had given her the distance she required to look back on the situation and see it from a more objective standpoint. Like a diver surfacing to check his distance from land, she was able to break away just long enough to gain a balanced perspective.

But defeating Nina was probably not possible. The woman was simply too tough and too savvy. There was only one possible route: an indirect attack.

"I know you're here, Nina." She pulled away, wiping at the ersatz tears. "You've always been there for me."

"And I'm here for you now," Nina said, an edge to her voice, "once you level with me."

"What do you mean?"

"I checked, Amanda. Your father's not buried in Arlington. That was some other loser's funeral you went to. Why did you lie to us?"

Amanda's mind raced. Her strategy had been cut short by what she should have considered the one obvious flaw in her plan, but she was prepared. Military funerals were highly publicized and easily researched. Again, Nina was punching and jabbing, circling the ring with her own flesh and blood, keeping her off balance and controlling the situation.

Not this time.

"Because he was Special Operations we handled everything quietly at Arlington. Go check it out yourself." This part was true as far as she knew. Matt had told her that he was the executor of her father's estate. In his documents there was a clause that asserted, in the event of Zach's death, that there was not to be a ceremony. He had already been buried once. In reality all they had handled at Arlington, was Sergeant Eversoll's funeral.

"I don't appreciate you questioning me." Amanda's temper flared, counterpunching. "You don't believe me? Here I come back to you for support, and you are suspicious of me? What in the world could I do to you, Nina?"

Nina stared at Amanda, her black eyes set upon her like a target finder. She watched her grandmother flinch, the tightness in her face eventually giving way to a more relaxed, if sagging, expression.

"You're right, Amanda. I'm sorry. You know, when I didn't see you-know-who's name in the paper for Arlington funerals I just began to wonder."

"Remember how crazy it was last time? They buried him, but he was really alive at Fort Bragg. I think they just wanted to get it over with. Yeah, we went to the ceremony for that guy, but it was right after that we sorted out everything about my dad."

It bothered her to call Lance Eversoll "that guy," but she transformed that feeling into a pained countenance.

"Come here." Nina clutched her again, her bony arms bruising Amanda's back.

She felt her grandmother begin to shake. "What is it, Nina?" Perhaps her plan was back intact. "Let's sit down."

They sat close to one another on the sofa. The television was turned to mute and the network news had begun, but the fire still replayed in a small inset next to the anchor's head as she spoke. Amanda wondered if Mary Ann had time to make the papers this morning.

"Grandma, talk to me, please?"

Nina looked at her absently. "Grandma." It was a statement, not a question. "That sounds nice. You always called me Nina because you couldn't say 'Grandma' as a little child."

Amanda knew this was a lie. Nina had named herself that and began reciting it with Amanda when she was three.

"I know, but, you know, Grandma just sometimes feels good to say. It's kind of like saying 'I love you.'"

Again, she saw Nina's features soften another notch.

"Well, I guess that's okay. Sure makes me feel good."

"You don't feel good much, do you Grandma? I mean, you always seem on edge like you can't trust anyone and you need to defend yourself."

Nina paused a moment and then spoke. "I suppose, Amanda. I've lived a hard life, you know. Came from nothing. Anytime I let anyone get close to me it seems they wound up hurting me. So I just quit letting it happen."

"But you know, Grandma, you won't even let me close to you. I mean, we're sitting here next to each other, close and all, but not emotionally close."

"I can't remember the last time I let someone get emotionally close to me, or me them."

"If you don't allow yourself to be fully happy, what kind of life is that, Grandma?" Again with the name, like a hypnotist.

"So many people out there, they want things. They take from you all the time."

"Come on, Grandma, it's not that bad. Just let it go. You've got so much held up inside you. For all these years you've just bottled it up. Remember that time we were at Six Flags, and we did the wet and wild ride? That was so much fun. That was the real Grandma that I grew up loving. Where did that person go?"

Nina sniffed. Perhaps it was possible to derive water from a rock, Amanda thought. She reached up and rubbed her grandmother's shoulder with her right hand. "It's going to be okay, Grandma. Just let yourself feel something. You've got to start trusting someone. Can you trust me?"

The aging woman began to show her years as if a computer imaging program had redrawn her. Amanda could see the demons that she carried waking and creating havoc. The tortured look on Nina's face told Amanda that somewhere in the basement of her soul a stagnant conscience must have emitted an electrical pulse. If only briefly, Amanda saw the look of absolute guilt cross her grandmother's face.

"Can you trust me, Grandma? It's important to me that you do."

Her grandmother lifted her hand slowly, tentatively, and reached toward Amanda, placing the leathery paw on her arm and then sliding it down and clasping her hand.

"I can try, Amanda. I guess it's time to start trying. We've been through a lot together, and I think if I were to pick one person in this world that I could trust it would be you."

"We make a great team, you and me, Grandma."

Amanda held her grandmother's hand and pulled her close so that they could hug. She noticed a picture of Mary Ann Singlaub appear on the television screen next to a Web site excerpt. The anchor was obviously referring to what Mary Ann had written. She knew it was time.

"Grandma, I'm really tired. I didn't sleep all night. Can I just go upstairs and take a nap?"

"Well, I'm up and I imagine your mother's going to need some help." She sighed heavily, blowing out a fraction of the stress she had been carrying for decades.

"Well, can you tuck me in like you used to do?" Amanda paused for effect and then pleaded. "Please, Grandma?"

Nina smiled at the thought. "You really are my little girl, you know. When you were born I stood right there and said, 'God gave me exactly what

I wanted.'"

"I know." Amanda smiled tightly.

Amanda grabbed Nina's hand and walked with her through the hallway and toward the foyer where she would turn and take the staircase up to her room. As she passed the front door, she paused and said, "What's this?"

"What?" Nina seemed lost in another time, perhaps a place she always wanted to be, ensconced in the love of a child.

Amanda opened the door, still holding her grandmother's hand with her opposite hand. Standing on the porch were two police officers from Spartanburg. They wore pressed gray shirts with creasing along the pockets.

"Hi officers, this is my grandmother. I believe she's the one you're looking for in relation to the prostitution of Brianna Simpson."

The rage came back into her grandmother's face instantly. The scared little girl suddenly became the fierce, hardscrabble Southerner. Snatching her hand from Amanda's, leaving a long fingernail scratch down her wrist, Nina reached for her granddaughter's throat.

"You little bitch!"

Blocking her thrust with a strong hand, Amanda grabbed her grandmother's wrist. "No, *Grandma,* I just wanted you to feel for one minute what it was like to trust somebody and have them screw you over. Take how you feel right now and multiply it by seventeen years. That's what you and your daughter did to me."

Amanda stared at her for a moment, wanting to snap the tender wrist in her hand. "How's it feel, *Gabrielle?*"

The look on her grandmother's face shifted from utter contempt to a blank stare. Without much fanfare the police officers had Gabrielle Hastings handcuffed and seated in the back of the police cruiser.

Amanda Garrett walked up the stairs and began surveying everything that she wanted to take with her.

After all, it wasn't her house anymore.

CHAPTER 82
YEMEN

TUESDAY MORNING (HOURS OF DARKNESS)

Matt could feel his face tighten with the pains of scarring and healing. He had a major cut across his forehead that had required stitches and two on his left cheek, his exposed side, where the doctor had gone in and removed the metal. One piece of shrapnel had penetrated his cheek and actually chipped one of his rear molars.

Considering everything, the doctor told him he was going to be just fine. Everyone who came to see him called him A-Rod, the nickname of Alex Rodriguex, star infielder for the New York Yankees.

"Okay, A-Rod, you're free to leave and do whatever you are going to do. I don't guess it's any use telling you not to jump out of airplanes, fight bad guys, or try to save the world, right?"

"Right," Matt grimaced, sitting up. The wounds on his legs were minor, like the scrape from a bad slide into second base.

He walked with some pain through the hospital corridor into the waiting SUV. The sun was bright and high in the sky to the west. Late afternoon. The fabled 100 days of wind had seemed to start as the hawking gales blew out of the mountains and swept across the plains, making air travel even more treacherous than normal.

The SUV pulled around a series of byzantine turns and then through a small gate, which opened onto the runway, finally stopping at the open ramp of a C-17 aircraft. Matt thanked the driver, walked up the ramp with a slight limp and was greeted by the Air Force loadmaster.

"Sir, A-Rod."

Matt stopped and looked at him, shaking his head. Apparently he was legendary for his toss. After all of the baseballs he had thrown in his career, perhaps he would be best known for tossing a four second grenade on its third second into an adjacent room, saving the database and his team.

"It's just A-Rod to you, Sergeant. Drop the 'sir,'" Matt said, smiling, which hurt.

Walking into the cavity of the C-17 he saw the command and control pod in the center and three sets of jump equipment. Hobart and Van Dreeves were sitting at the terminals looking at Global Hawk photographs and Predator feed.

"The Yemeni government wants to know what we're doing," Hobart said.

"We're not telling them jack," Matt said.

Hobart and Van Dreeves turned their heads, both saying, "A-Rod."

To which Matt said, "Bite me."

"Welcome back," Hobart laughed.

"Let's get this pig rolling," Matt said over his shoulder to the loadmaster.

Slipping on a headset he began to stare at the screen. On it were two pictures. One was a close up of a house in the middle of a residential neighborhood. It appeared to be Spanish architecture, complete with tiled roof. There was an empty driveway that led to what appeared to be an asphalt road. High shrubs of some type hugged the walls of the house and lined either side of the driveway as well as the entire yard. The yard was walled and gated, with swinging wrought-iron gates at the end of the driveway.

"This is Yemen?" Matt asked.

"Roger. We think this house is connected by underground tunnels to the houses on either side of it. When we do a thermal look, we get some shaded areas underneath that lead us to believe there are multiple escape routes through at least these two houses."

"The medics always come to the middle house though, right?" Matt asked.

"Right. But we can't follow them too well once inside."

"How did Dubai go?" Matt asked.

"About as expected. The pilot dropped a bomb from 40,000 feet. It hit the target, drilled about fifty feet into the substructure, and exploded. Multiple secondary explosions and many dead. Team jumped in and verified the identity of number five on the list, the chief financier. And the pilot gets a medal."

"This is starting to sound like the deck of cards from Iraq," Matt said.

"It's better though. The bad guys supplied the deck. We know it's right."

The aircraft buttoned up and began to roll, lifting into the sky and circling higher and higher until it had the altitude to soar above the Hindu Kush Mountains. The three men studied the target and wondered how they might neutralize the objective while capturing the individual.

"No sign of armed guards?" Matt asked.

"None. This is a small neighborhood in Little Aden, west of the port city of Aden," Hobart said.

"Kids, women?"

"Nothing."

"When do the medics arrive?"

"Usually at nightfall. They are there about an hour and then leave."

"Looks like a decent landing zone right there," Matt said pointing at the flat roof. "Or there." The second area was simply the backyard. They would have to land, forcibly breach their way in, and then fight whatever was on the inside. Not a good option, Matt thought.

"This is a tough nut. VD just wants to drop bombs on all three houses and call it a day," Hobart said.

Matt looked at Van Dreeves who had removed his headset and was eating a power bar. Van Dreeves just shrugged.

"Hey, a bad plan beats no plan," Van Dreeves said.

Matt, though, had an idea.

"Why don't we time this so that we're there when the medics go in? Kill/capture them before they get in, keep one alive, and then let him take us in?"

"We'll be over the target in three hours, which is about thirty minutes before the medics would arrive. You're suggesting landing off the objective and then moving toward the house," Hobart said as he played with the screen, rotating the view to wide. There was an empty lot, which gave way to miles of desert about a quarter mile away.

"There," Matt said. "Let's land there and move into position along the back," Matt said.

"As good an idea as any."

The three men spent the next two hours mapping out their plan of action, rehearsing, and checking their equipment. At the thirty-minute mark, they rigged their parachutes, pulled on their oxygen masks, secured their weapons and ordnance, and moved toward the aft of the C-17.

The ramp lowered, and Matt could see the Sea of Aden mixing with the setting sun. He imagined that it was a beautiful sight from the ground, but from 20,000 feet above sea level with fully loaded combat gear, he had other things on his mind.

The green light flashed and the three men were tumbling through the sky. The air was warm even at these altitudes in this part of the world. Van Dreeves was first to deploy at about 800 feet, then Hobart, and finally Matt. They were quickly on the ground and the darkness had settled over them during their descent. The landing zone had proven sandy and forgiving, which for Matt was a blessing. His injuries still smarted a bit and he would take all the freebies he could get.

They stowed their gear in kit bags, hid it beneath some palm fronds, and then Matt led them to a wall guarding the compound four houses from the target. They had exactly one hour on the ground before an MH-47 from the base in Djibouti would come screaming across the 150 miles of water where the Red Sea and the Gulf of Aden met. They would be picked up and raced back across the Gulf of Aden to a secure U.S. base.

They moved quickly along the shadows cast by the walls of the compounds until they reached their target. By Matt's calculations they had four minutes before the medics arrived. They had thus far been like clockwork, always showing up within a few minutes of darkness every night, indicative of a routine medical schedule where they were trying to mask their identity.

Van Dreeves moved across the driveway, hiding behind the high shrubs. Within seconds the sound of the gate opening was rattling through their ears. Matt watched as the ambulance dimmed its lights and turned into the driveway. The three men were immediately padding behind it as the gate screeched to a close.

The driver exited the vehicle and walked to the rear to be greeted by a stun gun from Hobart. He wrestled and writhed but there was nothing he could do against the high voltage being applied to his system. He would be lucky to live. Hobart flex cuffed the man. Matt watched and at first blush the man did not impress him as a medic. Matt moved up to the passenger door at about the time the passenger was exiting and used his Glock to knock him unconscious. The man fell into his arms, and again his instinct was that these men were not medics.

Van Dreeves opened the back door of the ambulance and he and Hobart dragged the flex-cuffed driver into the back. The ambulance contained a variety of gear, mostly toolboxes.

Matt gave the passenger a smelling salt, which woke him and the three men quickly went to work on him. Hobart flex-cuffed him. Van Dreeves held a pistol to his head, and Matt asked him questions in Arabic.

"Do you have the key?"

The man's frightened face gave away the fact that he did. Matt pulled a series of swipe cards and keys from the passenger's pocket.

"Who is inside?"

"No."

"Who?"

"No one is inside," the man said, visibly shaken. Matt smelled urine and saw the stain in the crotch of the man's white uniform.

"Who is inside? Where is he?"

"Cannot say," the man replied. "Cannot go in."

"You know we will kill you if you don't tell us," Matt said.

Either someone shot him from a distance or he had a heart attack, because the man simply slumped over. Not seeing any blood, Matt surmised that the man had fainted. He felt a weak pulse. They tossed him in the back of the ambulance.

"We've got 40 minutes," Matt said. "Time is burning."

They locked the ambulance and ran up to the front door in tactical fashion, weapons outward, scanning in all directions. Matt unlocked the door and rolled into the foyer calling, "One up." He heard Hobart and Van Dreeves come inside and acknowledge that they were clear.

They moved through a dining room, kitchen, living room, and study, all of it in pristine condition, as if done by an interior decorator, Matt determined that the house was like a Potemkin Village, the fake villages set up by the Soviets and North Koreans to trick its own residents, visitors, or both. The deeper they bore into the house the more convinced Matt was that no one lived here, especially the top of the Database.

"Found the stairs down," Hobart said.

The three men flew in unison down the stairs and through a door into an antechamber. There was a metal safe door that required a hand scan.

"I'll wait here. You two go get one of the two medics," Matt said. "Twenty minutes."

Hobart and Van Dreeves were out and back in less than three minutes, dragging the driver. They slapped his hand onto the scanning device, which didn't work so they tried an identical one next to it, which unlocked the door. Van Dreeves had snagged a toolbox from the back also and he opened it as Matt and Hobart went into the dimly lit room.

Air conditioning was blowing full blast onto a server farm. A room the size of a suburban basement housed server racks from floor to ceiling. Was this the actual database, Matt wondered? Or was it the center of operations?

"I'll be damned," Matt said.

"What's really behind the curtain?"

They heard the man mutter, "No," about the same time Van Dreeves said, "Holy shit."

"What?" Matt asked.

"There's a second hand scanner. I think both men had to scan at the same time."

Van Dreeves was looking at a series of red numbers falling all over each other to reach zero.

"Get the hell out of here," Matt said. But before he took a step toward the door, he reached in and grabbed two server boxes, really nothing more than small hard drives, stuffed them in his outer tactical vest, and followed Hobart and Van Dreeves up the stairs and out of the front door as the house exploded.

CHAPTER 83
SPARTANBURG, SOUTH CAROLINA

FRIDAY MORNING (EASTERN TIME)

Amanda spent the remaining nights until graduation in Jake's parents' home. She told them everything from start to finish. The sheriff had personally come by and removed Jake's security anklet immediately after the police had informed Harlan that they'd found a memory chip with pictures of the burning house on Dagus's desk. There was also a photo of an unconscious Riley Dwyer lying on the patio in her backyard. They were the trophy shots of a psychopath, the detective had told them. Like a hunter holding up a deer head, Dagus had captured his crimes on digits. Damning evidence for sure. "Slam dunk," the detective had said.

"How did you sleep?" Jake's mother asked. Mrs. Devereaux was a pretty, redheaded woman who could still wear petite junior clothes. She was definitely too perky in the morning, but Amanda had always liked her.

"Fine. That guest room mattress is super comfortable."

"Well, you've had a rough ride, honey. I don't know what comes next, but life should be a bit easier for you from here on out."

"Why do you say that, Mom?" Jake chimed in across the breakfast table. He quit chewing his french toast long enough to ask the question.

"I'm just saying that I see a maturity in Amanda now that I hadn't seen before. She's grown up a lot in the past few weeks."

"Mom—"

"No, Jake, she's right," Amanda countered. She put down her fork and looked at Jake. "I've changed. What my father taught me, what you helped me find out, has given me a new perspective. I'm not perfect by any stretch, but you know what?"

"What?" This time he had a mouthful of eggs.

"Jake!" His mother scolded.

"I'm ready to talk about my dad."

They sat in silence until Mr. Devereaux came into the house wearing an Egyptian cotton Bobby Jones golf shirt, tan khaki shorts and Docksiders. He was holding a newspaper in his hand. He was an older version of Jake. Tall, handsome, deep-set brown eyes, and thick, dark hair that was difficult to tame.

"*The Observer*. Front page." He put the paper in front of Amanda.

Amanda slowly opened the newspaper. The byline was Mary Ann Singlaub. The title was: "House Burning at Lanier Linked to Malicious Mother Syndrome." The subtitle read: "Melanie Garrett and Gabrielle 'Nina' Hastings Arrested on Charges of Child Prostitution."

She scanned the article and it read pretty much how she and Mary Ann had discussed it should. There were facts and figures about insurance fraud, visitation denials, and child abuse in the story. Riley Dwyer was quoted multiple times as the preeminent source on parental alienation syndrome. Amanda had specifically given her two quotes that she could use from her.

"My father was my hero until they changed everything. Suddenly I was living in a world where we were hiding from him; I was being used as a bargaining chip for more money, and I was going to the doctor about once a week. I didn't realize until I saw my father's files that my mother was making money off me every time she took me to the hospital."

She continued scanning and saw her second quote.

"My mother and grandmother robbed my father and me of at least ten years of our lives together. Once they are convicted in a court of law, those two women should get at least that for a prison sentence."

Those two women. She was sending a message to them in prison that she was completely disowning both of them. She would start completely on her own.

And she would be okay.

CHAPTER 84
SPARTANBURG, SOUTH CAROLINA

Amanda looked up at Jake as he brushed back some hair from her eyes then kissed her forehead. For Amanda, the days leading up to graduation had been filled with several visits to Harlan's office to discuss finances and the future. High school graduation had been rather anticlimactic and, perhaps, a harbinger of things to come. The time had passed quickly as she focused on preparing for adulthood.

They were standing on the porch of Jake's house with his parents sitting in the Lincoln Town Car, having already said their good-byes to Amanda. Jake was wearing a T-shirt that said "Metallica" on the front, and on the back, "Security."

Amanda was wearing khaki shorts and a light-blue polo shirt. The weather was sufficiently warm for her to wear her Teva sandals.

"It has been weeks and still no word on your dad's funeral?"

"Matt called last night and said there were some complications. The Special Operations command has opened an investigation. I should know something soon."

She saw Jake look away and then back at her. They locked eyes for a while, hers scanning back and forth between his.

"What?" she asked.

She felt him sigh as he spoke.

"I leave in a few minutes for The Citadel, you know. I don't necessarily agree with your decision to go to Africa for this program. I'd rather you go straight to Columbia, you know, so we'd be close."

"Jake, we talked about this yesterday—"

"Please just let me finish," he interrupted and emphasized the point by kissing her softly on the lips so that she couldn't speak anymore. "I was going to say that I support you, even though I may not agree. You know I'll worry about you over there. It's not a safe place."

"The world's not safe anymore."

"I don't agree, Amanda. We're safer today because of men like your father who go out and make the people who want to do us harm go away."

Amanda leaned into him, turning her head so that she could lean on his chest. "I believe that now."

"I know you do. That's probably part of what this Africa trip is about. You have to promise me, though, that you will be safe, okay?"

She pulled away and smiled that beautiful grin. "I promise."

With that, Jake got into the back seat of the Lincoln, which drove away, leaving Amanda standing alone in the front yard.

She had one task left to complete before she caught a ride from Riley Dwyer to the airport.

CHAPTER 85
SOUTH CAROLINA

Amanda summoned her courage, studied the Mapquest directions, and headed southwest toward the Georgia border.

She demonstrated her apprehension by missing the first parking attempt as her car straddled the yellow line of a visitor's space in front of the Leath Correctional Facility for Women in Greenwood. Harlan had mentioned to her that Leath was the primary facility for women in the state of South Carolina.

Before departing for Africa, she wanted to say good-bye to her mother and grandmother. As horrible as they had been to her and her father, she now realized, they were still a large factor in her life. She recognized if she were ever to be able to understand what had transpired during her childhood, that understanding would begin with her matriarchal lineage. She was also cognizant of the fact that one of the prime lessons she had learned was that no one was ever as bad or good as they may initially seem.

That point, though, was rather difficult to accept at this moment. She smoothed her khaki shorts and tugged at the collar of her preppie shirt as she exited the Benz. Having the lighter knocked from her hand onto the accelerant-soaked carpet wasn't supposed to happen. She had never intended for the house to burn. She just wanted the threat to be real enough to test her mother's motives. She had convinced herself that it was her mother's hand that had converted threat into reality.

Partly because she had chosen to press charges, Melanie and Nina were confined while the criminal fraud units continued to dig through the insurance claims. Not only health insurance, but jewelry, automobile, and homeowner's policies were all being reviewed. Harlan had told her that the initial report was that her father had uncovered only a portion of the racket that her mother and grandmother had nicknamed The Free Money Club.

"I'm here to see Melanie Garrett and Nina Hastings," Amanda said through the glass window in the outer foyer of the Metro. An African American woman smiled at her as she shuffled through some papers and then clicked a mouse on a computer.

"Number 945473 . . ." The woman stopped, recognizing Amanda's confusion. After a moment she asked, "First time?"

"Yes, ma'am." Amanda was embarrassed, but maintained her strength to continue with this process. It would be so easy to walk out now, but it wouldn't be right. And today she was all about doing the right thing.

"It's okay, honey. Let me see some ID."

Amanda promptly displayed her South Carolina driver's license, which satisfied the woman whose name she could see was Brenda.

"Okay, now, you're going to go right over there, and that nice man is going to open a door for you and sit you down at a table. After that, he will bring your mother in. The guard will be outside the door if you need him."

If I need him? All these years she had needed protection from her mother, and now the system was finally going to provide it when she was in jail. Her mind wrestled with the irony of that for a moment when she realized that the woman had said nothing about Nina.

"What about my grandmother?"

Brenda looked at the computer screen and asked, "Name?"

"Gabrielle Hastings."

After a moment, Brenda looked up and said, "Her lucky day, I guess. She was released this morning."

Amanda stood motionless in the center of the tiled foyer. One moment the double-lock barred door to her right seemed directly next to her, then far away, only to be followed by the thick clear ballistic door to her front zooming in and out.

How could this happen, she asked herself? She had provided the e-mails that clearly showed her grandmother had prostituted Brianna to Dagus as a way to blackmail him into cooperation in the nefarious scheme. What more did they need?

"Wouldn't they have both been released?" she heard herself ask Brenda.

The woman seemed to study the computer for a moment and then smiled.

"No two-for-one specials today, hon. Your grandma looks like she got herself that Russell guy. They tell me he can convince a judge to make a fish walk out of a pond."

Unable to even politely smile at the weak attempt at humor, Amanda chewed on that fingernail again, thinking. Okay, she had come this far. This was just an unexpected chess move. What was it that her dad always said? Something about the bad guys.

"The enemy always gets a vote," she whispered.

She determined that she had come here to see her mother, and so she would.

"Thank you." Amanda smiled at Brenda. She then nodded to the guard who had been patiently waiting while Amanda digested the new information. The guard was a tall man with a shaven head. Easily he could have been mistaken for a dark Mr. Clean, including the biceps.

They walked through a heavy-gauge steel door into a single room with a barren table and a chair on either side.

"This room's usually for attorneys and the prison—uh . . . and their clients, but the main visit area is maxed out. She'll be with you in a sec."

She sat nervously at the table, crossed her legs and began kicking the elevated foot to burn the adrenaline. *What am I doing here?* she kept asking herself. Springing forth was a new, or perhaps rejuvenated, sense of nobility. That's what she was doing here. She wanted to look her mother in the eyes and ask her, "Why?"

Why did she divorce her father? Why did she chase him away? Why did she love the house more than her? It was really that simple. At the critical moment when Dagus had held the gun to her head and the foyer was on fire, her mother chose to try to save her investment.

Perhaps she would never get an answer, but she had to try.

As much as she was prepared for the moment, her mother's presence shocked her. Melanie Garrett came into the room escorted by the dark Mr. Clean, his hand on her elbow. Her wrists were shackled with handcuffs that seemed longer than normal ones to her. She was wearing a flat gray jumpsuit with a number on the front. She looked down as she considered the thought that her mother was now number 945473. The number for some odd reason reminded her of when she and Jake had gone to see *Les Miserables*. Jean Valjean's prison number was 24601, she remembered.

Sitting in the chair across the table, she could feel her mother's stare locked onto her face. Slowly she looked up and their gazes fixed, mother and daughter, prisoner and escapee.

That's how she viewed the situation, anyway. It occurred to her that she had been the one in emotional shackles, cheated of the freedom to love her father. She weighed two competing emotions within her. First was enormous guilt about the role which she had played in attacking her father. Riley Dwyer had convinced her that it wasn't her fault, that she had never been given the chance. She had been imprisoned.

Second was boiling disgust with her mother's actions. Looking at her, she could not feel pity. Without makeup, her mother looked extraordinarily normal, even plain. No blonde highlights in the hair. No lip gloss. Even the botox seemed to be wearing off, leaving sagging eyelids and deep crow's feet around the eyes. In fact, it occurred to Amanda how well she seemed to fit right in with the population here. A model inmate.

"What took you so long?" Her mother fired the first shot across the table.

"You wouldn't understand," Amanda replied. She felt no further explanation was necessary. Another few seconds of awkward silence passed until her mother spoke.

"Well, are you happy?" Her mother's question could have been followed by . . . *with what you've done?*

Amanda was somewhat thankful that her mother had started out antagonistic. It might make this easier, she thought. "Truly? For the first time, I think I have a shot. But, no, I'm not happy."

Her mother glared at her, seemingly unsure of what to make of Amanda's new maturity. "Sounds like that shrink has been pumping you full of it, girlfriend."

"Mother, I came here to ask you why you did the things you did. That's all. If you want to fight, I'm going to leave, and I promise you I will never come back. You will never see me again except for on the witness stand at your trial when I tell the judge everything you did."

"Your word against mine, Amanda. Remember, someone burned your daddy's house down."

"Mother, have you ever heard of a flash drive?"

"What are you talking about?"

"It's about the size of my thumb and can hold about a zillion gigabytes of information. My father scanned every document, e-mail, receipt, you name it, that is proof of your insurance fraud and all the other horrible things you did to him and me."

Her mother watched her for a moment, and Amanda thought she saw something blink deep in her eyes. Perhaps it was the fear a thief feels when he recognizes that he left a major clue behind, having believed his tracks were sufficiently covered.

"No judge will ever believe that computer crap. Never heard of it."

She ran her hands along her pants and said, "Well, Mom, I guess that's it, then. If you can't admit to it—"

"What, are you wearing a wire? Is that it? You come in here trying to entrap me?"

Amanda looked over at Mr. Clean, who had stepped toward them. Holding up her hand, she turned to her mother. She stood and lifted her polo shirt and ran a hand down her bare midriff then twirled in place.

"See, mom, no wires. Just me. No games. All I want is for you to tell me why. I deserve that. You and Nina have screwed up at least two lives, and I can't believe that you are so self-involved that you can't tell your own daughter why you did it all."

Amanda kept her eyes fixed on her mother, who showed the first sign of cracking when she lifted her manacled hands from the gray table and covered her eyes. Accordingly, she felt herself giving in just a bit, hoping and praying that her mother would be able to give her some insight into what had driven her to the decisions that she made.

"You come in here and demand from me, your mother, a confession!" She was screaming now. "How dare you!"

Amanda remained calm as she gently pushed away from the table, turned toward Mr. Clean, and nodded. "I'm done with her."

The tall, dark man lifted Melanie Garrett from the chair while she was still screaming, "How dare you!" over and over again. Her face was contorted, veins popping out of her neck, eyes bulging, and teeth baring like a baying animal. And perhaps she was.

"Mother," Amanda said.

Mr. Clean stopped as they were half way through the door that would lead her mother back into the prison cell block. By now her mother was heaving and breathing rapidly. The guard stared at her as if she had exactly five seconds to make her point.

"Did you know that Nina has been released? Some hotshot lawyer named Russell."

That put Melanie Garrett over the edge. She began screaming, "Noooo!"

Amanda watched her disappear behind the hulking man and then the heavy steel door. The pervasive latching sound had the tone of finality.

As she departed the interview room, Amanda stared at the tile floor. Somehow she made it to the front door, never acknowledging Brenda's call out to her to "have a good day."

Outside, the sun blaring in her face, Amanda looked over her shoulder at the Metro Women's Prison. Could a man-made structure hold back her demons? she wondered.

Inside the Mercedes she leaned into the headrest and closed her eyes. With her hands on the steering wheel, she then leaned forward, resting her forehead on the leather.

She was overcome with sadness at the fact that her mother, in the end, was incapable of loving her. All any child, herself included, ever wanted was their parents' love. Every child deserved that unconditional love.

She sobbed into her hands, shaking softly in the comfortable leather seat.

Amanda looked up from her hands as the thought occurred to her that some things were inexplicable. Just as she believed in God, she had to also accept the reality that evil existed for its own sake—to destroy and ruin.

And evil it was.

CHAPTER 86
CHARLOTTE, NORTH CAROLINA

Amanda drove slowly past downtown Charlotte and into Dilworth to Riley Dwyer's house. After making one stop along the way to eat, she pulled into the cul-de-sac. Out of the corner of her eye something registered, but she became focused on Riley's open garage door. She eased into the open spot on the left, narrowly avoiding Riley's SUV on her right. It was a tight fit, but Amanda would leave her the keys if she needed to move the car while she was in Africa.

It was early afternoon and Amanda did not have to be at the airport for four more hours, but she wanted to get there early enough to get through security without any issues. She had never been to Africa, and traveling there with a small group of strangers was unsettling.

She locked her car with the key fob and then knocked on the door from the garage that led into the house. After a couple more knocks went unanswered, she opened the unlocked door and peered into the mudroom, which led to the kitchen.

"Riley? You there?"

Silence.

"Riley?" She called a bit louder this time.

Stepping into the house, she walked carefully into the kitchen. It was neat and well kept. On the kitchen table was an opened envelope which had a long piece of scotch tape on the outside. The tape had some whitish tailings on the adhesive side as if it had been used and then removed from something.

She lifted the envelope, turning it over in her hand. On the flat side she saw that Riley had written her name, "Amanda . . . I'm terribly sorry." Her writing was in wild, but neat, slanted cursive. Just how she imagined Riley would write, loose but in control.

Sorry? What could she be sorry about?

Perplexed and thinking that Riley must be upstairs, Amanda walked from the kitchen into the foyer. There were no lights on in the house that she could see. Eerily quiet, the home seemed empty, almost vacant. Looking down the long hallway into the den with the tiger-striped chaise lounge and the safari-themed plants, she saw that the mini-blinds were closed. The room was dark, save a few shards of the dull gray afternoon light sneaking past the gaps.

"Riley?" She jumped at her own voice, its sound foreign to the still home.

Her footsteps thudded dully off the hardwood in the hallway as she passed the lavatory on the left and the study on the right. As she approached the opening, she saw that the sofa across the den was vacant, as was the lounge chair across from the television.

She turned toward the tiger-striped chaise that she had lain upon when she first truly opened up to Riley several nights ago.

"Surprised?"

Amanda jumped back against the wall as if an invisible force was pinning her against the plasterboard. She tried to move her arms as Gabrielle Hastings stood from her secluded position on the chaise longue.

"What are you doing here?" It was all she could muster. Then a horrible thought occurred to her. "What have you done to Riley?"

Nina walked slowly toward her. She was wearing a dark-blue denim jacket and black pants. Old aerobics shoes on her feet, she appeared nimble and ready to leap.

"Thought you outsmarted me, did you? Should have learned, Amanda. You may have tricked me there for a minute, but I'm a survivor, and don't you forget that. I can be your best friend or your worst enemy. I know that there is no God and that the only life you get is this one. If you don't take from others, they take from you. It's the way life is, Amanda. Do you understand?"

Nina's words were the barren echoes of a despondent woman. That notwithstanding, Amanda noticed the glint of steel in Nina's hand as one of the slivers of light shone on it like a laser beam.

"What are you going to do, Nina, kill me? Where's Riley?"

Amanda remembered watching *Old Yeller* with her father. Her grandmother had that rabid look of a dog with hydrophobia. The only thing missing was the foaming at the mouth. No question that Nina had gone mental.

"I haven't decided what I'm going to do just yet. Maybe if that slut had been here I would have gotten it out of my system already. Maybe then I would be in a better frame of mind."

Amanda played with her purse a moment, suddenly remembering the story Nina had mentioned to her about the time she had stabbed her stepfather with a pitchfork. Fear bottled up in her throat.

She looked toward the chaise longue and saw an opened piece of paper on the coffee table. The note Riley had left for her. She felt a sigh of relief knowing that Riley was not a corpse in her own house, though the immediate danger to herself recaptured her attention quickly.

"You're sick, Nina. I never saw it before, but now that I'm free of you and Mama, it's like I never knew anything else."

Amanda looked toward the back door where she heard a noise. Gus Randel came walking in the double French doors that led to the deck.

"Gus, oh, am I glad you are here!" Amanda gasped, running toward her mother's boyfriend. She hugged him hard, remembering all the times he had sided with her against her mother. As she wrapped her arms around him, she noticed that he didn't reciprocate. She pushed away from his muscular frame.

Looking into his eyes, she instantly knew that something was wrong. He had a thousand-yard stare, looking through her. She had never seen evil personified, but at this moment she thought that he might be a good candidate.

"You know what to do," Nina said to Gus. "She's yours if you want her."
Then she said to Amanda, "Payback's a bitch."

Gus's grip tightened on Amanda. She temporarily broke free then pushed
him hard in the chest.

"What the hell are you doing listening to this crazy bitch!"

He was unfazed and continued to come toward her. Nina was to her
front now with something in her hand. Gus Randel was to her left toward
the back door and moving in her direction. She reached up and tilted the
sofa back, blocking Gus's progress, then ran for the front door. Nina looked
toward the door, her head moving like that of a predator protecting its kill—
a *T. rex* sizing up its prey.

There was a sound in the driveway. Amanda pulled open the front door
but saw no one. She then turned to look as she heard two car doors slam,
followed by, "Amanda?"

After a moment, she looked back at Nina and Gus.

Who were gone.

The back door past the sofa was slightly ajar. Amanda remained frozen
in place as Harlan Foxworth and Mary Ann Singlaub came into the house
through the garage.

"Amanda?" Mary Ann called out from the foyer.

Amanda turned her head toward the front door as a wave of relief washed
over her. "They were just here! My grandmother and Gus Randel. They did
all this!"

Harlan stepped outside, looked around the corner and then came back in.
"Calm down, Amanda. The police have them in custody."

"What? How?" Amanda stepped outside into the humid afternoon sun.
She saw a red mustang parked behind a police cruiser that was flashing its
blue lights. Two uniformed cops had Gus and Nina in handcuffs. They were
standing in the street. One uniform was talking on a Motorola radio.

Amanda could see a man dressed in civilian clothes holstering a pistol.

"Principal Rugsdale?"

Harlan nodded. "It seems your principal Mr. Rugsdale is a reserve detective in the police force. He worked the staged crime scene at Dagus's house

for what are now obvious reasons. The memory chip they found at your teacher's house turned out to be Randel's. Apparently Randel had planted it there. There were several deleted pictures that the digital exploitation team was able to recover. It seems that you never really erase something from a hard drive."

Amanda had been looking at the stone porch, leaning against Mary Ann, who was hugging her from behind.

"No, I guess not," Amanda whispered. "It's all still there."

"Anyway, Rugsdale reviewed the chip, and they found several deleted photos of Gus Randel with women, most of whom appeared unconscious. Of course, this led to a warrant to search Randel's condo in Spartanburg. He had downloaded all of these photos onto his laptop. We also found out that he had a contract with the *Charlotte Observer* to use the name Del Dangurs."

"How did Dagus get involved in all of this?"

"Simple," Harlan continued. "His media watchdog group had been pursuing Del Dangurs for years for publishing bogus stories. He had been collecting Dangurs' stories; that's what you found. The article written to compromise your dad's credibility finally gave him a causus belli with the editors of *The Observer*. The exploitation team found some talking points on his computer referencing unverified sources in the article. Dagus apparently believed he was going to be famous for using the story Randel wrote on your father as an example of journalists just making stuff up. He was fighting to show that the article was bogus when your grandmother offered him up Brianna.

"But don't have too much sympathy for him, either. Despite the nobility of his effort with the reporting, we have identified several fifteen- to seventeen-year-old girls he has manipulated and taken advantage of, based on his computer files. Some are stepping forward, others not."

Amanda slipped away from Mary Ann and sat down on the steps.

"What chaos."

"These are the types of people your grandmother and mother held dear."

Amanda stared at the bricks, an emptiness overtaking her.

"This was all so Dagus wouldn't expose the article about my dad as bogus?"

"That's the way it seems. Your father's house was burned down, Jake was set up for it, a man is dead, and your mother and grandmother stand to spend a very long time in prison, all because they wanted to suppress the memory of your father.

"Hence, my advice to—"

"Stay out of the way." All three of them said it in unison.

Mary Ann gave her a moment and then asked, "Ready to go save the world?"

"Just a second," Amanda replied as she regained her composure. Her heart was pounding like a war drum in her chest. She walked back into the house, leaned over the coffee table and picked up the note. She carried it back to the porch, where Harlan and Mary Ann looked at her. Opening the note, she read:

Amanda, I got called away on a very important mission, as your dad would say. I asked Harlan and Mary Ann to take you to the airport. I have your address in Africa. I promise I will be in touch . . . very soon. Never lose hope.

Love,

Riley

"Never lose hope," she whispered. She remembered opening the package from Matt, who had written the same words. *Never lose hope*. You have to have it to lose it, she thought to herself.

"And now I have hope," she said to herself as she felt Mary Ann's arm wrap around her. It wasn't much, but it was the best thing she'd ever had.

"Yes, I'm ready."

"One last thing," Harlan said. They began walking together down the steps of the porch. They stood on the sidewalk that led to the driveway and took in the beaming sun blessing them with its warmth.

"Yes?"

"My bill. We never finished discussing how you would pay me for this."

Amanda thought his timing was a bit inappropriate, but she recognized that he had done a tremendous amount of work for her.

"I understand."

"Maybe you do, Amanda." He handed her a piece of paper, which she opened at the folds. There was some printing at the top that stated this was the complete and final bill. She searched for numbers but only saw in big, bold print:

Grow up to be like your Dad. The Germans lost.

She started crying. Mary Ann hugged her again. That seemed to be her role.

"Thank you. I will."

CHAPTER 87
DJIBOUTI

SATURDAY

"A server farm?" Matt asked.

He, Hobart and Van Dreeves had been picked up by the planned MH-47 helicopter after their narrow escape from the target house in Yemen. The Chinook had transported them back to the joint task force headquarters in Djibouti, a destitute country 150 miles across the Gulf of Aden.

Consistent with their operating routine, they had been off the grid for several days. Invading Yemen was no small deal and immediately upon their escape to Djibouti, their orders were to go dark immediately. Surfacing this Saturday morning, Matt, Hobart, and Van Dreeves assessed the damage.

"The Yemeni police have been in there for days trying to figure out what the hell happened. Global Hawk's been snapping pictures. The place is a giant smoking hole," Hobart said.

They were sitting on a picnic table outside of the control tower of the airfield. Matt was staring at a Gulfstream 5 jet with two pilots who were probably becoming more pissed by the minute as Matt languished. He was hesitant to leave unfinished business, yet eager about what he intended to do next.

"How about the houses on either side? They go up in smoke?"

"Untouched," Hobart said.

That bothered Matt, big time. Hobart and Van Dreeves had spotted tunnels that ran from the center house to the homes on either flank.

"How about the prisoner?"

"Four days and he still hasn't said a word," Van Dreeves said. The three men wore their Revision ballistic eyewear, otherwise known as wraparound sunglasses. Matt kept staring at the Gulfstream and the pilots, he knew, were staring at him.

Matt had collared the "medic" that they had tossed in the back of the ambulance as they limped to the pick-up zone where they loaded their stowed parachutes and the detainee. Upon landing in Djibouti, the military interrogators swiftly moved him to a holding cell for questioning.

"Nervous about Rampert?" Hobart asked Matt.

"He doesn't have us along, how can I not be nervous?"

"He's got Samuels and Roberson. They're good."

"I'd rather be there," Matt said.

"You can't be everywhere, dude. And right now that airplane is waiting to take you where you should be," Van Dreeves said.

"You've got the list?"

"We've got the list, Matt. Your headquarters has the list. The issue will be keeping it out of the hands of douche bags like Assange and those Wiki-leak idiots."

"Add him to the list," Matt said, smiling as he stood.

"Roger that."

Hobart and Van Dreeves stood, each man shaking Matt's hand and giving him a half-hug, the shoulder to shoulder bump that signified respect amongst warriors.

"Wish we could go with you, but we've got to wait for Rampert once he gets Rahman."

"Don't go easy on him," Matt said, meaning everything he implied.

Both men smiled as Matt turned and walked toward the Gulfstream.

"Give him our best," Hobart said.

Matt acknowledged Hobart with a curt wave as he boarded the airplane.

QUETTA, PAKISTAN

Major General Jack Rampert was dressed in a traditional Afghan headdress and white man-dress. He had grown a well-defined beard and easily passed for a local. He twirled a cup of chai tea on his table in the mud hut restaurant in Jalalabad. Enough time had passed since the helicopter shootdown. They were back in mission rhythm.

His informant had told him to wait in this spot, as an important meeting was going to take place in the next building over. He studied his surroundings. There were two men dressed similarly to him sitting in the far corner at a small wooden table. Another man was squatting on his haunches smoking a pipe of some kind. Rampert figured it was hash.

The primary comforting thought for him was that two operatives were in concealed positions with long rifles outside of the building. With Hobart and Van Dreeves with Matt in Djibouti, he had decided to lead this mission. It was the least he could do for Zach. Samuels and Roberson were his team for this mission. They had clear shots if extreme measures were necessary. They wanted to capture this individual, but they would kill him if necessary.

Rampert could see outside of the open-air restaurant, which had two lambs hanging upside down in the front. They had been slaughtered and skinned.

"*Assalamu alaikum.* Peace be with you," the merchant greeted him. He bent over, blocking Rampert's important view, and refilled his tea mug.

"*Wa alaikum assalaam.* And on you, peace."

The man switched out the napkin underneath his mug and placed his hand over his heart. Rampert reciprocated the sign of good will. As the man departed, he lifted his tea mug and sipped the warm beverage. He then lifted the napkin and opened it.

The Scientist. Two minutes

Rampert folded the napkin and scratched his ear. As he did so he whispered into his cuff. "Two mikes." It was a simple transmission that they had rehearsed. The lack of additional information meant the Scientist was arriving according to plan. Rampert's drive to capture Mullah Rahman had been based upon his declaration of a *Fatwah* against Colonel Garrett. He wanted that over with so that everyone could move on. That was his promise to Matt Garrett.

Presently the black SUV in which the Scientist was believed to be seated stopped in front of the open hut. It skidded to a halt, dust flaring from beneath its rear tires. Immediately, security personnel from lead and trail vehicles swarmed the black SUV. Doors were opening and slamming with a *click* and a *thunk*. The clicks might have been the charging of weapons.

Rampert waited a brief moment and stood. As he did so he laid his hand on the silenced Berretta pistol beneath his tribal garb. He heard in his earpiece Samuels whisper, "Driver."

There was a barely audible whisper that hit the driver, who had made the fatal mistake of stepping outside the vehicle. The man slumped unceremoniously to the ground. It took the security detail a few seconds to comprehend what had happened. That gave Rampert the time to lift his weapon and shoot the lead security man, who was exiting from the front right passenger seat. He dropped to the ground dead. The guard who had been assisting the Scientist at the right rear door turned toward the restaurant, giving Rampert another clear shot at his forehead.

"Two down, right side," he whispered.

"Two more down left side."

"Three coming from behind." Roberson entered the discussion, followed by, "Not anymore."

Rampert made a quick move toward the vehicle, though he was certain that there were more security personnel. The two men at the table inside the restaurant made a quick move in his direction, snatching AK-47s from against the wall. Rampert had noticed though and quickly shot both men in the head. Directing his attention back toward the vehicle, he approached the right rear door. He looked inside, pistol first.

He saw the man they knew to be the Scientist, or Haqan el Lib Rahman. He was an Egyptian who was number three on the Database list just behind Zawahiri.

"Don't move or you die," Rampert said.

Roberson approached from behind and removed flex cuffs from his pocket, quickly zipping them across Rahman's hands. Rampert moved into the front right seat as Samuels closed in on the driver's side. With Roberson in the back, keeping his weapon on Rahman, Hobart gunned the vehicle and sped away under a fusillade of AK-47 fire. Thankfully, Rahman's vehicle was uparmored and the bullets pinged off the outer shell like BBs.

They drove through the Byzantine streets of Quetta until they reached a U.S. military operating base at the border checkpoint, where they were quickly waved through the gate.

There, they loaded a UH-60 Blackhawk helicopter for the short flight back to Kandahar. Rahman went without much of a fight, as usually happened with the senior leaders of the enemy. The plan had been executed perfectly.

Sometimes that happened.

General Rampert radioed Van Dreeves in Djibouti and said, "Jackpot. Give Matt the go ahead."

CHAPTER 88
LANDSTUHL, GERMANY

Riley Dwyer followed the uniformed security guard through the vault door at Landstuhl Army Medical Center in the southern part of Germany.

The last several weeks had been exceptionally challenging for her, but she understood her purpose. Every day she would come to this place and every evening she would go back to the hotel on the military base.

"Hi, Matt," she said, placing her coffee cup on the end table. "You look like hell."

"Riley," he said, standing and giving her a half hug.

"I'm told there's news?"

"Yes. I got word last night they got him—the one who put the *Fatwah* out on Zach. They compelled him to retract it this morning."

"*Compelled?*"

"I don't ask questions."

Riley looked away. Tears were forming in the back of her eyes. She had completely healed save for a small pale scar on her cheek. Now she looked at Matt who looked like he had been through a Mixmaster. What was happening to this world where good men like Matt Garrett had to look like he did in order for everyone else to be safe?

"Does this mean we can let Amanda know?"

"I think it's time, don't you? It's been killing me."

She looked back at Matt. "It's way past time, Matt. Who do you think should tell her?"

They looked at each other and immediately knew the answer. There was no question.

"Thanks again, Riley. Without you coming we couldn't have known whether to trust Amanda. Until we knew that we couldn't risk her having this information."

"I wouldn't say it's a done deal, but she's different. There's no doubt about that."

Matt said. "What you've done with her has been crucial. You can't deny that." He looked at her a moment, letting the compliment sink in. "About the other thing, I've talked to the insurance company. They made the donation to the village and are covering Amanda's college costs through a scholarship. When they heard the details, they were eager to assist."

"When do we leave for Africa?" If she was anything at this moment, she was impatient.

"Not soon enough."

EPILOGUE

TANZANIA

Amanda Garrett knelt in the tall prairie grass that swayed in the stiff African wind like underwater kelp flowing with the tug of the tide. Golden husks of wheat stood tall, nourished by the river that meandered behind her. Dressed in her khaki paratroop pants, an olive drab T-shirt and tan fishing vest, Amanda smiled as a young boy approached her with a pad of paper and a pencil.

"What would you like to draw?"

The boy, no more than twelve, clearly had a crush on Amanda, which she considered perfectly acceptable. She smiled when the boy was alternating pointing at himself and then at Amanda.

Laughing, even giggling like a little girl, something she had almost forgotten how to do, Amanda said, "Okay, Kiram, let's draw a picture of me and you." She helped him lay the paper out on the shaved tree trunk that doubled as a desk.

Kiram's artwork was surprisingly well done, like the coal drawings of Pervious. One thing was for certain, Amanda thought with a smile, he could make a mint drawing caricatures at Virginia Beach.

She watched him with intensity, feeling herself being pulled into his scene. She began to visualize another universe out there, ripe for collision.

Her demons apparently resolved, or at least at bay, she was free to think how she desired. Since her high school graduation, she had begun work at this small orphanage and had decided to attend Columbia University in New York next year. She had already been accepted, and they were going to give her eight credit hours for her time as part of a mission to Mwanza, Tanzania. Jake had written her every day so far.

She recalled with happiness the time she and her father had been working on the school project. She remembered what she had promised her dad; she had sworn to him that she would try to make a difference with the children of Africa.

She did not know what motivated her more; the fact that she had promised her father she would do it or the fact that she actually achieved great personal satisfaction helping these unfortunate children. It did not matter in her view what the source of her motivation was, because both were pure and gave her a good sense of purpose. She had never felt better.

Two weeks had passed since high school graduation, she distinctly recalled sitting in the chair on the football field wishing that her father was alive and would suddenly appear as the surprise guest speaker. Someone she couldn't remember had actually talked about purpose and meaning and finding oneself.

Yes, her father's love was a warming ray of sun breaking through the clouds after a storm. The memories were back in full clarity, easily recalled. The hard drive had been rebooted.

The little boy tugging on her leg snapped her from her wistful memory.

"Okay Kiram, show me what you've got," she smiled cheerily.

"Ma'am," Kiram said, pointing at the picture. He bowed his head as if to indicate that his work was not worthy of the eye contact.

As Amanda looked at the drawing, she was forced to take a seat on the very stump upon which Kiram had drawn the sketch.

One of the people in the sketch was definitely she; only he had managed to make her more beautiful. Her oval eyes seemed to lift off the page and hover in translucence. The face was a quarter angle profile shot, and she was looking up at a man who could only be her father. Here again, Kiram had done remarkable work. He captured her father's strong jaw line and piercing eyes. He had drawn her eyes and her father's almost exactly alike.

Amanda looked up. Near the village about twenty children kicked a soccer ball that she had provided for them. Kiram, though, was different than the rest of the children. Amanda had immediately liked him, partly because he gave her attention, she had to admit. But it was mostly because he seemed out of touch with the others, something she could relate to. Over the past two weeks of their presence in Tanzania, Amanda had noticed Kiram was a very intelligent young man, almost mysteriously so.

"How did you know what my father looked like?"

He wagged a long, slender black finger at her. "Miss Amanda, you find out. He protect you." Kiram hugged Amanda.

"You're such a beautiful child, Kiram. Maybe I'll take you home with me."

"No can go. Must stay here with my people."

"Well, the way you drew this picture of my father is just very strange. It's like you can see him, you know, in the other world. He's dead, you know."

Kiram screwed his face up at hers.

"Man not dead. . . ."

"I know, I know," she countered quickly, waving her hands as if to wave him off. "His spirit lives forever."

Kiram returned her stare.

"Well it does, Kiram, I've got my father right here in my heart."

She opened a gold locket hanging around her neck. On the left side was her face, smiling from a happy time with her father when she was nine or ten. On the right side was her father's face, square jaw set, green-flecked eyes radiant, and his beautiful smile locked on his face, the way she wanted to remember him. She tried not to think of everything that Matt had told her that day at the funeral for Lance Eversoll.

"I'll be in touch, Amanda, with more information about your dad. You just have to trust me." She did trust Matt and knew in time that she would find out his fate. And then there was the note from Riley that she kept with her. *Never lose hope.*

"What those?"

Kiram's skinny black finger was pointing at two medallions hanging in tandem next to the locket. Amanda pawed them without looking down.

"Saint Michael's medals. They say, 'Protect Us'."

"Why two?"

"One is from my dad. The other is from someone who tried to save him." Amanda felt tears welling as she thought about Sergeant Eversoll giving his life for her father.

"This man." He was pointing back at the drawing. At her father.

"You're too funny, little boy. Now go play."

"You'll see," Kiram said, lifting his drawing and then placing it back on the tree stump. "Time to go. See you tomorrow."

Then the part they had been practicing.

"Are you good to go?"

"I'm good to go, Kiram. Good job."

Amanda had taught him the exchange, and Kiram had picked it up easily, as he did with the rest of his English. He could be a leader for these people, Amanda thought. Her heart swelled with pride. Her short time in Tanzania had been cathartic in many ways.

"I don't know if this is what I'm supposed to do, Daddy, but it's the best that I can do right now." She had transformed enormous guilt into positive action. That was something.

She lifted Kiram's drawing and looked at the image of her father. Tears were streaking her face. In a way they were tears of happiness. Even in his absence he had been able to resurrect her. What she wouldn't give for a second chance with him.

"Are we good to go, Daddy?" She held the grainy artist paper in her hand and stared at Kiram's rendition of her father's face.

The wind shook the tops of the sturdy mahogany trees, a white cloud slid overhead as if it was a speedboat skimming the pristine surface of a crystal-blue lake. The thatch huts in which they were staying suddenly seemed deathly quiet, with no one in eyesight or earshot.

"We're good to go, baby girl."

It was as if someone had opened a zipper in time, reached in and somehow dragged him forward. She rose from the stump.

Watching the sun, a bright fireball diving beneath the descending tree lines that ran down the ridge, she mustered the courage to turn. Ever so slowly, she first saw the river flowing with its gentle, peaceful pace. It crossed her mind that her father was supposed to have been killed twice in the last four years. Surely she could not be so lucky as to have a father that resembled a cat in longevity performances.

Before she finished turning, she felt his hands on her shoulder. These were her father's hands, strong and gentle, protective. Before she came face to face with him, she closed her eyes.

"Daddy?"

MATT GARRETT SET up the satellite uplink from Mwanza, Tanzania and got confirmation of a secure satellite connection. He wasn't sure he could handle the emotional torrent that might release if he watched his brother, Zach, reunite with his reformed daughter. So, he got Zach from Landstuhl Military Hospital in Germany to this remote corner of the Serengeti and then removed himself from the picture. This was Zach's show, not his. Actually, it was Amanda's and he was damn proud of that young lady for having the intestinal fortitude to persevere.

While Amanda and Zach were embracing, Matt plugged the two hard drives he had snatched from the Yemen raid into USB cables that fed into a master computer that the Central Intelligence Agency could access and monitor. He could see Riley standing in the center of the soccer field, laughing as orphans ran circles around her with a soccer ball.

"Uploading files," Matt said into his satellite phone as he watched the green bar slide from left to right across the screen indicating upload progress. The files would take encryption experts in some cases minutes and in most cases hours or days to decipher. The haul from Yemen, while considered a bust in the operative communities, was anything but that. CIA Director Houghton had instructed Matt to secure the two server drives he had taken from Yemen until international attention on the raid ebbed.

Houghton was on the line with Matt and said, "Good job. We've got

Elsie Cartwright, our best techie already telling us you got a more current database than Rahman's of every Al Qaeda member in the first few minutes."

"There's a hell of a lot more there, Roger. And there are probably more databases. We have to keep the pressure on these guys," Matt said.

"Roger that," Houghton said.

"I want in on developing the plan to systematically go after these assholes."

"No question."

"And you were wrong, you know," Matt said.

Houghton paused. "About what?"

"Zach. He's good to go."

"I heard. I'm always happy to be wrong about shit like that. Now get your ass back here when you can."

"Roger that, Roger."

Matt heard Houghton chuckle and hang up. He looked out of the small cinderblock shack that Amanda had steered him toward for his "conference call."

Next he called General Griffin in Pakistan and after a few seconds got the general on the tactical satellite radio.

"Eagle six, give me a status," Matt said.

Matt heard a chuckle, then Griffin said, "Well, son, I'm in Miram Shah with my headquarters where Haqqani used to hang out, so I'd say we're doing some good. But it's going to take time."

"At least we're there," Matt said.

"Wouldn't have been possible without you," Griffin replied.

Matt smiled. No, it surely would not have been.

"Keep your powder dry, General."

"I'm just about out of powder we've been killing so many of these bastards."

"Stay safe, sir."

"Matt?"

"Yes, sir?"

"I'd follow you into combat anytime, son."

Matt paused at the strong sentiment from the seasoned soldier.

"Likewise, sir."

IN YEMEN, FOUR houses down from the raid objective of the Americans an ambulance arrived with a dialysis machine in the back. The medics disembarked rapidly and carried a stretcher into the suburban house, which was surprisingly unaffected by the blast of the server farm.

They found their way into the bedroom past several AK-74 toting security personnel who had materialized from the vapor. They loaded the tall patient on the litter and immediately hooked him up to the IV bags and heart rate monitors.

Securing him in the ambulance, they got the dialysis treatment underway, and under heavily guarded escort, sped away into the Yemeni desert night.

Make sure to stay tuned for *DARK THREAT*, book four of the Threat Series, where Amanda Garrett runs a clandestine U.S. State Department HIV vaccine program in Tanzania.

International terrorists and American pharmaceutical companies descend on the Serengeti Plain as the secret cure is leaked to the world. Protected by two Tanzanian orphans, Amanda evades the clutches of the Leopard and the Cheetah, a French sniper and Rwandan war criminal escapee, who have teamed up to steal the vaccine.

Matt and Zach Garrett are called into action with Amanda on the run and the vaccine in jeopardy, when a billionaire's fascination with a newly discovered 30,000-year-old text leads him to believe that Amanda's prize may not only cure disease, but offer everlasting life.

Author's Note:

The idea for *Hidden Threat* came from two places. First, ever since September 12, 2001 I have believed that we under-resourced the fight against Al Qaeda. As you have just read in *Hidden Threat,* I take creative license and put both Matt and Zach Garrett into the fight in Afghanistan and, more importantly, in Pakistan, where I believe we need to be to win this war.

Secondly, I have seen the impact of war on families and, in particular, on soldiers and their children. Amanda's struggle on the home front in parallel with Zach's in combat is symbolic of the agony I have witnessed in many different families and situations. The main point is that it takes courage to be a kid and have a parent in a war.

I would like to thank my editor, Shane Thomson, for his diligence, as well as Tim Schulte and Stan Tremblay at Variance Publishing. Also, thanks to the wonderful Jessi Alexander for allowing me to use her lyrics from the song "This World is Crazy" off her album *Honeysuckle Sweet.* Also, congratulations to Mary Ann Singlaub for winning the contest to have her name used in the novel during last year's USO sponsored book release for Rogue Threat.

And most importantly, thanks to you, the reader, for your interest and loyalty.

AJT